THE BIRDSKIN
SHOES

THE BIRDSKIN SHOES

JOAN TAYLOR-ROWAN

CREATESPACE

Published by CreateSpace

978-1477531082

Typesetting services by BOOKOW.COM

*For my loved ones
and Mary Le Blanc, an inspirational teacher.*

Acknowledgements

Cover image: Escuche by Teresa Villegas www.teresavillegas.com

Graphic design: Lulu and Rob at Dzine www.dzine.co.uk

I want to thank the wonderful writers of Brockley WOOA (Writers Of Our Age) for all their feedback, support and encouragement over the years; my wonderful sisters Marie and Rhona for all their patience, ideas and enthusiasm - Rhona who edited, proof-read (more than once) and constantly made me feel that this was worth publishing and Marie for helping me tease out plot problems, reading endless versions, listening even when I rang during Coronation Street and constantly thinking of new ways to promote the book; and my mum for being Irish and a very funny raconteur. Thanks to stalwart friends and who have commented and supported me in times of doubt who have shown an interest even at the risk of being drawn into a conversation that they knew might be one-sided and interminable - you all know who you are; the Forbes clan who I love dearly and whose names I have used in this book although in an entirely fictitious way (okay not entirely - Janice's Spanish is bad - but it brought us together. She has never worked for The National Geographic); and my work colleagues for their encouragement.

I need to thank Kate Shaw and Laura Morris for excellent professional feedback and Sally Lane for editing and proofing reading. Finally, I need to thank my partner Peter, for taking care of me and listening endlessly to me thinking aloud when he probably wanted to scream!

I found Katie Hickman's book A Trip to the Light Fantastic, to be invaluable in capturing the mood and day-to-day detail of a Mexican Circus. All of the characters in this book are entirely fictional, however Con Colleano - (thanks to www.circopedia.org, for excellent information about him) - was a world famous tightwire performer, the first to perform a forward somersault on the wire, and The Wallendas are an extremely famous (and world-record holding) circus family, renowned for performing dangerous stunts without a safety net. Descendants of the original Flying Wallendas are still performing today and as I write Nik Wallenda has just become the first person to cross Niagara Falls on a high-wire and has done it in a pair of elk-skin shoes made by his mother! Angel Milagro, and the other 'legendary performers' are pure invention however.

The Mexican earthquake of 1985 was the worst in Mexico's history killing more than 10000 people in Mexico City and the surrounding areas. While most of the scenes I describe from the Mexican earthquake are fiction, newborn babies were rescued days after the earthquake struck (www.bbc.co.uk.onthisday) by modern techniques, astonishing bravery and the skills of volunteer miners, firemen and the rescue brigades. The destruction wrought to named buildings also took place.

My main source about the earthquake, both the facts and the stories of witnesses and survivors was Elena Poniatowska's book, Nobody Nothing - Voices from the Mexican Earthquake. It was indispensible and heart-breaking. The astonishing bravery and stoicism and generosity of the Mexican people will stay with me. I found Wikipedia and BBC footage helpful for details about the earthquakes impact. I also must thank Jim Johnston and Nick Gilman - who love Mexico like I do and have made it their home - for their wonderful books and blogs; Mexico City, An opinionated Insiders' Guide, (mexicocitydf.blogspot.com) and Good Food in Mexico City: A Guide to Food Stalls, Fondas and Fine Dining (goodfoodmexicocity.blogspot.com).

Further thanks to Cobh Museum in Cork and Sheffield Fairground Archive for clarifying nitty-gritty details for me, also Dr Caroline Skehill, Queen's University Belfast, for clarifying the situation for children in care in Southern Ireland in the sixties - I hope I have not strayed too far from the facts.

It is not flesh and blood, but heart which makes us fathers and sons.

~ Friedrich von Schiller

How unhappy is he who cannot forgive himself.

~ Publilius Syrus

PART 1

1

Mexico City, 7.03 a.m., September 19th 1985

It was the silence that woke him. The birds with their raucous chatter had vanished. Joey jumped up and immediately fell back to the ground as an excruciating pain ran through his feet. His head ached from alcohol but his feet knew what was coming. Earthquake. The word formed, and then the world collapsed around him.

He clutched at the earth as it pitched and rolled and there he was, back on the ship that had brought him here all those years ago, lying on the heaving deck, praying that death would come soon. He scrambled under a bench and cowered there, his heart racing, eyes tightly shut.

It was the sound of screaming children that jolted him out of his own terror. They were running across the road towards him in their white shirts, school-bags bashing at their legs as they cried for their mothers.

'*¡Aguas!* Look out!' he yelled, as the windows above shattered, showering them in fragments of glass.

The first child dropped to the ground. The others, their shirts speckled with blood, stood in shocked silence surrounded by a sea of savage glitter. A young woman, her hair still in rollers, darted from her refuge and herded them away. Joey crawled over to the boy who had been knocked off his feet.

'It's okay, I'm here, I'll help you,' Joey whispered. He tried to staunch the flow of blood with his palm, but it surged out between his fingers. He stroked the boy's face. He couldn't have been more than five or six. The child opened his eyes, met Joey's gaze and blinked once.

'Hold on, hang on in there, *niño*,' Joey pleaded but the tiny hand was limp in his and the eyes framed with dusty lashes, stilled. Joey pressed his ear to his chest but there was no breath, no heartbeat. He spun around and yelled out for help as the ground shook again.

'*¡Córrele, córrele!*', an old man shouted to him from the other side of the road. Turning once to look back at the child, Joey covered his head with his arms and ran an erratic path in search of safety.

Cars slid forward and backwards, smacking together like marbles on a tipped plate. The pavement buckled and on either side of Calle Hidalgo the great stone buildings quivered. He needed to find a strong doorway or an open space, the *Zócalo* maybe, but he couldn't work out where he was; the landscape had changed, the sun blotted out by the dense grey smoke. He ducked for cover under the portico of an old church and tried not to panic. Around him mothers hushed their crying infants and teenagers clutched each other as the oscillations intensified. He was trying to focus on his body – his arms and legs the only controllable things suddenly in this shaking world – when a young girl grabbed his arm.

'Look!'

Two tower blocks were swaying from side to side, thumping together like a pair of wrestlers. He imagined the people inside, their beds sliding across the floor, their doors swinging open and slamming shut like toys in a shaken doll's house. And somewhere in all of this was his child. He pictured him alone and terrified. A howl climbed into his throat but he swallowed it back. No, Aurora would have kept Hijo by her side. They would be together. Had to be.

The ground juddered and then rested at last. Stillness hovered like a held breath. Abandoning the precarious safety he'd found, and ignoring the warnings of the others, he ventured back out. At

the junction, two cars lay tipped on their sides, a radio still playing lively salsa tunes. People began to step out of their shelters.
Some stood like dazed ghosts, unable to speak or move; others
grabbed passers-by, scrutinising their ashen faces for recognition.
Piles of rubble blocked the roads. Drivers, trapped in their cars,
pumped their horns uselessly. Buses had been abandoned, their
radios crackling with the names of buildings obliterated: *'Hotel
Regis destroyed... Super-Leche on fire...'* He'd taken Aurora and
Hijo there once. They'd ordered milkshakes and given themselves
moustaches with the foam.

Joey pushed through the chaos, with no idea of where he was
going. Ambulance sirens mixed with the cries of the trapped and
wounded. People scrabbled at the rubble, shouting for their children, wive, husbands. An old woman knelt by the body of a girl in
plastic shoes, her fallen ice-cream already swarming with ants. It
was like the end of the world – the end of his world, he thought.

He waded through the lost and the broken, searching every face.
He shouted their names until he was hoarse and as he walked the
smell of gas curled around each corner, followed by pistol shot
explosions and the shattering of glass. Police megaphones broke
through the air urging people to find a place of safety, an ineffectual bleating that signified nothing. Periodically the earth trembled, sending ripples of alarm through the bewildered crowds and
shooting pains through his heels. He was exhausted.

He turned into a small square and stopped. Cracked but still
standing in a sea of collapsed buildings, was a church. The stone
saints carved into the niches were worn smooth with age: they'd
survived this before. He went inside. The smell of incense and wax
was familiar and comforting but the flickering candlelight made
frantic shadows on the walls. At the altar a group of old *señoras*
wrapped in *rebozos* touched rosaries to their lips as they murmured
desperate prayers to the painted statues. His eyes roamed across
the faces of the kneeling figures and the small family groups. Of
course they weren't here.

Overcome by fatigue, he slid into a pew and rested his head on the wooden bench in front. He'd abandoned Aurora and Hijo, run away and left them. Yet still they'd come to look for him. If they were dead or injured it was his fault. He'd led them to this.

'*Mea culpa, mea culpa, mea culpa*,' he whispered thumping his hand to his chest. 'Take me God. Do the world a favour.'

As if in answer, a blast outside rocked the building. Cries erupted from the women as they ran for the doorway hoping the strong stone arch would protect them in a way that their prayers had not. The chandelier swayed sending pinpoints of light dancing across the walls. The glass pendants clinked together and Joey was struck by the incongruous beauty of the sound, like birdsong on a battlefield. Above him, a beam twisted beyond its limits, suddenly split in two. He watched as the golden altar-piece fractured and the angels, winged but flightless, smashed to pieces on the marble floor. He would join them, 'The Marvellous Joey Pachuca!', 'The best high-wire act in the whole of Mexico!', 'The hottest ticket in town!' Then the world plunged into darkness.

And there he was, back in the Ireland of his childhood the day he'd thrown God out of his mind and out of his heart, where he'd surrendered his soul to nothingness. He is lying in a field on his stomach. The grass is covered in dew. The sound of the water sucking at the soil is right in his ears as if he too might be sucked in. From his half-opened eye he sees a spider sprinting along a silver thread, its web a gleaming tiara in the wet grass. He remembers feeling just like that, that light and fast, before his da's fist knocked him through the air, breaking the joy in him into pieces. Maybe it had been the shock of seeing him, Joey, the clumsiest boy in all of Cork, hopping along the top of the fence like a bird. He'd been seven then, blue-eyed, and with a face that made old ladies stop and coo – until they saw him walking that is.

Why had he remembered that? Was this the end? Hah! Of all the times he'd prayed to God and now He chose to show himself!

He closed his eyes in the darkness and tried not to breathe. He wanted it over with.

'Run for it Limpy Joe. Joey Joey peg-leg.' A ball thrown deliberately out of his reach, the other kids shouting at him to fetch it, those schoolyard voices. He hadn't dreamed in his old brogue for a long time.

He'd thought it was the ground that did it. *'Ma,'* he'd said once, *'I can feel the earth breathing.'* The other boys managed though, striding effortlessly along as if they didn't even notice the fidgeting land. He'd coped with the earth's uncertainties by walking on the edges of his feet, his soles raised off the ground. For a time they'd had him in leg braces, like the plaster boy outside the chemist's. Adults let him be with that smile of his but the kids didn't. He'd learned very young that fear and shame could throw him off balance too and make his feet burn and ache.

So what had made him try that crazy thing? His feet had made him do it. They had forced him up on the fence post and out onto the thin wooden edge, as if they'd wanted to show him, just for an instant what was possible. Ciaran, the kid from next door, stood there, mouth open, watching him dance along the fence. *'Jesus'*, he whistled, *'how the hell did you do that, Joey?'*

At the time, he didn't know how he'd done it, had no idea then what his feet could do, yet somehow there he was, light as a cloud, clever as Superman. He caught sight of his father striding from the house and waved to him. Just wait until his da saw this, he thought. This would make him smile for once.

'Look da!' He'd shouted and he danced a little jig on the edge of the fence. His father's face whitened.

'Don't worry da, I'm fine, so I am.'

Wee Ciaran had seen the look of fury in that face though, and was running away. Then his father's fist came from nowhere, busting the wind out of him, knocking him through the air into the field behind the garden. The damp crept into his clothes and a sharp pain poked his side when he breathed.

Joey moved his eyes. He was sure they were open but there was nothing but blackness. He inched his fingers along the surface beneath him. It was wooden and gritty, the church pew he'd been sitting on before everything went dark. He lifted his hand, moving it through the emptiness until it touched his face but still he couldn't see it. Maybe it wasn't his hand at all. He tried to speak but his throat felt solid. His lids scraped against his eyeballs as he tried to blink. He closed them and tried to ignore the growing ache in his head. He'd been in a church, he remembered that. He'd been searching for Aurora and Hijo. An earthquake. Images sprang out at him suddenly

the business man stumbling to his knees clutching his briefcase to his chest, a tethered dog frantically trying to free itself from a street light, that dead child, covered in dust. He thought of his own child.

He had to get out. He moved his precious feet. A faint spark pulsed through his right heel but there was something heavy pressing on his left one. He prayed it wasn't broken. He had a show to do. He'd been in the papers. People had paid a lot of money to see him. He jolted up flailing against the debris but the dust made him choke and something creaked above him.

He stretched his hand upwards until it hit something cold. How much more lay above that? He imagined all the soaring ribs of masonry: the tiles, the wood, the glass, resting precariously above him. He stifled his urge to scream, afraid that if he gave in, it would never stop. He tried to turn but a hot pain lit up the side of his body.

He is standing in an office with his mother; the walls are speckled with a sickly green paint. He tried to blink the image away but it stayed there clear as a film. He is looking out of the window. The day is wet with sudden bursts of sun and the roads are black and shiny like records. The rain has freckled the glass so that people going past are blurred and grainy.

Underneath his shirt is a big bandage wrapped all around his body like a mummy. If he cries, the pain jabs through him and if he laughs it's even worse. But he doesn't feel like laughing or crying, he is too afraid to do either. In fact he is too scared even to take a breath. Perhaps if he doesn't breathe he might disappear. But when he doesn't breathe, the room begins to wobble and the welfare woman rushes away for water. His mother bites her lip and pulls at the skin around her nails. Sitting on a chair, his head swimming, he feels his mother clutch his shoulders as she stares into his face, her eyes large and frightened.

'Never ever do that trick again, not in front of anyone round here, especially your da. Never even speak to him about it, do you understand me?'

He hadn't understood, but the grip of her fingers was hard to argue with. When the woman came back, with a full glass and some smelling salts, his mother bent down towards him, her red hair catching on his cheek, and whispered in his ear,

'I love you Joey but you're safer away from your da.'

He drank the water and when he looked up she'd gone.

He batted his hands in front of his face. He didn't want these memories. Death had taken those others: that little one on his way to school, that grey-faced girl with the ice cream, and allowed him to survive. Why, to remember all this? The darkness around him jostled with words and images, swimming in close then vanishing. He tried to grab them but felt the sharp sting of raw skin.

He could smell something, Lily of the Valley, his mother's perfume. Had she come to him now? How many times had he waited for her in those homes, their windows full of rain? When at last she had visited, she'd held his wrists with her wiry hands and told him that she would take him back as soon as possible.

'Can't we run away?' he'd said. *'Come and get me in the night and*

we'll go together, we'll go to Hollywood or the Wild West. I've got money, look.' He'd held out his hand, two notes screwed up in it. She'd bit her lip, her eyes filling.

'You don't understand Joey, sometimes you have to make amends, pay God back.'

'Pay him back for what, mam?'

A teardrop darkened her skirt.

He could feel his own, running down the sides of his face collecting in a cold pool in his ears. If he just kept quiet in the dark, disappeared into some other place, all this would go away. His mother hadn't learned how to do that. She wore her pain on her sleeve along with her heart, all her inner life exposed as if she'd been born inside out.

Something shifted above him. He heard another noise, an unfamiliar croaking. Excited, he called out and then realised it had been the sound of his own weeping. The loneliness of it frightened him. He'd thought he was ready to die but now he wasn't sure. He wished there was a light, just a scrap of it, something to define his edges and make him believe he still existed.

He had sought out darkness as a child, hiding in his wardrobe among the clothes when the fighting started. One night he heard a shriek so high that it seemed to fill his skull. It could not be his mother he told himself, it must be a wolf. He closed his eyes and pressed the soles of his feet together, squeezing until the pain numbed them and lights floated in front of him. Then, suddenly he found himself in cowboy country. It was daytime and the red rocks rose out of the yellow sand like upturned strawberry jellies shimmering in the heat. Tumbleweeds blew across his path and the horse beneath him whinnied. He whispered in her ear, *'It will be alright, don't worry.'* She calmed down and started trotting towards the small town on the horizon.

Mind-floating, that had got him through some of the nights when his da was riled, or in the children's home where the big ones moved around in the dark. It was always the same place he escaped to, that big empty desert with a blue sky, a small town rising out of the emptiness, music tinkling in the distance and his horse taking him there across the silence.

He hadn't done it since he was a kid, maybe because his feet had learned so many other marvellous tricks: how to sense vibrations through a taut high-wire, how to know the exact moment to take off into a leap, how to find the rope again when he landed and how to make an audience leave this world and taste the next. His feet had felt the writhing of the earth and the tremors of love. Still he yearned for the simplicity of that childhood experience, the belief in the power of escape.

In that moment before the church had collapsed there had been other people inside this building. They must be trapped in pockets of air just like him, fearful and alone. He began to shout into the darkness then stopped abruptly. How much air was there? He might use it all up before someone found him.

He thought about his performance. All the tricks he'd practised, the costumes that Aurora had made, the silver one with his name on it. Was the circus caught up in this? He imagined the Big Top of Circo Robles, flattened, the caravans and trucks tossed across the site. It had been his home for eight years, more of a home than anything else he'd ever had, the place where his life had truly begun. He pictured the jugglers and the acrobats, Rodrigo the strongman, and Negrita and Blanca and their beautiful horses, scrabbling on a bucking earth. All of his family gone. All his achievements come to nothing.

Falling in love, Hijo, the roar of the crowd, that's what he wanted to relive now in this dark place, not his childhood, not the terrible thing he'd done. But the past was closing in, its fragments kaleidoscoping around him. He could see it all, the synchronicity of bad luck and mistakes, the dance of destruction that he had been rehearsing since he was born, all for that moment that he didn't want to remember. When his soul finally floated out of his body through the ruins of this church and into the chaos outside, he hoped there would be a moment of illumination, like the phosphorescent bloom of a struck match, when he'd know what it had all meant.

'Ma,' he called out into the darkness. 'I'm sorry.'

Part 2

1

August 1975, Atlantic Ocean

The first night, dog-sick and swollen-hearted, he stared down into the rolling sea and thought about jumping. He pressed his forehead against the railing of the ship, trying to remove those images of her that sprang out at him like the terrors on a ghost train. He hadn't meant it to end like that and now there was nothing he could do.

On his second night holed up in the damp hull of a lifeboat, he tried to talk himself into a future, convince himself he could have a new start in America, but he was talking through his arse. All he really wanted was to close his eyes without seeing his mother's face, her red hair slipping in and out of his head like a drift of blood in a bowl of water.

After he was kicked out of his lifeboat hideaway three days out, he thought he'd had it. They'd send him back, let the cops have him. Snot-filled and miserable to the core, he didn't care. The captain wasn't having any of it though. He set him to work in the charge of Seely, the ship's cook.

'I want you ta mop not mope,' Seely barked, shoving a stinking bucket into his hands.

The fumes nearly burnt out his nose and made his eyes stream. He cleaned until his arms ached and his fingers were raw, until he was too exhausted to think. Leatherhead, a stammering Kerryman, bald and ugly, shared his cigarettes, but also gave him the news that made him want to climb the railings again.

'We're going to M-mexico,' he said.

'Well we go to the States in the end,' Seely added, 'but yer won't want to be there as a stowaway, you'll be deported quick as shit.' He rubbed his stubble. 'Better to jump ship in Alta Mira, take your chances there. You got a bit of the foreigner about you, so.'

Joey groaned and dug his fingers into his eye sockets.

'Sure t'heres c-cowboys in Mexico,' Leatherhead said, 'and g-girls, fine ones, black-haired, byootiful, speak f-feckin S-Spanish t'ough.'

Joey sighed. Mexico.

'They play football,' Seely added, rolling his chef's hat into a ball and heading it in Joey's direction.

'Don't like football.'

'Wha… are you a nancy or what?'

'Seen him doin' de b-ballet,' Leatherhead said, 'he tinks I d-don't but I do. For someone who c-can't even walk right, he's got balance I'll give him that.'

'Juggling, I do juggling and magic. I'll show you if you want,' Joey snapped, pulling the cards out of his pocket and waving them in Leatherhead's face. Leatherhead put his hands up in a gesture of conciliation.

'Don't worry son, I'll teach you some of the lingo, enough to get you by,' Seely said, 'some curse words are always handy.'

'Christ Seely, he should g-go home. What are yer, f-fourteen?' Leatherhead said.

'Nearly sixteen and I can't go back.'

Leatherhead and Seely exchanged glances. 'Why?' Seely asked, his beady eyes travelling over Joey's small, skinny frame, his mouth twisted into a smirk, 'have you killed someone?' Joey rolled his eyes but felt his chest tighten.

'Or maybe you've robbed a big bank with a saw'd-off shotgun,' he added, winking. The other crew members laughed, their eyes disappearing into their sunburnt cheeks.

Leatherhead put an arm around Joey's shoulders. 'Come on, that's enough now boys, I bet he's aff t'mek his f-fortune, aren't you son, with those blue eyes.' He ruffled Joey's hair with his huge hand. 'You've bin watching t-too many f-f eckin films, so you have.'

The police hadn't checked the ports yet then, or put an alert out for him. Maybe he had a chance after all. If he could just get off this ship and into a new country, he would change his name and then no-one would ever find him.

He spent the long sleepless hours practising magic and perfecting his card tricks. And as he scrubbed floors and smashed cockroaches with the back of the broom, Seely drilled him in survival Spanish. Despite the food and the cold and the sickness that plagued him there was one blessing to being at sea: his feet, separated from the earth by tonnes of steel and ocean, registered little more than the swell and the occasional bout of terror when a storm lifted the ship and dropped it back with a shudder. Here it was only his fears and anxieties that his feet responded to, searing his arches and flooring him in unguarded moments.

When they docked, the crew slapped him on the back and wished him luck. For a second, as he looked at their familiar faces, Joey thought about staying put and risking his luck in the States. Then Seely pressed into his hand some *peso* notes that the crew had scraped together and a slip of paper with an address in Mexico City.

'Unless you've other plans made, she'll put you up, if you can get there. Hitch a ride in a truck, you'll be fine. Her name is Lupe. Tell her Seely says, yo *tay keero*.' He placed his hand over his heart in a mime of love.

2

He slept through most of his rides, his head drooping on his chest as he struggled to understand the drivers who stopped and picked him up from the roadside. In the stifling heat of their cabins hung with flags and religious knick-knacks, he dozed and dreamed, waking only when they stopped at dusty taco stands that appeared from nowhere amongst fields of cacti and rocks.

Mexico City began with shacks that tumbled down hillsides where cows still grazed on livid grass. Then gradually the sprouting fields shrank to small patches which in turn became window-boxes until finally there were just corn-oil cans filled with dusty geraniums in dirt yards guarded by tetchy dogs.

Here and there, majestic houses, their beautiful balconies like artfully arranged hair, their crowns a confection of scrollwork and stucco, stood out from the surrounding tangle of gleaming offices and modern residential blocks. As they idled in a jam, he imagined himself living in such a place with wrought-iron gates and a sprinkler in the garden, and then the truck rumbled on its way again, blasting its horn fruitlessly at the traffic and shattering his dreams.

Joey was sure he must be in the centre but still the truck jolted on, under huge roads, past empty lots jagged with the skeletons of demolished buildings or the sprouting rusting bones of new ones and everywhere he looked there were people. Youngsters much younger than him, wandered in and out of the traffic selling gum and newspapers and jellies and biscuits, and older ones pushed their wares through the windows of chugging buses and cars as they slowed down at junctions. He looked in their eyes and saw fleeting glimpses of himself.

In the distance glittering skyscrapers pointed up into the clouds as if drawing the new visitor's attention to the yellow smog that lingered there. At last the truck driver dropped him at a bus station, and with a brief wave ground back into the traffic.

Horns blared and buses creaked; a frightening din assaulted him. New words leapt off buildings, bubbled from mouths, and everywhere streams of people swept around him, selling, buying, eating, hauling, cajoling and gesticulating. The forecourt was swarming with travellers of every age and income: business men in crisp short-sleeved shirts and dark glasses, students with backpacks, old people with walnut faces and bulging bags tied with string, and all about him the reek of diesel and the grinding of brakes. Battered microbuses lined the street, destinations painted in white on their windscreens.

'*A dónde va?*'

Joey looked around him. A teenager was leaning out of the window of one of the buses, a big eagle-headed ring on his little finger.

Joey put his hand up, '*Uno momento. Yo tengo...* I have an address.' He dug into his pockets for the slip of paper wrapped around the peso notes that Seely had given him. The boy waited, drumming his fingers on the window as Joey patted himself all over and turned each pocket inside out.

'*Momentito,*' Joey said. He ran back, retracing his short journey from where the truck had dropped him, weaving his way through the milling people, scanning the ground for paper. The floor was spotless though, each dropped fragment swept away by a team of cleaners easing their brooms across the pavement.

He ran, checking his pockets one more time but the address and the notes were gone. Joey wanted to punch someone. He'd had it in the last truck he'd been in. That fella wouldn't have taken it, he was sure. He'd been a kind old boy with pictures of his granddaughters in his wallet and a sun-strip that read – if he'd got the Spanish right – *God is the driver of this truck.* The old man had even bought him food when they'd stopped. When they'd stopped. Shit! He remembered taking his jacket off after a wee one bumped into him with a jug of water. He'd put it on the back of the chair to dry.

The driver's assistant, a skinny boy with long feathered hair leaned back and shook his head.

'Can you remember any of it?' The boy said in Spanish.

Joey shook his head. '*Nada.*'

'I'll take you to the *Zócalo*. All foreigners go there. We'll be leaving soon.' He looked Joey up and down, '*Turista ou estudiante?*'

'I'm a performer, a magician,' Joey muttered in English, searching in his pockets for some change.

The boy stayed his hand. '*No problema*, get in, I know what it's like to be new in town.'

'I'm from Chiapas in the South,' he continued as the bus pulled out, 'came up here two years ago when my father died. It was a struggle, man, but now, I've done well. I've made it.' He straightened the collar of his worn shirt and adjusted his mirrored sunglasses. Joey understood his body language even though he didn't get all the words.

The bus stopped frequently to pick up passengers but Joey, disconsolate, took no interest in them; he rubbed the dirty glass with his sleeve and stared out of the window. The roads were full of buses and taxis competing for passengers, cutting in front of each other and pumping their horns in warning or triumph. He was convinced, as they struggled down yet another traffic-choked road, that they were going in circles. The bus stopped again and the driver's assistant tapped Joey's shoulder and pointed,

'*Aqui. ¡Buena suerte!* good luck.'

Joey nodded, grasped the proffered hand and climbed out.

The *Zócalo*. The square opened up like a field in front of him. He stood for a moment trying to take it all in. Magnificent buildings lined its perimeter and across its vast space, vendors of balloons and baked sweet potatoes, tee-shirts and beads, moved in slow circles, trying to tempt the strolling tourists. And over it all like an awning, a bright blue sky. So this was Mexico City. It wasn't what he'd expected. Where were the bandits, the sombreros, the black-eyed girls with bare shoulders and the rest?

Music and drumbeats floated from a small crowd. Moving gingerly through them, trying to keep his balance, he came upon a group of dancers. Their costumes were bright, their broad faces framed by straight black hair. He'd seen those faces before in the *National Geographic*, Aztec faces. Wasn't it the Aztecs who practised human sacrifice? Surely they couldn't still exist. Joey thought they'd died out like the Romans. The dancers were staring ahead, as if in a trance. The smell of incense lingered though, reminding him of home, of churches on dark evenings.

The square was impressive but overwhelming. The scale of it alone made him weary. And his feet! Each step he took sent shocks up through his body. He'd noticed it the moment he'd set foot on the shore, but he'd been suffering from the sea legs then and mistook his difficulties for that. The tide had long since drained from his bones but his instability was even worse. He lifted his feet up and massaged them even though it made him wince.

He made his way to the edge of the *Zócalo* and followed it around. A straggling line of men leaned against the iron railings, their faces impassive, each in his private world. Some carried bags: others wore belts dangling with unfamiliar tools. '*Plomero.*' '*Electricista,*' their signs read. He saw himself there in a few weeks, with his own hand-made sign. As he walked past them they stared at his hobbling gait. He took cover under a colonnaded walkway.

Here was another world altogether. In the shade, the tapping of a dozen typewriters filled the air. The typists sat in a long row and next to each stood a queue gripping letters and documents. One typist, balding, but with a big moustache read out a letter to a young woman with a baby. She wiped her eyes with the back of her hand but she didn't make a sound. She dropped a coin on the table, took her letter and left. He understood then. He walked away suddenly embarrassed by his scrutiny.

He followed a street lined with shops and cafés wishing he had enough for a cold beer. His head throbbed. Perhaps it was the altitude, Seely had warned him about that. Peering inside the *Café la Blanca*, he noticed the walls were covered with old black and white photos of film stars and there he was, back on the couch with his mother on a wet Sunday afternoon watching Gene Kelly and Frank Sinatra. She loved those old films, with the soppy songs and the dancing, so he watched them with her though he preferred The Man from Uncle and The Virginian. He blinked the image away and hurried on.

The window of the *Dulceria de Celaya* glittered with crystallised fruits and sweets of every colour. His mouth filled with saliva. It was sixteen hours since he'd eaten. Kicking at a rotten orange he wondered how long it would be before that started to look appetising. He turned away from the street with its tantalising windows and took a side road which eventually opened out into a small plaza at the centre of which was a clump of shade trees and a circular bench. He threw himself onto it and rubbed his face. Above him invisible birds squabbled in the dark leaves but in between their shrill cries he heard the unmistakeable sound of running water. He shuffled along the bench and peered around the thick trunk of the tree. On the faded blue wall on the far side of the plaza was a stone angel's head, a metal pipe wedged into its mouth. The great gob of its spit cascaded into a pool lined with tiles. Joey ran across and stuck his head under the flow, filling his parched throat and soaking the front of his shirt. Only an angel could spit as well as that! His skin cooled and his thirst satisfied, he stretched himself out on the bench and closed his eyes. See, all he'd needed was a bit of luck.

3

By the third week though, the luck he'd imagined had faded and Joey was sick of his own stink. It was more than just sweat and dirt, it was fear and hunger. His stomach juices desperate to work had seeped into his mouth and his tongue burned. Hunger was no longer the gurgling reminder he'd become used to, it was a constant, nagging presence.

Tired and light-headed, he drifted into a market. The stalls pressed in on him and the mountains of spices made his head swim. Glad of the cool, though, he dawdled in an aisle stacked on either side with fruit and hung with bunting in the red, white and green of Mexico. The aisle opened out and in front of him was a stall piled high with pieces of roasted pork. Before he knew it he had stretched out and grabbed a handful. In an instant there was a shout, and a man in a bloodied apron came at him.

Joey froze as the jowly face disappeared and the smooth one of his father replaced it. He ducked and then ran as best he could, past the dripping heads of pigs, the shivering piles of maroon livers, the coiled innards, the grey crimped tripe, the gleaming bones, past the rank smell of decay and sawdust and old blood out into the street where the light, sharp and hard, blinded him.

There was nothing to stop his legs though, and he ran on until a blaring horn and a chorus of shouts stopped him. He collapsed on the road in front of a waste truck and a bus that had screeched to a halt inches away. A crowd quickly gathered.

'¡*Policía!*' someone called.

'*Y ambulancia tambien.*'

He lay on the ground stunned, looking up into a circle of faces. He pulled himself up to a sitting position and dropped his head between his knees.

'Ay, he's okay.' He heard disappointment in the voice.

'He's not hurt?'

'Nah, no blood'

'*¡Que cabrón!* He nearly killed himself.'

The crowd began to disperse as he crawled to the kerb. A couple of worried mothers grabbed their children's hands and turned back to look at him, but too busy with their own errands, they left him to dust himself down leaving only a dog to bark at him.

'You okay brother?' A thin teenager peeled himself from the wall of a building and offered him a cigarette. He took it, accepted a light, puffed, and choked.

'*Me llamo* Paco. Let me buy you a drink.' The boy disappeared and then was back in a moment with a bottle of orange soda.

Joey took a gulp, nodded, '*Gracias.*'

'You're hungry?'

Joey shrugged. The boy laughed, slapped his shoulder. 'Come on, come with me, my auntie sells *carnitas* and she'll do anything for me.' He winked at Joey, grabbed the empty bottle from his hand and dropped it in the gutter.

Joey tried to keep up as Paco wove in and out of the crowds that hung out on the pavements. He stumbled as a sharp spasm shot through his arch. Maybe this was not a good idea, but he thought of the promised food, ignored his feet and tried to catch up. Paco turned his head to chat, slap someone else on the back and offer another a cigarette, his eyes darting from side to side. Once or twice someone peered around Paco's head to look at him and words Joey couldn't understand and laughter were exchanged but Joey didn't care. He was thinking about the *carnitas*, hoping the auntie existed and really would do anything.

'Nearly there, brother,' Paco said, slowing down a little. 'What's your name anyway?'

'Joey... Pachuca.' The surname seemed to come from nowhere. He liked the sound of it though. Perhaps he'd seen it on a road sign. Paco stopped,

'Hoey? What in hell kind of name is that?'

'A gringo name.' Joey said then wished he hadn't. The boy peered at him closely then spat on his thumb and wiped it against Joey's cheek.

'Blue eyes, brown skin – American mother, Mexican father,' Joey lied 'Both dead.'

'Half a gringo then, and you speak a little Spanish but your accent is *loco*. So Djoey,' – he had difficulty with the sound – 'what's half a gringo doing fighting with the traffic in Mexico City then?'

Joey hung his head and looked away. Paco wagged a finger at him and grinned.

The glass-fronted shops had given way to hole-in-the-wall kiosks hung with cheap household goods. Signs painted on plastered walls advertised clutch shops and tyre centres. Paco made him sit at a metal table whilst he went up to the counter. He heard chatting, the hiss of an opening bottle, a woman's high sing-song voice. His head felt like it might crush his neck. He rested it on the table.

'Here you go, get your teeth round those.' Joey woke from his doze. On the plate in front of him were four tacos bursting with succulent crisp-edged meat and pale jalapeno peppers. Joey looked up at him, mouth open. Paco waved at him,

'Go on, eat.'

'I haven't any money to give you.'

'*Amigo*. Did I ask for money? No, so eat.'

Joey picked up the taco and took the first bite: an explosion of chilli, the chewy softness of the tortillas, the crisp coolness of the lettuce. He wanted to hold each mouthful and savour it, but his teeth had other plans and soon he was staring at an empty plate. Paco, playing with a plastic key-ring in which was embedded a figure of a praying Christ, had been watching him all the time.

Paco's auntie came out and joined him for a moment. *'Es un muchacho muy guapo,'* she sang to Paco, her big bosom bumping against Joey's shoulder as she ruffled his hair. He caught the savoury smell of her and decided he would only marry a woman who smelled of hot roasted meat.

'You need somewhere to sleep?' Paco said, stirring three spoons of sugar into his coffee and lighting up another cigarette. Joey nodded.

'I can help you with that too.'

'Another auntie?' Joey said.

Paco gave a brief grin. 'An uncle,' he said.

4

Under a street light an old woman nursed a tub of *tamales* – aromatic morsels wrapped in corn husks – which steamed like laundry. Children played in the road dodging the cars and motor bikes that bowled along over the potholes and muddy ruts. Nobody took any notice of him.

He followed Paco into a courtyard. Through an archway he could hear the sound of muffled voices. A doorway led into a room crammed with furniture where a huge television blinked in a corner casting blue flickering light across the walls. They were covered with pictures of Elvis Presley.

'Uncle.'

A man in a white shirt turned from the television. He was wearing loose pyjama bottoms and his feet were bare.

'*Tío*, I have a friend with me, he can stay in my room, is that okay? Joey, this is *Tío* Alejandro, *Uncle* Alejandro.'

The man turned and stared briefly at Joey, nodded at Paco and then returned to the television.

The bedroom was small and windowless, separated from the corridor by a ragged curtain.

'You can sleep over there.' Paco pointed to a mattress with a pile of blankets on it. 'Toilet is down the hall.'

'Where are you going to sleep?'

Paco turned from the door. 'Me? I don't need to sleep.' He laughed and Joey heard his voice echoing down the hallway.

The room smelt stale but he didn't care, he dropped onto the bed, on top of the blankets and was asleep in minutes.

It was there on the edges of his dream - the sensation creeping up, forcing him to remember; his blood pumping, himself shouting and she sitting on the couch her face pale and waxy. His father is looking at him, a look that has made his knuckles white with anger, a look that he can't find a word for but even now he wants to strike it off his face.

Joey's eyes shot open and the dream vanished like vapour. He could hear breathing. Someone else was in the room.

'Paco?'

'You want a drink?' It was *Tío* Alejandro. He was holding up a glass.

Joey shook his head. 'No, *gracias*.'

'I don't like to drink alone.' He didn't move. Joey lay still, his stomach tight, pins and needles in his feet.

'You like Elvis Presley?'

The question took Joey by surprise. He laughed slightly. '*Claro*. He's the King.'

'The king!' the man said in English and laughed. 'Come and listen to the king, come, come.'

Joey, unable to think of a reason to refuse, got up and followed Uncle Alejandro to his room where the television still played in the corner. *Tío* Alejandro chose a record from a stack and held it under the light.

'*Esté*.' He jabbed his finger at one of the titles on the back cover 'Ar djew lonee-somee tonite.'

'Are you lonesome tonight?' Joey said in English.

'*Qué significa?*'

Joey tried to explain in Spanish. *Tío* Alejandro stared at him, put his hand on his shoulder and squeezed it. 'Good boy.'

Joey shrugged it off, wished he weren't so small.

'*No tiene miedo*. Don't be afraid, we only listen to music.' He turned and put the record on the turntable and cursed twice when the needle skipped the surface. 'There.' He stood up, ear cocked, nodding his head as the voice crackled out of the speaker. He hummed along.

'*Gracias*, but I need to go,' Joey said, turning, '*Necesito dormir.*'

The humming stopped. 'Go?' he said, 'I don't think so. Food must be paid for, and I think you have eaten, no?'

Despite the heavy accent Joey understood. How could he have been so stupid? He glanced around the room looking for a means of escape. For a moment he thought of fighting his way out but Alejandro was a big man. If he called for help others might come, more boys like Paco. Alejandro took his arm and dug his fingers into the muscle making Joey wince.

'*Yo quiero dinero*, money,' Joey said boldly rubbing his fingers together.

Alejandro tutted, 'You are a greedy boy.' He ran his other hand across Joey's forehead, lifted a thin lock of his hair, 'but *guapo*, pretty.' Joey flinched and tried to pull away.

Keeping his grip tight, Alejandro rummaged in his pockets, pulled out two notes and put them on the table. Joey went to grab them, but Alejandro's hand came down hard on top of his fingers crushing them tightly in his.

'After,' he said, and pushed Joey over to the mattress that lay on the floor in front of the speakers. It was slashed and marked as if murder had taken place.

Is your heart filled with pain, shall I come back again…?

'Sit.' The man forced Joey's shoulder down, and he sank onto the mattress. Rigid with fear Joey sat bolt upright trying to block out what was going to happen, staring at the television that ranted in the corner like the town drunk. Panic rose in him but his cold, resigned self, pushed it down.

'Here.' Alejandro gave him a tiny glass full of clear liquid. Joey sniffed at it.

'It's tequila,' Alejandro said. 'Drink it like this.' He tossed his head back and fired the drink into his throat.

'I know how to drink tequila,' Joey said, and did the same, felt his mouth burn, and as his senses returned he took another glassful, hoping he might pass out, or at least numb the dread that was threatening to turn his stomach to liquid.

He'd focused hard on the television, a quiz show, the contestants squealing and clapping as their numbers came up, and beneath its jabbering, the animal grunting, the stink of sweat, and the bite of fingernails in his shoulders.

When it was over Alejandro sat back on the armchair, and changed channels. 'Ah, Magnum,' he said, 'I like this guy.'

Joey turned his back and wriggled into his trousers.

'Tell anyone and I'll kill you,' Alejandro said, without taking his eyes off the screen.

Joey took the money and left the room. Back in the bedroom he pulled on his shoes and grabbed his bag. He crept down the corridor, past the room where Elvis was now singing *Heartbreak Hotel* and slipped into the alleyway.

It was still dark outside and the street was empty. He limped along the pavement, keeping to the shadows, afraid he might meet Paco on his way back from some business. He needed to find somewhere to clean himself up. He followed the wall until he found an opening. He squeezed through the gap into a piece of waste ground where long-spined *nopales* and *agaves* had grown up among the collapsed brickwork. He hoped there were no wild dogs or snakes. In one corner he found a tin bowl half filled with water. It smelled stale and insects puckered its dusty surface. He bent to clean his face and pain dazzled him, a raw weight that dragged at his abdomen and made him giddy. He leaned forward and tried to take some deep breaths but his bruised body protested. He rested for a moment to let the earth stop moving and washed the blood from his thighs. His clothes were damp now but it was worth it to feel clean. He found a sheltered corner between two pieces of masonry and lay down. The alcohol was wearing off and the night's ordeal was returning in flashes.

Perhaps he could mind-float if he tried hard enough. He clenched his fists and gripped his feet, trying to clear his head like he had as a child. For a moment the desert plain loomed into his vision and he felt the old sensation of being on horseback with the comforting movement of the animal beneath him and the clip of its hooves on the rocks. Then it was gone.

He hoisted himself up, rested against the wall and felt the notes rustle in his pocket. Barely sixteen and already he'd become the piece of rubbish his father had predicted. It was almost a relief. There was no coming back from this. He stared up at the night sky and took a deep breath. The scents of earth and shit and vegetation shot up into his head. For the first time in ages his mind felt clear and empty. He fell asleep and didn't wake until the sound of a rooster blasted out of a September sky and six peals of a church bell clanked him out of his stupor.

5

August 1977

Joey threw himself at sin – as Father Michael would have said – and it happily embraced him. At night he joined the other hustlers on the street corners and watched them watching him, waiting for their opportunity. He acquired enough Spanish to scrounge and charm and enough work to stave off that consuming hunger he'd felt when he'd first landed in Mexico City. Leftover *pesos* were spent in pursuit of oblivion – anything to block those memories lay in wait, ready to paralyse him.

There had been moments during those first eighteen months when the secret he carried seemed too much to bear and lying in some ill-lit room, he longed to confess everything, clutch some spent girl's arms and tell her how he'd grabbed the knife, but he imagined their frightened eyes and their stiffened sinews as they drew back from him.

In those nights, bawling from a barstool, he would goad some poor fool into a fight with him. For a few moments he would feel electrified at the sound of excited men betting all their wages on his clumsy gait, convinced he'd fall in a moment, only to shake their heads as he hammered some teenager with the force of his anger.

The cuts and the bruises were worth it for those moments when, focused on that one thing, he pounded away until the red sea inside him subsided. At first he rode the wave, relishing the handshakes and the free drinks. Then, his mind empty and his fists stinging, he'd stare around him at the gathered group, despair seeping into him as their eyes scrutinised him with curiosity and admiration. At last the wave would recede, leaving the flotsam of those emotions behind and the need to do it all again.

He probably would have got himself killed if it hadn't been for Teresa.

He'd found himself a room, at the back of a shop, a tiny place no bigger than an outhouse with a rickety bed and a table. Just having somewhere ready and waiting for him made it worth the money he had to earn to rent it. He felt safe there, free from the possibility of random violence and the paranoia of those high on drugs. Here after a bout of drinking he could sleep disturbed only by his own demons. But after a particularly raucous night he returned to a stony-faced landlady, a crying baby in her arms.

'You must go,' she said, 'my brother gets out in two days and I need the room, I'm sorry.' She thrust a plastic bag at him stuffed with his few possessions.

He walked a block or two and found a bar he recognised. A couple of old guys were playing cards in the corner. Two more at the counter were glued to the *lucha libre* wrestling on the television. He watched with them for a while, the fighters in their capes and masks like superheroes, rolling around in the ring like a pair of giant battling flies. There was money in fighting but he didn't want to punch someone in a mask, he wanted to see their faces. He caught sight of his own in the mirror above the bar. Would his mother recognise him? He barely recognised himself. His face had become chiselled with hunger, his cheek bones sharpening his oval face, making his blue eyes seem bluer still. His light olive skin was burned brown and scarred in places from his injuries, and his lips, once full and sharp-edged, were dry and scabbed in the corners. His dark hair had acquired an auburn cast, bleached by his hours in the sun. He cut off the curls and kept it short, giving nothing for his opponents to grab onto. He pulled back his lips, at least his teeth were intact and his nose hadn't been broken yet. It was still the small snub nose he used to press up against windows, rubbing spy-holes with it on the misted glass, through which he was convinced he would see his ma running down the road to fetch him.

He drank slowly and methodically until his anxieties began to lessen their grip and his feet began to numb. Addled with booze he talked it over with himself, deriding his foolish choices and cursing his bad luck. Two young men turned from the bar and laughed at him. He stood up unsteadily and swore at them. They mimicked his accented Spanish and awkward posture, before turning back to their drinks.

'*¡Que chinga*! What a loser,' one of the boys sneered in his up-town accent. Joey lurched towards them. They wavered in front of him like figures on a hot road. He swung his fist, but the rich boy ducked, laughing.

Joey staggered forward and tried again, catching one of them on the side of the head. A moment later Joey found his arms pinned behind his back. He twisted and wriggled and struck out again but the boy was tougher than he looked. The other one lunged at him and Joey felt a hot pain in his leg. He looked down. A dark stain was spreading through the cloth of his jeans and he could see the glint of red through the slit in the fabric. His arms were released and as he struggled to stand the room spun. He tried to pick out the two boys from the blurred onlookers, but they had vanished. He spat out insults hoping his shouts would reach them in the street.

The barman lifted him by the collar, and pushed him out of the door. Face down on the pavement he felt that old bump on his rib against the stone. He wanted to be sick. He rolled onto his back and glared at the passers-by who'd stopped to stare at him. A police siren whined as it closed in. Someone broke through and pulled at his arm.

'*Pobrecito*, what are you doing? Look at you, you are a mess.'

Did he know those eyes, he didn't think so. No-one he knew

had eyes as beautiful as that, except his mother. 'Is it you, mam?' he said blurrily in English.

The girl – her lips gluey with gloss – tutted. 'If I was your mother I would thrash you myself.'

'Am I dead then, *muerto?*'

She swore and pulled him up. '*Levàntese*, get up before the cops come. Come on.'

He got to his feet, and limped after her, trying to staunch the flow of blood with his hand.

The street was jammed with stalls and people. Noise buzzed in his ears and a giddy collage of faces zoomed and retreated in front of him. He followed her into another bar. The music was throbbing and only the press of bodies kept him upright. Lights played off the sweating dancers, covering them in patches of colour, turning their smiling mouths into grimaces. His feet ached and he let her lead him through the crowd to a patio at the back strung with lights. She pushed him into a chair in a corner.

'*Quién es?*' he said, looking up at her smooth face, with its thin eyebrows and smear of sparkly eye shadow.

'*Me llamo* Teresa, now stay there while I get a cloth.'

'...and a drink.'

'You've had enough to drink,' she said. A few minutes later she returned with a wet rag, and pulled back the cloth from the wound.

'*Es loco*! What did you think you were doing?' she chided as she carefully wiped the blood away, ignoring the stares of the other drinkers.

The coldness of the cloth sobered him up a little. 'I'm just a loser. I should go back home and take what's coming to me,' he mumbled. He'd enjoyed thumping that bastard though. He'd felt a rush better than a drug. Is that what his father had felt, that bliss of violence? But like a drug, the downside was a great empty hole. Was he going to beat the hell out of every lowlife in Mexico City, keep on thumping his way through them just for some moments of peace? Christ, what had he come to? She stopped dabbing at his wound and lifted his face with her hand. He stared into her eyes which were filled with tears.

'Why are you crying?' Joey said, confused. 'Don't waste your tears on me. The bastard bladed me, that's all.' He closed his eyes. 'I didn't see it coming. I'll be okay.' A burning sensation seared his leg making him wince with pain.

'Those stinking *fresas.*' Teresa sniffed. 'I need to fix you up, you don't want an infection.' She took his hand carefully in her own and the warmth of her touch made his head spin. He began to fall sideways.

'Hey, don't faint on me, I can't pick you up on my own. You live near here?'

'Not any more, I got kicked out.'

'Then you better come back with me.'

6

They stumbled through the narrow streets to a single storey building, with boarded-up windows and words he couldn't read in the darkness, painted over the façade.

'It's a dump, but it's all I've got to call home at the moment,' Teresa said. She knocked hard on the door and it opened with a clanging sound as someone slid it back. The smell of urine and decay made his eyes water. It took Joey some time to adjust to the dim yellowish glow from a single bulb. It hung from the centre of the room, shielded by a tee-shirt draped over the skeleton of a lampshade.

'It's connected to the wiring from down the street. It doesn't always work but it's better than the dark.'

It must have been a garage at one time. He looked around, trying not to breathe through his nose; advertisements for engine oil and brakes, covered with a patina of dirt and age, were pinned to the wall and hub-caps dotted the ceiling and gave Joey the feeling he was being stared at by the eyes of a huge insect. The concrete floor was scattered with stained mattresses, car seats and sofas with stuffing popping out of the seams. With his leg out of action he had no idea what to do next. He would end up on the street again. Panic gripped him and he began to shake. Teresa pulled back a ragged curtain that blocked off an area not much bigger than a cupboard. A young boy was lying there. She kicked him in the side.

'Hey, Rigo, shift, *rápido*.' The boy swore but moved away, and Joey sank down onto the mattress. She lit two candles that sat on a shelf above the bed. The red wax was printed with images of the Virgin Mary and the words *Madre de Cristo*. The flickering flames undulated over the green flaking walls, creating soft mountains and valleys over the plaster. The smell of the wax began to pervade the atmosphere.

'Take off your trousers and let me see the damage.'

He did his best to wriggle out of the jeans which were heavy with blood. Trails of it streaked down his pale thighs.

'It's drying up, but I will put some stitches in it.' She opened her bag. 'I have a needle in here somewhere.'

He watched her as she pulled out tissues, a rosary and a couple of bottles of nail varnish. Her possessions spread over the bed glittered in the candlelight, worthless treasure, but more than he possessed at this moment. The sparkle from her eyes had spread to her cheek, and her eyelashes, thick with make-up, cast fluttering shadows on the wall. Her oiled hair was fastened with clips. He reached up his hand to touch her face.

'Are you real?'

She laughed, a sound that pierced the rank air like the smell of citrus and smiled down at him, her teeth white and even and he felt his panic subside.

'Here it is,' she said holding up a fine silver needle.

'Have you got a sewing machine in there too?' Joey asked, hoping she might laugh again. She grinned and shook her head.

'I used to make a bit of money piercing ears so I got into the habit of keeping one in the lining of my bag.' She placed it in the flame from the candle. 'How is it feeling?'

'Like someone stabbed me with a sharp knife,' he said.

She laughed. 'You speak Spanish so funny. Where are you from?'

'Ireland,' he sighed.

She stopped what she was doing.

'Irlanda? A gringo!' Her eyes narrowed. 'So how come you've got no money?'

'Not all gringos are rich.'

'You haven't been here long then. Why do you think so many Mexicans want to go to America? You should see the tips the tourists leave in the cafés! I'd get work in a café if I could. Nice smart clothes, one of those little books to take the orders, and free food, and no tricks.' She sighed.

Joey listened carefully. It was hard at first picking through her street slang.

'So what's stopping you?'

She turned back to her needle, which had blackened slightly in the flame. 'Can't read or write,' she said.

'But you can sew, right? So what are you going to use for stitches?' She lifted the bottom of her tee-shirt in reply, and pulled at it with her teeth. He watched as she threaded a curly piece of yarn and then brought it to his wound.

'This is going to hurt, so I will help you with the pain. You need to trust me.' She settled her hands on his head and he felt a warmth seeping down through his skull as if someone had poured oil on him.

'Keep breathing slowly while I do this and you should not feel so much pain.'

He did as he was told, and winced as he felt the point enter his flesh. Perhaps it was the touch of her fingers against his skin distracting him from the sharp intrusion of the needle or maybe she really had worked some magic on him but he was surprised when she broke the thread then leaned back to admire her work.

'There, all done,' she said wiping the needle and putting it back into her bag. Joey peered down at the gash joined with little knotted stitches. He'd have a good scar.

'These are some herbs to stop the infection.' She placed a small wet cloth bundle on his thigh. 'You'll need a week or so of rest, then I'll take the stitches out.'

'How do you know all this stuff?'

'Me, I'm from Catemaco, near Veracruz. It's famous for witches and *curanderas*.'

'And I thought I'd found an angel.' Joey said.

She pushed her head through the curtain and he noticed now the sound of a radio and some voices in the background. 'I'm with a customer,' she yelled, 'don't disturb me.'

She pulled her head back in and lay down next to him. 'There, we have some time alone.'

He felt the press of her along the side of his body. The ache from the wound was forgotten as his nerve endings abruptly changed their focus, alert to this unexpected touch of flesh with all that it might promise. The face of a girl he'd been with when he was just fourteen drifted into his head. There had been a fight then too, on his way back from school. They'd cornered him, dragged him into an empty shed and kicked him to shit. She'd hung at the shed entrance pulling at her brother's belt, whining at them to stop. Brona her name was, a sickly thing with dirty-blond hair and bitten nails. She'd clung to him afterwards weeping and they'd fumbled with each other, neither of them really knowing what to do. Saved by girls, it was turning into a habit.

There had been many more since then. But it wasn't like in the films: physical relief and animal comfort was what it came down to. Sometimes he'd felt something more and his head filled with dreams and stupid ideas but usually he'd got it wrong. There had been no-one he'd really cared for and no-one who'd really cared much for him. That's just how it was, how he was.

'Here, give me your hand,' she said.

He stretched out his arm and she turned it over, rubbing her painted nail along the lines in his palm. He felt electricity run through his body and down into his groin. She was so close he could smell her breath, a mix of bubble gum and toothpaste. He turned his head away, aware that his own mouth was sour and stale. As she circled his palm with her finger, he shivered slightly then moaned as the involuntary movement sharpened the pain in his leg. He closed his eyes and saw the ghosts of the candle flames dancing into view, each one savage and hot. He pressed the herbs to the wound and waited for the pain to subside.

She sat up a little and opened out his hand, 'Let me see what I can find out about you. Hmm...a long journey by boat.'

'Well, you can't get from Ireland by bus, for sure.'

She ignored him. 'And your family line is badly broken.'

Joey yawned, 'Yeah, I come from a broken home,' but his stomach fluttered.

'That is strange,' she said, pointing to something invisible to Joey. 'Your hand is telling me something special about your feet.'

Joey pulled his hand away. 'Okay, so I'm a cripple, you've seen that already, you don't need witchcraft to tell me that.' He screwed it up into a fist, felt pains rush through his feet. Special? Special pain in the arse, more like.

'What else can you read, tea leaves, chicken guts?' he mocked. She began to get up but he grabbed her arm. The thought of her going filled him with dread.

'I'm sorry. Don't go Teresa. Stay with me.'

She leaned back, resting her head against the wall. He curled up and settled his head on her stomach. He could feel the thud of blood rushing through her.

'Why did you help me?'

'I heard you calling my name.'

Joey leaned up on his elbow, bewildered. 'But I didn't know your name. I've never even seen you before.'

'I know, but still I heard you calling, like a little song in my ear.' She leaned forward and kissed him on the mouth. The touch of her lips took him by surprise and he froze for a moment. Was this her racket, her patter? He didn't know for sure but he wanted to give into it. She opened the curtain and wriggled away but he could still feel her breath on his face. He watched her go and a fizz broke out in his feet like fireworks.

7

In the morning he lay on his back watching the dust motes dance in the chinks of light that penetrated the holes in the curtain. Had she really been there or had he dreamed her? He closed his eyes and thought of her body.

'Hey! Time to get up, *chingado*. Other people need some privacy.' Rigo, his teeth a broken fence in his grinning mouth, stood admiring Joey's wound as he pulled on the blood-stiffened jeans and hauled himself out.

The only sunshine came in through the door and hovered by the entrance, too weak to travel further. The room in the gloom looked even more ramshackle. Dirty blankets were dumped in twisted heaps and in one corner a young woman sat feeding a baby. He could hear the sucking sound it made. The mother was staring up at the ceiling, her hand tapping her thigh to some inaudible rhythm. Two boys, trousers trailing around their thin legs, were stretched out on a mattress, a pile of playing cards laid out between them.

'You know where Teresa is?' Joey asked. One of the boys shrugged. Joey was about to ask again when a loud screech of brakes made him jump. It was followed by the growling rev of an engine. The two boys jerked their heads up, startled out of their indifference.

'El Tigre!' one of them said, his eyes alight. Bodies emerged from the blankets. Only the woman with her baby remained unmoved. Joey limped after the boys to the open doors of the garage.

Leather trousers, a denim jacket with rolled-up sleeves, a gleaming motorbike – El Tigre. His arms from elbow to wrist were tattooed with tiger stripes. A red bandana was knotted around his nose and mouth. He looked like something from a comic book. He pulled the bike onto its stand and climbed off, pulling the bandana down around his neck.

Off the motorbike, El Tigre was short. His naked, muscular chest tattooed with a grinning skeleton. Joey could just make out the word *Muerte*. The news of his arrival spread quickly and a swarm of teenagers appeared in the street.

'Rigo, Berto, Chaco my man, and where is Paulina? Gone? I'm sorry for you, but there are plenty more where she came from.' He shook their offered hands in a complicated fashion, responded to their questions and jokes like some minor celebrity and then he caught sight of Joey.

'You must be Teresa's latest fuck,' he said shaking his head as he took in Joey's ripped jeans, 'just remember she works for me and if you want to stay here you can work for me too.' Joey's fist itched to take a swipe at him.

'I got into a fight and I just need to stay until I'm fit, I don't need any favours.'

'Where is that accent from?'

Joey shifted his weight. 'From *El Norte*,' he lied.

El Tigre grinned, 'Okay, okay whatever you say. Anyone got a drink around here? Christ, a man could die of thirst.' He disappeared into the garage followed by a slew of hangers-on. Three or four of the younger ones lingered to admire the motorbike, daring each other to climb on, before an older kid in dark glasses came and chased them away.

Despite the pain in his thigh Joey decided to get out and walk a little, his head bursting with images of Teresa. What did she mean that he had called to her? It was impossible and yet as soon as she'd said it, his feet had responded. They'd pulled him towards her and he hadn't wanted to resist. He needed to see her again. He inched his way along a tree-lined street packed with tarp-covered stalls selling everything from baby clothes to porn.

He wanted to buy her something. She'd rescued him, saved his life or at least saved him from the police. He stopped at a stall where the hair-slides and the elastic ties were laid out in rows. He felt in his pockets, he had enough to buy Teresa something for her hair. Every colour, every flower, how would he ever choose? He closed his eyes and let his hands decide for him. The old woman behind the stall smiled as she wrapped the clips covered in white roses. He tucked them in his pocket and made his way back, aware of the pain nagging at his thigh. He wished he had the money for new trousers.

By the time he reached the garage his head was pounding and his leg was on fire. He'd been a fool to walk at all. If he got an infection now he might lose his leg, then he'd be good as dead. He dropped onto a mattress that reeked of chemicals and closed his eyes. The smell of the solvent made him nauseous. Voices boomed around him. He tried to open his eyes afraid that if he slept, *it* might get him, the thing that loomed in the darkness. He struggled but his eyelids felt heavy and stuck. If he could just open them a little more then maybe he'd see Teresa coming to him through the ether, floating on her angel wings. Perhaps she'd come and save him again. Sweat trickled down his neck. He wanted to pull his clothes off and press his hot body against the cold walls. Through his lashes he could see the glow of the *Madre de Cristo* candle; someone had lit it but the flame was struggling. *Madre*.

It must have been a Sunday afternoon because his da was out. She was squeezing his arm and talking in that sad way she had some-times. He can feel that urgent press of her hand even now, knead-ing him like something she hadn't finished making. They were curled up on the couch watching Fred Astaire.

'*He used to dance like Fred Astaire.*' A big sigh shook her body so that his own shifted with hers. *'My girlfriends called him "Quickstep Charlie", though Charlie wasn't his name. Everyone wanted to dance with him. But it was me he chose.'*

He gave in and closed his eyes and immediately he felt the swift current of unconsciousness tugging at him. He struggled to resist it, whispered to her over and over to help him but his voice sounded hoarse and not like his own at all.

Is he still there with her at home? He's sure he is, but the room is vast and a thin curtain blows inwards from a distant, unfamiliar window. He leaps off the couch, and stands awkward in front of the television. *'When I'm a famous magician, I'll take you dancing and buy you gloves up to your elbows like Ginger's.'* The eyes looking back at him are sharp and accusing.

'You're just the same as him,' she shouts. *'He promised me impossible things, silk dresses and white castles, and instead I got you, and look what you've done.'*

Her face is right next to his. He pulls himself away from her eyes and stares at the cluster of freckles on her cheek. A tear distorts them as it lingers on her skin. He wipes it away for her and the room darkens and blurs. He feels the wetness on his fingers.

'I was trying to save you from him,' he is crying out, but she has vanished and he is doubled-up under a tree, his hand sticky with blood.

Joey woke, his breath scratching in his throat, the pain in his feet making his eyes roll back in their sockets.

'You look like shit, man.' El Tigre was standing over him, his arms folded across his chest. 'Chaco, get this guy some water, and some pills, there must be aspirin somewhere. I don't want another corpse here.' He bent down.

Joey stared into the yellowish eyes. *'Gracias,* I owe you,' he muttered.

'You do indeed, *hombre,* you do indeed.'

Chaco came over with water and Joey swallowed the offered pills, not caring what he was taking. 'Shit,' Joey breathed.

Teresa was suddenly kneeling next to him, her face anxious. Others stood around exchanging curious glances. 'Shoo,' Teresa said, turning. 'The show is over.'

She pressed her hand to Joey's head. 'You had me worried there, I leave you for a few moments and next thing you're screaming the place down.' She lay down beside him cradling his head. Joey, weak and exhausted, failed to stop the tears that slid silently from him.

It was dark when he woke up and she was still asleep, her lips slightly apart. He tried to shift his arm from under her body without waking her. Her eyes fluttered, and she smiled at him, a half-lidded smile. She rubbed her eyes and yawned.

'Sorry,' he said stroking her cheek with the back of his hand. She kissed it, and he felt the warmth of her breath, spreading down through his body.

'I need to go outside.' He climbed over her, trying not to step on the other sleepers. It was raining. He could hear the patter of the drops on the corrugated roof. He stood out in it while he relieved himself. It felt good to be in the rain, to feel it on his skin. He glanced back and she was standing at the door, a blanket over her shoulders, her hair a charcoal wave.

She stretched out her hand, 'Come back, I don't want you to get sick again.'

'The sickness is gone, I'm sure of it.' He joined her in the doorway wrapping his arms around her body, burying his chin in her hair. He felt light-headed, emptied as if the fever had burned something out of him.

'It'll soon be autumn in Ireland,' he said, as she stuck her hand out to catch the rain.

'Why did you leave, Joey?'

'Long story. Long, long story.'

'Was it a girl?'

'Is it always a girl?' Joey said looking down at her.

'Not always, sometimes it's money or murder.' She laughed. 'You didn't murder anyone did you?'

He grabbed her neck and pretended to shake it. She squealed, and he was glad that he didn't have to answer any more questions.

8

September 1977

'*¡Feliz cumpleaños*' Teresa sang, her voice husky from smoking and
the early hour. She yawned and wrapped her legs around his. 'It's
your special day. You can do anything you like as long as it's free.'

A couple of hours later they were with the jostling crowds in
the *centro*, and his feet were nagging him, a mixture of the buzz
that being with her always seemed to generate and the throb of the
ground beneath him.

'Can we go up there?'

She followed his finger. 'The *Torre Latinoamericano*?' she shrugged.
'Tourists like to go there.'

He'd said it almost at random but now, despite her lack of enthusiasm, he felt a real urge to go. The skyscraper was often shrouded
in smog, but today was clear and bright.

'Oh come on, Teresa. How often do we get a sky like this! We'll
see the whole city laid out. I'll look after you, I promise.'

He craned his neck at the base of the building. The forty-two
floors soared above him, like the Beanstalk. He scraped together
enough for their two tickets and they got into the lift. They looked
out of place amongst the workers and tourists, and more than once
he saw someone clutching their bag close to their bodies.

Teresa clung to his side. He was surprised at the tension in her
arms but something else surprised him more. As the lift slid up-

wards his feet seemed to lose their weight. Several times he had to check that they were still on the ground. As soon as the doors opened, he leapt out, Teresa reluctantly in tow. The observation deck was open to the air, although potential jumpers were thwarted by a lattice of wire mesh. Teresa hung back, her face drawn. Joey had forgotten all about the view, he was concentrating on the sensation – or lack of it – in his feet. He twisted his arches, allowed his feet to rest flat for once then he held his arms out to steady himself but it wasn't necessary. He called out to Teresa.

'Look.' He began to walk. With each step he felt he might take off. She nodded weakly and returned her gaze to the ground.

'Can we go now?'

He took her hand. It was shaking.

'Don't you want to see the view?' He walked towards it, felt the absolute resistance of her grip. His own feet then responded with a sharp needling pain – the sting of disappointment. The intensity of it surprised him. Without the interference from the earth and the traffic, the quality of the sensation was quite different. He looked out through the mesh, across the city which spread in every direction, a jumble of blocks split by straight roads and in the distance the white tops of the volcanoes.

Behind him, Teresa was crying. 'Please Joey, I'm frightened.'

He put his arms around her and led her back to the lift. On the 37th floor was an aquarium. He walked her around its languid tanks until her anxiety subsided. He watched the fish moving seamlessly through their natural medium, elegant and easy. He wondered then what his own natural medium was. On land he seemed to be a fish out of water, a being designed for something else. Maybe the only way his feet would find peace was to be at sea or high above the earth like this. He thought of the cranes around the city. Was he destined for that solitary existence, the eye of a long-legged bird watching the city beneath him?

Back on the street, the contrast made him fall on his knees but Teresa's mood had improved with every floor they had descended, and her spirits were high. They spent the rest of the day in the *Zócalo*, walking hand-in-hand, eating *chicharron* and drinking cola by the *Templo Mayor*, the mythic competing with the mundane. He smiled at her as she ran after the birds that landed in the square and his heart filled. Despite her fear, she had gone up there with him to that eyrie where his feet had experienced a fleeting calm.

That night, monsters emerged from the dark to frighten him but then she wrapped herself around him, taking him into her, until there was nothing else but her heat and her beating heart. His skin prickled constantly with desire. He was restless with it and it frightened him. This wasn't like the movies either, no Fred and Ginger romance. The intensity of his feelings overwhelmed him. He was driving downhill in a car with no brakes. While she slept he watched her, running his fingertips along the curve of her spine, lifting the hair from her face to stroke her cheek in the darkness unable to leave her alone. And when she woke, he covered her in kisses, his breath mingling with hers, their tongues like flames.

When daylight arrived and she left him, the hours without her dragged along, seconds as tortuous as hours, and hours long enough to kill the soul. He sat in the garage lifting his head like a lonely dog each time he heard a noise at the door, hoping she'd be there. Some nights she never came back and they were the worst of all.

Unable to sleep, he laid awake listening to the snuffles from the lost and the broken, tangled in the blankets around him, itching with bugs and crying for their mothers or their drugs. His reverie was disturbed by Berto banging on the glass jar where he kept the fabric soaked in solvent. He was 'keeper of the rags'. A cluster of strays gathered around him as he doled out the bits of cloth. Joey was tempted for a moment. He'd tried it on the streets. You went up like a rocket and came down just as fast. He preferred the long gentle drop into drunkenness. There was a scuffle as two kids fought to be next.

After threats from Berto, the two boys disappeared into their corners with the wad under their noses, their upper lips coated in a silvery trail. Joey stared at those that still waited. Their eyes were already dead. Paradoxically, looking at them gave him hope. It was a constant reminder that he hadn't quite reached the bottom, a marker by which he could judge the extent of his desperation. He'd found Teresa and she would keep him from that. He felt it like a truth from birth. He had to get them both away from this place, but what could he offer her without money?

9

He was the only one up when the light changed from indigo to a clear blue. She hadn't turned up. He tried not to imagine where she might be, who she might be with. He was drawn back into the garage by the feeble cry of a baby.

There was no sign of the mother, Liliana. The infant, wrapped in a grubby blanket had been placed in a cardboard box that reminded Joey of a coffin. He looked down into its old man's face, the eyes closed and puffy. He pulled the bundle out. The blanket as it fell open gave out the tell-tale chemical whiff. The baby stirred slightly, widened his mouth in a tiny yawn and stretched his fists out. He opened his eyes and on seeing Joey his mouth dipped and his eyes began to crease.

'Oh no *niño*, don't do that,' Joey whispered, and songs came to him then from his childhood. His mother must have sung them to him, but Joey heard them in a man's voice, the slow cultured brogue of his father. He sat with the child in his arms singing quietly to him until his eyelids closed again and with a small huff of breath he'd fallen back to sleep. It was strange having that tiny body against his. His da must have held him like this. Had he looked up into his father's eyes and listened to those songs, and how had he got from that, to the broken rib and the welfare woman and the mother who'd let him go? He put the child back and felt the small chest rise and fall under his hand.

It was nearly dark by the time Liliana returned, and more youngsters had gathered there. Joey, unable to sleep, got up and tried to stretch. The electricity was out. The acrid smell of candles and a paraffin lamp permeated the air. The fading radio was playing some dance music and the DJ kept butting in with gags that made two of the younger boys burst into croaky laughter.

Joey picked up a chair and headed for the doorway. He lit up a cigarette, and blew the smoke into the night. An unexpected cloudburst had washed the scents out of the brickwork and the gutters, a ripe cocktail that made his nose quiver. He watched and waited, willing every approaching figure to be Teresa. At last he saw her running towards him.

'You're back,' he smiled, as she stood in front of him. Her hair was slick to her head but the fringe stuck out in a stiff roll as if it had been wrapped around a tin. Her eyes were thick with make-up, but still had the glitter in them that thrilled him.

'Where have you been? I missed my nurse.'

'I have to work,' she said looking away. 'I have debts to pay.'

His heart shrank. The thought of others touching her made him breathless with jealousy. He pushed himself from the chair and out into the dark, and grabbed her in his arms. Lights from passing cars flashed over her, catching the sheen of her skin. She ran her fingers over his lips, a look of sadness in her eyes. He held her face in his hands and felt the brush of her tongue.

'I think you've cast a spell over me,' he said laughing a little. He wanted to have her right there, feel his hands slip over her warm body. He pulled open his shirt and wrapped it around her, feeling her snug against his chest. Kids whistled at them, yelled things he didn't understand. She turned and swore at them.

He remembered his first week in Mexico City, stumbling into the *Zócalo* one night and seeing a hotel lit up on the corner of the square, a chandelier in the foyer like a frozen fountain. He wished he had the money to take her there, somewhere that didn't stink of piss and failure. She rested her head against his chest, her hands clutching his arms.

He lifted her chin. 'What is it, Teresa?'

'I don't know. I feel sad that's all.'

'Why? I was the song in your ear, remember, and you found me. It is fate.' He rummaged in his pocket 'Here. I bought something for you.'

She took it eagerly, a smile suffusing her face as she undid the package. He slotted the clips through her black hair. The white flowers looked like fallen snow.

'When I am rich and famous I will buy you something better.'

'Maybe I won't know you when you are rich and famous.' He didn't understand the melancholy in her voice. He ran his finger along her collarbone; she shivered.

'The rain is making you cold. Let's go back in,' he said, taking her hand.

The weather had brought more of the destitute to the garage and the smell of unwashed clothes and bodies was nauseating. A gloom had descended upon him as if she had transferred her anxieties to him. He watched, subdued, as she played with two of the children, tickling one of them until he begged for mercy. She turned to him, a grin breaking across her tired face, but even the crystal cadence of her laugh couldn't jolt him out of the dark mood that had gripped him.

That night, as she lay asleep, he found himself staring again at the silver skull she wore dangling next to her crucifix. That grinning head mocked his hopes and made his feet ache with foreboding.

Teresa didn't want go to work the next day. She seemed restless and irritated. Finally El Tigre appeared and she disappeared into the room he called his office at the back of the garage. Joey paced the room, lit two cigarettes that he didn't smoke and chewed his nails. What would happen if he just broke the door down? He imagined finding them there together and shooting Tigre – not that he had a gun. He looked towards the door. Chaco, his biceps bulging, stood guard, his head buried in a comic book. Joey shifted a step towards him but Chaco slowly shook his head without lifting his eyes from the page. After ten minutes or so Teresa reappeared. She smiled at him, and grabbed his arm.

'I'm free for today at least. How is your leg?' she said, 'could you walk to the *Metro*?' He nodded. 'I want to take you to a special place but let's go and see the *ofrendas* for The Day of the Dead first.'

He allowed himself to be led along the busy street in the sun. She was chattering and giggling, skipping in front of him as they walked and soon he was infected by her high spirits. He couldn't help noticing the skulls though, leaping out at him from every window and every market stall: sugar skulls with names on them, dancing skeletons, operating theatres of skeletons, a pregnant skeleton giving birth to a skeleton baby.

'*Mira*,' she said pointing to an altar set up in a shop window. The table top was edged with cut paper flags, featuring Doña Catrina, the skull with the wide-brimmed hat, like the one she wore around her neck. The surface was covered in marigolds and red coxcomb flowers and there were bowls of food set out on it. Why did skulls always seem to be laughing, what did they know that the living didn't? He turned away.

'Don't you think it's beautiful?' Teresa sighed.

'It's creepy. Mexicans are in love with death. It's not natural.'

'It's the most natural thing in the world. Death is just a fact of life,' she said, shrugging.

'There are lots of things that are facts of life but we don't celebrate them,' he snapped, 'shit, disease, prostitution, but where is the Day of Disease, when do you celebrate that?' He let go of her hand and walked on ahead. There it was again, threatening to spill out of him. He felt his hand shake a little.

'Joey, come back,' she called out running after him. 'You don't get it; we can't keep death away so we may as well have fun with her.'

Joey stopped and stared at her. 'You're the one who doesn't understand. Death is the end of everything: of hopes, of dreams, of love, of answers. When you die everything is gone.'

They had reached the Metro.

'We'll get the train to Observatorio,' she called. 'Quick!' She ran towards it, dragging him with her, refusing to be infected by his cynicism.

. 'You said you wanted to be alone with me,' she said out of breath, as they squeezed onto a train. 'Well, I am taking you somewhere beautiful, a house in a town called Malinalco and we can stay there all night and all day if we want to.'

'Who does it belong to?' Joey said, suspicious.

'It is the home of two artists, Nicolás and Jaime. Nicolás pays me sometimes to be a model.'

'And what else?' Joey grumbled.

She laughed, 'They are not interested in girls, don't worry.'

'But they let you use their house?'

She twisted her mouth into a sly grin and swung coquettishly on the hand strap above her. 'I know where they leave the key, and I know they are going to be away. We will be like ghosts. They will never know we have been there.' She leaned forward and pecked him on the cheek.

The journey on the second class bus took most of the morning, and as they rolled west out of the city, Joey felt his mood change. The air became cleaner and life confirmed its superiority over death in the glossy trees and the fields full of crops. They drove through dense pine forests and rolling pastures dotted with sheep that reminded him of home.

They got out of the bus in the centre of the town where the usual vendors milled, selling ices made from papaya and mango. The streets of neat adobe homes with their white walls and red-tiled roofs reminded Joey of houses in the story books of his childhood. And at the end of every street, hillsides thick with trees stretched up towards the sky.

The house of Teresa's friends was in a small cobbled street, quiet except for the birds chattering in the trees.

'We need to be careful. You never know who might be watching. I don't want anyone calling the police.'

Giggling and hushing each other, they approached a blue door in a terracotta wall that was overgrown with dark pink bougainvillea. She pushed her hand up under the foliage and after a minute or so of searching, pulled down an iron key. They stepped into a lofty hallway, disturbing swifts that were building a nest under the eaves.

'Wow!' Joey breathed. An archway on the left led to a colourful kitchen, and ahead of him stretched a courtyard garden full of plants.

'What do you think?' she said, jumping up and down. He gasped, struck by the sheer surprise of it. From outside it was nothing but a door in the wall, and yet hidden behind it was all this. Things were never what they seemed in this country.

'And there is no-one here but us!' She grabbed him and danced him around the tiled floor. Hand-in-hand they explored the white living room with its domed brick ceiling and delicate cut-tin lanterns dangling from chains. It was the smell that was the best part though, clean and dry, a faint odour of soap and limes.

'They must be rich!' he said rubbing his thumb and forefinger together.

She dropped his hand. 'Joey, we mustn't take anything from here, do you understand me? These are good people and I do not want to steal from them. Promise me.'

'What! But you steal from everyone, *mi pocita ladróna.*'

Her eyes flashed a warning. 'This is different. Shops and people I don't know is one thing but these are my friends. I do not steal from my friends.'

'You're crazy. They wouldn't miss anything. You could pay off your debt.'

Her brow furrowed and her eyes grew anxious. He put his hand to his heart. 'Okay, okay, I promise.'

The walls were hung with paintings, pale watercolours, that reminded him of pressed flowers found in old books. 'Helen Gillen,'

Joey read from the corner of one of them.

'Nico's mother. She used to come here to paint, and when she died he bought the house and filled it with her work.'

One of the paintings was huge, at least six feet long with three rows of people, each one perfectly painted in shades of brown and white, standing outside an old wooden schoolhouse on a sunny day. Joey put his hand up to the glass.

'It's a painting of an old school photograph!' She took his hand and joined him in front of the painting.

'When I was a kid, we had to have these taken every year, standing on benches, trying not to squint or frown, knowing that if you did, that face would be there forever, your mouth all screwed up, your finger stuck up your nose or down your trousers; I was always terrified that someone would push me off the bench.'

He remembered back to days like that when so many competing emotions flooded him, it was impossible for him to remain upright and he'd be hauled off to stand on his own. He peered at one of the children in the front row. A small, pale, round figure with spectacles like an owl, knee-length shorts and an old-fashioned knitted jumper looked back at him.

'Whatever happened to you?' Joey said quietly.

Teresa squeezed his hand. 'Let's imagine that all of them are very happy. That one there,' she said pointing to a tall, thin girl with an awkward look about her, 'she had seven children. And those two teachers at the back – they got married and ran away to start a tango school.'

'A tango school?' Joey laughed. 'But that old man's already seventy if he's a day.'

She squealed and clapped her hands. 'But her passion has given him new life!'

'And that one?' he said pointing to a stout matron with a sharp nose.

She thought for a moment, 'She killed a man in a crime of passion,' she said, her eyes widening, 'and then she crossed an ocean to escape. She is in disguise in this picture. They think she is just a dry old virgin full of facts and figures but at night she lies in her little bed and dreams of the man who broke her heart.' Joey's own heart was thumping.

'And what about that wee girl there?' Joey said, nodding at a child who was looking away from the camera, up and into the distance.

Teresa stared at her. 'She has lost her way that one. She is missing her mother. She is looking for someone, but he hasn't come.'

'Maybe he is just out of the picture, gone to get some cigarettes,' Joey said.

Teresa nodded, 'I hope so.' He leaned forward and kissed her.

10

By the time he awoke, it was dark. He could hear her moving in the other room. She returned with a tray of lit candles, and a bottle of tequila.

'Come and see the moon. It's huge,' she said. Wrapped in blankets against the chill air, they sat in the garden listening to the cicadas.

'All that noise and yet you can't see them,' Joey said.

'Often the things that disturb you the most are the invisible things, my mother used to say.' She was sitting in his lap, her body warm against him.

'What happened to your mother?' Joey asked.

'Would you like to see a picture of her?' She eased herself up and disappeared in to a little *casita* at the end of the garden, returning with a wooden container the size of a shoe box.

'Until I met them I used to bury it like a squirrel in different places in the city and I was always terrified someone would find it.' She opened the lid, pulled out a photo, and shuffled up next to him.

'Can you see? This is my mother, and that is my father. And this is me in the front, with the serious face.'

Joey stared at the image with its bright colours. Her mother was small, her hair in a long plait braided with flowers. She was looking off to the left at a man who was standing stiffly, his hands resting on a chair.

'Who took the picture?'

'My grandmother. It was just before everything fell apart. I think I must have sensed it. Look at the way I am staring up at my mother as if I am trying to remember everything about her. She had lipstick on, and I had never seen her with lipstick.'

Joey looked again at the picture, and felt a jabbing pain in his feet; he shifted uneasily.

'My mother was able to cure people with medicines that she made – everyone but herself of course. My grandmother was a *bruja*. She believed in spells, but only for good purposes. Now tourists go to Catemaco to meet the devil, *que tonto*! Why go all that way? He is on every street corner as far as I can see. It is all gimmicks, but the real healers are there too if you know where to look.

'My father made things from wood and paper: furniture, flowers for the altars, toys for *El Día de los Muertos*. He had skilled hands.'

'So how did you end up in Mexico City with Tigre?'

'Quite soon after this picture was taken – I must have been about twelve years old – a group of men arrived from Texas. They came into the village and set up a green tent with a big banner across the front. I thought it was a carnival. They were bigger than any of the local men and freckly. I thought they were covered in cinnamon like the *pan dulce* in the bakers. I'd never seen freckles before, ha ha.' She kissed the few that dotted Joey's nose. 'They were evangelists, come to save us.'

Joey watched a moth dance in the candle light, and brushed it away. Teresa took a gulp of tequila and passed the glass to him. He took a mouthful, felt the burn in his throat, thought for a moment of his dad, going to church every Sunday, suave as James Bond, leaning forward like he was taking in every word.

'All the children went down there when we heard the music. They had soda and cakes and an electric guitar. I peered in and there was my father, his arms raised up to the sky, tears rolling down his face, singing along with these strangers. I'd never even seen him inside a church before. He'd spend Sundays in the square, or lying in the hammock. At the end of the week they packed up and left and we woke up to find that my father had gone with them.'

'What did your mother say?'

'She said they must have bribed him and she was better off without him. But she wasn't. She loved him, had done since the day she set eyes on him. She tried to keep herself going without him but she couldn't. She stopped brushing her hair. That's when I knew something was very wrong. She had beautiful hair you can see how long it is in the picture. In the evenings she would untie it and it would drop all over her shoulders – and those flowers, my father made them for her.'

She touched her hand up to the clip he had bought her, crushed from their love-making. He straightened out the petals, wishing again he could have bought her something better.

'Then one day I came home from school and there was a smell in the air like burning feathers. She was sitting in the garden with her back to me. I called out to her but she didn't move. At first I thought her hair was tucked into her dress then I noticed chunks of it lying on the path. I cried out and she turned her head. I saw the rest of her hair smouldering in a pan next to the fire. She leaned forward, picked up the ashes and rubbed them onto her face. I screamed at her but she just looked up at me as if she didn't know who I was. A month later I found her hanging from the tree in the garden. In her hand was a bunch of roses, and where her body had jerked as she died, the petals had fallen in a pattern beneath her. I swear nothing ever grew on that patch of earth again.' She fell silent and Joey didn't know how to comfort her.

'Soon it is the Day of the Dead and then I can call her back to me.' She put the photo back in the box. It made him shiver, this talk of the dead returning.

'At first I lived with my *abuela*, my grandma, but she died soon after my mother. I slept in the woods, and lived on what I could find. I scavenged and I cleaned houses and did laundry but people were afraid of me. They thought I was possessed by something and

I suppose I was. I wanted my mother so badly. Every day I cried for her, but I was angry too. She didn't think I was worth staying alive for, I wasn't enough.'

'Your mother was sick. She didn't know what she was doing.'

'It is simple. If you love someone you care for them. That is it.'

He felt her body stiffen and although he understood exactly how she felt, he could offer nothing but platitudes that felt stale in his mouth. He thought of his own mother with her skin all picked and scabby from pulling at it and her pupils dark and bright.

Teresa leaned forward and rescued a beetle that had fallen onto its back.

'Men didn't seem to care what my family had done. They didn't worry that I might bring bad spirits into the house, but their wives did, so I came to Mexico City. That was two years ago. I was fourteen then and I ended up in bad company.

'Sometimes I walk down the streets of Coyoacán and La Condesa and I see the couples buying ice cream, and eating meals in restaurants and celebrating birthdays, and I think they do not know what is going on under their noses. Is it the same where you come from?'

Joey looked around him, 'I think the whole of life is like that. Here we are in this beautiful garden and yet that beetle you rescued will be eaten by a bird, those vines are choking that tree and see there, those ants are cutting up the roses. By the morning there will be nothing but stalks. That's how life is, a struggle that ends in death. Some people's struggles just come with better furniture than others,' he said gazing around at the pink walls dancing with shadows.

'Do you really believe that?' she said.

'I don't know.' He massaged his temples. Emotions surged around in his head, a sea of conflict that he could drown in. He looked across at her shoulders hunched under the blanket. He'd thought she was the boat that had come to rescue him, now he wondered if it was perhaps the other way around. Maybe they were both drowning and death would be the one to save them.

He took her hands and pulled her up. They walked in silence around the garden. She took him into the room where she kept her box and turned on the light. It was a studio, a half-finished painting sitting on the easel – Teresa's face, with a banner rippling above her, on which was painted the words, *'Dios encuentra una boca que te diga lo que necesitas oír',* 'God finds a mouth to tell you what you need to hear.' Was she the mouth that God had chosen for him? His feet flinched. There was no God. There was only death.

Teresa grabbed his hand. 'Do you like it?'

'It looks just like you.'

'My hair had been plaited. Nico likes it like that, says it makes me look like a child of nature.'

Joey studied the paintings. In one a burst pomegranate spilled its juice onto a white tablecloth. In another a hand holding scissors was about to snip the ribbon linking a birdcage to its chain; the cage was open but the bird was still inside with its back to the open door. As his gaze roamed over the paintings – the vase of dying flowers, the worm in the bowl of golden apples, the cracked mirror in a pale hand – he grew increasingly uncomfortable. But it was the last painting that stopped his breath. A woman, life-size, her face cold and grey, lay on a bed, a blanket covering her body, as roses rained down on her.

'It is a portrait of his mother, on her deathbed.' Teresa said.

Joey felt his throat constrict. 'Why would he paint that?' Appalled, he looked away but like a hall of mirrors the other paintings seemed to reflect the same image back at him.

'I think it is beautiful.' Teresa said. 'Her ashes are here too, buried under the rose tree in the garden. Her spirit is in those roses. It is what I like best about this house.' Joey turned and headed for the door. This room was suffocating him. He needed some air. Teresa ran after him and grabbed his hand.

'Don't you see? Death isn't the end. Sometimes, when I am with a customer, this is the only thing that keeps me sane. He thinks for that moment that he owns me, but he only has my body, my soul is with these roses.'

He took hold of her and buried his face in her hair. Was this the message that God had sent her to deliver, that Death wasn't the end? It was too late. He knew that it was. He didn't want to be dragged into that world with her. He wanted to be the one to pull her out of it, bring her into the thrashing, tingling world of love,

'Teresa, I'm not one of those men, you know that don't you?'

'Oh Joey, of course I do, oh I didn't mean…' she covered his face with kisses as he walked her back into the house.

Holding her in his arms as the light filtered back into the sky, he wished he could stay here in this room forever, in this bed with the blue light and the sound of birds and the faint booming voice of the corncob seller as he ambled along the road looking for customers.

11

He was quiet on the bus back to the city. The thought of returning to the squat filled him with despair.

'Why haven't you tried to run away and start again, Teresa?' he said as the bus sped along the busy roads.

'It's not that simple.'

'You could learn to read and write, and become a waitress.'

'I can't leave Tigre, not yet.'

Joey looked out of the window. 'So you love him then?'

She took his hand 'Love? Are you crazy? Of course not! He got me out of a bad situation. If it wasn't for him I'd be dead by now. I owe him my life. That is a big debt.'

Joey grabbed her by the arms. 'You sell your body and he gets most of the money. You must have paid him back by now. He has bought you like something in the market!'

'Get your hands off me. You don't understand. Nothing is straightforward.'

They sat in silence for the rest of the journey and even the out-of-tune wailing and hopeless card tricks of two dirty children who tried to earn money on the bus, failed to pull them out of their separate worlds.

She said goodbye to him at the bus station and disappeared into the crowds. He called after her but she didn't turn. Things changed so quickly, one minute they were staring at the moon together and the next they were cold and distant. He thought again of Teresa's mother, happy in her garden with her braided hair and the next day abandoned. Is this what love was like?

When he was small and his parents were fighting he would creep into their bedroom. He'd pull open the bottom drawer of his ma's dressing table and feel around at the back until he found the loose corner of the drawer liner. He'd peel it back, heart thumping, and withdraw the old black and white picture he knew so well. He wished he had it now. It had fascinated him that photo. He always had the feeling there was something he had missed in it, something he hadn't quite understood. There she was, his ma, laughing at the camera, her hair flying away from her face like she'd just done a fast spin. The light was in her eyes, two little stars, and her teeth so white and his da – just out of focus, bigger than he seemed in real life – holding up his mother's hand. He could see their fingers touching.

His father's face was in shadow but even his hair looked free, like it too was having a ball, flying around with the music. And his feet. Joey remembered squeezing up his eyes and peering closely at the photo. His da's feet were a blur, like someone had suddenly moved the camera. He couldn't recall seeing them dance, not even when his da had had a few, although sometimes he grabbed her and tried. Then his mother looked stiff and moved her head away, although she never stopped him.

He knew he was somehow to blame for the way they his parents had become with each other. He closed his eyes and allowed his mother's smile to linger on in his head, the dancing stars of her eyes and the crescent moon of her mouth. Then he blinked it away before the other image replaced it, the one he didn't want to see.

Teresa returned the following day. 'I want you to come with me to the 'Day of the Dead' altar at Bellas Artes,' she said. 'It is the best one in the city and if we pray, the dead will return to spend time with us.'

He shook her hand away. 'I don't believe in any of that stuff,

Teresa.'

She smiled, her eyebrows lifted. 'If you don't believe, you have nothing to fear. If you do believe, then why would you be afraid of seeing your loved ones?'

'I haven't any loved ones.'

Teresa took his hand, 'You don't stop loving your parents just because they are dead.'

'I don't want to talk about them,' he said, beginning to panic. 'Look, you go, I'll stay here and if any spirits drop by, I'll point them in your direction.'

Alone, he lay on a mattress staring at the ceiling. Devils and demons, skeletons and skulls, why would he want to seek them out when he was awake? It was bad enough that they haunted his dreams. He didn't understand this country: he didn't understand her.

When she came back she seemed withdrawn and distracted. He couldn't bear the distance between them. He needed to see her smile.

'Do you want to see a trick?'

She looked up, shrugged. He searched around for something he could use, reached past her and grabbed her make-up, some lipsticks and bottles of varnish.

'Hey! What are you doing?'

He grinned. 'Watch!' He began to juggle, ducking his head every so often to let a lipstick sit between his shoulder blades then he'd jerk and send it back into the circle.

'Man!' she laughed, her mouth open in admiration. His spirits lifted.

'That's pretty good! Now give them back to me.' She checked the items for damage and put them back into her bag.

'What else can you do?' Two of the other boys who'd been listening to a football match on the radio had come over to watch. Joey tried out some of the old tricks he had taught himself on those long hours on the boat when he'd been afraid to close his eyes.

'I'm very out of practice, but let me see…get me a rope,' he said. Someone fetched him a bandana.

'This do?'

He nodded. He wrapped it around his hands, got the boys to check the knots. Then he stood up, took a couple of deep breaths, and with a twist of his wrists had freed himself from the bonds.

'Ta-ra!' He responded to their applause with a deep bow. There was a shout from the corner. He tried another trick, made a coin appear from behind Rigo's ear, everyday stuff but for a minute, Rigo, his eyes wide with amazement, looked like a five-year-old.

'Shit! You should give up the cards and do this for money.'

'Cards are easy, you can do that in any bar, this needs a bit of room.'

'Tigre would find you a great spot so long as you give him a cut.' Teresa said.

'I could be your assistant,' she added, suddenly animated, 'I could get one of those shiny dresses and a tiara.'

The rest of the evening Joey showed off all the tricks he could remember. Finally worn out, he went outside to think. He liked the rain at night when the streetlights became watery and the gutters ran, cleaning everything up and getting rid of the filth. But it wasn't like the rain in Ireland. Here the rain was warm and heavy, big fat drops of it that never cooled anything down but dragged the dust out of the air, and in the morning the sky would be blue again, swimming pool blue and sparkly. In Ireland the rain was cold and seeped into your coat, through your hair, onto your scalp making you shiver until your teeth ached. And when you walked, the fields were sodden and squelched and the smells came up at you and sought you out like old friends. He was thinking of those days when he'd walked the lanes with his mother before it had all gone so wrong.

'Hi.' He felt a hand tentatively touch his.

'Hi, Teresa.'

'I'm sorry about today.'

'Me too.' His feet ached and he shuffled them on the floor trying to shake off the pain.

'What is it, Joey, what is your problem?'

12

Lying on the bed in that womb-like space separated from the rest of the squalor, she listened as he tried to explain what had happened with his father, what it had felt like on that fence, to be like a bird for once instead of a clay-footed oaf. He tried to explain how he'd struggled to capture that sensation again. He'd got a sense of it on the boat and high up in the *Torre Latinoamericano* with her, but even then his feet had jangled with pain, and then his father's response, the beginning – it seemed to Joey – of something cruel and incomprehensible.

She scrabbled to the end of the bed, and swung her legs around so she was at right angles to him.

'Take off your shoes and put your feet in my lap.'

Joey, happy to feel her smooth thighs beneath his legs, did as he was told. He kicked the old leather sandals from his feet. They left a ghost of themselves, white against his grubby skin.

'Some people believe that each part of your foot responds to a different part of your body, so by massaging that area there ...,' she pushed hard on the right side of his foot and he howled in pain. She bit her lip to stop from giggling, '... I am massaging your liver.'

'There is nothing wrong with my liver, but I think you've just broken my foot.' Joey said. He rubbed his ankle but didn't look at her. When she'd pressed the side of his foot an image of his father had appeared sudden and sharp.

'Sorry, I'll be more gentle.'

He tried not to cry out as her fingers followed his arches and her hands prodded and kneaded the soft fleshy parts of his toes. This was not an enjoyable experience. He tried to pull away.

'Relax! I have healing hands. Close your eyes and empty your mind.'

'Why?' he said, trying to squirm away from her. He felt afraid suddenly. She tugged his toes, making him wince again.

'Oh don't believe all that stuff I told you. It's rubbish!' Teresa said, tossing her hair back. 'Don't make such a fuss. It's only a massage. You want to be helped or do you want to spend the rest of your life in misery?'

Gripping the edge of the bed he closed his eyes and the moment she pressed her hands to the soles of his feet a memory came from nowhere and ambushed him.

He is in his parents' house so he is six, maybe. He can see his hand in front of him, shaking and white. Where is his mother? She is outside. He can see her face at the window. He turns back, dread swirling in his stomach and there is his father looking at him across the table.

Between them is a butter dish, with 'A present from Tralee' written across it in bright jaunty letters, but his father doesn't look jaunty. His father has a funny look on his face and his shirt is open at the neck. Joey is looking at that little triangle of skin, covered in thick hair but clipped neat at the collar. With his tie on, Joey thinks, you'd never know that he looks like a wolf-man, like a werewolf. Joey wants to giggle. His father is a werewolf. But he can't giggle because he isn't breathing. His father has taken one of his hands and is holding it very tightly. Joey is too afraid to cry. He is thinking about Tralee and wondering if it is a happy place. It sounds happy, Tralee, tralaa. His bones are grating against each other, conker-knuckles, finger-sticks, rubbing together and burning.

His father is pressing his hand into the table with the heel of his own. Joey is shocked at his strength. And his father takes the lit cigarette from the ashtray and holds it over Joey's hand. Joey is breathing again now, short sharp gasps. His father takes a puff of the cigarette. It glows, a tiny dragon in his hands. He blows the smoke at Joey who coughs. Bam! His father hits him on the side of the head.

'Where are your manners? Keep your mouth covered when you cough.'

Joey's ear is ringing and his head is very light. He tries to float without closing his eyes. He knows that if he closes his eyes he is done for. The desert drifts into the foreground but he can't hold onto it because his da is there in front of him, in the way of the mesas and buttes and the bright blue sky.

'You're not listening to me,' he says

'I am, I am!' Joey says, hating the quaver in his voice. His father lifts his hand sharply, the cigarette still burning and Joey cringes thinking he is in for another wallop, but instead the cigarette floats down through the kitchen air and lands like a butterfly on his knuckle, where it stays. His father watches him watching it, and the smell of burning is suddenly in his nose, and the pain is white and terrifying.

Joey tries to pull his hand away, but his father holds fast to it. He writhes and twists. His mother is at the window her mouth open. She must be shouting but he can't hear her because the sound of his own screaming is in his ears. There is a banging, banging at the door, and he knows it is his mother. His father takes a puff of the cigarette, cool as anything and gets up to open it.

She is standing there fists balled-up, breathing fast, staring across at him, across the present from 'Tralee, Tralaa' and the bread and butter, and the table with the ash and the smell of burnt skin. She lets out a sob and tries to drag Joey from his chair, but he can't move, all his focus is on his trembling hand.

'You bastard!' she cries.

'I'd put some butter on that burn, so I would,' his da says, 'That'll teach him to play with cigarettes.'

His mother wraps her arms around him but he can't feel her, he can't feel anything.

When Joey opened his eyes, and looked into Teresa's, they were dark and wet. She gave him a shaky smile, a look of bewilderment on her face.

'*Madre de Cristo*, Joey! What happened, what did you see?'

Joey hunched his shoulders and tried to stop shaking. 'Something I've tried not to think about for a long time.' He took the cigarette she offered him and inhaled deeply. He'd broken out in a sweat. He wiped his arm across his forehead. He felt as if something had passed out of him, as if she'd flushed out an infected wound.

'My grandma used to feel the weather in her corns, and I used to think my feet were like that, but mine were more sensitive. I could feel things I could hardly see. A speeding train or a rumbling truck could trip me over. It hurt so. That's why I started walking like I do on the outside of my feet. I was sure I could feel the earth itself moving, like water diviners can sense water underground I suppose.' His heart was still pounding and his mouth dry. He licked his lips and tried to steady his breathing.

Teresa was staring down at her hands, turning them over as if she had surprised herself. When he stopped talking she looked up, 'Don't stop, I'm listening to you.'

He passed her the cigarette. 'When my granddad died, things at home took a turn for the worse. My parents started to fight a lot. I'd run upstairs because they were having a huge row and agonizing pains were shooting through my heels and along my arches and I knew that my feet were hurting because they were fighting about me. I knew a kid who got so anxious he'd throw up. Me, I'd fall down. Then once, after a particularly violent fight I hid in the wardrobe and realized that if I squeezed my feet together, I could short-circuit the pain, and in the process escape into my dreams. I called it mind-floating. It was comforting, like thumb-sucking, but I can't seem to do it now.'

'It's vibrations,' Teresa said, her eyes excited, her hands plucking at the air as if she saw them wreathed around her like coloured smoke. 'You are picking up emotional vibrations and I could feel what you were going through.' Her eyes sparkled.

'But unlike you Teresa, I don't feel other people's emotions, only my own, what use is that?'

She shuffled up to him and took his hands. 'Don't you see? You have something more. You told me! You pick up vibrations from the earth too. ¡*Que raro!*'

'The ground in Ireland was asleep compared to this place,' he said slapping the ground. He went quiet for a moment, unsure whether to share something with her or not. He glanced up and she was waiting for him. He began to speak again, avoiding her eager eyes.

'Do you remember back in February, I had that day when I was so dizzy I couldn't even get up and I thought my head was about to break open? Then the next morning we heard about the earthquake, the one that started in Guatemala…'

She was listening intently.

'… I had a feeling that my feet knew before we did. Sounds stupid, doesn't it and there is probably no connection and anyway it was no use because I didn't recognise what they were feeling until it was too late.' Uttered aloud, it sounded completely crazy. He felt his face flush. In this pulsating city the sensations in his feet were a baffling assault. He struggled to explain it.

'There is so much going on, it's all mixed up. It's like ten radios playing different stations at the same time, sometimes you think you've understood something and other times it's just noise.'

She whistled, 'Joey, this could be a great gift.'

'Yeah, great! Well, you can keep it! What use is it to me if I can't understand it? How do I know if it's a bad memory or an earthquake! What kind of gift is it if it makes me walk like a cripple? Shit!'

Teresa stroked his face gently, 'Gifts always have a price tag, trust me. My mother came to me at the altar in Bellas Artes,' she said suddenly.

'What do you mean?' Joey stiffened. 'Your mother is dead, you couldn't have
seen her.'

Teresa opened her hands and shrugged her shoulders. 'You can believe what you like but she came to me as I was praying. I closed my eyes and I heard her talking to me like we are talking now. She knew your name. She said '*Tell him his feet are silver and gold*'.

Joey was aware of a silence closing in around him, a still sensation in his feet, in his heels, as if every cell was listening to her. He tried to swallow. 'What does that mean?' he said hoarsely, trying to conceal his sense of unease.

Teresa looked at him, as if it was obvious. 'It means your feet are your fortune, the key to your past and your future.'

Joey shook his head. He wanted to run as fast as he could away from this place and her talk of the dead, but he knew her words would follow him.

'I know a woman,' Teresa said. 'She used to live near my family when I was a child. She also lives in Malinalco, but in the hills, a good walk from Nico and Jaime's house. She is a *bruja*, a witch. I went to her once after my mother's death and she helped me. I think she could have helped me more if I'd let her.'

'You think you can fix my feet with witchcraft?' Joey said, unable to hide the disbelief in his voice.

'They don't need fixing. They are not broken. She'll help you to make the best of the gift, to understand it. Trust me, Joey. I've seen what she can do with my own eyes. She is *muy intuitiva*, she is a sensitive. When you are ready, you tell me and we'll go there.'

13

The clouds settled on the city for three more days, and it was cooler than normal. On the third day Tigre turned up with two of his 'cubs'. He was on a new motorbike. He sat astride it, revving it hard, pumping clouds of blue exhaust into the shack.

'Hey man, what the fuck you doing, you want to poison us?' Chaco called out. A group of kids gathered round him. Tigre climbed off and lit a cigarette. As he turned, Joey saw that his denim jacket now sported a tiger's head in black ink, slightly lop-sided as if it had toothache.

'Cool jacket,' Teresa said. 'You are getting so flash, *muchacho!*' She giggled. Tigre pulled her towards him and kissed her. She stiffened up and pulled away.

He shrugged, 'No problem. A tiger can always get pussy.' He stared around at the circle of faces. They all laughed.

'So Joey, I hear you're a regular magician.' He wondered how Tigre had found this out already. Where had he been anyway? He was clean and smelt of after- shave. Someone had been caring for him in a nice dry place.

'So what do you say we find you a pitch?' Tigre said. 'Whatever you make I get fifty per cent.'

'And what do you do for that?' Joey said.

'Protect you, of course. I'll keep the pitch clean, get the right crowd around you, and draw in the pesos. What do you say?'

Joey shrugged.

Tigre cracked open a bottle, 'So, give me a show. Chaco, line up some seats here. Let's make our own little *teatro*. Hey, it's like Las Vegas.'

Joey went through a brief routine making things appear and disappear, mind-reading cards and a pickpocket trick where one person's watch appeared on someone else's wrist. He'd spent weeks working it out, getting the movements of his hands really precise. The effort had paid off. Tigre made him do it four times standing alongside each volunteer trying to catch Joey out. He squeezed his temples and shook his head in disbelief as he failed to spot the secret of the trick yet again.

'You are good Joey. You, *hombre*, are good! I think we could really make some money here and I mean really make some money.'

'I do other stuff too, acrobatics, back flips.' He did one to demonstrate, and Teresa, taken by surprise, shrieked.

'Yeah, yeah, *hombre*, enough now. I need to work out some stuff here.' Tigre got on his motorbike, revved until he'd created his own cloud of smoke and then disappeared into it.

'Was it something I said?'

'He's got plans for you,' Rigo said, his grin flattening his wide nose further. 'Thing is you're gonna need some heavy magic to get you out again.'

Joey jolted awake. Teresa was breathing quietly beside him, and another, tiny young girl with a long thin plait lay curled in her arms. He stared at her face. Free of make-up, she looked so young. He got up, careful not to wake them, and crept out.

The sky was turning turquoise between the buildings, and the mechanical roar of the city had not quite started. That's what had woken him, the peace. It was beautiful: clean, fresh and chilly. An old man in a baseball cap pushed a wide broom along the gutter, the scratch, scratch of the bristles, and the clang of the rubbish collector announcing his arrival, sounded new, as if he was hearing them for the first time.

The women were already up cleaning the front steps, shaking

out their dusters. Even here, in this part of town, where the buildings were not much more than sheds with corrugated iron roofs and plastic sacks covering holes in the brickwork, the women still cleaned every day.

His nan had done that though, shaking out the doormat, walloping it against the wall, making him cough. His granddad would come out and pretend to slip on the step, making big windmill circles with his arms and uttering moans of doom, making Joey laugh until he got a stitch. Funny that laughter could hurt.

His granddad was sixty-seven years old when he died, which had seemed ancient to Joey then. He always wore a suit and a starched collar with a stud. He owned a gentlemen's outfitters, and even though Joey's da had managed it for five years his granddad paid a visit every day. He'd even gone there on the day he took sick, though he'd only stopped for a wee while.

His granddad's funeral, he must have been five then. They were sitting in the parlour at the big house. There was quiet chat, a ticking clock, the smell of cake and sandwiches. He was under the table fascinated by the shoes: the tiny ones of his grandma with their bunions bulging and the cracked leather ones of Mr Metcalf that looked like burnt pastry.

He saw his father's well-polished feet get up and walk away from the table. He crept out and followed him to the garden. His father was quiet, sad, Joey thought at first. As he stood staring into the field, a muscle jumped in his jaw. Joey had shuffled, making the gravel crunch, and his father had turned, a look of fury in his eyes and something else... Joey tried to put a word to it now, despair was it, or desperation, like a dog cornered for the pound. A look that he knew, even then, was focused on him.

Tigre was as good as his word. He found him a pitch near the *Zócalo*. Ever since the proposal had been put to him, Joey had been practising the routine that he hoped would make him enough money to pay off Teresa's debt and buy their freedom.

The tricks he'd developed were impressive, and the gasps of the kids in the shack sent a shiver across his skin. Teresa had found a sequined tutu and a gold plastic tiara and insisted on helping him when she could.

By Christmas they had developed quite an act. Tigre collected his half without dispute and Joey's share was amassing comfortably. The city was full of tourists and shoppers generous with their money. He discovered he had a knack for performance. It was not enough to have good tricks. You needed to know how to attract a crowd, how to keep them interested and make them feel that the trick was just for them. He didn't hassle, he charmed, and his awkward gait made them feel sorry for him.

He'd been performing for several weeks, when Tigre stopped by to discuss his new plan.

'Hey, *compadres*.' He strode in, an oversized leather motor bike jacket slung over a white vest emblazoned with a large cannabis leaf.

'*Madre de Dios*, this place smells like a donkey's bollocks, why don't you clean up around here?' He dragged up a chair and sat down next to Joey.

'I got a proposition for you,' Tigre said. 'Good money, get you out of this hole.'

Joey turned. 'Is it legal?'

Tigre laughed, 'Is it legal? *Compadre* you make me laugh. 'Course it isn't, I have my reputation to think of.' He passed Joey a joint, shaking his head, still chuckling. 'Is it legal? Ha ha.'

Tigre had worked out a way of selling hard drugs in broad daylight right under the noses of the *policía* using Joey's sleight of hand, and avoiding the use of runners. The buyers had a signal that Joey would recognise. They would be persuaded to offer him a big note as part of a trick. Joey would fold it small and make it reappear behind the guy's ear or from his sleeve. It was a schoolboy trick, but the note the 'volunteer' got back, was a fake bill wrapped around a fold of cocaine or heroin. As long as they moved around the city a bit, the police wouldn't catch on and neither would his rivals. It would work for a while, until he thought up a new scam.

'It's risky so I want to discuss a deal of my own,' Joey said, 'It has to do with

Teresa.'

Tigre smiled a little. 'Anything I can do to ease the path of love. I'm sure we could come to an agreement.'

14

April/May 1978

Joey was shifting thirty or forty wraps a day and making a good cut. He was constantly on his guard though. Some of the junkies looked too rough to be shelling out big notes on the street. Anyone with a sharp eye could see something was going on. Still he'd jack it in soon. He squeezed the money pouch which hung on a thong around his neck.

Keeping his plan from Teresa took every ounce of willpower especially when she disappeared out into the streets to work. Sometimes when she came back, she sank into a dark mood and no amount of magic could pull her out of it. She would lie on a mattress staring at the wall, her eyes open, playing with the skeleton around her neck. She was so changeable. One minute buzzing and excited, teasing the passers-by, persuading them to stop and be amazed by his skill then the following day she would sink back into the despair that left her silent for hours or humming quiet off-key tunes that had no beginning or end. Watching her then, his love was like a pain in his lungs, making it hurt to draw breath. If he could just get her away for good he was sure she would recover.

It was Saturday evening, the atmosphere crackling with energy and anticipation. The pavements were jammed with people spilling out onto the streets from bars. The thrum of pumping music made his pulse race.

'Free *Margaritas* for the ladies.'

Blond female tourists on their vacations responded with drunken shouts, as they staggered in the street, the boys watching them, waiting. Joey quickly found a new way in this frenzy of hedonism to increase his profits. He'd found his own supplier and had extended his customer base. No third party now and the takings were good. These gringos were crazy with their money. They didn't know what they were buying and didn't care. He'd never see them again anyway so what was the problem. He was surprised Tigre hadn't gotten into this market. He'd missed a trick there. He was on a fast train to riches and soon she would be on it with him heading for the moon.

It was the fight that changed everything. Tigre had found himself a new girl and sent his lackeys to collect his commission, which meant his gifts of booze and drugs had all but disappeared. Luckily one of the younger kids had managed to knock off a dozen bottles and they'd been drinking all day.

Joey had been dozing in a corner, a heavy, drugged sleep that he couldn't quite leave in which he was trying to pull away from someone who wouldn't let him go. Then he'd heard a woman shouting. It had become part of the dark dream and then had woken him from it.

'You bastard!' He lifted his head and saw, in the guttering yellow light of a kerosene lamp, the quiet mother, Liliana. She was yelling at a skinny man who was leaning against the wall. One of Tigre's boys was holding onto her. Joey leaned up on his elbow to find out what was going on. He saw her baby, Eduardo, lying awkwardly on the mattress, a soft liquid noise coming from his throat, his small face patchy in the half-light. That creep had hurt the baby. He felt a rush coming up from the pit of his stomach and scrambled to his feet. He pushed past the drunk and dozing bodies to where the man stood pressed back against the wall, still yelling back at Liliana. Joey grabbed him by the shirt and dragged him across the floor.

The place was suddenly in an uproar, someone was banging on a hub cap with a knife. His brain was on fire, metal wasps buzzing against the sides of his skull. Joey had him down on the floor trapping his throat with one hand whilst he punched. There was laughter and catcalls. He felt the nose crunch under his knuckles. He kept on even though the body beneath him had stopped fighting back. The yammer of voices swelled in his ears. Two pairs of hands grabbed at him. He tried to shake them off but they held onto him more tightly, dragging him back.

'Stop!' Liliana shouted. 'What are you doing? This is Eduardo's father. You want the cops here?' Joey his chest heaving, looked across at her,

'You mean the baby's okay? He hasn't hurt him?' Liliana frightened, shook her head.

'Fuck,' he spat and stared down at the man, whose face was bruised and swollen. Joey let go and turned his head away. The others were staring at him in silence. He wiped his hands down his bloody shirt.

'You crazy son-of-a-bitch,' the man said, sitting up slowly, gingerly touching his nose with his fingers. 'I give her good money.'

'It isn't enough,' Liliana shouted at him. He staggered up buckling his belt.

'You bunch of animals.' He pushed past Joey out into the night.

Joey stared after him then dropped to his knees. He felt faint, and the smell of the fight was still in his nostrils. Eduardo was curled up asleep, his thumb in his mouth.

Teresa ran into the room, dropped her bag and screamed at the sight of Joey covered in blood. Her hands were shaking and her face was white. He calmed her down and tried to explain what had happened.

'I thought she'd finally got you instead of me,' she whispered.

'Who?'

'*La Muerte*.' She began to cry and Joey took her in his arms.

'I can't do this. I can't be here anymore,' he said, kissing her hair.

'Me neither, Joey. It's this place. No matter what I do, I can't seem to find a way out.'

Joey squeezed her hand, a worm of doubt uncurling inside him. She hadn't mentioned him. She hadn't said 'no matter what *we* do.' He looked at the dark shadows under her eyes. Maybe she was just exhausted.

'I need to be out of here, Teresa,' he said.

She smiled wearily, and stroked his face with her chilled hands, 'We'll be out of here in the morning. Tonight you need to sleep.'

She was right. He was too tired to do anything tonight. He crawled onto his mattress and lay down, his swollen hands behind his head, looking up at the metal-plated roof. His feet were on fire and a dead weight had settled on his soul.

'We'll go tomorrow, Joey, we'll go to Malinalco,' she whispered.

15

It was growing dark by the time they arrived. Joey's memories of Malinalco were mixed. That night in the artist's house with Teresa, he'd felt overwhelmed with its beauty, but like the paintings he'd seen there, it was accompanied by a feeling of unease. Teresa's face when she'd gazed at that image of Nico's dead mother had disconcerted him. She was drawn to it as if it spoke to her personally. He'd seen nothing but the cold emptiness of death but she'd seen something else, something she wanted.

On the bus he stared out of the windows, captivated by the bent figures of people working the fields. They would still be there planting and weeding for years to come. Joey didn't know what might happen in the next few hours. He yearned for some certainty, some peace.

'You will need money, Joey. Doña Marta is good, you will have to pay her. How much have you bought with you?'

He held out a wad of notes. He'd brought all his money with him. Tonight he would tell her about his deal with Tigre and ask her to come away with him. They could leave the city tomorrow if they wished. When he imagined the look on her face, excitement buzzed in him and the fears about the night ahead began to subside. He squeezed her hand, and kissed the top of her hair.

'You know when I was young I was a little afraid of her. She lived alone in a house by the lake. She knew about herbs and medicines, but also about the sicknesses of the soul and the heart. Then she left my village and moved to Malinalco.' Teresa sighed and turned away. 'I sometimes think if she hadn't left, she might have been able to save my mother and then all the bad things wouldn't have happened.' They sat in silence together for the rest of the journey watching the countryside gradually swallowed up in the darkness, each lost in their thoughts.

The bus finally ground into the main street, halting with a dry rasping of brakes. Joey's feet were already jittery.

'I need to buy some gifts to take with us, and a torch,' Teresa said. 'That shithead Rigo thieved mine but then I suppose I stole it in the first place.' She was edgy, her eyes darting and bright. He offered to join her, but she insisted he sit still and reflect, so that his mind would be clear and open. He smiled weakly at this, knowing his mind was not open at all and he watched her run across the road and disappear into a small, run-down kiosk.

He was just beginning to become anxious when he felt her hands close around his eyes. He grabbed her wrists, and swung her round onto his lap. Her pupils were huge and there was a slight tremble in her hands. She wrapped her arms around his neck and kissed him before jumping up and dragging him across the square. The moon was no more than a sliver and didn't provide much light. She was several paces ahead of him walking backwards, illuminating the branches with her flashlight and carving an erratic silver path in the night sky.

'This was the home of the goddess Malinalxochil who was a sorceress, so the place is very powerful,' she said breathlessly. She disappeared down a small track to the left and he had to jog to keep up with her. Monsters hiding in the shadows turned into foliage silhouetted against the sky. He thought of telling her that he'd changed his mind and that he would put up with the problems he had, but she was still ahead of him, chattering and buoyant as if they were on their way to a fiesta.

The path petered away into clumps of tall trees through which he could see the tin foil gleam of water. Noises emerged from the undergrowth, squeals and unnerving rustlings, sounds unfamiliar after two years in the city. Despite his anxieties, the aluminium cans that glinted in the torchlight and bits of litter caught on the bushes reminded him that they were not far from people. It didn't seem like a path to the mystical, more a road stamped with the impatient footprints of the gullible.

The path became a track and the undergrowth turned into a tangled forest, forcing him to duck branches and pull sharp boughs away from his face and his clothes. The air buzzed with the sound of insects. At last they came to a clearing, where three or four candles sputtered in painted tin cans. In the red light he could see the door of a small house. Pictures of saints, encased in plastic, their identities obscured by a film of condensation were pinned to the wooden door.

'Are you ready?' Teresa said, squeezing his hand.

'As ready as I'll ever be,' he replied, as his stomach clenched.

The first knock sent something scuttling into the bushes. Joey wiped his hands down the side of his trousers and wished he'd never agreed to this. Teresa knocked again.

He'd been half expecting to tumble into a dark pit, or be jumped by a thug with a gun but the door was opened by a tall woman with full lips, a high forehead and hair pulled tightly back from the sides of her face. She took Teresa's hand, and held it tightly. Teresa's eyes filled as she stared up into Doña Marta's face, answering her questions in a breathless gush. It was the expression he'd seen on holy days, as the faithful stared into the plaster face of the Virgin.

Doña Marta stepped aside and invited them in. The clop of her heels accompanied the ferocious singing of cicadas. She was dressed like a neat secretary in a plain skirt and green blouse. Heavy gold earrings hung to her shoulders and her eyebrows were thin and arched. She pointed out chairs to them and offered them water.

The two women chatted to each other in a dialect he couldn't understand. Doña Marta held Teresa's hands and listened to her answers with the tilted head and furrowed brow of a doctor. Whatever they were discussing, the effect on Teresa was significant; she nodded and wiped her eyes, and kissed Doña Marta's hands.

Embarrassed, Joey got up and explored the room. It was lit by candles, which cast their glow across shelves lined with unlabelled bottles of liquids and assorted natural objects: rocks, dried flower heads, bunches of herbs, even, he noticed, a group of animal skulls. An archway led from the main room to another smaller space which was also lit by candles. He turned back to the two women. They were still engaged in earnest conversation; Marta was stroking Teresa's bowed head. He ducked into the second room. The smell of wax was suffocating and the walls were plastered with peculiar drawings, and prints of the most revered saints of Mexico: Santa Lucia with her eyes on a plate, El Niño de Atocha, The Virgin of Guadalupe. They stared at him as he entered their space, and followed him as he picked up twisted branches and wizened seedpods that sat in clusters on the low shelf. It gave him the creeps. He returned to the room, where Doña Marta and Teresa were quietly waiting for him.

'Tell me about yourself, Joey.' Doña Marta was sitting with her hands folded in her lap, her feet tucked under her chair. He saw his face reflected in the window, he looked white and tired. He was glad Teresa was there.

'When I walk it's as if my nerves are exposed and I can feel everything. The ground, especially here in Mexico, is constantly moving but it's not only that. I feel weighed down as if things are dragging at me or cutting into me, it was the same back home.' God, it was so hard to explain. He looked up.

'What kind of things Joey?'

'It's going to sound so stupid, like one of those spaced-out *gringos* you hear in the *Zócalo*.' He bit his lip, shoved his chin into his hands and let out a deep sigh.

'I feel emotions: anger, fear and…' Teresa smiled encouragingly at him.

'And?'

'Memories. Things I don't want to think about, but they won't let me go.'

'And when do your feet feel at ease?'

'When I'm far away from the ground, and when I'm happy or excited, then they feel good but most of the time the pain gets in the way.'

Doña Marta listened patiently and asked him many more questions. Each time he answered she nodded and asked, 'And how do they feel now?' His feet seemed to be responding to her comments with tiny sensations, as if they were separate entities. He bent down several times to feel them, to make sure they were still connected to him.

'And your father and your mother, did they have these feelings too?'

'I don't think so.'

'Tell me about them.'

He shook his head. 'I thought this was about me. It's just my feet I need help with.' He had the familiar sensation that he was being sucked into something dark and impenetrable.

'Let's talk about your father.'

Joey looked her in the eye and felt his resistance weaken. 'A bastard. Sadistic. Cruel to us both.' He felt the sweat trickling from his armpits just thinking about his father.

'No-one would believe it. He was clean-cut you see, well-dressed and smooth, but me and my ma we knew what he was like.' He glanced at her face again. She was staring right through him. He didn't want her eavesdropping on his thoughts. He looked away.

'And are you like him or like your mother?'

Joey swallowed. The question was not what he'd been expecting. He felt a hand pressing on his heart, a weighty burden of inevitability.

She reached forward took his hands. He pushed them away, wiped his face.

'We can be better than our parents,' she said.

'And worse too.'

'Better or worse, these are our choices.' She knelt down in front of him, eased off his shoes. 'Let's see what we can do about this.'

She undid her hair, wrapped it around his feet and rested her forehead on them. Joey gasped. The sensation was bizarre, shocking and unexpected. He leaned back as something opened up in front of him, a crack in a huge wall. Through it he could see everything, the house, the old tweed couch and his mother. No! He put his hands up to block it out, pressed his fingers to the sides of the fissure. He squeezed his eyes shut, his blood rushing through his veins.

'Don't resist it Joey.'

He felt his feet trembling in her grip. 'No!' he shouted, struggling up. 'Let me go, if you can see something then you just tell me. What is this, Teresa? What is she trying to do?'

Marta let him go, and watched calmly as he jumped up and gulped in the air around him. He clenched his fists and felt his jaw tighten as the muscles in his chest constricted. He had seen it, just as clearly as the day it had happened, right there in front of him. He'd felt it with all his senses, and she had too. He stumbled, opened his mouth and a long groan slid out of it, like a foghorn, warning the ships of the past to stay away, but too late, too late. He fell to the floor. Teresa cradled his head on her lap. He felt his ankles lifted and then strong, hands pressed against the soles of his feet.

'I didn't mean to kill her,' he whispered. His body shook violently. The pain in his feet made him cry out. Doña Marta poured something onto them. He felt it both hot and cooling like a peppermint in the mouth.

Lying on the floor of Doña Marta's house, the night's frenetic song ringing in his ears, the sweat cooling on his face, he saw his old house hovering like a planet in the darkness. He'd managed over the years to bury his childhood. Even the memories that burst through unbidden had become removed from him. He could look at them as if through a window at someone else's past. But here with her strong hands on his feet, it was as if that window had been smashed and the people and smells, the feelings and voices had climbed over the sill and gathered around him, forcing him to remember them all again.

December 1970, The Beatles singing 'All You Need is Love', on the radio. He is eleven years old, sitting in a taxi with his ma, on the way home for his first Christmas in years. He remembers hearing her voice, breathless with pleasure. He'd almost been fooled, but his feet hadn't. When his father came back from work that first evening, his smart shoes clicking on the pavement, pains had shot through his feet, aggravating his muscles, until the only relief was to squeeze them together as tightly as he could.

There she is. He can see her now clear as anything with her patterned apron and her floury hands. Christmas Eve and the house full of the scent of mince pies and anxiety, her pupils shining, as she buzzes around the kitchen like a trapped fly.

She jumps at the sound of the door as his father walks in. His chin is stubbly, a blue-black shadow across his face. Joey puts his hand to his rib, the bump still there from the time his father had knocked him into the field. His da hasn't changed. Joey can feel it in the atmosphere, in the jarring gaiety of his ma.

'Sit yourself down love. Was it a good night?' She says.

'What's it to you what sort of night I had?'

She drops back in her seat like she's been punched. He walks past her and heads up the stairs. She turns her eyes back to Joey and stretches her mouth into a grin.

That night in his wardrobe hideout, his feet clutched in his hands, he'd floated to Cactus Gulch. Cactus Gulch was small, with one main street and a general store. Luckily the store was open when he arrived. They had a wonderful magic set on the counter, and because he was the hundredth customer they gave it to him for free. It was the most fantastic magic set he'd ever seen. It came with a live rabbit and twelve white doves, each one named after one of the apostles. The rabbit was called John Wayne.

When he woke up in the wardrobe, his neck was stiff and his feet were twitching. It was Christmas Day. He crept downstairs. The living room door was wide open and the Christmas tree lay across his path, dull in the daylight. He pushed past it. There were presents scattered across the floor. The mirror had a long crack right down its front that made Joey look like Frankenstein's monster. He knelt down in the middle of the mess, and picked up a playing card and a magic wand that was bent in two.

His mother was asleep on the sofa. Her eye was squeezed up like a raisin in a teacake. He went to the kitchen to make her a cup of tea but by the time he came back with it she was on her knees trying to clean up. If his da had walked into the room at that moment he would have killed him.

Back in his room, he pulled his bag out from under the bed. Later when it was dark, he would run away and never come back. He didn't want to leave his mam but he couldn't stay with his father anymore and he wouldn't go back to those children's homes. He would run as far as he could and get away to America. He headed back downstairs to help his mother. She was at the hall mirror, dabbing make-up on her face.

'There, that looks better,' she said. He stared at her. She looked like a doll from a rubbish dump with a poked-in eye.

'Yeah, much better,' he said.

She went into the kitchen and started to chop the vegetables as if nothing had happened.

Dinner with the three of them had reminded him of a puppet show. It seemed as if they were mouthing words from their wooden jaws, which someone else had written. He'd struggled to eat anything at all. There was his mother with her paper hat and her best dress and her black eye. He wanted to get up and scream at them both but he didn't. Instead he'd just chewed his way through the turkey, its fibres settling in his stomach like a shipwreck.

Christmas night, and his father was asleep in the study. This was it. He wasn't ever coming back here. He went downstairs, and peered into the front room. His mother was nodding off in front of the television. The pain in his feet was almost unbearable. He yearned to curl himself in her lap, but he knew he could never be safe with his da.

He opened the front door and a blast of winter air struck him. He had an errand to run first. He hurried down the lane along the main road towards the centre of town to St Patrick's. There was a light on inside and the door was open. The smell of incense was soporific. He headed down the aisle, to leave his note on the altar.

My da is a bad man, please take care of my mam, yours sincerely, Joey Flight.

Now Father Michael would know, and maybe he could do something. He turned to leave and noticed the stable set up in the side chapel. The hay was real and nestled in it were the figures of the Nativity. Light flickered on them from a wrought-iron stand full of candles. He sat on a bench in front of it and stared at them. This was a family, The Holy Family. They'd had a good Christmas you could tell, all those presents. Well, if God was so great, why couldn't he have struck his da with a plague of boils, or sent a big tidal wave up the lane and drowned him?

Joey glanced around but the church was silent except for the trickling of water in the radiators. He picked the baby Jesus out of the manger and held it in his hand. It was the size of a hand grenade. He turned suddenly and hurled it at the wall. It smashed into pieces with a crunch that echoed around the stonework. He held his breath but no giant hand came through the church roof to strike him down.

He stared up at the statue of Jesus, with his heart on display and thorns all around it. Joey had never understood it. Why would God let his son be crucified? Maybe he was a bad da like his own, one who didn't know the rules.

'You should have told your father to feck off,' he said to the statue. He felt the swear word lingering in the still air of the church. He wanted to say it again. Instead he picked up the statue of the Virgin Mary. She was heavier but he threw her at the wall too. He needed both hands for that. Next it was Joseph and the three wise men in stupid hats and then the shepherds and the silly angels with their fairy wings. One after another he hurled them at the wall. The noise was fantastic. The air was a blizzard of dust and the pews were scattered with painted debris.

Shaking a little, he swung his legs up onto the bench. He held onto his feet and watched the dust motes waltzing in the light from the candles. Fatigue washed over him. He closed his eyes and felt his horse carrying him across the desert to that town with its glittering lights. If only he could just sleep there, stretch out and…No! He shook his head and sat up quickly. Although the air was pearly with plaster he could see the enormity of what he'd done. Christ! He had to get away fast. His heart thumping, he scrambled off the bench and ran down the aisle and out into the night.

But they'd found him, followed his ghostly tracks, and hauled him out of the shed he'd hidden in.

He opened his eyes and buried his face in his hands. He had to finish this, let it all go. He breathed in. The smell of the warm wood and incense was like a confessional box, except there was no-one he could ask to forgive him. He felt Doña Marta's hands gripping his feet.

'I'd been sent to a place for bad boys like me, bad boys who smashed up churches on Christmas Day. When I was fifteen they decided to let me come home to spend my last month before my release, with my family, like it was a treat! I would rather have stayed in the prison, although they didn't call it that, it was supposed to be a reform school, where we'd learn to be good citizens. I think they wanted the bed and so they kicked me out telling me they were helping me to adjust.'

He looked up into Doña Marta's calm face. 'I tried, I really did. It was good to see my mother, what there was of her. Maybe if granddad and my nan had still been around it would have helped, but ma was on her own with him.'

'Da was still working at the shop and that was the rub. He thought that when my granddad died he'd get the business, but he didn't. Granddad left it to his own brother. My father said there had been a promise.' Joey leaned back, his head ached and his neck felt tight as if the unsaid words were crowding at the back of his throat, waiting to spill out.

'While I was away he'd started drinking and he was not an easy drunk. I was used to insults, but when he spoke to her like that, calling her terrible things.

Don't stand for it ma, I said to her. *Tell him to go to hell.* She looked at me with these drowning eyes, as if she didn't know what I meant.

My da just shook his head wearily. *Don't tell her what to do. She'll do as I say, won't you Maureen?* and I saw her flinch.

You don't have to stay here mam, we'll go away, come on now, I whispered pulling her up next to me.

Sit down, da said firmly, the muscle in his jaw jumping and she looked from one to the other of us, bewildered. I held onto her, all skin and bones. I was ashamed of them both.

Sit down Maureen, and tell that bastard to leave this house, my da said again.

I am what you made me, I shouted and he looked at me, his eyes wide with surprise and he laughed and laughed until his eyes watered. I couldn't stand it. I saw the knife on the table; it was there to cut the ham. And there was his throat, clean-shaven and white. I grabbed the knife and went for him.

Ma screamed, *No!* And then it was her face in front of me, those freckles on her cheek. Her mouth open suddenly, shocked. I could feel it in my wrist, the sensation of the knife hitting bone. She fell back into his arms, folded-in, like a puppet and all that red hair... Da looked down at her, his face almost grey. I was still rooted to the spot, my brain trying to catch up with what I'd done.

You know you've killed her, he said quietly, *you crazy wee bastard, you've gone and killed her.* And then I ran.'

He felt the force from Doña Marta's hands surging up through his body, like a rush of water flushing out each tiny vivid detail. He opened his mouth and a cry flew from his throat, a white bird dragging with it the ribbon of guilt that had lain coiled inside him for so long.

And he was right there, doubled up under an old tree as his lungs struggled for breath. Above him the black clouds rolled like tanks across the night sky. He covered his eyes as the rain thrashed down on him. He was drowning in a field, red-handed, his heart in splinters.

He saw that blossoming stain, her white chest split, the strange heap of her, and then he and his da staring at each other by a kitchen table set for tea. And somewhere back there, his mother's *No!* still echoed, spilling out across the grass, across the fields, across the sky and into his head filling it with its anguished note.

Without looking back, he'd followed the hidden furrows, tripping and falling and picking himself up, snivelling into his sleeve and cursing the dark and the rain and the luck that had led him there. And what was he now? Nothing but a stinking coward, the son of his father. The son of his father.

16

Teresa rubbed his back as his breath steadied.

'Okay, okay' Marta said. '*Basta*, enough.' She helped him to sit up. He hung his head unable to look at them.

'You are a wild country Joey Pachuca, and what you have just experienced was a major earthquake.'

He remembered pictures from the *National Geographic* of volcanoes exploding in a shower of boiling lava. She was right. It was as if some terrible poison had been flushed out of him, some enormous force released and he was exhausted.

Even though her eyes were full of energy, her sallow skin was drawn and waxy. She helped him onto a chair and he noticed that her hands were shaking. She rubbed them together twisting them over each other in a sequence of circles as if washing something from them.

'You have a great gift, Teresa was right.'

'A gift? Most of the time I can't even see things coming. I can't even help myself let alone anyone else. I only feel things that affect me.'

'You have to let them go, and then you will feel the other things too. At the moment you are overwhelmed, the earth is speaking, others' emotions want to be heard but loudest of all is your own heart, shouting at you to hear it. Each of us carries our emotion in a different place: the stomach, the mouth, the chest, even on the sleeve but you, you carry it in your beautiful, powerful feet.' She closed her eyes for a moment and became very still.

Joey thought of all those crazy women whom he'd listened to on the buses or in the market with their potions against the evil eye and their clairvoyant soaps. He couldn't believe he'd found himself in the hands of one and had just confessed everything. What a fool he was, gullible like every other desperate person in this world. It was Saint Jude of the hopeless cases and Saint Anthony for things lost, all over again. What would she give him: a foot powder to be taken on the full moon, a cream to rub in when a lizard crossed his path?

'Maybe not a lizard,' she said.

She crossed the room to a large chest of drawers, opened the bottom one and pulled out a box. She undid it with a key that hung on a chain around her neck and stared in at the contents. She pulled out a roll of something, blew on it creating a cloud of dust. Dragging her chair closer, she sat down next to him. She untied the roll and flattened the material with her hands.

'I've had these for a very long time. People are always bringing things to me for rituals or purifications: dead animals, vegetables that have grown into strange shapes and things that have been found in the wrong place. Someone once bought me a wizened ear that she claimed to have found at the bottom of a goldfish bowl!' She rolled her eyes.

'Most of them went straight into the rubbish but sometimes they brought me something astonishing, something powerful or frightening, and I had to wait for the right time to use it. These came to me by a different route.'

She peeled off one of the pieces of fabric and laid it on his lap. Lightness overcame him. He closed his eyes and above his head he saw a large blue space, full of stars like white birds. Colours blinked down at him, then vanished; he felt slightly giddy. Doña Marta was watching him. She smiled and nodded. He touched the material with his finger tip. It wasn't fabric, it was a fine leather, silvery in colour, with tiny little pinprick holes all over it.

'What is it?' He was almost afraid to find out.

'It is the skin of a bird,' she said, 'a quetzal. Have you heard of a quetzal?'

He shook his head.

'If you visit Guatemala where I was born you will find it on the banknotes but you will never find it in a zoo. The quetzal dies in captivity. For that reason it is a symbol of freedom. They are rare now, hunted for their extraordinary feathers.' Joey studied the skin more closely. It was soft and velvety.

'This particular bird lived in the cloud forest. They have been revered as sacred by the native peoples of Mexico and Guatemala, by my people. The villagers knew it was there and were proud to have it live close by. In fact, a cult grew up around it. People would go to the tree where it nested and leave little offerings hoping, that their prayers would be answered. Then the bird found itself a mate and the villagers were delighted. This tree then became a place of pilgrimage for those searching for a new love or trying to rekindle an old flame.'

'Soon, so many people came to the forest that the birds no longer felt at peace, and one day the villagers discovered that the nest had been abandoned and the female had flown away. For days they searched but couldn't find her, and then a young boy, on his way to school found her body in a clearing. He picked it up and hurried down to the village. He was not able to find the village elder, so he took the bird back to the tree where it had lived, climbed up and laid it back in the abandoned nest.

'He couldn't stop thinking about it though, and after his supper he went down to the tree with a lantern, and climbed into its branches. Balancing his light, he reached up to the nest. The body of the bird was still where he'd left it, but as his hand moved along in the dark he felt something else. He picked up the lantern and raised it above his head. There, lying next to the female was the dead male, his head across her neck.

'The boy was so shocked that he jumped out of the tree and ran back to the elder's house. This time the door was opened and the elder accompanied him, soon followed by a cluster of curious and excited people all intent on seeing this beautiful tragedy.

'In a long and complex ceremony, the two hearts were removed and buried in a hole at the root of the tree and the skins of the birds were tanned, painted with Mayan silver and kept in a special casket.'

'So how did you get these?'

'That boy was my cousin and the elder was my father. I inherited them and when I moved to Mexico many years ago with my first husband I brought them with me. These are for you,' she said, 'a gift of freedom. I will have them made into a pair of shoes, and whenever the sensitivity in your feet becomes too overwhelming, put them on. They will filter out the extraneous and leave only the true and important.'

There was a sudden change of tone in her voice, 'but if you don't forgive your father and your mother and yourself, those emotions will always be clamouring, dragging at you, stopping you from becoming the person you should be. You will always be a prisoner.'

'Forgive my father? I can't, not that, not ever.'

Marta sighed, 'I can only tell you what I know. The shoes will help you, but they are not a permanent solution. That lies with you. Leave your own shoes with me, and borrow these,' she said, passing him a pair of sandals. 'I will give them to someone who can craft the shoes you need. Come back tomorrow and collect them from me.'

She put his shoes on the bird skins and rolled them into a bundle which she tied up with the cord. He didn't know what to say. It was a fairy story from the brothers Grimm, but here in this room, he almost believed her. She looked at the money Joey had left on the chair.

'I don't know if it's enough,' he said.

'It won't be.' She picked it up, folded it and tucked it into her pocket.

'Aren't you going to count it?'

'Why? What I am giving you is priceless and I hope you realise that.'

Unable to sleep, Teresa and Joey walked up the hillside as the morning light slowly diluted the darkness. They sat down on a table of rock and stared at the world unfolding beneath them. He could hear the sound of a church bell, the barking of a dog some-where down below, an engine revving in the distance – the sounds of everyday life.

'I don't know what to make of it but something strange happened there.' Joey said.

Teresa shrugged and stared into the distance. He moved closer to her and placed his hand on her arm. He sensed her stiffen slightly and his fingers turned cold as if the chill of her response had spread through them. She pulled away and stood up.

'Joey I, I… what you did to your mother… I keep thinking about it. I am so confused. You did that, you took your mother's life and yet right from the start you treated me like a proper person, a real person who had something to give apart from her body. Doña Marta does the same thing. She saw what I could be. When I'm with her I feel there might be a way out.'

Joey, his skin turning to gooseflesh, dug into his shirt and pulled out the money pouch and a small squashed roll of paper.

'We have a way out. Look! I planned to give you this in a smart restaurant or somewhere. But here….'

'What is it?' She opened the roll of paper. 'What does it say?'

I, El Tigre confirm that you Teresa, are no longer in debt to me. Joey read.

She looked up at him puzzled, 'I don't understand.'

'I paid off your debt to Tigre with my earnings, and a little more.'

She stifled a gasp with her hand. 'You never said anything. I don't know what to say!' Her brow furrowed, she bit at her knuckles as she stared at the paper that she couldn't read.

'I agreed a price with Tigre. You won't have to work for him anymore, you won't owe him anything,' he said in a rush. 'You gave me my freedom, and I am giving you yours.' Teresa's eyes told him what he didn't want to hear but he ploughed on.

'I have more, look.' He opened the pouch as if there were an amount that would change her expression.

'It's enough to get us a new start. I love you Teresa and now we can go anywhere, maybe even the United States. I've got myself a passport, it's fake but it's a really good one, you can get one too, there is enough money here. There are so many places in the world, beautiful places we could see.' He stood up, felt the sun on his face and tried to draw her back, convince them both with his stories that they still had a future together.

'When I was little, my mother would get all these *National Geographic* magazines from the jumble sales, they are like the flea markets here, and she would call me down and we would play this game, "whereshallwego".

'Now, Joey, where would you like to go?' she'd say and I would peer up into the ceiling as if there might be a map of the world printed on it.' He stared at the sun, its gleaming optimism made his eyes water. His disembodied voice hung between them. He could feel the despair percolating through his veins.

'I think I'd like a turn around the Anti-podes.' I'd say back.

'The Anti-podes now is it?' She'd say it like I'd made an amazing choice and then we'd spend the next half an hour as the rain poured down imagining ourselves on the Great Barrier Reef or strolling among the kangaroos. We even went to Mexico once,' he said turning to her, desperate to see her smile. But she wasn't smiling.

'I can't go away with you Joey. Here, take this back.'

'I don't want it back. It's for you. I don't understand. I thought you loved me.'

'Joey I do but I'm going to stay here with Marta, and learn to do what she does. You know until I met you, I thought I was worthless, just a cheap *puta*. She told me that I have the gift of my grandmother and of my mother. Maybe that is why I was able to help you. This might be my only chance to do something useful with my life.'

'Let me stay here with you then, we can live here together, I can be a performer, earn money,' he begged. He grabbed her limp hands. 'I know what you must be thinking but I would never hurt you. What happened… it was an accident.'

She shook her head. 'It won't work Joey. I have problems that you can't help me with, but I think Doña Marta can. There is so much I can't even explain to myself let alone to you.' Tears slid down her cheeks. 'There is something much greater for you, Joey, my mother told me this. And… and she told me that I am not the one for you.' A small sob escaped from her and she covered her mouth with her hands.

Joey kicked at the ground. 'How very convenient! So, you have a ghost to advise you. Me, I only have my stupid heart.'

He started back down the hill, breaking into a run lifting the dust with his angry feet. By the time he got to the bottom, he was hot and dirty, and tears streaked his face. She was afraid of him. She could invent any excuse she liked but that was the real reason. He'd never tell anyone again.

Later that day, despite his protests she walked with him to the bus station. He yearned to take her hand but he couldn't touch her, afraid if he did, he wouldn't let her go, or even worse that she would shrink from him. The shoes were in a cloth bag tucked into the big loose pockets on the sides of his trousers.

The sensation when he'd first tried them on was still with him and he didn't know what to make of it. Doña Marta had made him sit down and warned him to take it easy, not to wear them for too long at first. He'd slipped them on and stood up. He'd tried to explain the feeling of them to Teresa.

'It's like when you are at a party, and everyone in the room is chatting and suddenly one voice comes over louder than the rest.

Maybe it's an accent or perhaps it's just someone with a microphone. Well, without these shoes it's just a mess, but when I put them on I can hear individual rhythms very clearly.'

'Rhythms, you mean vibrations?'

'Well, that's what you and Doña Marta call them. Jesus, I don't know what they are. She says if I practise I'll know what the different vibrations are about, one might be something inside me that I need to sort out, or it could be the earth moving and maybe one day I will learn what's going on in other's hearts. Anyway, Teresa, you'll soon know all about it when you become the witch's apprentice,' he sneered.

She stared at the ground. 'I will never forget you Joey, and what you did for me.'

He climbed onto the bus. It pulled away from the station but he didn't look back. What good was it having miraculous feet if he couldn't see what was in front of him? She was just a girl of the streets; you could buy her love for a handful of peso notes.

17

His only aim now was to make as much money as possible, buy a truck and start a new life. He expanded his business and took risks. He was eighteen and ready to break away. Rush-hour was in full flow as he headed from the streets to escape the melee.

The sunset was a slap on the brash blue face of the sky, and his mind, dreamy with alcohol, was somewhere in Colorado, among the violet hills and the scented pines and streams that trickled down from the mountains, full of fish. He was thinking of the log cabin he might build where he could live his solitary life, when he became aware of two figures closing in on him from either side. He turned but one of them grabbed his arm and twisted it up behind him. The pain made his eyes water. He struggled but they held him fast. Questions stumbled around in his addled head. He felt his feet lift off the ground as they marched him down a small side street and into a doorway.

'Who are you, what do you want from me?' he said.

'It's too late for talking. Tigre doesn't like it when his friends leave him out.' Joey tried to answer but one of them slapped a hand over his mouth. He could taste the alien sweat. The other jabbed something hard between his shoulder and his chest. Was this it? Were they going to shoot him here in this alley? Christ. Sweat trickled down his forehead and stung his eyes. His feet were a tangle of stabbing pains. If only he'd had his shoes on he might have seen this coming, if only he'd been sober. The kid with the gun was smaller than him and half his face was obscured with a yellow bandana advertising a taco restaurant. There was something ridiculous about this pint-sized bandit, and Joey in his panic felt a laugh roll up through him but the gun felt real enough.

'Don't shoot me,' he tried to say through the fingers clamped over his mouth. The hand loosened slightly, and Joey swallowed.

'He wants to say something,' the kid with the gun said, jabbing him again 'a last request maybe, an apology even.'

'You know what, Rico? I don't want to hear it.'

They were kids speaking like TV gangsters and Joey felt reassured but only for a moment. Their inexperience could make them even more unpredictable and dangerous.

'Wait,' Joey garbled, and ducked his hand into his tee-shirt for his money pouch.

'What the fuck…!' the boy with the gun shouted and kneed him in the groin. White pain flooded Joey's body and he doubled over, dropped the money, and vomited all over the arm and hand that held the gun.

'*Ahh! Chinga!*' the gunman swore, recoiling in disgust and dropping the weapon. It clattered to the ground. He bent down to make a grab for it, Joey kicked out. The taller kid tried to regain his grip around Joey's neck but Joey took his opportunity and bit down hard on the arm. He felt the muscles slacken and a howl escape in a stink of breath and then he ran.

He knew this area well, he had the advantage. He had nothing left but his shoes and his loose change, but he couldn't think about that now. There was a shot, followed by a loud crack and ping as the bullet hit a metal object. His heart pounding and his balls aching, he darted down an alleyway, dodging bags of stinking rubbish and came out behind the back of a market. He thought for a moment of sneaking inside, hiding under a stall all night but the traders often slept in there, they might make a commotion and hand him over. He'd have to find somewhere else. He needed crowds to get lost in. He had to get back to the busier streets again, they wouldn't risk firing in a busy street. He was in the Zona Rosa. He fled up

Roma, came out onto Insurgentes. The main drag was packed as usual. He jumped on a bus going north.

He hunkered down, next to a heavy man in a baseball cap. He peered out to get his bearings then pulled back. He'd spotted the two figures, close to his bus. One was running along the pavement peering into doorways, rough-handling passers-by, checking their faces for a resemblance. The other was standing in the road, looking directly up at him. It was the one he'd puked on, he'd seen him. Both of his attackers ran out into the traffic to an outburst of horns and shouts. He turned and saw them hop on the bus behind his. He jumped up, dashed to the front.

'I need to get off quick! I'm going to be sick.' The passengers all drew back. The doors opened and he leapt off, ran in front of the bus hoping that the boys chasing him hadn't noticed. He darted between the late-night strollers, trying to blend in and then jumped on another bus. It took off up Insurgentes Norte, joining a stream of bobbing lights and growling engines. He leaned back and caught his breath, his heart so loud he thought the drowsing man next to him might wake up. When he'd calmed down, he looked out of the window at the unfamiliar buildings and when the bus came to a stop, he got out. He peered back along the road; he needed to be careful, they might be following him still.

It was bright here, too bright maybe. Strings of coloured lights flashed and shops poured music out onto the street. There were vendors peddling balloons and toys, and there was singing coming from somewhere, not drunken songs from a cantina, but hymns or prayers – that's what he could hear.

He pressed forward into the crowd, slipped down a back street behind a *ferreteria*, trying not to disturb the stacks of metalware outside. He grabbed an abandoned blanket and wrapped it around his shoulders, comforted by its animal stink.

The alley twisted sharply but after a couple of turns it opened onto a plaza, hung with bunting and thronged with people. He'd found himself in some kind of procession. He managed to squeeze himself between two stocky men whose faces and hands told of long days spent working in the fields. One looked down at him with dark earnest eyes and nodded a greeting. His shirt was open and a large crucifix was fastened across it with chains. A crackling voice amplified by a megaphone led a chant and all around him women pounded their chests with their fists and responded in dry, tuneless voices.

Above the crowd, a statue of the Virgin floated. Several times he was convinced it was about to topple but it always righted itself and sailed on, leading the crowd forward. Huge banners hung over them, dipping and rising with the swaying pilgrims. They were stitched with the names of co-fraternities and women's groups and villages he'd never heard of.

He looked over his shoulder, his heart slowing. There was no sign of Tigre's hired hands. He edged forward with the crowd and nearly tripped over a woman walking on her knees, her eyes gazing at the heavens.

'Sorry, señora,' he muttered, but she ignored him and carried on with her incantations, and the counting of her beads,

'*Mea culpa, mea culpa....*' No-one else was looking at her. They just slipped around her like a stream around a boulder. He turned back. She was still there on her knees. The road here was cobbled, and he wanted to tell her to save her knees, that she'd be better off talking to the clouds, but the crowd had swallowed her up.

'*Dios te salve María, llena eres de gracia, ...*' It was the Hail Mary. They were chanting the rosary, like they did at home. He knew these words by heart. Despite his resistance it picked him up and he drifted along with the river of people, protected by its gentle rhythmical flow. The density of the crowd increased and in the distance he could see they were heading towards an enormous church. Huge banners fluttered from scaffolding, painted with the Virgin of Guadalupe.

She was everywhere you looked in Mexico City, light bursting around her and roses tumbling from her cloak. Some of Tigre's

boys wore tee-shirts with her face on it, one of them had her tattooed on his back; buses had her image in the clear resin of their
gear sticks. She dangled from car mirrors and he'd even seen her
image on bath towels and face cloths in the market. He allowed
himself to be swept inside the famous basilica, safer there, than on
the streets. Tigre's thugs would never find him among these crowds
and even if they spotted him they wouldn't take out a gun. Even
gangsters respected the Virgin of Guadalupe.

By the time he left it was dark although the streets still bustled with
souvenir sellers. Families lay on the ground asleep under blankets;
they must have walked miles for this. What would he pray for if he
still believed in praying – a new start, a family, money? But you had
to be forgiven and who was there to forgive him now? If prayers
could be answered he'd pray that he could go back and change that
terrible day, change the things that had led to that moment. But
how could you pray when you didn't know what needed to be un-
done?

He had wandered away from the pilgrims and found himself in
a small street that opened out at the end into a large piece of waste
ground. Lights hung in space like fallen stars, but as he moved
closer he realised they were rigged up on a frame, and formed an
entrance above which a huge banner fluttered, with the words,

'Circo Robles'

Ahead of him the Big Top billowed like a giant lung. A crash
of music, a roaring crowd, and thunderous claps and whistles burst
through the silence. In the darkness, the shadows of trailers loomed
ahead of him, forming a circle around the tent. He stood and stared
at it, and his feet were utterly still.

'It started an hour ago. You can have a ticket half price if you
want to see the last bit,' an old woman in the ticket booth said,
without lifting her eyes from her book.

PART 3

1

There was an elephant, an elephant right there in front of his eyes and sitting astride it a beauty in sparkles, waving at him. Then the *tantara tantara* of a trumpet and the cymbals' giddy clash, and four men fighting with pillows tumbled past him in big red boots and giants' coats and covered him in feathers. Oh, the roar of the crowd, their necks craned, giggling at him turned into a goose! The elephant though, was real, like something in the *National Geographic*, as big as a truck and rough as a shoe in a ditch. Oh, this was good, this was good!

Joey slipped into a seat right at the front and brushed the feathers from his shirt. A girl gawped at him like he was an angel descended. Her mouth, mid-lick around a lollipop, hung open for a moment until another roar caught her attention. Joey followed the gaze of the crowd to the roof of the Big Top. The elephant had gone, the clowns had driven into the wings and now high above the sawdust floor, two men and a girl in shimmering suits leaned out from a small platform, silver moths against a blue roof painted with stars. He knew this place from somewhere. He closed his eyes. Doña Marta's house, the bird skins on his lap. His heart contracted as the face of Teresa slipped into view. He pulled out his silver shoes and put them on. A sensation spread through his entire body, as if he'd been drenched with cold water on a hot day, and his feet stilled on the wooden boards beneath him.

'And now,' a voice crackled, 'all the way from Chihuahua, the best high-wire you will everrrr see, the most Gracefullll, the most

Darrrring, the most Dazzling, Las Estrellas del Circo Robles, La Familia Alvarezzzzzzz.'

The music flared, full of blasting horns and strings and the iridescent gods skipped along the high-wire, dipping and dancing, long thin poles in their steady hands. He didn't care about the patches in the awning, the splits and the tears covered in tape, the splintery seating, the sweaty reek of old lard, the sweet stench of spun sugar, the under-whiff of dung. No. Joey had tumbled into the dazzle of the circus and for now he wasn't going to get up for anyone or anything.

He stared up into the roof of the tent as if he'd been offered a glimpse of heaven. He clapped until his hands stung as the performers jumped into the net and somersaulted back into the ring. Cheers accompanied their swift bows to the crowd. The woman curtsied, her eyes glittering in the stage lights. Joey stretched his hand and touched her cloak.

He was still looking hopefully into the wings when live music suddenly burst from the aisle and a band of mariachis strode into the ring followed by three jugglers dressed in gold, tossing lit torches to each other. The crowd whistled and clapped as the clowns reappeared, all five of them balanced on a tiny car with a horn as big as a vacuum cleaner. The children squealed as it tipped to the right on two wheels and tumbled back only to do the same again on the other side.

And then the horses trotted into the ring, one black, one white, and Joey was lost. A girl in black stood on the back of the white one, a silver rein in her hands and behind her a girl in white stood like a snow queen on her black horse. Joey stood up, or rather his feet forced him up and he had no choice but to obey them. A rush of energy surged up through his legs into his heart, into his arms and they shot into the air.

'Yes,' he shouted, 'bravo!'

The people around him smiled indulgently and he dropped down again. He stamped and hollered, hoping the riders would look in his direction, but they stared ahead, steely and regal, monochrome Amazons, making a prisoner of his heart.

Outside, a dry, cool evening wind blew litter across the site, trapping it under guy ropes and flattening it against the windscreens of trucks: the plastic bags and straws, the *helado* cups and ticket stubs and the flyers for Circo Robles, '*El Circo Mas Famoso en Mexico*'.

It was out into this dusty ground with its excited children and its sticky offerings, that Joey wandered dazed and bewitched. In that moment he forgot the fact that he'd lost all his money and had nowhere to go. Every cell in him was alive and focused. This was the place, this circus, these people. Now his real life would begin. If only Teresa had come with him. They could have stood here together and she would have understood what this meant. She had made a choice though, and she hadn't chosen him. He came back to earth with a thud that even his birdskin shoes couldn't soften. He needed to lie down. His throat ached from the brutality of El Tigre's thugs, and the spot on his chest where the gun had jabbed him was aching beneath his tee-shirt.

The crowds were still clustered around stalls selling clown noses, flashing wands and *palomitas* but he needed to sleep. He settled for a gap between a washing tub and a fence. The grass was soapy in places but he wedged himself in, hoping no-one turned up too early to do their laundry. From this vantage point he watched the families dressed in their best clothes, clutching their children's hands and posing for photographs with the clowns who strolled around in their garish costumes, until eventually the last stragglers left and the circus lights went out one by one like stars consumed by clouds. Soon the only glow came from the caravans and trucks dotted around the site, where he imagined fire-eaters and jugglers massaged their muscles and boasted of tricks and terrors.

He rolled onto his back and put his arms behind his head. Tomorrow he would find the boss and discuss his plans for a permanent job here. Two and a half years he'd been in this city and yet he'd never even seen a circus and then out of nowhere it had appeared in front of him, the sparkling tent with its music rising out of the dark like a wish he'd longed for but never even uttered. His feet, this was their doing. They had brought him here.

2

A growling dog woke him. Joey flattened himself on the ground, afraid to move. A strong hand held onto the collar as the dog fought against the restraint.

'Jesus! Call him off! I'll come out,' Joey said. He began to wriggle and the dog dropped its head and snarled.

'*Basta*,' the man said smacking its muzzle and it dropped to its belly, its eyes unflinching. Joey dusted himself off and eased himself up to the sound of a low growl. The dog's owner was a colossus, a vest stuffed with muscles and a neck as thick as a tree.

'Thanks.' Joey said. He offered his hand, 'I'm Joey Pachuca.'

'I'm not planning for this acquaintance to be a long one,' the man replied. 'You've no right to be here. You're lucky no-one else found you first and shot you.'

'I'd nowhere else to go, I'm sorry. I was the victim of an armed robbery.' As Joey pulled at the neck of his shirt, the circular bruise in its stormy colours drew a raised eyebrow.

'Huh. You don't look like someone worth a bullet.'

Joey looked down at his dirty jeans, and his scuffed sandals. 'I'd been saving up my money for months. I wanted to buy a pick-up, get myself out of this city but now I have nothing, all that graft and they got it. Shit.' Last night's euphoria had left him. He was cold and hungry and his head ached.

'That's enough, you're making me cry.'

Joey looked away. 'Stupid thing is, it's all true. I got on the wrong side of the wrong people, story of my life.'

'I'll get you some breakfast,' the man said, his voice softening, 'and then you can head off and find yourself some other place to stay.'

'No, you don't understand.' Joey swallowed and keeping an eye on the dog he stood up. 'There isn't anywhere else for me to go. This is where I'm meant to be. This is my destiny.'

The big man looked around at the scrappy field with its rolling litter, its faded banners and the assortment of well-used cars, and sighed. 'We don't need any more nutcases, place is full of them.'

Joey protested. 'I can't explain it. Let's just say I need to join this circus. I'm nearly nineteen. I've travelled a long way and now I'm ready to stop. You will never regret it.'

'Great, just what we need – another starry-eyed nobody who can't even look after his own money.' He strode away, his big arms swinging by his sides and the dog trotting next to him staring up at his face.

Joey had to run to keep up. 'All I want is a chance. Tell me where the boss is and I'll speak to him.'

The man turned and looked him over. 'What do you do?'

'You first, what do *you* do?' Joey said.

The man stopped, and clenched his fists. 'I would have thought that was obvious. I'm 'Rodrigo El Fantastico', the strongest man in Mexico, maybe even the world. I can lift up a family car with one hand – with the family still in it,' he whispered bending down and peering into Joey's face, waiting.

'Wow! That's incredible!'

'*Claro que si.*' Rodrigo said, thumping his chest. 'Whatever you might hear about me in this place you just remember that I am incredible, I am fantastic,' he pounded his chest again, coughed a little, and the dog barked and wagged his tail.

'So?'

'I am going to be the best high-wire act in the whole of Mexico.' Joey said.

'Going to be? When, exactly?' Rodrigo asked, taking in Joey's odd stance.

'When I start learning,' Joey grinned. Rodrigo shook his big head and his laughter reverberated across the site like a depth charge.

3

Señor Robles' trailer was bigger than the others, painted a pale blue with wrought-iron shutters on its windows. From inside came the sound of soaring orchestral music. Rodrigo knocked on the door and then opened it, the caravan tipping with his weight.

A plump man sat behind a table, his shaggy grey head between his hands. Without moving, he held up his finger and they stood waiting as the music rolled over them, its yearning notes filling the space with melancholy.

Joey glanced around him. It looked like an executive's office, clean and neat with dark furniture. Apart from the table, there were several chairs, a bench upholstered in subdued stripes and a metal bead curtain that suggested hidden living quarters. The walls were covered in framed pictures of performers in tights and spangled costumes, with arms flung upwards. A poster with the grinning face of the man himself surrounded by smaller circular photos of contortionists and jugglers hung on another wall. Joey peered closely at two muscular young men who appeared in several photos, *Los Diablos Volandos* –The Flying Devils. They hung from trapezes, dressed in red, one holding the other by the feet, arms outstretched into the future, a pair of superheroes.

Rodrigo coughed, and Joey turned back. Señor Robles closed his eyes as the last bars of the music faded and then he shook his head. He knotted his hands in front of him and leaned back in his chair.

'Yes, Rodrigo, what can I do for you?' His voice was deep and crackly like the sound of a very old record.

'Another runaway who wants to join our happy family.'

Robles pushed his chair back, stood up and stared out of the curtained window behind him. His hands were surprisingly slender except for the knuckles, which were swollen and arthritic.

'And what exactly can you offer a great circus like this?' He said turning and pinning Joey with a glare.

Joey cleared his throat. 'I want to learn the high-wire.'

Robles shook his head and rubbed his eyes. 'Take him away Rodrigo. We are not a school and I have work to do.'

Joey sprang forward and leaned his hands on the big table. 'Please, I can turn my hand to anything. I arrived in Mexico with nothing, and earned enough in one year to buy a truck except it all got stolen by thieves. I taught myself card tricks and magic. I'm good with my hands. I can be a clown or I can sell things and clean up. I'll work for nothing, try me, please.'

Robles stared at him for a moment, and Joey saw the tired lines in his face, the dark watery eyes, and a mouth that struggled to hold its shape. Robles picked up a picture from his desk, stroked the frame with his thumb.

'I don't have the stomach for a fight today. You can stay for the moment and if you do something that makes you worth keeping, I'll reconsider. We are not a charity; we are a business, a family business. Rodrigo here is my nephew. I trust family. Where are your family?'

Joey looked out of the window. 'I have no family, they are dead.'

'Ah, an orphan, there are many of these in the circus. Strange, isn't it, there is no word for a parent who has lost his children.'

He put the photo down and turned back to his tape machine, pressed the button and the mournful music poured out of it again, filling the room. Rodrigo grabbed Joey's arm and dragged him out.

'What's his problem?' Joey said.

Rodrigo slapped his head. '*Madre de Cristo!* Today is the 28th. It's the anniversary of the death of his sons, you and your problems made me forget!'

'What happened to them?'

'They were killed in an earthquake in '73. The police reckoned they panicked when the ground started to shake and lost control of their car. They were always more at home in the air than on the ground. He's terrified of earthquakes now.'

'Why doesn't he leave Mexico then?' Joey thought of the time he'd fallen in the street from a tremor that rocked the ground, six months after he set foot in the country. People for a moment or two had stood in the street, trembling like peas on top of a drum before running for cover.

'His boys are buried here, and his wife. His heart lies in Mexico and so his soul must stay here too.' Rodrigo scratched his moustache. '*Hombre*, I've work to do. Look around. Don't go into any trailer or touch anything. If you meet anyone, introduce yourself,' and he strode off, his huge arms swinging away from his body.

Joey stood in the dirt and watched him go. The vicious dog he'd encountered earlier licked his hand and then returned to scratching itself with enthusiasm.

4

The air was tostada crisp, the sky a turquoise blue and cloudless with only a hint of yellow at its base where the pollution gathered, suffocating the city with its noxious vapours. The site was up and active even so early in the morning. The air rang with the sound of voices and radios, the DJ's yammering about the virtues of washing powder and toothpaste – and then there was the traffic.

The site was nothing more than a piece of scrubland next to a busy road. Trucks hurtling by whipped up the dust, scouring the ground, casting grit in his eyes. In the unforgiving daylight the circus had the look of a pretty girl after an all-night party, bleary and disarrayed. Faded canvases hung from scaffolding sporting huge paintings of a rosy-cheeked Señor Robles, not a trace of the dolorous man he'd just met. Another showed a curvaceous girl on the back of an elephant, its trunk holding a Mexican flag. Finding them would be his first job, he decided, and that shouldn't be difficult; an elephant wasn't an easy thing to hide after all.

He headed towards the Big Top and peered inside as he passed. Four men in shorts were engaged in a ferocious argument. It would have been more intimidating had one not been seated in a baby bath and the other gesticulating with a giant yellow watering can. He let the canvas drop and continued to walk around the structure.

A little girl crouching between the trucks put her finger to her lips and he smiled and nodded as a gang of screaming youngsters hurtled past them both, and scattered in different directions. He winked at the girl in her hiding place. Then he heard it, the shrill animal blast. In a couple of turns he came to a trailer with a huge grinning elephant head painted on the side. He peered around the truck. The elephant tethered to the ground by a chain spotted him from the corner of its black-ringed eye and gave another blast. It unrolled its trunk in his direction. It was the biggest living thing he'd ever seen this close up. Ears flapped like sails, creating a draught he could feel on his hot skin. As he inched closer, its soft muscular trunk poked at his chest. He laughed in surprise.

'Hey! Who are you?'

Joey jumped.

'Circus doesn't open yet, and this isn't a petting zoo.'

A small pugnacious man, a hat pushed to the back of his head, appeared from behind the elephant, a bucket of water in his hands.

'I'm Joey Pachuca, *buenos dias*.' He offered his hand. 'Señor Robles knows I'm here. He said I can stay for a week.'

'Of course, it's the 28th August,' the man muttered.

Joey said nothing, but touched the trunk that nosed into the neck of his tee-shirt. He couldn't help smiling.

'You like elephants?' the man said, putting the bucket down.

'I don't know,' Joey said 'this is the first one I've met.'

'Ha ha, first one you've met, that's a good one. I'm Gustavo,' He extended his hand. 'This here is Dora, and she's ready for her morning wash. There's a broom over there, you can help me. Normally my daughter does this but I think she's still asleep.'

Joey took the broom and began to brush Dora's sides. She trembled at the force of the bristles and leaned her weight into him, her eyes closed.

Gustavo chuckled. 'Yeah, she likes this, don't yer girl.' At the sound of his voice, Dora opened her eyes, and stroked Gustavo's face with her trunk.

'*Si, guapa, si, mi amor,*' Gustavo murmured.

Joey had never had an animal of any sort, not even a goldfish. It seemed almost impossible to believe that he was here standing next to such a beast. He rested for a moment, the sweat trickling from his forehead. His arms ached already. 'Have you had her since she was a wee 'un?'

'No, it's a sad story. I wasn't an elephant trainer by background although of course I am *del circo*, I come from a circus family. My family used to work in North America in one of those Barnum and Bailey circuses. I looked after the zebras, trained them up. You know at one time they had more than six hundred animals. Those were the days of the big circuses, but I don't miss them. I changed my mind about those wild animals, especially the big cats. When you've done time like me it puts you off cages. A cheetah in a cage, it's not God's way, is it? So that's what I'm saying and I can see you thinking, the man has an elephant! That's not a domestic type of creature, it's not a pet!'

Joey wasn't thinking that at all. He was wondering what this talkative little man had done to end up in gaol.

'I'm soft-hearted, love animals. I bought her from another circus, she was already an adult, and used to people but she'd been mistreated. I fell in love with her. They are very sensitive creatures, elephants, very clever. How could anyone mistreat a lady like Dora?

'It was rescuing animals that landed me in gaol. I liberated a seal that was covered in scars, that's what I told the judge. He saw it differently. I couldn't pay so I ended up in the slammer. I learned my lesson. I paid for Dora. She cost me every penny I had, but she's the best investment I ever made.' He patted her cheek, and rummaged in his pocket for a scrap.

'I don't like chaining her up, hurts my heart to see that cuff around her leg, but she has no road sense. I think she imagines those trucks out there are odd-shaped elephants. Ha ha! One day I expect to hear she has run away with an articulated lorry, eloped with a pick-up.' He roared with laughter, stopping only when the laughter turned into a cough.

'What can she do?' Joey said, rubbing the brush behind her ears.

'I call her *The Entrancer*,' Gustavo said, clearing his throat and spitting into the dirt. 'She dazzles the kids and they pester their parents, the parents buy the tickets, that's Dora's job. My daughter, Concepción, is the cherry on top of the cake.'

Joey fetched more water, and Gustavo checked the bristly skin for mites and cuts and rubbed some stinking ointment into the ones that he found.

'Those toenails of hers are going to need cutting,' he muttered picking up a foot, 'then I suppose those girls will want to varnish them!'

By the end of the first day Joey had introduced himself to everyone he'd met. He'd cleaned Dora's pen, washed down a truck, fetched water for three girls in leotards, touched up a wooden sign advertising popcorn, stuck tape over a new split in the entrance to the Big Top and generally exhausted himself being useful. His feet ached but only from tiredness, and although the little children had called him names as they watched him hobble awkwardly around the lot, no-one had asked him about it.

The evening clear-up over, Joey crawled back into his space. No mattress, just the hard ground beneath him. All around him the caravans glowed with life and sound and he was outside of it, his nose pressed up against the sweetshop window like one of those urchins in a cheesy Christmas card. Only a few months had passed since he'd beaten Liliana's boyfriend in the squat and had felt the thrill of violence possess him again. Maybe that was the only kind of place he deserved to call home, a place for the lost and the damaged.

He yearned for new experiences now that would lay themselves down in his mind, cover the past like a snowfall. Teresa. If he closed his eyes, those memories were there, those thin layers of joy. She'd given him his freedom but just when he thought happiness was at last within his grasp, she'd left him. Now the past was beginning to protrude again, revealing itself in sudden ominous flashes that made him stumble and extinguished hope of salvation. He wouldn't let it. He opened his eyes and recalled the feel of Dora's soft trunk against his cheek, the glitter in the eye of the high-wire walker.

He wriggled out of his sleeping place and stood up. The smell of the animals was in the air, rich and ripe and mixed with the aroma of spun sugar. He walked around the site, his hands in his pockets. Behind the closed doors he heard voices, laughter and radios breaking into lively tunes as he passed. Animals snuffled and huffed and shadowy figures moved around behind curtained windows or darted across the shadows.

A big tent in a black field. There are coloured lights and the darkness is full of voices and laughter that seem brittle and crisp in the winter air. Dodgems. He can hear now the rubbery thunk of them and the squeals of children as the cars bump against each other. His mother squeezes his hand as she gazes about her.

He is staring at the cars with their hunched grinning fathers and wild children, but she is dragging him away across the grass to the tent where people are queuing. She is asking someone a question. The old man with the red jacket mutters something then shakes his head. His ma gasps, looks into the distance and digs her hands into her pockets. His feet are tickling him. He giggles. She'd gazed down then and oh, how sad she'd looked. He'd taken her in his five-year old hands, tried to swing her around and around, his feet bubbly like orangeade, but she was heavy, a weight that anchored him to the spot with her sadness.

Hey ma, let's dance, he'd said, *I'm just like Quickstep Charlie.* She'd let go of him abruptly and he'd fallen on his backside. He can still feel the shock of it now. He'd twitched his mouth in a tentative smile, waiting for an answering one to show she'd been joking, that the pain in his arse was just a bit of a prank.

It seemed an age before she smiled back and then bent down and scooped him up, wrapping her arms around him and hugging him so fiercely he could hardly breathe. He put his hand to his cheek.

He remembered the press of her coat button on his face and the hot dampness of his breath against her sleeve.

Don't tell your da we came here she'd said as she let him go, *he'd say I was wasting his money.* He'd wanted to tell her that they hadn't spent any but he didn't. He knew the weight of his father's hand.

He had trotted alongside her, his hand numb from her grip, as she strode with him across the field, thrusting him forward into the night away from the lights and the tinkling music, with his feet wanting to go back there, back where his toes danced in the grass and sparked with a wild joy.

5

The trial week slipped past and then a few more and Robles didn't seem to notice. Joey made himself essential but inconspicuous, living on donations and leftovers. He was the first up and the last to bed. He never got a chance to watch the show, eager instead to be seen as a working wonder, a tireless model of diligence.

But he was an outsider. At night the *cirqueros* disappeared into their trailers or gathered together to share food and conversation. Occasionally he would hang around the fringes of these gatherings absorbing the jokes, trying to remember the names, enjoying – if only at a distance – the atmosphere of intimacy. People were not unkind, they were just indifferent. He was invisible to them, a minor misshapen planet outside their orbit. Most nights he returned to the small nest he had made for himself and stared at the stars until, exhausted, he fell asleep. He was lonely but after all that he'd endured it didn't matter. He still had the feeling that this was his destiny and when, after an insult or slight he felt despondent, his birdskin shoes soothed him like a mother's hands.

He was clearing up the Big Top after the afternoon performance when Doña Rosa – the old woman who'd sold him a ticket on that very first evening – came in with a plate of food for him. Hungry and alone he was moved by her kindness. He had seen her several times scolding the children, or chasing them away from her trailer, a book in her hand and her hair wild. He'd had her down as a mean one.

He rested his shovel and broom against the ring and sat in the front row with her.

'I saw you looking into the rubbish bin and that is no way for anyone to live.' Joey hung his head.

'You have no family?' she said, poking at the filling of an enchilada with long, curved nails.

Joey shook his head and smiled. 'I'm a poor wee orphan.'

She screwed up her eyes. 'But you are not from here, though your skin is *moreno*, maybe Colombia, Italy?

'I've been travelling all over, but I want to stay here. I'm going to be a performer.' He looked away from her not wanting to see the incredulity in her face.

She shrugged. 'You can do many things in a circus: there are tickets to be sold, *palomitas* to be made. I do all of this now, although I used to be a brilliant contortionist.' She stretched out her leg and raised it until it touched her forehead. Her grinning face appeared from behind her knee, 'I still have the flexibility but who wants to see an old creature like me in the ring.'

He stared into the empty space, its roof laced with wires and ropes, imagining himself up there, *light as a bird, as amazing as Superman,* dazzling the crowds with astonishing stunts. The whine of a drill and the startled response of the elephant broke his reverie. Doña Rosa balled up the napkin and dabbed it at her mouth.

'Maybe I can help you. I can certainly feed you.' She stood up and brushed down her clothes. 'We must have dreams but we must also do our more humble work,' she sighed, pointing to the ring. Joey laughed, and picking up his shovel, he loaded the piles of elephant dung into a bucket and carried it out of the Big Top to a far corner of the site, where someone even poorer than him would come and collect it and sell it for a few pesos to the gardeners of Xochimilco.

It was good to have a friend in this place, and Doña Rosa latched onto him, preparing meals as she'd promised and stopping for a few words whenever she saw him. The old gals at home had always gone crazy for his dark curls and his dimples. He'd been pale then but Mexico had given him a colour and the contrast with his blue eyes was unusual. People stared at him sometimes in the street. It had made Teresa both proud and jealous.

Under Doña Rosa's tutelage he began to understand the routines of the circus and its gossip. At first he was enthralled, but after visiting Doña Rosa's trailer he began to wonder if any of it was true. Her home was lined with books. The counters were covered and unstable stacks threatened to engulf him every time he visited. *True Detective* magazines with shocking headlines and garish covers lay on every surface, and piles of yellowing newspapers gave off their distinctive musty smell. He wondered how she slept at night with those stories circulating through her head. He saw his own story in those pages; the image that infiltrated his dreams turned into a titillating cover page.

Each week Rodrigo drove Doña Rosa to the bank. One day she invited Joey to go along with her for extra protection. He was happy to join them and stood waiting by the truck. Doña Rosa arrived with a bulging shawl wrapped around her, like an *indigena* carrying a baby.

Rodrigo sighed. 'Doña Rosa, you look very suspicious. Why not just carry the cash in a bag and put some oranges on the top?'

She shook her head, 'a bag can be grabbed from your hand. Someone could spray something in my eyes and snatch it! No, this is the best way.' Rodrigo glanced across at Joey and rolled his eyes. This was obviously a regular argument.

'It's a dangerous world out there,' she whispered to Joey as they climbed into the pick-up, 'you can't be too careful. She pressed a wrinkled finger to her lips and offered him a cake. 'I read the papers. You'd be surprised at what the most innocent people are capable of. I'm not taking any chances.' The cake turned to clay in his mouth and he shifted uneasily, afraid she might feel the rush of blood through his veins.

As they wove their way through the traffic, she forgot the crimes of passion and the drug barons and instead regaled him with her achievements: how she had turned a mutinous audience into a crowd hungry for more, or saved a performer from the jaws of death.

He was a good audience and it was clear that Doña Rosa relished these new ears eager for her stories. Most performers, he discovered, were *del circo*, there by birth, by marriage, or by extended family connections. Some had been with Robles for years while others left to marry, to progress up the billing or to escape scandal. There was no exclusivity at the circus, everyone had several jobs; jugglers danced as equipment was cleared and changed costume to breathe fire or swing hoops or ride horses around the ring, and in the interval children were served popcorn by the mind-reader and found their sweets in their hands before they'd even uttered their requests. It was a strange and complicated family, sprawling but loyal, and Joey longed to find his own part in it.

He'd hoped to have more time to watch the performers, especially the high-wire troupe and maybe even talk to them, but he only caught brief glimpses on his way to a job, glancing over his shoulder as acrobats practised a complex pyramid, or peering in through the flap of The Big Top as the *trapecista* swung and flipped. The *chamacos* – the circus hands – delighted to have someone lower than themselves, worked him hard barely giving him time to relieve himself.

Then he was assigned to work with Otavio. He'd heard about Otavio from Doña Rosa and it was clear that she held him in high regard. He lived in a trailer next to Robles with his two sons – the clowns he'd seen arguing on the first day. They were a big draw, especially after the shows when the children clustered around them tweaking their noses and stepping on their big shoes. Feeling positive and hopeful, Joey presented himself to Otavio ready for the day's work.

Otavio looked him up and down with a sneer and shook his head. 'I suppose you're the new one. Why am I given all the dregs? I can't believe they'd give me a cripple to do the heavy work!'

Before Joey could defend himself, Otavio slouched off, beckoning Joey to follow him. The old anger rose up inside him and he wanted to knock him to the ground. He'd have to start wearing his shoes during the day to improve the way he walked, but he was afraid of wearing them out.

He thought back to those words of Doña Marta. If he didn't get rid of all that bitterness within him he'd always be awkward, always be assailed by violent pains. But how could he change? Forgiving his father was out of the question and it was too late to save his mother. He wished he still believed in God. He could have joined the other performers on their Sunday trips to mass. He could have knelt with them in the pews, a rosary wrapped around his hands or stepped into the confessional and unburdened himself to the sleepy murmurings of a hidden priest. Then he'd be forgiven, in the name of the Father and of the Son and of the Holy Spirit, and everything would be clean again, except of course, his mother would still be dead.

He stumbled along behind Otavio, muttering to himself. God the father - and that was supposed to be a comfort? God could have been any father he liked and what did he do? He had his son born a bastard so everyone would despise him, gave him special powers that put him under suspicion and then sacrificed him. What kind of a da was that? Joey knew exactly – one just like his own. Well, God was supposed to have made man in his own image after all.

Just thinking of his father gave him the familiar nagging in his arches, the pains in his head and the feeling of faintness that accompanied them. Joey had no time for God, but Jesus, Jesus was different. He had a feeling Jesus would understand him if he'd been a real person and not just a hippie made out of plaster and paint.

Joey managed to catch up with Otavio just as he entered the Big

Top. Three small muscular figures were standing next to a safety net, engaged in earnest conversation. It was the Alvarez family.

'Ah, Otavio, we need you to do a second check on the supports. Margarita thought she felt a slight wobble at the top.'

Otavio scowled and looked up. Margarita immediately darted forward and clutched his arm in her own. 'Let me show you,' she said. 'Perhaps it was me. I was a little anxious today.' She crossed herself. 'Maybe I am superstitious, but you can make me feel better, *claro que si*.'

The scowl softened, and Joey caught a faint smile and an exchange of glances between the two brothers.

Whilst Margarita took Otavio aside, Joey watched the brothers limber up. He'd have to do some serious working out if he was ever going to be more than an odd-job man. He was aware of something in his feet, not a pain exactly, a sensation, as if his feet were also listening and watching with him, tuning in to the performers. Joey yearned to get up on the wire himself.

Otavio disappeared up the ladder and tinkered with the bolts and fixtures for a few minutes before he came down again. 'Seems fine to me, but I've tightened everything again, just to be certain.'

Margarita kissed him on the cheek and sprinted up the ladder. From the little platform she sent a thumbs-up and Otavio sat back down with Joey, offered him a cigarette, and lit up. He leaned back against the bench, his arm spread along the wooden backrest.

'We'll watch for a while just to make sure.'

Joey nodded, thrilled to have the chance to observe their routine. 'How many performers do you have here?'

Otavio thought for a moment. 'About forty, plus stage hands and casuals that we take on at each new site.'

'Sounds big,'

Otavio, the cigarette balanced on his sagging lip, glanced at him. 'Big! Huh! We've been far bigger than this. This is nothing. We are just a boil on Mexico's behind at the moment.'

'The audience seem to like it,' Joey said remembering the night of his own seduction.

'What do they know? Peasants and cowboys.' He spat onto the floor and wiped his mouth on his sleeve. The performers had stopped again and were now on the ground discussing some intricate manoeuvre, sketching it on the earth with a stick.

'How come you're in the circus then?' Joey asked, enjoying the feel of the smoke in his lungs. It was weeks since he'd smoked, and he felt a little light-headed.

'Circus family,' Otavio said. He leaned forward over the front seats and knocked the long trembling ash of his cigarette to the floor. 'My family had its own circus, Circo Sanchéz but when my father died, our stars left us, snuck out in the night like rats despite all the things my father had done for them – see, no loyalty.'

'Maybe they couldn't stand it without him?'

Otavio rolled his eyes. 'Maybe they couldn't stand not being paid. My father left the circus with big debts; we had to sell all the animals.'

'So it wasn't any good?'

'Good? It was the best, but my father was cursed with bad luck. He fancied himself as a Mexican impresario, but sometimes, his ambition was greater than his intelligence. Have you ever heard of The Humming Birds?'

Joey shook his head. Otavio stamped on his cigarette and spat another ball of green phlegm with such precision that it landed on top of the dying ember and extinguished it. His drooping mouth reminded Joey of an old dog that had followed him in Tepito. Its wet, grey lips with their constant look of disappointment had made him so uncomfortable he'd tried to hide whenever he saw it. It had filled him with a sense of dread. Then one day he'd crept out, peering up and down the road ready to dodge it, but it had gone. His spirit had lifted, like his sins had been wiped away. After three days he finally felt he'd got his old self back again. *That was a bad spirit fighting God for your soul,* Teresa had said gravely. He'd laughed at her. She wagged her finger at him. *You may laugh but we both know it's true. You're lucky God won.*

She was right. He'd been saved, pulled back from the brink by something. But he also knew how easily he could find himself back at the edge peering in and longing for its darkness. Otavio's jaded view of the world could infect him, and he had enough bad thoughts of his own to torture his waking hours.

'The Humming Birds were a troupe of acrobats, perfectly formed but tiny adults, four women and four men. They were so small they barely reached my knee. They were the best tumblers in the Americas, and my father signed them up but what should have been the making of the circus turned into our undoing. He brought them over from Finland on a cruise ship, one of the best, 'The Princess of the Fjords'. It had only top-notch passengers, a show every night with famous stars, chandeliers, wood panelling and a top class chef from a Helsinki hotel. They don't make cruise ships like that now. In those days my father would travel halfway across the globe if he got wind of a new act, and bargain like a pro to get them. He'd made some good finds, did y'ever hear of Señor Reptile?' Joey shook his head. 'That man could make a Nile crocodile lie in his arms and coo like a baby but that's another story.

'In this instance my father won the bargain and there they were, on board ship, speaking nothing but Finnish, their suitcases bigger than themselves and their faces the colour of *salsa verde*.' He chuckled, the rasping sound of a sandpaper tongue in a wooden throat. 'The weather was so rough they were confined to their beds the whole voyage.'

'¡*Que mala suerte*!' Joey said remembering his own long voyage with its bouts of furious nausea that turned him inside out.

'They were sick for the entire voyage, a voyage that had not been paid for. You see my father had bargained with the captain, their passage in exchange for performances to entertain his passengers. But bilious acrobats can't tumble, stands to reason. When they got off the ship and hit *terra firma*, they were so relieved they climbed one on top of the other in a human pyramid and sang the national anthem of Mexico. It was in all the papers. I have a cutting somewhere. When they recovered, they earned their keep no problem. Their act was something special. It was the first time I'd seen anyone do a triple somersault from the ground and land on someone's shoulders, whilst playing a waltz on the trumpet.'

Joey looked up. At that moment, Lazaro was walking across the wire, with Margarita draped across his shoulders. He'd never seen anything so beautiful.

'If they were so good how come the circus made a loss?'

'They moved on, got an offer from an outfit in Florida, and my father never recovered from the cost of their voyage,' Otavio said, his sour countenance returning. 'They were real stars though, not like the rubbish we have now, amateurs, like that scumbag Dimitri, crook-legged Johnny-come-latelys, fit only for street corners.'

He threw the half-smoked cigarette to the ground and mashed it in with his heel.

6

Whilst the evening show was in full swing Joey's job was to patrol the site. He saw a group of *chamacos* sitting on some crates smoking and chatting. After two years in Mexico, he was almost fluent and could just about keep up with their conversation, richly seasoned as it was with slang from all their various dialects, but that wasn't the kind of company he wanted tonight.

Watching Margarita Alvarez in the arms of her brother on the high-wire had filled him with a longing to be up there. He was impatient to start on this journey but could see no way of beginning and then there was Margarita herself to remind him of his other desires.

The moral code here was just as strong as in the rest of Mexico. The circus girls were not easy. They were heavily chaperoned, always watched by brothers and cousins and uncles. Pure as *The Sound of Music* by day, they made up for it late at night when the married couples were tucked away in their beds. He'd often heard the stifled moans from the dark corners of the Big Top. At those moments, he was like a fox catching the howl of another across the night air. He felt the desire almost before he heard it and he'd lie and imagine Teresa's lithe body in his arms.

Margarita was out of the question. He thought of the others, the three jugglers, beautiful but fiercely protective of each other, and the acrobats but they were all attached. There was the girl he'd seen once or twice with the strange clothes, pretty but oddly dressed in long skirts and high collars like a Victorian governess.

He had no idea what she did. He'd have to ask Doña Rosa.

He was sick of his own imagination. He'd have to find a girl out-side of the circus, someone without a brother or a cousin watching over her. He rummaged in his pockets. Not much in the way of cash but enough for one beer. When the show was finished he would go and spend it.

After the final straggler left, he stripped off, and slipping be-hind the makeshift curtain, he stood under a plastic water container rigged up for the itinerant labour and took a cold shower. One of the clowns had given him an old shirt, faded but fresh at least, and he'd rescued a pair of jeans from a pile of clothing he'd found in a plastic bag at the roadside.

He was sure in a mirror he would look like a tramp, but at least he felt better. He smoothed back his hair and rubbed his hand across his face, wishing he had more need to shave and could lose that bloom that made him look so young. Still, his face was tanned and despite the blue eyes he might pass for Mexican until they heard his Spanish.

After a short walk he discovered a bar that was inconspicuous and simple where the beer was cheap and the barman's wife, clad in a frilled pink apron, was quiet but welcoming. Most of the *cirqueros* didn't drink much. They'd nurse a beer all night. They found drunkenness grotesque and shaming, all except Rodrigo, but then Rodrigo was not like other men. Joey without a family or friends was grateful for the solace of drink, for the comfort of a bar, and besides, drinkers made the best audience for magic tricks. Soon he had several beers lined up and someone had bought him a pack of cigarettes.

He didn't tell them he was with the circus, wasn't sure he was yet and didn't want to tempt fate. As he waved goodbye to his benefactors and took a swig from one of his beers a woman pulled up a chair and sat down next to him.

'*Buenas noches,*' she crooned, '*soy* Isobella.' She fondled the cards on the table with her pink fingernails. He nodded and offered her one of the beers. There was a tang of sweat about her and a flowery smell on top, like furniture polish. It wasn't unpleasant. She ran her hand along his leg.

'Sorry señorita, *yo no tengo dinero*, only beer and cigarettes,' he said pointing to the cluster of bottles. She shrugged her shoulders. It was hard to tell how old she was. Her eyes looked weary but her skin was smooth and her teeth were white except for the two capped in gold. She was pretty enough but it was her cleavage that held his gaze.

'Maybe we just have a talk and some fun,' she said pushing back a strand of sprayed hair that had escaped its complicated arrangement. A dance tune poured from the radio. She called to the bartender to turn it up, and then she dragged Joey onto the floor.

'I don't dance,' he said.

'Come on,' she purred, and wrapped her arms around him, moving him in time with the music. He felt like he should be able to do this, but something was stopping him. He closed his eyes, rested his head on her shoulder.

'You have good rhythm,' she said. 'I like a man who is good on his feet and good with his hands.' He shuffled around the floor enjoying the feel of her warm body and when she whispered for him to follow her he didn't take much persuasion.

The sex was swift and awkward but Joey didn't care. As he fumbled with her stiff bra and the tight fabric of her jeans he closed his eyes and thought about Teresa. But as he tripped over his own trousers, his stomach churning with booze, it was Isobella who forgave him when he came too suddenly. He looked into her face and for once he didn't see Teresa, and when they kissed, her mouth as lush as a peach, he felt like crying.

She waved to him as he stumbled out onto the street. It was still hot and humid. He walked back towards the circus, his hands in his pockets, a smile playing around his lips. Change was on its way. Beneath his feet, the ground rumbled and he tripped up. He stood and re-gained his balance, unsure of what he'd just experienced.

7

The circus was quiet by the time he got back, even the insomniacs seemed to have taken to their beds. The night was still beating with the love-calls of insects and the frogs sang down in the wet culverts that stank and fermented after the heat of the day.

The moon was up, half a moon at least – scaly and fish-grey, it gave a silvery tint to everything. He rested against a broken section of concrete wall and thought of his old *compadres* back in the shack. The feeling of that girl in his arms had awakened something in his heart, something his body had been pestering him for, sex of course, but more than that, an intimacy – even a fleeting one – being the object of someone's eye. Teresa. What if she changed her mind and wanted to be back with him, how would she find him? But she wouldn't, would she? She had other ambitions. Well, she wasn't the only one. He would be famous and one day she'd see his name plastered all over Mexico.

His feet were aching. He felt the ground shudder beneath them. It might just be his mood, memories stirred by his encounter with Isobella but it seemed more intense than normal the needling shocks more frequent. He would put on his birdskin shoes later, try and practise what Doña Marta had told him about listening to the earth, though he was too tired and too drunk now to think about anything much except sleep.

He stood up straight again, staggered slightly and began to walk. He stopped by the refrigerated food truck and lit another cigarette. He heard a voice from one of the trailers slightly out of the circle.

It was deep, emphatic, but he couldn't make out the words. He stopped for a minute, waiting to hear the reply but there wasn't one. He began to walk on but he heard it again, the muffled voice louder and more insistent. As he stopped to listen there was a thud, then the sound of falling. Instinctively he held his breath willing every cell to shrink so that he could render himself invisible.

He wiped his clammy hands down his trousers remembering those nights when he and his mother flinched at the sound of his da's key in the lock. They could tell before they even saw him what kind of mood he was in. It was the way he closed the door, the way he'd let it click shut and then pause before taking his first step into the hallway. Joey imagined in that moment of silence, his father gathering himself, summoning whatever memories or imagined slights he needed, to justify what was to come.

That familiar dread possessed Joey, urging him to run and hide but knowing there was nowhere to go, watching his father's eyes raking around the room like grim searchlights and that sick feeling of inevitability when they came to rest on his mother's huddled frame. But he wasn't at home anymore. He walked on, unclenching his feet, letting his held breath go. Whatever was going on in there, it was none of his business. He hesitated and then he turned and walked back. He put his ear to the trailer door. He could hear the sound of a woman crying. He knocked.

'Are you okay? Did you fall?'

There was no answer. He knocked again, but all he could hear was his own breathing, the hum of the generator and the insect throbbing of the night. He waited for a moment longer, straining to hear any sound but there was nothing.

His sleep was interrupted by dreams which vanished each time he jerked awake. Finally, as the light bleached the night sky he gave up trying to sleep. He wandered over to the mess tent. The wooden benches and tables were covered in dew. He wiped one off with his hand and sat down. Maybe someone would be up soon, making coffee and *huevos rancheros*. His mouth tasted bad and his head hurt.

Negrita and Blanca, the bareback Amazons, ran the mess tent for those *chamacos* and performers who didn't have a place to cook. He looked hopefully in the direction of their trailer and saw the curtain twitch. It was Negrita who came out first, her hair bleached white and her dark eyebrows forming two perfect arcs. She blew onto her fingers then wrapped her dressing gown around her.

'*Hace mucho frio!* You are up early. Let's make some coffee.' She disappeared into the kitchen and soon he could smell the familiar whiff of propane and hear the tiny roar of the flames as they licked around the pot. Blanca skipped down the trailer steps, fully dressed, her long black hair pinned on her head in a messy pile, except for the fringe which was straight and long and touched her dark brows. She was more petite than her sister, delicate and doll-like. She nodded to him and joined Negrita in the kitchen. Soon the sizzle of the griddle reached him along with the yapping of the radio.

Whilst he waited, he mulled over the events of the previous night. He knew he hadn't imagined the sex – he could still catch a scent of the girl on his body – but what of the woman weeping, had that really happened or had he dreamed it?

Negrita brought him over some eggs, and coffee and he began to eat. A few other bodies attracted by the smell of cooking had drifted in and were sitting at other tables, in twos or threes.

As Joey nursed his hangover, a tall, lean figure came and occupied the table in front of him. He was dressed in knee-high riding boots and a khaki jacket. He turned as Negrita put some coffee on the table. Joey saw a white face, long hair, dark eyes, and a patchy shadow of beard growth. He didn't look Mexican. If he spoke to Negrita, Joey didn't hear him. He sat on his own, and no-one came and sat with him as the tables began to fill.

What could you discern from a man's back about his profession, Joey wondered? He was too tall for an acrobat and too thin for the trapeze. He could be a juggler or a fire-eater though. The posture was imposing, the manner slow and deliberate. Joey had recently managed to watch the whole of one show but he didn't recognise him.

Just as Joey was ready to leave, a thin woman barely more than a girl, carrying a toddler came and sat down at the stranger's table. She said something that Joey couldn't hear. The tall man stood up and strode away. The infant started to whimper and she dropped her head and started to rock it. Joey saw quite clearly a darkened area on the side of her face.

He couldn't take his eyes from her. She was as dark as the man was pale but she had the same deep-set eyes. He could see her collar bones sticking out from the wide neck of her black tee-shirt. She tucked her dark hair behind her ears and rocked the baby absently then her eyes suddenly alighted on him. Caught staring, he lifted his hand and waved; she ignored the wave and gave a half-smile back, glancing around her as she did so.

He stood up and took his dishes over to the kitchen, where Blanca was sitting reading a magazine. A small girl up to her elbows in water was explaining the plot of some dramatic soap opera in a high birdlike voice. Joey offered the dishes.

'Thanks, sweetheart,' Blanca said.

Joey hesitated, 'That woman over there with the baby.' Blanca peered over his shoulder,

'That's Elena, Dimiti's wife.'

'Who is this Dimitri?'

'The tall man in the boots, Russian.'

'What does he do?'

Blanca raised her eyebrows, 'He calls himself Papa Afrika on the posters, works with Don Carlos – you know, the lion.'

Joey furrowed his brow. He remembered now, second billing, so he must be quite a draw. He'd caught a little bit of the act before he'd been pulled out to do some work on a trailer. He was surprised Doña Rosa hadn't mentioned him, but he was beginning to realise that for Doña Rosa the past was as real as the present, and many of the people she talked of avidly no longer even worked at the circus.

He'd looked so different in the ring, a bandana around his head, his eyes ringed with make-up, his pale face tanned and daubed with tribal markings. He'd seemed powerful, noble even. It was so easy to be deceived by appearances. He thought of his da, serving the customers, the smell of good cologne lingering around him and that solicitous manner that made the old ladies in church fuss too much when he was around. There were two people inside his da and you never knew which one would come home to supper.

The rest of the day he couldn't snap out of the mood he'd awoken in. His feet plagued him, made him a laughing stock amongst the *chamacos*. A dark shadow hung over him, casting a grey pall, a sooty residue which tainted everything he heard or thought. He was glad when the day ended and he was able to put his feet up and sleep.

8

But Joey had not been able to sleep. It wasn't just Dimitri or the November weather bothering him: it was the ground under his feet. As he walked back from his last job – readjusting the poles that supported the Big Top – he felt as if he was walking across a rolling ocean.

As soon as he made it to his sleeping area, which he'd now improved with a piece of tarpaulin, he kicked off his *huaraches* and put on his silver birdskin shoes. Like a familiar hand in a busy crowd, they made him feel safe in their grasp. He stretched out his toes, and wriggled them, felt the fine leather softening. He pulled up his knees, planted his feet firmly on the ground and closed his eyes trying to recall Doña Marta's exact instructions. He settled his breathing, focused entirely on his feet and tried to concentrate on each point of impact on the patch of ground they covered.

He began to be aware of patterns like interference on a television, and then they formed images in his head. Of all the bars he could see, a strong violet-coloured one occupied most of the space. As he stilled, the purple dissolved into cracked lines, the grey turned into smoke.

The pain in his feet and head had been acute before that first tremor he'd experienced in Mexico but in those early days it had made no sense at all. The underworld of drink and drugs into which he'd plunged soon dulled and distorted his senses and he'd forgotten about the tremor until his experiences with Teresa.

But now he had his shoes and he was sober. Still he couldn't be certain; there was so much seismic activity in Mexico. The subterranean growling was like the churning guts of a great beast. Would it be just a slight shift, the kind he felt quite frequently but no-one else seemed to notice, or could it be something more significant? Perhaps they were memories he felt; the violet of bruises, the grey of regrets. He closed his eyes again, hoping to re-capture what he'd seen.

9

29th November

He woke up too late for breakfast. The day was overcast and heavy and everyone seemed to be irritable with each other. Dora was bellowing, and Gustavo said it was toothache and made Joey rub wintergreen on her gums. The horses were skittish too.

'Must be a storm on the way,' Rodrigo said to Otavio, peering into the foaming sky.

'Just what we need, freak weather to put off the crowds.' Just the same, he climbed into the Big Top and triple-checked all the equipment for the performances. A flurry of warm wind picked up litter and sent laundry somersaulting over the lines. Robles came to the door of his trailer and peered into the sky. His brow crinkled and he rocked on his heels and sniffed the air.

'Strange,' he said, 'unseasonal.'

Joey needed to find a quiet place where he could stand and focus again. He wished he was better at this. At that moment there was an eruption of voices. Several children came hurtling towards him laughing. Above him, he heard a high distant ringing. He looked up as a flock of white birds with tiny bells on their legs swept by, the sound diminishing as they flew in increasingly wide circles. The children jumped into the air, grabbing handfuls of sky in a vain attempt to catch them.

The girl in Victorian dress was chasing them, calling in annoyance but then dissolving into laughter at the children's futile efforts. She stopped, pressing her hand to her side, as a particularly keen boy ran straight into a line of the girls' laundry.

Her stage name, he'd discovered, was 'Santa Francesca', a female St Francis of Assisi who made the birds come at her beck and call. When he'd asked Doña Rosa about her he'd detected a certain change of demeanour, a shrug of disapproval.

'I know nothing about her, she comes she goes. She is not really one of us. And she lives on her own. It is not natural.'

He'd been mesmerised when he'd seen her perform. She'd worn a long white dress that covered her body from wrist to ankle. Her hair was a nest of curls held in place with a band of white feathers. The birds had swooped and grouped to her commands. In the end she had danced with them to haunting music that had hushed the entire audience.

Now she was hot and flustered, her long sleeved-shirt had come loose from her ground-skimming skirt and her wild hair had worked its way from its tie.

'Don't scare them! I don't know what's got into them,' she said, out of breath, gasps of laughter still escaping from her.

'Won't they just settle somewhere?' Joey asked. She rolled her eyes. 'Yes, but if it's Monterrey, they won't be back in time for this afternoon's performance, then I'll be in trouble.'

'They'd go that far?' Joey said.

'They'd go hundreds of miles if they got the urge, but they never usually do. That's the last time I put cocaine in their water bowl.'

Joey's eyes widened.

'I'm joking!'

She'd stopped near him and watched them circling above the site, their wings tipping and gliding, the bells creating an eerie sound. He could see the outline of her breasts through the thin white fabric of her blouse.

'Something's got into them though. Birds of peace! Huh. You should have seen them!' She pursed her lips.

'We can make them do all sorts of things, but in the end they are creatures of the wind.' She turned and looked directly at him, and her gaze was so intense he wanted to look away.

'I'm Aurora. I don't think I've seen you around before. Are you a *chamaco*?'

Joey nodded then shook his head. 'I want to join the circus, to be a high-wire artiste.' There, he'd said it. 'For the moment I am waiting for Señor Robles to make a decision about me.'

She looked down at his feet. 'What strange shoes.'

Joey shuffled. 'They help me with a condition I have.'

She tipped her head. 'Silver orthopaedic shoes, now that's what I call style.'

'Well, yours aren't so regular either,' he said, peering down at her old-fashioned boots with their hooks and laces. She laughed and as her cheeks puckered, he was suddenly aware of his filthy old jeans and stained shirt and the withered husk of his heart.

'Well, good luck, maybe we will bump into each other again.' The earth suddenly seemed to shake beneath him and he reached out his hand to stop him falling right there in front of her.

'*Estás bien?*' she said her face full of concern.

'Didn't you feel that?'

'Feel what?' she said, her face now a mixture of wariness and pity.

'Nothing. I think it's just pins and needles, I need to sit down.' At that moment the birds glided towards the earth.

As she and the children ran to catch them Joey hobbled away. He headed into the scrubland on the other side of the culvert. A concrete bridge covered part of the overflow, and despite the stench it provided a quiet spot, where it was possible to sit and see nothing but sky and reeds, and sometimes the frogs even drowned out the sound of the juggernauts thundering north.

He sat on the ground and concentrated hard. Almost immediately the purple reappeared cracked and pulsing, the grey plumes blooming into thunderheads. He focused harder trying to gauge the strength of the hue and the imminence of the earthquake that his feet seemed to tell him was coming. The colours flared and died. If he could feel it now, they would all feel it later, he was sure of that. The horses would go crazy – and Dora – she even flinched at car horns. Robles would have to cancel the show. He stopped mid-thought. This was ridiculous. How could he know when or even if, an earthquake might come? He'd had so little practice with the techniques Doña Marta had taught him and yet here he was about to go and ask Robles to close the circus down. The man would kick him out on his arse, send him packing. Yet despite all this, he found himself walking towards Robles's trailer.

Aurora was standing outside as Joey approached. Having managed to coax some of the birds back with grain, the children had caught them and returned them to their cage. Once half a dozen were in, the rest had come too. As she stretched her arms forward to place the stragglers inside, Joey noticed a blue mark between her shirt and the top of her skirt. As if aware of it, she pulled the shirt down. He tried not to stare at her as she picked up a final bird that had retreated under the trailer but he couldn't help it. Distracted for a moment by this unexpected train of thought he'd almost forgotten the reason he was visiting Robles. Outside the door, he was overwhelmed again by the outlandishness of his proposal.

Usually the trailer was full of comings and goings, nieces and nephews, aunts and uncles, visitors from other circuses. It was amazing Señor Robles ever got anything done. Today, however, he was alone. Sitting in a straight-backed chair, his silver hair gleaming, cufflinks shining on the crisp cuffs of his shirt, he exuded confidence and authority. Joey cleared his throat.

'Yes, what can I do for you?' Robles boomed, without looking up.

'I'm Joey Pachuca.'

'Pachuca, of the Puebla Pachucas, who have the "*modern*" circus?' he said lingering spitefully over the word.

'Ah, no. No relation. I came some time ago, do you remember? You said I could stay on trial for a week and if I made myself useful...'

'...I'd let you stay on. Well, you've been here longer than one week already?'

'Three months,' Joey said sheepishly.

'Well?'

'I don't quite know how to begin. Can I sit down?' Robles indicated an empty chair and Joey pulled it up to the table.

'Señor Robles, I have this uh, this...' he didn't know what to call it. He glanced at the fierce grey eyebrows, the blue vein pulsing in the mighty temple, the sceptical eyes fixed on him.

'I have a special skill, which is why I think I could be master of the high-wire. My feet are extremely sensitive. I can feel all sorts of things that others can't feel, vibrations, emotions...'

'Emotions?' Robles eyes narrowed. Joey jumped in with both feet,

'...and I can tell when an earthquake is going to come.' Robles' expression hardened, anger suffused his cheeks.

'What have they told you? That I am a gullible fool, that because of my sons you can pull the wool over my eyes? Christ.' He stood up and ploughed his hand through his hair.

'No, no' said Joey, 'that's not it at all. Look everyone's muttering about a storm, but my feet have told me there might be a tremor, not a serious one, but we will feel it, the audience will feel it, and so will the performers. I'm telling you because you might want to cancel the performance this afternoon, just in case.'

'*Just in case?*' Robles leaned forward his face thunderous. 'You want me to shut up the show because your *feet* have told you something? What do you take me for?'

Joey stood up too and faced him. 'I know you to be *muy inteligente*. Look, Aurora's birds sense it and Dora does too, you can hear her now. Even the horses are restless, and the frogs... listen.' They both stopped.

'I don't hear anything.'

'Exactly, even the frogs know. I think it will happen this afternoon and you can do with that information what you like.' Robles mouth dropped open.

'Look, Señor Robles. I know it sounds crazy and I can see you don't believe me and if I were in your shoes I suppose I'd feel the same but I have another idea. Just change the order of performances, don't let the high-wire or trapeze take place after the interval, have them on first, and the horses too. The clowns and the acrobats and the jugglers they can all go in the second half. That way if I'm right there is less risk of an accident.'

Robles sat down. 'I have never heard such nonsense in my life.'

Joey nodded, 'I know, I know, but look, if I am wrong and I may be – I'm not very good at this yet – I will leave here tomorrow and you will never see me again, but if I am right….'

Robles stared at him, his twisted hands clenched together in front of him. When he spoke the anger had gone out of his voice. A hint of the melancholic had returned.

'I don't know who you are, boy, but I will think about your suggestion. I lost my sons in an earthquake, you know that.'

Joey hesitated then nodded. 'Yes, Otavio mentioned it.'

'Did he tell you that my sons were also his godsons? No, I thought not. He wasn't always the man you see today. Acts of God have a way of transforming a person, and rarely in my experience for the better.'

At 1.00pm, an hour before the show, Robles called all the performers together and gave them the new order of performance. There were grumbles, but not from those who now had a chance to appear in the prestigious second half. Robles blamed the unusual weather, suggested people might leave in the interval to escape a downpour, and that appeased some. Still there were complaints. Joey kept his head down.

The new line-up caused a few technical hitches, things weren't where they should be, and Joey began to wonder if he'd misread everything entirely. Then at 2.52pm just after the interval as he had predicted, the ground juddered, followed by a cracking sound as all the posts supporting the Big Top shifted.

An undulation rippled under the seating. The jugglers, who were in the middle of their spectacular finale, dropped the china dishes on the ground. Luckily, the fact that they bounced was missed by most in the hubbub that followed. The audience, startled, stood up in their seats, children began to cry, and from outside, Dora's loud anxious blast pierced through the tinny mariachi music that had been turned up to mask the distressed murmurings of the audience.

Robles voice crackled over the loudspeakers. 'Ladies and gentleman, take your seats please, you have no reason to be alarmed. I have it on good authority that this was only a minor tremor. It is over now. See the performers are continuing to entertain you. Look the clowns have come in full of joy and laughter. See how BuBu's knees are knocking, ho ho ho! But who is this coming up behind him, children?'

The children, watching ZuZu creeping up in his huge red boots, a pair of cymbals ready and open in his hands, had begun to laugh. BuBu, pretending now to be asleep, leaned his head against the wall of their cardboard house. At the shouts of the children he opened his eyes and looked around. Unable to see anything, he closed them again and settled down to sleep. The children transfixed, squealing with anticipation, had forgotten the tremor, although their parents still shifted nervously in their seats, and when ZuZu finally smashed the cymbals together, the parents roared with the children.

By the time Aurora and her doves had performed their somewhat chaotic act to the sweet music of Debussy, it would be hard to believe there ever had been a tremor at all. The only casualty was Dora. She was too nervous to appear in the final parade. The applause was fulsome, but people left more rapidly than usual, pulling their children from the ice-creams and the toys and the pink candyfloss, plump in its plastic bags like captured clouds.

Around the steps of the trailers, talk buzzed into the night. The radio reported that an earthquake originating in Oaxaca had caused extensive damage even to some buildings in Mexico City.

'Thank God, Robles changed the order.'

'If that had happened when we were up there...'

'Robles must have developed a sixth sense, after you-know-what,' someone

whispered.

Joey said nothing. A sense of calm enveloped him. At last the future lay ahead of him, secure and clear.

10

Robles never forgot the name Pachuca again. Christmas came and went and Joey joined the payroll and though he received barely enough to live on he didn't care. The New Year saw him one step closer to his dream. He made time to practise his skill, and learned to sift out the deep vibrations of the earth from more human vibrations of anxiety, foreboding and memory – but still he needed his shoes; without them the babble of the world confused him, and he knew he had a long way to go.

He remembered that moment in his childhood when he'd walked along the edge of that fence, and was punished so harshly. It had left him fearful of trying it again, even though he longed to do it. Now he had his shoes he was sure the tight-rope would be different.

He got his opportunity one March morning when, finding himself with an hour to spare, he plucked up the courage to speak of his hopes to Lazaro Alvarez. They were resting after practising a complex lift. Margarita, wearing a loose wrap over her torn fishnets, was massaging her feet, and Franco, was flexing and rotating his massive shoulders.

Joey coughed.

'Hi there Joey, how's things?' Lazaro said.

Joey nodded, 'Good, good thanks.' Lazaro continued with his practice as Joey studied the angle of his feet, the pressure of the cable between the toes and the balancing of his body.

'Is it hard to learn?'

Lazaro, skipped to the end, jumped off. 'I couldn't tell you. I've been doing this all my life, like all my family. My grandmother was a Russian, from Tsovkra. They did nothing but train tight-rope walkers there. It was their biggest export and one of them was my grandmother.'

Joey sighed, *del circo*, of course. 'I'd love to do this. I think I could have a knack for it.'

Lazaro laughed, glanced at Joey's awkward feet. 'You need ex-cellent balance, focus, strength and… your feet, ah.'

Joey didn't wait to hear more. Stung by the comment he hobbled out into the sunshine, ready to blame it for the tears stinging his eyes. He wanted to kick something or someone.

Lazaro came out after him. 'I'm sorry, Joey, I didn't mean any-thing. Come back, come on, I'll give you a lesson, but don't be disappointed if you can't stand on it for more than a second.'

Joey swallowed his pride and returned to the ring. He put on his shoes. He was extremely nervous. The cable was different from the fence. That had been solid and his ecstatic promenade along it, impulsive. It had come from nowhere, an instinctive response to an inner urge. Since then, each time he thought about that day the shadow of his father hung over him, the sense of shame, of having done something unspeakable. Despite this, the yearning to repeat that experience, to have that feeling of abandonment and release, came to him often. Now at last there was a way. He just had to get over his anxiety, show he had the latent ability and then he could re-enact that moment or even surpass it.

He stepped onto the cable. It had some bounce, some sway, but the instant he stepped on it, it felt right. Lazaro coached him and after an hour he could not only stand he could walk the length of the rope with assurance.

Lazaro whistled. 'You know, I owe you an apology. That's re-markable. I really didn't think you could do it, but it's odd, up on the cable you are so much more stable than you are on the ground. It's always the other way around until you are an expert. Are you sure you are not from a circus family?'

'Do you think I could become an expert?' Joey said, catching his breath. Lazaro squeezed his shoulder, 'Joey, I'm sure of it but it will take time.'

Joey grinned, 'I'm a rich man when it comes to time.'

11

As Easter approached, the circus thronged with visitors, not only those who'd paid to see the show, but family and friends, bringing gifts and news from all over Mexico. Joey felt alone. Despite the thrill of his lesson with Lazaro, the life he hoped to have seemed a long way off.

And then there was Aurora. He'd hardly seen her since the earthquake. She seemed to be in and out of the circus like one of her birds, settling and then vanishing just when he got close. And when he did manage to catch up with her, his feet tripped him up, his head seemed to loll like an idiot and his fluent Spanish eluded him so that any question he asked resulted in a smirk and a roll of her eyes.

He sat with Doña Rosa as she stitched some ribbon back onto a costume. Her trailer smelt of used paperbacks – the smell of imaginary lives. He picked a book at random, flicked through the pages then put it back with a sigh and picked up another.

Doña Rosa, looked over her glasses at him. 'Please settle down, you are making the place look untidy.'

He threw himself onto the padded bench and stared out of the window.

Doña Rosa snipped a thread with her teeth and put her work down. 'Tell me, what is it, what's bothering you?'

Joey shrugged. 'Nothing. Other people's happiness. Why do you have so many books?'

She stretched her old knuckles. 'More reliable than a husband.

A husband tells stories to conceal the truth but books tell stories that reveal the truth. And did you ever hear of a book rolling home at three in the morning!'

'Can they tell you how to get a girl?'

'Ay! They are all about that. They are all full of sighs, and tears and pattering hearts. Every type, every country every century, but it's all the same. A man thinks he is chasing a woman, but really she is chasing him. Open any one of them and the wishes fall out of their pages and stick all over you. It's very simple, Joey. A woman likes a man who is strong and skilful, a doctor, a hunter, a *trapecista*. Women? Ah, according to these books all we have to be is young and beautiful, of course. We can do a lot to stay beautiful but almost nothing to stay young, except die.' She sucked her teeth.

'Why are you worried anyway Señor Pachuca? Look at you. You are *muy guapo*, very handsome, with those eyes like bird's eggs and that smile of yours. I am sure little Florita is heartsick, she follows you all over the place. You must have noticed.'

He shook his head. She was one of the jugglers, always blushing and giggling when he passed. She was just a child as far as he was concerned.

'Tell me about the girls here. Aurora, for instance,' and his heart thudded faster at the mention of her name. Doña Rosa pretended to check her sewing, her mouth drooping at the corners, her eyes avoiding his.

'Well, she is a pretty girl, if a little eccentric. You know of course she was married.' Her eyes darted upwards for a moment checking for the impact of her statement.' Joey couldn't keep the disappointment from his face. Doña Rosa held him with her gaze, '...but she left him for another man apparently. Yet she is always here on her own.'

Joey's eyes widened, 'but she can't be much older than me!'

'Maybe, maybe not,' Doña Rosa said, lifting her own chin, to straighten out the wattle that hung beneath it. 'She must be twenty-five, and you are just a boy of nineteen.'

'So what happened?'

Doña Rosa shook her head. 'I don't know. There are only rumours. You'll have to ask her.' She beckoned to him conspiratorially and whispered, 'No-one I have spoken to has ever seen the first husband. And when I've asked Robles and Rodrigo about the other one, they go quiet. Perhaps she left him as well!'

Joey pursed his lips in irritation. 'So what if she did leave them? Maybe they beat her, maybe she didn't like the way they ate. There are lots of straightforward reasons.' He stared through the window at the children laughing and playing outside with nothing at that moment to worry about but winning tag.

'You know me, Joey, I don't like to speak ill of someone, but still. One bad marriage you can forgive, anyone can be unlucky, but two…that looks suspicious.' She balanced a sequin on the end of her needle before running it through with her thread. 'If she is still married, why doesn't he ever visit?' She looked up at him, her eyes gleaming circles of conjecture. 'What is she hiding?'

Joey shook his head in disbelief, but a cold chill slipped down his back. 'Just because she is young and pretty and doesn't share her problems with you, you think she must be up to something. Maybe she just doesn't want people gossiping about her.'

Doña Rosa put down her sewing and sighed. 'Oh dear, you're hooked already. Nothing I can say will make any difference now. I've read many books and I know all the signs. I only want the best for you Joey but I can see heartbreak on the horizon.'

Joey thought of Teresa. Was this to be his punishment for what he'd done? Would he go for the wrong girl, over and over again, until his heart gave up trying?

'When I am a great high-wire artiste she will fall for me,' he said, the quaver in his voice belying the bravado of the words.

'If you don't fall first.' Doña Rosa picked up her sewing again. 'She has other secrets too,' she said, stabbing the cloth with her needle.

'What secrets?'

Doña Rosa, removed her glasses and rubbed her eyes. 'Joey, I need to get this costume finished but you are like a detective, you squeeze these things out of me and I am unable to resist.' Her beady eyes popped open. 'Haven't you noticed that she never shows her arms and legs?'

Joey thought back to the glimpse he'd had that day of blue marks on her back, were they bruises? Had someone beaten her?

'There are rumours that her skin was badly damaged in a fire. Her second husband or lover or whatever he is, was once a fire-eater, apparently. Others believe she has a disease that leaves her skin covered in scabs. One of the acrobats accidentally saw her while she was washing and says she even wears a dress in the shower!'

Aurora's body covered in scars, her flesh melted like wax into ridges and valleys, his first instinct was disgust and then he thought of his own awkward posture and his clumsiness and was seized by a desire to defend her.

'What about what's inside?' he said, 'surely that is the most important thing.'

'You're not telling me you only are interested in Aurora for her personality and brains are you?'

Joey grunted. 'There are lots of pretty girls.'

'True, but I'm sure her curves had something to do with it. I bet you've hardly spoken to her'

'I would if I ever saw her.'

'Joey, you have to understand – outside of the circus, people have a low opinion of us. They think we are dirty, immoral and even stupid. It stands to reason that a girl inside the circus, even someone with as dubious a background as Aurora, wants someone who could hold his head up anywhere.'

'So you're saying she wouldn't want someone like me?'

'Joey, you are a good-looking boy, but at the moment you are just a pair of hands. You have to do something to make her see you. They tell you not to judge a book by its cover but we all do.

We are illusionists. What do we do in the circus except turn sweat and hard work into something extraordinary? You have to find a way to make her look at you in a different way.'

If only he could admit that it was his special skill that had helped prevent an accident at the circus, and not Señor Robles' sixth sense, but he couldn't and she wouldn't believe him anyway. He'd just have to practise with Lazaro and await his opportunity.

12

The tremor had affected Robles deeply and as the anniversary of his sons' deaths rolled around again, rumours spread through the circus that he wanted to move away from the endless battered *terrenos* of the city and travel the country – San Luis Potosí, Zacatecas, Monterrey, cities up in north and east away from the fault lines – until his nerves settled.

'Who will stay and who will go?' Negrita and Blanca looked around at the circle of old hands. Rodrigo was old for a strongman and he wasn't planning to leave Robles. Gustavo and Josefina, and their daughter Concepción would stay, as would the three young jugglers and Otavio. Negrita chewed her pencil, 'I'm not sure about ZuZu and BuBu. They have ambitions.'

'Yeah, they're sick of that cardboard house,' Rodrigo said 'they want a proper house – made of plastic!' The others laughed but Joey stumbled.

'Watch out, Limpy,' Negrita said. 'Those are genuine china plates you are drying there.'

Blanca tousled his head and cooed. 'Oh *hermana*, don't call him that. I have a feeling our Joey will be great one day, ay?'

He ducked her sympathy and picked himself up. He knew what that had been about, the Alvarez family. Would they be leaving? He'd never be able to learn on his own. And what about Aurora? Joey's twentieth birthday had come and gone with no more than a few sentences exchanged with the elusive Aurora but she constantly intruded on his thoughts.

He walked away as straight as he could, his heart heavy in his chest. They were just rumours; maybe it wouldn't happen and maybe the Alvarez troupe would stay. After all, it wasn't a bad place to be, not grand like some circuses but still they got full houses in the festival times, and…

'When you've finished day-dreaming, you can go and see Dimitri.' Otavio said. 'We will be making a big move in a few days, and he wants some repairs made to Don Carlos' cage.'

In the year he had been with the circus he'd never spoken to Dimitri, but he'd not forgotten that night when he'd heard shouting and had seen the bruised face of his tiny wife in the morning. Now he was going to have to work with him.

Whenever he passed their caravan, especially at night, he would pause and listen, his nerves tensed for any sign of distress. He imagined bursting in and finding Elena cowering in a corner, protecting her baby whilst her husband, his eyes red and raging, loomed over her. Joey, like a private eye on the cover of one of Doña Rosa's *True Detective* magazines, would wrench him off and then he would be everyone's hero. But he never heard another sound from the caravan although the eyes of Dimitri's wife were still circled with dark shadows and suspicious patches and bumps appeared from time to time on her face.

The lion, Don Carlos, was old and mean and roared as Joey approached the enclosure where he spent his days. The cage inside seemed too small and Joey always had the feeling Don Carlos might burst out one day and savage him. But his fear was tempered with pity.

Sometimes at night he could see the animal pacing up and down with barely room to turn. Once, unable to sleep, he had gone out to gaze at it, as it rested its huge head between its paws. Through the hot night air the howl of a dog rang out, a lonely echoing cry. The lion sat up, its ears twitching. Silhouetted against the moon, Joey could imagine for a moment that its cage bars had become long blades of savannah grass and at any moment he might pad through their rustling fronds and disappear, out into the living night. Now though, Don Carlos looked patchy and moth-eaten. His nose, scuffed and grey, dilated at his scent. In the corner of the cage, a blue-white bone shone and stank in the heat of the day. He looked around but saw no sign of Dimitri. He moved a little closer, the yellow eyes watched him, the tongue pink and heaving in the open mouth. It snapped its jaws shut, swallowed and the lips pulled back in an angry snarl. Joey jumped, but moved in closer still. The tail began to twitch and slap, sending dust up from the floor of the cage. Joey took one step more and it was on its feet, its mane a wild, tobacco-coloured halo. It threw its head back and roared. Joey leapt back. There was a clearing of a throat behind him,

'Don't worry, these bars will hold him.' Dimitri was standing with a small riding crop in his hand. '*Venga*. You are here to help me.'

Dimitri had a long stride and Joey struggled to keep up with him as he walked to a scrubby area on the far side of the site, where the transit vehicles stood in a small group. One of these was a cage on a wagon, with painted bars and a sign across the top in faded letters announcing, 'Don Carlos, King of beasts! The most terrifying lion in the Americas!'

Two of the bars were bent and even from here he could see that a strong chew would destroy the others in a matter of minutes.

'I have new bars made, here,' he pointed to a package wrapped in canvas, lying on the bed of the truck. 'You pull out fucked old bars. Use this,' he said handing him a crowbar, 'then clean out holes. We fit new bars. After, Otavio will make strong with blow torch.'

'You're Russian so I've heard.' Joey said to make conversation. 'Whereabouts?'

'Omsk, you know?'

Joey shook his head and grinned. 'It sounds so strange listening to someone speaking Spanish with a Russian accent. A bit rich coming from me I suppose! So how did you end up in Mexico?' Joey watched him as he worked, wondering if Aurora liked him.

Dimitri grunted as he unloaded more bars from the truck. 'You ask so many questions, you are nosy boy.'

Joey laughed. 'The circus is my family now. I like to get to know my family.'

He said the words but at some level they still didn't sound true to him. They

felt like his family but he wasn't sure the circus saw him in the same light.

Dimitri spat in the dust. 'Families. My father was college professor, he studied the frozen trees in ground, got paid little but thought it was good to work for science. He was fool, head in fucking clouds.'

'Did you always want to work with lions?'

It was Dimitri who laughed this time. 'It was not idea of schoolteachers, no. They said, engineer, great scientist like your father maybe. I said hell no, man! I am not my father. I want to see the world. This was not easy in Soviet Union, so I escaped my country. No more family for me.'

Joey was surprised, another runaway like him and not from a circus background. No wonder people were suspicious of Dimitri.

They spent the rest of the afternoon swapping stories as they repaired the cage.

'Finished now, I think. You like to see new trick with Don Carlos?'

Joey nodded. Despite himself he had enjoyed his company. They returned to where the lion was now snoozing in a patch of sunlight. At the sound of Dimitri's voice, Don Carlos sat up and mewed.

'The *chamacos* have set up rehearsal cage inside tent. We attach this cage to rehearsal cage.' Dimitri jumped into the truck and reversed it.

Inside the Big Top Joey could see a circular caged enclosure with an opening the exact size of Don Carlos's cage. Once they were lined up, the cage and ring were bolted together. Barriers were attached at the sides, so the lion could not escape. Don Carlos whisked his tail. Dimitri hopped out.

'Now, I have to get in to rehearsal space first. He knows I am dominant male, I am in charge.' He pulled himself up and puffed out his chest. He flexed a large whip in his hand. Two of the *chamacos* waited for the nod.

Once Dimitri was in, they operated a lever that raised the door of the lion's cage. Don Carlos moved forward suddenly and Joey felt the hairs lift on his arms. The muscles rippled under its honey-coloured fur. With one stroke of that huge paw, Dimitri could be killed. Dimitri stood tall, arms outstretched, to one side of the ring. Don Carlos dropped onto his belly.

'See, he knows I'm boss,' Dimitri shouted and the lion snarled and rolled over. For the next twenty minutes, Joey marvelled while Dimitri coached the lion to jump over him from one coloured spot on the ground to another, using the whip only to indicate direction.

'Always you must watch,' Dimitri said, 'I am master but he is wild animal.'

After the rehearsal was over and the lion was back in his cage, Joey returned to his sleeping quarters for a rest before supper. As he lay there dozing, Doña Rosa walked past.

'Phew, you stink. You need to wash, you smell like Don Carlos.'

'That's because I've been helping Dimitri with him all afternoon.' Joey said with a yawn.

'Hmmm. What did you make of him?'

'Dimitri? I liked him.'

'Well, Mr Pachuca, he is your competition. Dimitri has his eye on Aurora and he tames lions!'

Joey swallowed, 'But he's married to Elena.'

'So Aurora and Dimitri are made for each other, they are both secretive and unfaithful.' Doña Rosa said spitefully.

'Why do you say that, what has he done?'

Doña Rosa, shrugged, 'Things have happened.' Doña Rosa sat down on the ground next to him with a grunt, her legs neatly folded under her. 'I've been here many years, Joey. I was here when Dimitri arrived and his first wife fell in love with him. I knew her, she was not *del circo* but she was a sweet, bubbly girl, like a bottle of cola shaken up. We nicknamed her Estrellita, little star, because she sparkled. I have never seen someone change so much. She became quiet and withdrawn, she even stopped performing. I tried to talk to her but she shrank away.

'I met her once in the market. She didn't see me at first. She was at the *herbalista*. I watched, tried to see what she was buying, but I couldn't. When she left the stall I went to see which packets had been disturbed. I think she was looking for powders to help her conceive, but that is just my guess. I was here when they left for a year to travel, paying us to look after that mean old lion while they were gone and I was here when he returned with this new wife Elena and the baby. How he crowed about his son!

'When Rodrigo asked him about his first wife, he said she'd stayed in Mérida because she'd had enough of the circus life. Rodrigo was of course sympathetic. When you marry out of the circus it isn't always easy.' She sighed and looked away.

'I have seen Elena cower like Don Carlos when Dimitri is around, and when he speaks to her at all it's always in the sharpest way. Something is very wrong with that man. He has barely spoken to me in all the time I have known him. Circus people aren't like that, we depend on each other.'

Joey thought of the bruises on Elena's face and tried to square that kind of aggression with the man he'd met. 'But the way he manages Don Carlos, it's amazing, he doesn't shout or anything!'

'That's why he is still here, he is a big attraction but do not be swayed by his skill. He has a story that one. I have many magazines, newspapers and journals in my trailer. I read them every day and soon I will find an article, a detail and then I will have him.'

'Maybe I can help you look?'

Doña Rosa's mouth twisted slightly, 'So now I am not just an old gossip, Mr Pachuca. Maybe I do know something after all.' Joey felt colour rise to his cheeks.

'Just be careful who you choose as friends,' she said, 'Not everyone is what they appear to be.'

13

February 1980

After months of indecision, the day had come. Joey felt wretched as he gazed around the site. The trucks had been loaded up, a huge brown circle scattered with sawdust was all that remained of the Big Top, and Joey's dreams of becoming a high-wire legend had expired. The Alvarez family were leaving.

Tomorrow, when the circus wove its way to the next site in Mexico City, on its journey north, the Alvarez family would be heading for the airport and Miami. As Joey bust a gut, hauling guy ropes out of the truck, remembering his first dazzling encounter with Lazaro, Franco and Margarita, they would be unloading their suitcases in a fancy hotel more interested in the restaurant than some nobody they once met called Joey Pachuca.

Posters fluttered across the open ground in the gentle breeze with the scraps of litter and the brittle remnants of dead undergrowth. Of course there was excitement at the prospect of a new location even if it was still inside the city limits, but it was underpinned by the sadness of imminent departure. Some of the *chamacos* would say their goodbyes here too and love that had sprung up would now be tested by distance and time.

With so many of them to cater for, they had decided to celebrate on site, and Negrita and Blanca had prepared a party. With an empty heart, Joey had helped them rig up the bunting and the candles on the tables. The children had made paper flowers to decorate them, and the *chamacos* had returned from the supermarket with crates of beer and soft drinks. As night descended, the generator kicked in and the candle flames flickered in the darkness, creating a magical scene in the otherwise drab location.

The trailers lit up by their occupants stood like a desert caravan ready for departure in the morning. Dora bellowed and the horses whinnied, sensing excitement in the air. But despite the squeals of anticipation from the children and the sight of shy Florita and her more exuberant sisters in their clinging dresses, Joey couldn't summon up enthusiasm for the night's festivities. The Alvarez family were leaving.

He would carry on as the odd-job man, always an outsider, with no way of proving himself extraordinary. But it wasn't just that. He hadn't realised how much he would miss the city. He'd fallen in love with Teresa here, and lost her, because he'd confessed what he had done. Every time he'd walked through Parque Alameda, or sat on the steps of the Bellas Artes, he'd hoped he might bump into her, looking for him in their old haunts. Now that would never happen. The final cord that tied him to her would soon be cut.

His feet felt it too. Several times he found himself rooted to the spot unable to decide in which direction to go. In those moments of confusion he knew the only solution was to rise above it all, not only in his heart, but literally. But without the Alvarez family to help him, even that avenue felt cut off from him.

The party was exuberant and tearful. People sang and the musicians played tunes that rent the heart. That night Joey took himself to the edge of the site where the traffic could drown out all sound, and he cried. He cried for his lost opportunity, for the friends who were leaving, and for Teresa. He wept for all the slights he had endured, the mockery, the taunts, the sly looks from girls as he stumbled and tripped and he cried for his mother knowing that whatever he managed to achieve she would never be there to see it. He wished he'd been able to throw her a lifeline when she needed it, save her when she couldn't save herself, but instead he'd robbed her of her life. He sank his head into his hands.

'Can I sit here with you?' It was Aurora. Joey looked away, appalled that she might have heard his weeping.

'It is too much all these goodbyes, isn't it?' Joey nodded, still unable to look at her.

'You are carrying on with the circus?' Aurora said. Joey stared at her smooth brown feet peeping out from the bottom of her skirt and as she leaned towards him he could smell her perfume,

'You're not, though,' Joey said, his voice dry and scratchy.

'I'll stay until the circus leaves the city, but I cannot go with you after that. I have family responsibilities, although I will try and visit once a month. I miss the little ones.'

Joey thought of her husband, if he existed, waiting at home, unbuttoning her long-sleeved blouses and loosening her skirts. He stood up. 'Families,' he said with a bitter edge, 'they must come first.' He walked away cursing his luck that she should come and talk to him then, when all he wanted to do was to kick the shit out of someone.

Before they left the following morning, Lazaro Alvarez sought Joey out.

'I want you to have this,' he said, and gave Joey a parcel. Inside was one of his costumes, a silver one, with red stars scattered across the chest.

A lump sprang up in Joey's throat. 'I don't know what to say.' He put the parcel down and took Lazaro's strong hand in his.

Lazaro shook it then hugged him. 'Joey, I have seen a lot of performers on the wire, and you have something special. I know we only had just a short time together but I felt it. I am so surprised you are not of a circus family, the kind of ability you have can't be taught, only developed. You must promise me that you will carry on. You can do it without me, you know.'

Joey's head was buzzing. 'How can I learn the proper techniques without a wire, without instruction?'

Lazaro rolled his eyes, and then bent down and picked up a stick. Beckoning Joey to squat next to him, he talked through how to rig up a low wire to practise on, how to get the tension right and a few tips about progress. Joey repeated it and committed it to memory.

'Find out about other high-wire artists, go to as many circuses as you can, look up in those books of Doña Rosa's, she has quite a collection on the circus, you know.'

Joey's eyes widened.

'Doña Rosa is a dark horse, she may read romances but she has a lot more upstairs...' Lazaro said, pointing to his head '...than love. Her trailer is always the last one to extinguish its lights at night. She is working on something in there but don't tell her I told you.' He winked.

When Joey took his costume to Doña Rosa and asked her to take care of it, it was with new eyes that he scanned the shelves and took in the titles that she had there, and between the romances he spotted the philosophy, the Greek myths and the histories of the circus. It was so easy to look and not to see, to miss what was staring you right in the face.

14

February 1980

The new site was to the north-east of Mexico City. It had taken a couple of days to ready everything for the move, and even on the morning they were due to leave, Robles still hadn't quite decided where they would go. Joey sat astride Dora's back as they came through the *barrios* and the clowns tumbled along the streets giving out flyers announcing the imminent arrival of the '*Uno Circo Espectacular.*'

The site did not look much more promising than many of the previous ones. Sandwiched between a scrap-yard and a cattle market, they were bothered the first night with the frightened bawling of cattle disturbed by the scent of the lion. Don Carlos, full of fresh meat that he hadn't had to chase, was not in the least bit interested, but for all their sakes, Robles insisted he be moved.

As the trucks were unloaded Joey looked around to see where everyone had pitched their trailers. He'd spotted Rodrigo's, Gustavo's and Josefina's and Robles's, of course. The one he was looking for had not yet arrived – Aurora's sea-blue van. Aurora, he'd discovered never slept on site. Every afternoon after the matinée she left, presumably to return to her husband. She rarely took part in the evening performances.

Joey tried to imagine this man, for whom she'd left her first husband and crossed the lines of social acceptability. He would be tall and handsome, with a mighty chest and great skills. But if he was a performer, why didn't they work in the same circus? Doña Rosa didn't know and he could see that it bothered her.

'She is close to Robles, so she has special privileges. She is not *del circo*, but she knew his wife very well, too good for the rest of us.'

It didn't matter what Doña Rosa thought of Aurora, Joey's groin still ached every time he heard the swish of her skirts across the dry earth of the site, and when he passed the Big Top and heard the ethereal tinkling of her show music, he had to stop because his feet, entranced, would not let him go a step further.

By the end of the week, he'd carried and hammered and cleared and cleaned and his arms ached and the dirt and grease became ingrained in his skin. He'd spent the first few nights sleeping in the Big Top but now he'd decided to look for somewhere more private. He wasn't the only one without a proper place to sleep. Some of the younger couples had makeshift tents and the hired hands slept in the trucks and in the back of the trailers now emptied of equipment. Doña Rosa had offered him a bed in her caravan, but he'd refused. He couldn't sleep surrounded by all those romances. He imagined the type drifting off the pages at night, buzzing around his head like midges driving him mad with lovesickness.

As he explored the new site searching for an alternative sleeping place, he heard the sound of a crying child. Instinctively he stopped. It was unusual to hear a baby cry at the circus. They had so much freedom, and so many people to whisk them up and pet them, they never seemed unhappy. He found the toddler at last under a trailer, half-dressed, a smear of dirt down its face. It was Elena and Dimitri's son.

'Oh now, where's your mama, *niño?*' Joey said, coaxing the boy out. The small face framed with tangled hair stopped mid-wail and the brow puckered up. Joey managed to pull him out and jogged him on his arm until the crying became a weary grizzle.

He liked the weight of him, and the damp sweaty hand clutching at his neck. He remembered that day back in the shack with Liliana's baby and wondered what had happened to that little soul. He tried not to think of the fate he might have suffered. He thought about his own father holding his hand, its soft fleshiness, not gripping it so that Joey felt his bones crunch, simply holding it. Why then? Why had he changed?

'Mama,' the baby's arms reached out as the thin figure of Elena hurried forward and grabbed him.

'*Gracias,* I, I must have left the door open, I was sleeping,' she said. She buried her face in the child's neck. Happy and confident again now that he'd found her, the toddler struggled to free himself. She put him down, but held onto his hand, her hair falling across her face.

'What's his name?' Joey said,

'Sasha,' she replied without looking up. He felt that same unease he'd experienced the first time he'd spoken to her, this familiar evasiveness. It crept back to him from Sunday mornings in the moody grey of home, his father in the armchair and his mother at the sink, her skin the colour of the dishwater.

He bent down as if to speak to the baby then looked up directly into her face. Startled, she looked wildly from side to side.

'Don't be frightened, I'm Joey Pachuca, I work here, I'm part of the circus. You must have seen me around?'

'I'm not frightened,' she whispered avoiding his gaze.

'Thank you, for finding him,' and she grabbed the child and darted away, her sharp hip bones sticking out through her jeans. As he watched he saw Dimitri standing in the clearing, his shadow stretching along the ground enveloping his wife, until she became invisible.

15

'Come in.' Doña Rosa was on her back on the floor her legs up against the wall.

'What are you doing, are you all right, did you fall?' Joey said kneeling next to her. She waved him away and he heard her counting. She finished, groaned and shuffled herself back to a sitting position.

'Just keeping fit, I don't want to become one of those brittle old ladies complaining about their arthritis.' She stood up with a flourish and slid into the splits.

Joey clapped.

'Now, are you here to sell me something or do you need a favour?'

'Neither, I need to discuss something.'

'Sounds like thirsty work.' She got up again to get them some cola from her refrigerator and popped the caps.

He took a swallow. 'It's Dimitri's wife.'

'Ah.'

'I found their child wandering on the site, and then I saw her. She was trying to hide her face from me but it was covered in fresh bruises.'

Doña Rosa shook her head, caressed her bottle. 'See, I told you,' she sighed. 'Some men are brutes, and some women marry brutes, and stay with them.'

Joey tutted in exasperation, 'Maybe she is afraid. Can't we do something?'

'I've tried, Joey. I spoke to Robles about him once.'

'And?'

It was Doña Rosa's turn to laugh this time. 'You don't understand Mexico yet. We still have a macho culture here. There are many who turn a blind eye to men who beat their wives. Robles, might not like it much, but he won't do anything, not yet anyway.'

'It's not just in Mexico that men beat their wives,' Joey muttered. Doña Rosa raised an eyebrow but said nothing.

'So we have to wait until he kills her?'

'He won't kill her, he needs her.'

Joey took another gulp of cola. He couldn't understand why Elena didn't stand up for herself. With all these other people around wouldn't they help? Then he thought back to his own mother. How many times had she been to the hospital, with excuses so feeble that even as a small child he'd had to look away in shame? It was clear the staff knew what was going on but nothing was done. Once, a policeman had come to the house after a report from a neighbour. Joey had been with his mother in the front room as she held a wet cloth to her bleeding mouth. Together they'd heard his father laughing and as the policeman left, Joey saw them in the hallway shaking hands. The policeman hadn't even spoken to his ma.

Rosa was staring at him, a half-smile on her face. 'I thought you liked Dimitri?'

Joey shrugged. 'Well, I was wrong. I think I was just impressed.'

'She too, poor thing.'

'If he does anything more to her, I'll …' Joey muttered. 'Do you think he ever hurts that kid?' he added suddenly.

'Probably not, what man beats his own little son?' Doña Rosa said.

16

There were three aspects to wire-walking: focus, height and balance. The most important part was the focus but his daily practice with his shoes had already improved his ability to concentrate. He'd learned to tune out external noise and visual distractions, whilst keeping his eyes open and alert.

The shoes and the pole helped with the balance, but the height would have to wait. He loved the feeling of it, hovering above the world, barely in touch with it. He felt most at rest here, with nothing but the vibrations of his own body. Without his birdskin shoes it was more difficult, his own emotions got in the way and confused him. Up on the cable the shoes gave him freedom. He was above the ground and all its seething turmoil, its grudges and upheavals. What must it be like to be way up in the Big Top looking down at all those faces, shiny discs of anticipation and fear? Lazaro had promised to take him up to the top platform just to look down, but he had left before the promise had been fulfilled. He took down the wire and went for a wash.

At lunch in the cook tent, he read the local newspaper, with its gruesome pictures of murdered gang members and drug dealers, throats cut, or blood draining from holes in their foreheads. For an instant he was back there on the night when he'd been accosted at gunpoint. If he'd not found the circus that could have been him lying in his own blood, it could have been his image in the newspaper crumpled into a ball in the street, or used by a mechanic to wipe an oily spanner. Who would have even cared? He turned to the sports pages. They were full of headlines about football and pictures of masked men with clenched fists facing each other across the wrestling ring.

As he was turning the pages over, trying to make sense of the more unusual Spanish words, he heard Aurora's name mentioned. In the kitchen trailer, Negrita was leaning across the counter talking to two of the jugglers, young sisters with a copper tinge to their hair and skin. Negrita was gesturing animatedly and blowing smoke from her cigarette over their heads, as she bent closer to listen. He rose quietly, studying the newspaper as he walked.

'I heard her crying,' Negrita said, 'she told Robles it was all over.'

'Well, what did she expect, if she spends her days at the circus, on her own, what husband will put up with that?' one of the jugglers said, 'and she's so weird – those clothes!'

Negrita hushed the girl. 'You're just jealous, Florita, because you saw her talking to Joey that time.'

'I'm not interested in Limpy,' Florita blushed and the others laughed.

Joey walked out from under the shade of the awning. The sunlight was falling on everything including his heart, and its edges too were silvered and glittering. Now he had his chance. He would offer to take her out and console her, and maybe he would show her some of the magic tricks he used to do. She would see what he was worth and what he had to offer a girl like her. He looked down at himself. He needed more than magic to stand a chance.

Later in the afternoon, before the preparations for the show, he took a bus into town. The streets as usual were thronged with people and traffic. He felt like a bumpkin in his dirty overalls. He peered into a couple of shops but was too nervous to go in. He turned into a side street, and found a market in full swing, stalls selling bags and hardware, caged birds and clothes. The stall holder looked at him up and down as he searched through the rails, eyes flitting from one thing to another, his hand stroking fabrics but not understanding them.

'*Mira*,' the vendor said pulling a simple shirt off the rail.

'*Classico*, see label Raff Lawrin, Polo, *muy bueno*.' Joey took it and held it up. Was this good? He tried to remember back to what he wore at home – never a shirt unless he was going to school. What did the other boys wear?

'Try, try.'

Joey slipped it on over his tee-shirt as the trader chewed on a pencil and scratched his belly with a weathered hand.

'*Muy bien*, you look smart, *elegante*.' Joey thought of that word and immediately thought of her and her frilled white shirts. *Elegante*, would she like that? He pulled at the collar, it was a button-down. Joey nodded, and he pointed to his overalls.

'*Necesito pantalones*.'

'You need Levis gins.' He studied Joey his head on one side.

'These, and belt. Don't want to lose gins, heh heh.'

A smile fluttered across Joey's lips. He handed over the money and immediately felt his confidence return, and then he looked down at his feet – filthy old work boots! He scanned the crowds walking around him. Cowboy boots and trainers. He wandered in and out of the stalls until he found a place selling second-hand leather goods. He chose a dark brown pair, with a low heel and a square toe. He'd momentarily dallied with two-toned snakeskin with fancy cutwork, but then changed his mind, especially when he saw the price tag. When he was top-billing he'd come back and buy a pair of those, two maybe.

Armed with his new clothes he returned to the site. The lights were already up, and he realised he was late.

'Where the hell have you been?' Otavio said his jowls quivering.

'I had to go into town.'

'Had to?' Otavio spat on the ground and walked past him. 'Get in there and start working or I'll have Robles kick your lazy arse to the other side of the city.'

Joey stashed his goods under Doña Rosa's trailer and got to work. He tried to concentrate, but as the show progressed he found it harder and harder. His stomach was knotted up and it seemed as if the show would never end. Finally the parade music sounded and there she was, wearing a black dress this time, diaphanous and sleek, her wild curly hair loose but pinned with red roses.

She did not seem like her normal happy self though, her eyes under the make-up looked tired and her painted lips and rouged cheeks seemed even more of a mask than usual. He began to have second thoughts. Maybe this wasn't the time to approach her; maybe he should wait until she had recovered from her marital break- up.

Why had they split up? Maybe she had chosen to leave him. If that was the case she might be happy to have a new man in her life. He would wait until she had changed and then he would knock on her trailer and ask her out for a drink in town. He would be in his new clothes and she would say yes, even just to be polite and then he would make her laugh and leave her thinking of him when she returned to her home, wherever that was.

Finally the last performer left, the final trickle of claps subsided and the crowds gathered their belongings. Joey wanted to rush up and shoo them out with his broom.

It was dark by the time he found himself outside her caravan. The jeans felt stiff and unfamiliar. His hair was slicked down, and his boots creaked a little. He didn't know how he looked, he had no mirror, but the clothes fitted and he felt like a different person.

He'd crept through the shadows, afraid that if he met anyone they'd make fun of him and he'd lose his nerve. He stood on the threshold, his hands damp and his mouth dry. A light glowed at her window. It was unusual to see her still on the site after dark. It must be a good omen. He cleared his throat, and then knocked on her door firmly, twice. He heard movement within and he felt his stomach roll and tumble. The door opened. Aurora stood in her long wrap, her face cleansed of make-up.

'Yes?' she said. He cleared his throat.

'Ah I was wondering...' he saw her eyes travel up and down his body noting his clothing, 'I was wondering if you would like to go into town with me for a drink or maybe a coffee?' She tapped her foot, bit her lip and looked away. Joey persevered. 'I know we haven't talked very much, but I'd like to get to know you and have some fun maybe.'

'Have fun?' her voice broke, and to his dismay, tears collected in her eyes.

'Sometimes the best way to get over a loss,' Joey said trying to sound like a man of the world, 'is to have some fun with a new man.'

A little cry broke from her lips, and she put her hand to her mouth. 'Just go away,' she said, her voice harsh, 'go away and leave me alone,' and she slammed the door shut.

He threw back his head and swore at the stars. He'd blown it. Such contempt in her eyes! He felt ridiculous in his new clothes. She'd seen right through him. He stuffed his hands in his pockets and looked around. He didn't want to stay here waiting for someone to spot him, waiting for her to spread the news. He'd go and drink on his own, get smashed and find a girl, someone who'd be pleased to spend the evening with him.

17

The main road did not look promising: electrical goods shops, old auto scrap yards, and the stench of stale blood and sawdust from the cattle market. He turned down a side road, where light bulbs dangled from a cable and rows of blue and white bunting fluttered in the light evening breeze, a tattered remnant of one of the many fiestas that enlivened the city.

A sweet scent filled his nostrils. A jasmine plant spread over a crumbling wall, but couldn't quite hide the dereliction. As he continued along the road it widened out and smartened up into a picturesque plaza. Waiters ruffled pads at crowded tables, as customers dithered over menus.

He drifted past taking in the clear-skinned girls with gold on their ears, leaning across the tables giggling together. This wasn't his sort of place. He'd never find a girl here, not unless he was prepared to buy her dinner, and he didn't think his pesos would extend to that.

Across the plaza the roads fanned out in several directions, and he followed the darkest one. The neat shop fronts and dripping window-boxes soon gave way to less salubrious buildings, empty lots, tinny music, the glow of cigarette ends picking out a silver capped tooth, a fake ruby ring.

He went into the first place he found, a brightly lit cantina, with a grinding and ineffectual fan. A television with the sound turned up, blinked in the corner. A group of men watching a football match stamped their feet and then banged the tables in disappointment. He ordered a beer and found a quiet corner. The sound of accordions and a heart-wrenching vocal poured out of a speaker above him, a confection of misery and failure that matched his mood. He ordered some *tacos al pastor* and another bottle.

He finished the beer and pushed the tacos away half-eaten. A fly sizzled on an insect-o-cutor above the bar. Bored with the television, he tapped his boot restlessly against the floor. He shouldn't be here alone. He left some pesos on the table and walked out. The street was livelier now. People were sitting on front steps and the air was hazy with the smoke from braziers. He scuffed along the pavement looking for somewhere else to spend his last few pesos, and someone to spend them on.

'Hey, hey, Joey!'

He turned around.

'Here, here, *hijo de puta*.' He caught sight of two big muscular arms waving. Rodrigo was standing outside a bar, lighting a cigarette. Close-to, his moustache showed traces of food and his eyes, red-rimmed and rheumy, told Joey he'd been here for some time. He offered Joey a cigarette. Joey took one, lit it, took a long drag and gave an explosive cough which doubled him over.

'What are these?' he croaked his throat burning.

Rodrigo chuckled. 'They're a brand called Strongman. I've just been out for them, not many places sell them.'

'Christ, you won't be strong for long if you smoke these.' Joey gasped.

'Come inside and join us.' Rodrigo said. 'We're having a party.'

Joey followed him into the bar and pulled a chair over to the table. Rodrigo sat down next to him. 'What's the party for?'

Rodrigo leant forward and placed a huge finger over his pursed lips. 'Secret. Don't tell anyone,' he whispered loudly. 'It's my birthday.' The crowd on the next table cheered.

'Why's it a secret?' Joey laughed.

'Because I'm forty years old, and that is a lot of years for a strongman.'

A door next to the bar squeaked open and Joey's heart sank. The other member of the party was Dimitri.

'Pachuca!' he said slipping into his chair. 'You've joined us. We plan crazy night. You want to play, *da*?' He looked Joey over, his eyes a solid black.

Joey bridled. '*Claro que si!* Why do you think I'm out here? Bring it on. I want a night I won't forget.' His words sounded no more convincing when they'd left his mouth than they did for the half-second he'd considered them.

They cheered and clashed glasses together. Rodrigo lumbered to the bar and soon returned with his hands full of bottles. The table was already groaning with empties. A waitress came over to clear them, and Rodrigo seized her in his huge arms and nuzzled her.

'Leave her alone or I will break your legs,' the barman shouted.

Rodrigo guffawed and sat back in his seat, wiping his moustache against his sleeve. 'I want a woman,' he said to Joey, 'something special.'

Joey grinned. Dimitri said nothing as he carried on drinking, slow measured gulps. Joey was aware that he was being watched but he didn't care. What was Dimitri after all but a bully, and he wasn't scared of bullies.

They left in the early hours and headed for a little place Rodrigo knew, 'where the pussy is so hot, it leaves scorch marks on your cock,' he slurred in Joey's ear. Joey sagged against a wall, spluttering his beer over the pavement. Dimitri strode ahead in long even strides that showed no evidence of his drinking. Rodrigo hollered a loud, sad song, which required him to stop regularly to act it out between gulps from an unlabelled bottle.

Progress was slow, but Joey was elated, his head awash with alcohol. The blood slipped through his veins and everything shone with a luminous blurred quality. His stumbling felt natural in this state and no-one thought to comment on it.

Rodrigo stopped at a blue door, which showed signs of damage at the base. There was no name or number on it. He banged it with his fist until it opened and a round, gleaming face looked up into Rodrigo's.

'Hey Rodrigo!' The door opened wider, and a small stout man with greasy skin, threw up his arms.

'*Amigo*! I seen the posters, wondered when you'd be in, you old dog!'

Rodrigo hugged him back until the man scrabbled to be released. He stood back, straightening his waistcoat and ushered them all inside.

Joey's blood was racing as his eyes became accustomed to the dim light. Crimson curtains hung awkwardly from the windows. A maroon rug lay over a tiled floor and his feet seemed to stick to it as he walked. The corners were dark and shadowy except for one where a television babbled, casting its flickering light over everything. As the doorman moved back a flurry of girls approached them.

He'd never been to a place like this, even when he'd lived in the squat in Tepito. His thoughts were instantly distracted by a girl in lace underwear offering him a drink, whilst another, wearing nothing but a tiny skirt, lit him a cigarette. He turned to Rodrigo and burst out laughing. His cock was already pressing itself against his jeans, a fact that was immediately picked up on by the girls. He shuddered as one of them ran her finger down his fly. He knocked her hand away afraid that he would come before he'd even left the room, making a fool of himself in front of the others but the hand returned like the limb of an octopus, her fingers moving in thrilling circles inside his ear.

As he twisted his head away, his gaze was halted by an enormous woman, her thin wrap revealing that she too was almost naked. She saw him staring and grabbed his head forcing it between her breasts. He pulled away, his face glowing, as Rodrigo bellowed with laughter.

As Joey pulled himself together he saw Dimitri disappearing upstairs holding the hand of a slight girl in a dark slip, her hair hung in a plait laced with red ribbons that nearly reached her knees. He was consumed with a mixture of anxiety and desire, as the blood rushed through him fuelled by the rat-a-tat-tat of his heart.

Dimitri and the girl had gone and the fat girl had dragged a laughing Rodrigo down another corridor. Joey, alone suddenly, realised his head was spinning and he tried to quell the lurching in his belly. The girl in the miniskirt took his hand and he followed her. He lifted her long straight hair and kissed her neck as she fiddled with the door. Inside the room, she leaned back against the wall and adjusted her stockings. She unfastened her skirt and it fell to the ground. Thuds and muffled groans were clearly audible in the adjacent room as Rodrigo tested the furniture. Joey smiled awkwardly, but his hands were sweating as he glanced down at her again.

'You can have what you want, he's paying,' she nodded towards the adjoining wall. Joey dropped to his knees and wrapped his hands around her waist, pushing his cheek into her belly. What did he want? He felt the press of her pelvis against his chest. He licked the skin of her stomach, it was smooth and salty. He opened his eyes against it, felt the thud of her blood beneath him and then from the corner of his eye, he spotted the tattoo on her hip, two doves, their wings open. 'Aurora', he whispered as his fingers slipped down the girl's body, pushing their way into the soft plum flesh.

The girl let out a cry, and swore. She grabbed his hair and tried to pull him to a standing position. He squeezed his eyes shut and tried to block her out. She knocked his hands away and he felt suddenly angry. His pushed her against the wall forcing her cheek against the hard surface, enjoying the feel of her trying to squirm away. But as he fumbled with his zip he felt the heft of her heel, against his groin and he doubled over. He opened his eyes, and tried to focus. In a slow, heavy blink, he saw that tattoo again and he began to weep.

'I'm sorry,' he slurred.

'*Cuál es tu problema? Es muy borracho,* so drunk, tch,' she muttered. Her eyes narrowed then grew weary as she saw the tears on his face.

'*Venga*', she said pulling him towards the bed. He stood looking down at her. She lifted her knees let them fall to either side. A crooked smile playing on her lips, she let her hand drop between her thighs in a practised move.

Perhaps it was the alcohol, or the realisation that for a moment he'd really wanted to hurt her, but something had changed inside of him. Gold eye-shadow had smeared her face and her lipstick had smudged. Close up she was just a kid probably younger than Teresa, whose name he didn't know, who didn't know his name. That had been okay once, but now it was different. He zipped up his jeans and left her there as the neon sign from the building opposite left its glowing imprint on his retina.

18

Dimitri had already left by the time Joey and Rodrigo stumbled back out into the night. Joey thought about Dimitri's girl again and that innocent red ribbon dangling from her plaits. He wondered if Elena knew where her husband was. Rodrigo offered Joey a bed for the night but he shook his head preferring his isolation and the freedom to gaze at the stars if he wanted. But he was too tired to do much star-gazing.

He woke up late with a hangover big enough for two men and an overwhelming urge to vomit. He lay still and hoped the feeling would pass. It didn't and he managed to stagger a safe distance away before hurling his guts into a drain. His stomach felt better then but when he thought about his encounter with Aurora the night before, a different sort of sickness enveloped him. He looked around the site but her van had gone. He sat on a bale of straw and let the sun warm his face; his stomach felt raw and crinkled like tin foil.

'Hey, whassup?' Joey opened one eye, 'Must you shout, Rodrigo? I've three heads today and all of them are in pieces.' Rodrigo roared, a noise that made Joey wince.

'So you had a good time last night? Those girls are fantastic aren't they?' Joey nodded.

'Liar, Lupita told me your tree wilted. She said you were angry and then you cried like a baby.'

'Christ,' Joey said about to get up.

Rodrigo pushed him back with a heavy hand. 'Alcohol gets all of us sometimes, it's no big deal, but if you ever get rough with a girl again I will break each of your bones.'

Joey stared at the face of his friend and knew he meant every word. 'My da was a violent man, and I'm always afraid that it is there in me,' Joey said quietly.

'That is so much shit,' Rodrigo said. 'My father was a priest but do you ever see me praying, no! We don't have to do what our fathers did.'

Joey kicked at a can and watched it roll into the scrub. He rubbed at his eyes with the heel of his hand, saw the world twist and fracture.

'It's Aurora,' he said at last. 'I heard that she was on her own again so I asked her out and she slammed the door on me. Obviously I'm not good enough for her, seems I'm not good enough for anybody.'

Rodrigo's face fell. 'Oh God,' he groaned. 'Aurora left this morning. I thought it was because of Dimitri, he's been sniffing around her, but it was you.'

'I only wanted to take her out and show her some fun,' Joey said lamely. 'What's so bad about that?'

Rodrigo yanked Joey off his feet, fury distorting his features. His arms screamed in pain as Rodrigo's iron fists squeezed the muscles, he tried to wriggle free but it was pointless. He stared into his cold eyes.

'Don't you know why she doesn't stay here at night, why she goes home every evening and has so little time to hang out and chat with us all?'

'Doña Rosa said it was because she's married and doesn't want her husband to mix with trash like us.'

Rodrigo dropped him, and he fell to the ground. 'You should know better than to get your facts from her. No wonder Aurora keeps her life a secret.' Rodrigo sat down again next to Joey his voice quiet and measured. 'Aurora was nursing a very close friend, a man, yes, but not her husband or even her lover as it happens.'

The colour drained from Joey's face.

'He was a performer too, a fire-eater. He cared for her when no-one else did, found her work in the circus and then he contracted throat cancer, the result of his art. During the day, her sister took care of him while she earned money here, and then she would return and take over. She has been doing that for nearly two years.'

'So when Aurora told Robles it was all over, she meant…'

Rodrigo nodded his head in despair.

19

But that was only the first shock of the day. It was Negrita who told him about Elena. As soon as Joey heard he ran to Doña Rosa's trailer, rapped on the door and didn't wait for a reply.

'Hey hold on a minute, let me put my dressing-gown on.'

'Sorry,' Joey muttered and turned his back for a moment.

'What's got into you?'

'It's Elena, she's run away. She left a note saying she missed her family.'

'A note?' Doña Rosa said, puzzled. 'Well, that explains why I saw Dimitri searching around the site this morning. He spoke to Robles too.'

'She's left Sasha though.' Joey was unable to sit still.

'I suppose she couldn't look after him herself and she'll be faster on her own. That must have been hard for her, she adored that boy.'

Joey stared at her, surprised at her matter-of-fact tone. 'How could she leave him then?' He felt his head churning.

'She thinks he will have a better life with us, than on the road, sleeping in doorways, begging and worse, and she is probably right. She doesn't know what her future may hold, and she knows she can trust us to look after Sasha.'

'But she has left him with Dimitri! How could she do that after the things he has done to her?'

'She knows we won't let Dimitri harm him.'

'Yeah,' Joey spat, 'he can beat his wife and we all look away, but if he touches the child, that's different.'

Doña Rosa sitting on her couch, her feet tucked beneath her, was studying him. 'Well, a baby can't defend itself.'

'And you think she could?'

Doña Rosa sighed. 'She has defended herself, she's run away. Not every form of defence involves fighting.'

Joey looked up at her. He wondered what his mother's form of defence had been. It had seemed to him that she'd never fought back at all.

'There are many ways to escape when you feel trapped,' Doña Rosa continued, 'Elena's is an understandable one. I escaped from my family to marry my husband – God rest his soul. I gained my freedom and the love of my life, but I lost my family. Elena has sacrificed her child in order to save it. Let's hope she will find some peace through that sacrifice.'

'My mother never left my father, she gave me up instead.'

Doña Rosa reached her hand across the table and took his. 'Trust me Joey, she did what she needed to do, you don't know the whole story, I'm sure. Maybe that was her way of being a good mother. You have to forgive her. You can't carry this around with you forever. You don't know why she did what she did. Why not believe the best of her? What harm can it do you? Let it go.'

She was right. He would never know what really lay in his mother's heart. He saw her now in his mind, cleared of all his accusations. There she stood, a frightened girl, like Elena, with no place to go.

20

Joey kept hoping that Aurora would return that he would have a chance to apologise, but as they moved out of Mexico City to Querétaro, San Miguel De Allende, Guanajuato, she did not appear.

In the summer, these towns were full of tourists, and Joey could see why. The buildings competed with each other to be the most beautiful, with their balconied façades in shades of gold and terracotta, cascading plants and cool central squares with cafés and fountains. They could have walked together and made up stories about the passers-by. He could have held her under these trees in the dark shelter of night like the other young couples he stumbled upon, his hands under her jacket, her hair soft against his cheek. He had to get over Aurora and find someone else

Despite the beauty of the towns, the circus sites were invariably on the outskirts, next to a sports ground, or near an industrial plant but at least he could find his way into the *centro*, while away an hour and still get back in time to prepare for the afternoon show.

Of course, some of the smaller towns they took in on the way were stinkers, squalid little places with nothing to recommend them but a few scratching dogs and a market that had lost its will to live. Joey wondered whether Robles just stuck a pin on a map when they arrived at these dumps.

'You'd be surprised at how big the audience is in these small towns,' Otavio said, 'you wait and see. When there is nothing else to entertain you, the circus is a big deal. The smart towns with their big festivals, cinemas and theatres, they may not even notice us until we've gone, but the little places they will talk about us for months. It is those raggedy children who will turn up at our gates wanting to join us.'

He was right, of course, and it was in one of these small towns, the Big Top packed with an appreciative audience, that Joey finally told his dream to Otavio.

'I want to be a circus star. I plan to develop a brilliant act before I tell Robles. I want to be more than just good.'

Otavio grunted. 'Joey, this is something you must have in your blood. These trapeze artists and high-wire walkers have fathers and grandfathers and great grandfathers who have nurtured them from the day they were born. You know I even heard of one family who placed each of their babies on the wire when they were just two days old, to see how long they could balance there, how relaxed and calm they were, and from that they could judge just how great a performer the child would be. They never got it wrong.'

They were sitting in the empty ring, the smell of sawdust in the air, the big airy space echoing to the sounds of the boys taking down the trapeze and sorting out the musical equipment. Joey, looking into that huge roof space, felt a longing in his feet.

'Lazaro Alvarez said I had something special. I have been working hard and one day soon, I will show you what I can do.'

Joey practised late at night when everyone else had gone to bed, when there was no risk of disturbance from giggling children, no chance of snide comments and mockery from the boys, waiting for him to fall.

He'd begun with a long balancing pole and he could perform a number of tricks with ease. Once his confidence improved he'd abandoned the pole, it felt like an encumbrance. He wanted to be as free as possible – just him, the cable and his birdskin shoes. Even suspended just a few feet off the ground, the relief washed through him.

Those nights he spent in the dark shadows of the tent, a small glow from a lantern to guide him, were some of his happiest moments on the Grand Tour as they all began to call it. Surrounded by empty seats and swags of cables, the smell of warm wood and the sweep of bats that flew through the empty space in search of insects, Joey found himself. His feet alighting on the cable began to tingle and as he closed his eyes, he imagined every cell in his feet aligned and alert, busy and single-minded as a colony of ants, with one purpose – to convey to Joey exactly where to stand and how to lean, where to shift his weight so that he could move himself across the glinting stretch of wire. In these moments he found escape. Feet on the wire, eyes closed, he heard the clip-clop of the horse hooves beneath him, saw, rising out of the rosy distance, the red rocky structures of his childhood refuge.

It was during one of these practices that he was disturbed by the sound of a car approaching the site. It was late for visitors. He ignored it and returned to his task, he had so little time. He was determined to perfect a new move he'd been working on. He climbed back onto the cable but his feet despite his shoes felt jittery. He swore and jumped off. When he looked up Aurora was standing in the light of the entrance. He flushed and his blood shot around his system like a pinball.

'I didn't mean to startle you,' she said.

Joey straightened up, cleared his throat and tried to speak. He was sweating and his hair was stuck to his forehead. 'I'm so sorry about…' he stammered, 'I didn't know, I didn't understand.'

She dismissed his months of anguish and regret with a wave of her hand. 'It was Rodrigo who told me about your mistake. He's a good friend to you. It must be nice to have a good friend.'

Joey hoped Rodrigo hadn't said too much. 'Well, I am still very sorry. I've thought about it every day since you left, and hoped I would have a chance to see you and say so.'

'Your timing was terrible, but please, let that be the end of it,' she said shaking her hands in a show of awkwardness. 'It's my fault. I didn't tell anyone, because I hated having to talk about it. We can start again as friends, can't we?' Joey nodded, but the word friend struck him like a slap.

'Tell me what you are up to?' she said, pointing to the wire. He explained his desire to become a high-wire performer. He saw her eyeing his shoes again and he shuffled uneasily, not ready to share his dreams with her yet.

'So, are you back with the circus for good?' Joey asked.

She sat down on a bench and stretched her hands above her head as if trying to find the answer in the still air above her. 'I really don't know. There is my family to consider. I have only one sister that I am still in touch with and she lives in Mexico City. She has a daughter, and I help to support them. My sister got a job in the garment district and hardly earns enough to keep them both. I miss the circus life though, I pine for it when I am in the city and I miss the children. I'm afraid they will forget me if I'm not here and then it will be as if I never existed.'

So she didn't miss him then, but why would she, she just wanted to be friends.

'Ernesto – Señor Robles, said I should come when I can.' she continued. 'I won't perform of course, it's not fair to take another's place when I am so unreliable but I am good with a needle and thread and there are always costumes that need fixing. I will try and come once a month, if only to bring the mail from Mexico City.'

Joey had hardly heard a word she said. He was transfixed by the way the light caught her cheek and by the patterns that he was sure he could see between her ankle and her trousers. When he looked again, however, she had pulled the fabric down. Perhaps he had imagined it, and it was merely the shadows from the tangle of cables in the roof that he had seen.

She yawned and stood up. 'I better go and get some sleep. Goodnight Joey and I am glad we talked.' She lingered for a minute as if she was about to say something else. He moved towards her. He wanted to kiss her just where the light caught her lip.

She turned away then as if she'd thought better of it and in her indecision she stumbled over a guy rope and fell. He rushed to help her, his hands grasping hers as he pulled her up.

'Not the exit I planned,' she said, giggling. She brushed herself down, and a smile suffused her face.

Not the exit she'd planned. The phrase ran through Joey's mind. Did you plan an exit from a friend? He smiled to himself in the darkness.

'Good luck with your practising, Joey, and when you have learned how to walk on the wire, perhaps you can teach me how to walk on the ground!'

21

1981

No-one heard from Dimitri's wife Elena again. Joey hoped she would return at Christmas, to spend time with Sasha, even sneak back and take him away in the night but the year rolled on and there was no news. Sometimes a performer would claim they had seen her in the audience but all these sightings came to nothing. No-one ever spoke to Dimitri about it and he never shared his feelings about the disappearance.

As for Sasha, in the beginning he cried frequently for his mother but as the months went by and he was showered with love and affection by everybody in the circus, he stopped calling for her. Whilst others spoke of the resilience of children and how they bounced back from a crisis, Joey knew that Sasha had not forgotten her. Deep down in his five-year-old soul was a place where his memories lay stored and one day he would be gazing into the distance or studying an insect or staring at the patterns oil made on the wet street and one of those memories would bubble up and burst inside him, showering him with longing.

Aurora kept her promise to be friends, a bitter-sweet state of affairs for Joey. When she arrived his days were brighter, as if the sky had been polished. She made him laugh until his sides ached. From Aurora he learned how to cheat at cards, and when they gambled with potato chips and he won, she would lean across defiantly and eat his winnings, her cheeks full and her eyes laughing at his outrage.

Sometimes she arrived with a picnic, and they would take the little ones to a park where he would try and teach them hurling, a game he'd played as a child but in truth, could barely remember. And when they were worn out with running she would make Joey learn Spanish tongue-twisters until the children fell over in uncontrollable paroxysms of laughter. If he lost his dignity he didn't care, he would roll onto his back and howl at the moon if it pleased her.

Once as they travelled on the *Metro* after an afternoon out, her head had fallen against his shoulder and he had felt his body go rigid. He'd dared not move in case she awoke. A thousand fireflies fluttered in his chest and the heat of her breath through the fabric of his shirt made him break into a sweat. When she did wake and smiled up at him, he moved towards her, not caring how many other bodies were squashed around them. All he could see were the lips on her upturned face. But what he saw in her eyes stopped him, something fleeting, fear maybe, reluctance, but it made him draw back, and the rest of the journey passed in a loaded silence.

The memories of those few hours he spent with her each month, accompanied by the children or other performers were eked out in the dark restless hours of the night, picked over for evidence of love or desire. He couldn't carry on like this; he was young and might die of frustration waiting for her to change her mind.

It was at a party for his twenty-second birthday in San Luis Potosí that he started a relationship with Florita. When Aurora found out, he watched her face, eager for signs of dismay. One flicker and he would have ended it instantly, but if she felt disappointment she hid it from him, speaking sweetly to Florita as she stood possessively in Joey's reluctant arms.

He did his best with Florita but his heart wasn't in it and he ended the relationship as gently as he could a few months later when he realised she was falling for him. She cried for several weeks, and she and her friends stared at him reproachfully whenever he passed but then she met another juggler and promptly forgot all about him. He was relieved. It was easier to love fruitlessly Joey decided, than to be the unwilling object of someone's love. One's own pain was easier to bear than the pain of others.

Doña Rosa was preoccupied as the year ended and the new one began. Joey confided in her less and less but he did visit her library and together they spent hours reading. She was looking for evidence against Dimitri and he was reading as much as he could about the high-wire.

Doña Rosa had convinced herself since Elena's disappearance that she had been murdered. 'You see, Joey, according to Dimitri she left a note saying she couldn't cope with the circus life and she was returning to her family. But I know for a fact that she couldn't write.' She tapped her pencil on the table to reinforce her point.

She combed the newspapers for descriptions of unsolved murders and corpses unearthed. There were a surprising number of them, and each time she read one out, her voice savouring the details, Joey's own heart shrank. There were nights when he was pursued through his sleep by *those who knew*, unnamed faceless individuals who were onto him, watching him go about his daily existence, waiting for that moment when they would confront him. He awoke from these dreams coughing and struggling for breath, his feet in spasms. He was afraid then to return to sleep, convinced she would appear to him with lifeless eyes and that stain spreading across her chest. Once daylight burned away these phantoms, he regained his equilibrium, thankful for his own life and unable to do anything about the one he had taken.

Dimitri was possessed by his own ghosts. His behaviour had become erratic. It worried Joey. He wondered what happened to the boy when no-one was there to watch. When he wasn't practising, working, or keeping a quiet eye on Sasha he followed Lazaro's advice to visit as many circuses as possible. Some were huge with parades that took hours to pass; others were no more than a handful of performers in scrappy costumes, barely managing to make ends meet. Whenever he spotted a new circus he checked the flyer for high-wire artists, and if he found one, he did his utmost to see it. He'd seen performers who cycled across the wire, supporting someone on their shoulders; others who danced along it to the rhythmical claps of the audience and some who performed complicated acrobatics to the Mambo.

When he saw them he knew he had much to learn but he also knew that he had something else to give, something that they didn't. When he watched the crowds, their eyes were filled with fear, with anxiety for the performer. What he didn't see reflected in their faces was what he felt up there, the feeling of ecstasy and of release.

It was a member of Otavio's extended family, his nephew Tito, who'd invited him to the circus in Gómez Palacio. Their own circus was on the other side of the state border in Torreón: both modern cities, and disappointing to Joey after the glories of central Mexico. Rodrigo thought otherwise,

'Wine-growing region,' he said rubbing his hands together. 'We'll go to the *bodegas* after the performance, do some serious quality drinking.'

'You drink too much,' Gustavo said.

'Who are you, my mother?' Rodrigo shouted, cuffing the side of his head.

Gustavo tutted, 'you are a performer, you have responsibilities. I have Dora so I wouldn't drink.'

Joey, Rodrigo and Otavio had all squashed into Gustavo's car. It was unusual for Gustavo to join them, he hated leaving Dora on her own especially when he knew Concepción was out for the evening too.

'We're going to have a wild night out for Crissake,' Rodrigo yelled from the back seat. 'Stop talking about that bloody elephant.' There was laughter from the others, but Gustavo hunched over the steering wheel in a sulk.

'No-one invited Dimitri, did they?' Otavio said. Joey hoped not.

The others shrugged,

'I didn't think there would be room for him in the car,' Joey said.

'So you mean he is still at the site and we are all here?' Gustavo said anxiously.

'You think he's got his eye on Dumbo? Just waiting until you'd left so he could fuck your elephant?' Rodrigo said winking at Joey. Joey bit his lip to stop himself laughing and even Otavio fought to keep the smile off his face.

'You may laugh but he is like Rasputin,' Gustavo whispered, turning from the wheel to look reproachfully at the others, 'all females are mesmerised by him.'

'You only say that because he is Russian,' Otavio said.

'Who's Rasputin?' Joey asked. Rodrigo punched him. A huge truck whipped by, its horn blaring, Gustavo swerved the car back to the right side of the road.

'Every place we stop, he's out all night and anyone who goes with him says he finds a new girl, thin, fat, rich or poor,' Gustavo's round head shook, 'but all very young.'

'He's got money,' Otavio said, as he wound down the window and spat out.

'No, he doesn't always pay for it,' Rodrigo added, 'I've been out with him many times, and I tell you Gustavo's right, he is like a *brujo*, he looks with those dark staring eyes and they come.'

They were all silent for a moment, the hot car filling with the smell of aftershave and petrol. Joey thought of Sasha. Young ones were so much easier to push around.

'But *is* he Russian?' Gustavo said suddenly. 'I have never heard him speak it and he doesn't teach it to Sasha.'

'What, you think he is a fake?' Rodrigo said.

'Doña Rosa definitely thinks he is hiding something,' Joey added, excited suddenly at sharing this information, 'she thinks he killed his wives.'

Rodrigo clicked his tongue and swore. 'I can't believe you still listen to a word that old woman says!'

'He better not come near my wife,' Gustavo said 'or I will kill him,' and he raised his hand from the wheel and plunged an imaginary knife back into it. Joey closed his eyes. The mention of it was enough for him to feel that momentary resistance of bone. He was jolted out of it by a dig in the ribs from Rodrigo whose face was an expression of exaggerated disbelief. Gustavo's wife Josefina was a harried mother, small and grey and always cleaning. She barely had time to look at her own husband, let alone be seduced by a man young enough to be her son.

Rodrigo patted his friend on the shoulder. 'Don't you worry *amigo*, if he comes near Josefina I will tear him apart for you, and feed him to Don Carlos.' The others cheered but Joey was still thinking about Sasha.

'Tito is family but Christ, what a dump,' Otavio said, as they walked out of the performance. A small child in cheap clown make-up thrust a flyer into his hands. Otavio peered at it before screwing it up and throwing it aside.

'He thought he was so special when he told me he wouldn't work for nobody but himself but I know where I'd rather be,' Otavio spat on the ground, buoyant with disgust.

The high-wire was also disappointing but Joey left knowing that with only a few months' more practice he could easily develop such an act himself and in a couple of years he would be a show-stopper. He left with the others, hopeful and enthused, a little light glowing inside him.

22

After Florita, girls flitted in and out of his arms, but nothing matched the feeling he experienced in the presence of Aurora. Still, he had other ambitions in his life. Her occasional visits distracted him from his training regime, and sometimes even though he knew she was on the site, he avoided her because her effect was so disturbing.

In her presence, his feet played up and he struggled to keep still. He had to keep his birdskin shoes on just to talk to her. He skittered about, made her laugh, showed her tricks and used all the poetry his soul could devise to leave an imprint of himself on her memory but still she kept a certain distance.

There were times when this aloofness infuriated him, and angry and resentful, he tortured himself with the reasons for it; his awkwardness, of course, his status at the circus, his poverty. In those moments he was glad she didn't stay for long because he wanted to argue with her, snub her and make her feel as wretched as he did. Yet there were times too, when he stood outside her van like a forlorn dog, yearning to be on the other side of its doors. Another couple of days in her presence and he would have been hammering to be let in.

Friends, that is what she wanted them to be and she was sticking to it. He wasn't even a performer and the only extraordinary thing he'd ever done for the circus he couldn't talk about. But at least he was working on his performance skills. He could now walk forward and backwards on the wire. He could lower his body so that one leg remained bent, the other stretched out before him, and he could jump and land back absolutely still on the wire. That was his favourite move. Jumping felt like flying, but on the ground he always had the hard crunch of earth beneath his feet. On the wire, he was a leaf settling on the current of a river.

Visitors brought news of amazing performers from Russia, from China, from *El Norte*. He combed newspapers and circus magazines wanting to find the impossible thing, the thing that no-one else had done. He loved leafing through the magazines that Doña Rosa collected. The smell of the paper was addictive, and with each turn of the page there was the possibility of a new discovery. Joey studied photographs of circus trains, thirty or forty carriages long that had travelled across America and Europe. The days of the huge circuses had long since passed. Cinemas and television offered more instant pleasures but what a life that must have been!

He turned another page and stopped. He read the caption, *'A Spanish circus in Cork, Ireland 1950's.'* Of course, he remembered – his mother had taken him to one, and that unsettling memory returned to him of his agitated mother in the darkness. There were times when he'd thought he'd imagined that, had seen it in a film perhaps but no, here was evidence. He lifted the magazine to the light, his hands shaking a little, to peer more closely at the photo. There was no information, not even a list of acts, but just the sight of that familiar place unlocked something in him. He put a marker in the page and returned it to the pile.

He pulled down another book and continued to look for ideas for the high-wire. He felt restless, though, as he searched the pages. Performers had done everything that could be done. The high-wire wasn't about gadgets, it was about human ingenuity and that had always existed. Over the centuries artists had pushed that inventiveness to the limit. The Dancing Diamonds were a perfect example. He'd never seen them but the family were legendary. They had given everything to the high-wire, and several of the troupe had died pushing their stunts to the edge. Other performers spoke of them with awe. What could he possibly add?

He closed the book and leaned back. On his own he couldn't match any of these stunts, and he wasn't sure he wanted to. Was it worth dying to provide the audience with a thrill, to make a man gasp, a woman hide her eyes? Life was too precious for that. He wanted to give them a moment of bliss, not terror and to do it on his own, without fuss and without props. That was the only thing he could do, and as far as he was concerned, the only thing worth the risk. He said goodbye to Doña Rosa, who barely looked up from her newspaper. She was busy copying down details into her little notebook.

23

It was May 4th 1982 when Joey first heard about Angel Milagro. It was a warm afternoon and he was in Robles' trailer, discussing the options for their next site. Concepción was next to Robles, her arm around his neck. Two little ones were scrabbling on the floor squealing over a toy that someone had bought for them. Josefina was there too, lipstick on her anxious mouth, a pretty dress showing her surprisingly neat figure and there was a visitor.

'You'll be interested in this, Joey,' Robles said. 'Let me introduce Francisco Sánchez Lopez. We go way back. I think forty years. My, oh my! Where do the years go?'

Joey stood up and shook hands with Robles's friend. He was a tall slender man, with receding hair and a perfect, thin moustache. He was dressed immaculately like Señor Robles, smart and elegant, right down to his two-toned cowboy boots.

'Francisco, was a friend of Angel Milagro, God rest his soul.' The others in the trailer murmured their approval. Joey looked blank.

'High-wire artist, only one of the most famous in the world,' Concepción said rolling her eyes.

'What was he like?' Joey asked, over the din of the children, whose friendly play had become something more violent.

'I didn't know him very well. I performed with his family in Argentina and then met him again in the 1940's in the US. He was a huge star then.'

Joey winced as a high-pitch scream burst from one of the children. 'Are you around for long, can we talk later?'

Francisco nodded, and resumed his conversation with Robles.

Joey had to wait until the end of the final performance before he had a chance to catch up with Francisco. They sat on a pair of upturned beer crates and opened some *refrescos*.

'He was of mixed-blood, West-Indian, Irish, English, Uruguyan – a tricky combination in the old days, so his father billed them as Tahitian and in America he was passed off as an Egyptian! It was alright to be a complete foreigner, you just couldn't be a mixture; the public didn't like it especially in the US.'

'I better steer clear of El Norte then,' Joey laughed, 'People here look at my skin and think I'm Italian, or Colombian – they can't believe I'm Irish 'til they take a good look at my eyes.'

Francisco stubbed out his cigarette. 'Different times Joey, different times. Angel did what he had to do to give his gift to the world. I worked with him there. We were both with Ringlings. He was earning $1000 a day then. I met him again just after they returned from Europe in '37, but once war hit, he never went back there. He was remarkable, the best I've ever seen; if you want to be the best, he's the one you have to find out about.'

'Why, what did he do?' Joey's heart was in his mouth, perhaps what he hoped to achieve had already been done. Perhaps Angel Milagro had already given the world that special something.

'His reactions were astonishing. He once told me that his father would take him and his brothers fishing and make the kids catch fish with their hands to sharpen their reflexes. The thing with Angel, he had no-one to imitate, he had to teach himself, work out his individual response to the wire, maybe that's what made him so special.' Joey remembered back to that moment when the Alvarez troupe had left, how full of self-pity he'd been. He was ashamed – Angel Milagro would never have let that get in the way.

'He was inspired by the great Con Colleano–have you heard of him?' Joey shook his head. 'You have a lot of learning to do, my boy. We grow up with this knowledge. We drink it in with our milk, and live it in our dreams!'

'Colleano was the first person ever to a forward somersault on the wire. Now that doesn't sound very dramatic does it, but let me explain. People had done other things: the splits, the high kicks, they'd even done backward somersaults, but before Colleano, the forward roll had never been done, he is even in the Guinness Book of Records. It is very difficult, especially on the tightwire. As soon as Angel saw it he was determined to master the move.'

Joey tried to imagine it as he drank. The crowds were milling at the stalls, the sound of tinny music blared across the site, and a gang of boys swaggered past them shouting insults at each other. Joey was seething with questions. His feet burned and ached.

'To do a forward somersault the performer's feet must lead the arc over his head. The feet must have an instinct for the wire. They must find it before the performer can actually see where to place them.' Joey held his breath. *The feet must have an instinct for it.*

'What else did he do?' Joey asked excitedly.

'Oh, he was a real showman, wore a small pair of gold wings attached to his back. They called him 'Wonder-Wings'. He did some exceptionally difficult acrobatics. He brought poetry to the wire. Maybe it was that little bit of Irish blood in him,' Francisco winked.

'He was like Mozart and the rest of us were the diligent orchestra, competent and hard-working but lacking that extra thing that makes a genius. Part of me hated him but only because I wanted to be him.'

'Francisco, I want to be him. I know I can be that good. Señor Robles has no idea what I'm up to, but soon I will show him, and you will see my name begin to climb from the bottom of the posters to the top. Milagro brought poetry but I will bring magic! Remember me. I am Joey Pachuca.' He stood up, and his feet overburdened with excitement, floored him.

Franciso helped him up, 'I suggest you cut down on the drinking then,' he said.

24

Joey unable to rest, wandered around the *terreno*. The evening was warm, a few birds were still exercising their throats but he didn't know what to do with himself. He wished Sasha was about. Playing with the boy always grounded him.

Whilst outwardly happy and spoiled by everyone, the boy was often bruised, but in places that could be put down to the rough and tumble of a circus boy's adventures. All the same, Joey worried. Only yesterday he'd had a water fight with him when they were cleaning out the animals and his father's voice had boomed for him to come. Immediately his smile had evaporated and a small crease had split his brow. When they sat in the mess tent, Joey would watch the boy quietly eating his food, looking up occasionally as his father made a comment and then looking back down at his plate.

The only time he saw Sasha happy in the company of his father was when Dimitri rehearsed a new trick with Don Carlos, then his eyes shone. Dimitri had boasted on more than one occasion that his son also had the gift and would be a great lion-tamer too. In fact, he was already working on something spectacular, 'I will show all that he is my son,' he'd said, 'that he has my great gift in his blood.'

Joey met Otavio standing by the empty Big Top, smoking, and they walked together to the mess tent where several of the other performers were yawning and stretching after the afternoon show. BuBu was still in his make-up, and the acrobats Romulo and Remus who had joined them in Zacatecas were discussing politics with ZuZu, their spangled clubs glinting on the table.

From a huddle of people at the back, he could hear a voice that sounded like Aurora and he felt the familiar lightness in his body, the rush of blood to the heart that her proximity brought about in him. When had she arrived? She was so far from Mexico City; did that mean she was planning to stay? He worked his way into the group. There was some sort of argument going on. He nodded to Otavio who had stopped working and was wiping his hands on his overalls. Aurora's voice high and querulous rose momentarily above the others.

'What the hell did he think he was doing?'

'What's all this?' Otavio said.

Aurora turned and Joey saw a defiant expression that he'd rarely seen in her before.

'Today Dimitri took Sasha into the cage, he sat the boy on the lion's back and he dangled him over the lion's jaws.' Her face was flushed with indignation.

'This woman knows nothing of animal behaviour,' Romulo said, no longer interested in politics. 'She struggles, when she performs at all, to manage a bunch of birds.'

Joey wanted to punch him.

Aurora's eyes blazed. 'I know a lion can kill a child in a moment,' she said.

One of the hands spoke up, 'But surely Don Carlos would not harm Sasha when Dimitri is there?'

'But Dimitri cannot look in two places at once. Tell them, Juan, you felt it didn't you? That maybe the lion was different with the boy there?'

Juan, one of the new hands, looked away. 'Well, what do I know?' he said scuffing the earth with his shoe.

Aurora pushed her way past the assembled group. 'I hoped you might support me, but I see that it is not just the girls that Dimitri has hypnotised.' She stormed off in the direction of Robles' trailer.

'Someone ought to take that woman in hand,' one of the new *chamacos* muttered. 'Who does she think she is talking to us like that? If she had a husband, he'd have taught her a lesson by now.'

'Or she would have bitten off his *cojones*.' There was a burst of laughter. Joey ran after her and caught her arm. She spun around.

'Oh, it's you Joey. Coming to see Señor Robles with me?' her smile flickered and then vanished. He nodded when he saw the despair in her eyes and yearned to take her in his arms and bury his face in her neck. A few of the other women had joined her at Robles' trailer. At the sound of Robles' voice, Negrita, Blanca, Aurora and Joey crowded in.

Robles sat behind his desk. He stood up as they entered, his hands outstretched. '*Buenas noches*, a wonderful show as always, and what have I done to deserve a visit from my beautiful ladies…and gentleman?'

Aurora laced and unlaced her fingers. 'We have come to talk to you about Dimitri.'

'Would you all like a drink perhaps, some nice cold sodas? It is so hot.'

'We haven't really got time for that,' Joey said. Robles' eyes turned on him, fierce and dark. He tugged at his crisp white shirt cuffs.

'We always have time in Mexico, for a civilised drink between friends,' he said.

Negrita jumped up and ran to his side. 'Of course we do, *compadre*, and it is really hot tonight.' She fanned herself in a way that was both submissive and alluring. 'Joey didn't mean to be impolite; we are all a little tense - that is all.' She squeezed Robles gently on the arm.

His face softened and he tweaked her chin. Joey watched him pour the drinks and could see in his graceful movements the performer he had once been. It was only through Blanca that he'd learned about Robles's past. She'd shown him cuttings of their travels around Europe, when she and Negrita were just children.

'So how can I help you?' Robles said, handing out the glasses.

'Señor Robles, Dimitri has started putting Sasha into his act, and I'm sure you must feel, as we all do, that this is too dangerous.'

Robles nodded, 'He said he was going to involve the child, yes.'

'And you agreed to this?' Negrita asked incredulous.

'Negrita, little one, you and Blanca were on horseback when you were only four years old.'

'But with all respect, *compadre*, that was different, a horse doesn't bite, the worst that would happen is a fall.' Blanca said.

'True, but a fall can kill.' The two sisters exchanged glances, and their shoulders dropped slightly. Negrita sighed, already resigning herself to the outcome.

'It's not the same, Ernesto, and you know it,' Aurora said, her exasperation getting the better of her. Blanca grabbed her thigh and squeezed it, shot a look across at Joey.

'I'm sorry,' Aurora said, 'it's just that I am afraid for the boy. Lions are unpredictable and that one is worse than most.'

Robles nodded again. He turned to the window and looked out. 'Dimitri is highly skilled. He knows the risks he is taking. Do you think he would let Sasha do this if it was dangerous? Fathers love their sons. They are like their own heartbeat.' The room fell silent. Joey looked down at his feet, lifted them slightly.

'Dimitri is not like you Don Ernesto, he is a volatile, even dangerous man. You know that.' She spoke softly, cajoling.

'A man is in charge of his own home and his own family,' Robles said. Aurora pleaded silently for support but the sisters wouldn't meet her eye.

'Aurora, bravery and skill, that's what people want. If we take that away they might as well stay at home.' Robles picked up a pen and doodled on his blotter. His fingers moved restlessly over the desk.

Joey leaned forward and gripped the edge. 'Please, Señor Robles, we are adults, we can make choices about the risks we want to take but Sasha is only six, he still thinks the lion is a pussy cat. He doesn't understand that he is potential prey to that animal.'

'Well, let's just see how it goes,' Robles said, coming out from behind the desk and standing by the open door. Negrita and Blanca kissed him on the cheek as he helped them down the steps. Joey followed.

Aurora hesitated, 'So you will do nothing? If that boy gets killed you know it will just up the ticket sales.' There was a break in her voice, 'I can't believe you are going to let this continue, Don Ernesto.'

'Ticket sales are good for all of us,' Robles said, his cheeks drawn and his mouth rigid, 'and lions, my dear, are more exciting than doves.' Aurora turned and left the trailer.

Joey walked with her to her van. Her frustration filled him with misery and he longed to say something to help her. She turned to him and placed her hand on his chest. He wondered if she could feel that his heart had stopped completely.

'Thanks for speaking out, for supporting me. I know you have ambitions and you took a risk. You're a brave boy.'

Joey clenched his jaw in irritation and pushed her hand away. 'Christ, Aurora. I'm a man, not a child, why do you always speak to me that way? My childhood ended when I was seven years old.'

She stared up at him, her eyes anxious. 'God, I'm sorry Joey, I didn't mean anything, I'm not thinking straight. I wish I could do something, persuade him to change his mind. Sasha, that child just pulls at my heart. Come in,' she said opening the van door, 'come and have a drink with me.'

Joey's blood beat a polka as he climbed in behind her, wondering briefly who might be watching him and judging her.

The tiny space was stuffed with fabrics for new costumes. She gathered them in her arms, looked around for a place to dump them, but there was none. She dropped them back where they were.

'You'll have to sit on them, watch out for pins.' She searched in her fridge, found some juice and poured them each a drink.

'Dimitri is a strange man,' Joey began, 'the boys tell me he finds women everywhere we go.'

Aurora pursed her lips. 'Well, it doesn't seem to stop him pestering me,' she said. 'See that roof?' He looked up and realised that there was a window under the draped fabric.

'I had that window put in so I could see the stars but one night I open my eyes and there is Dimitri looking down at me. I was terrified, which is why I put the fabric up there. Dimitri apologised the next day, told me he sleepwalked. Huh! He gives me the creeps. I'm not surprised his wife left him.'

'He hit her,' Joey said. 'I saw the marks on her face.'

'*¡Que malo!* I was so wrapped up with my own problems I didn't notice anyone else. Poor Elena. Do you think he hits Sasha?'

'He's frightened of his father, I recognise the signs.'

Aurora took his hand and squeezed it. Joey, changing the subject, suddenly blurted out a question that had been plaguing him. 'Aurora, the man who died, was he your husband?'

She looked up, her eyes suddenly full of tears and Joey wanted to suck the words back out of the air where they hung suspended between them. She shook her head quickly. 'He was my saviour,' she said, 'one day I'll tell you all about it, but I can't at the moment, I'm sorry.'

Joey nodded, thinking that for the second time in his friendship he'd blundered on in and made a mess of things. He wanted to take her crumpled face and cup it in his hands, wipe away those tears but he was too afraid. He left her van and the sound of the door closing behind him lowered his spirits.

Sasha came running towards him. 'There you are. I've been looking everywhere for you.'

'Hi Sasha,' he said bending down and tousling his head.

'I went in with Don Carlos.'

'So I heard. He is not a kitten though and he hasn't grown up with you.'

'But he knows I wouldn't hurt him.'

'It's not him I'm worried about, Sasha.' But the boy had already skipped away again to play with his friends.

'What gets me,' Negrita said later as he sat sharing a drink with her, 'is why Dimitri is doing it. Is he trying to prove something?'

'What do you mean?'

'We all know that Elena ran away. He knows that we know, she left a note after all. So now he is dangling this in our faces. It's like he's saying, the boy belongs to me. He is my property. I can do what I like and you can't stop me.'

25

Joey yearned for the buzz of Mexico City. He'd enjoyed Monterrey and they were at least heading south – Doña Rosa had told Señor Robles that 1982 was a good year for southward journeys and 1983 promised stability. She spoke with such confidence and authority you'd think she'd made a study of the heavens her life's work.

Still, he should thank her; each mile nearer Mexico City was a mile nearer to Aurora. If they returned to Mexico City she would be able to stay with them. He would see her every day rather than endure her fleeting visits with the mail when he had to share her with so many others. The longing to see her was a constant nag in his body.

Maybe by the time they returned, his skills would be the phenomenon that he dreamed of. He had researched Angel Milagro and found pictures in Doña Rosa's magazines. He'd read about his dance steps and added that to his repertoire. In the snatched hours that he had, he'd mastered a range of acrobatic moves, and his jumps had become longer and higher. This required enormous strength and control so in addition to the morning practice he was working out: lifting weights, limbering up, stretching and refining his muscles. He'd also managed to persuade Otavio to set up the high-wire and net for him when he could.

Others had begun to realise that he was in training, but they weren't prepared to stay up into the small hours and watch him. Quietly they were bemused, especially when they watched him lumbering around the site, tripping over invisible stones.

Joey thought the height might worry him, but on the contrary, it made him joyful. Once he had focused, his feet took control. The special thing, though, the extra ingredient was still missing; it would come, once he was confident with the techniques and the complicated moves, it would come.

Sasha did not go into the ring again. Aurora, Joey and Negrita quietly toasted their success but over the next few months Dimitri's behaviour changed. They were pitched in San Luis Potosí. The *centro* had looked beautiful as they came through calling out to the citizens of the town that the best circus in Mexico was on its way. Its elegant colonial buildings and magnificent churches were set around green squares, its wealth a result of the silver that riddled the landscape. Joey had thought about going down into one of the mines but didn't think his feet would stand it.

He'd been enjoying the sunshine, watching a father with his sons buying jointed wooden snakes from a street vendor to play with. He remembered the first square in Mexico City where he'd slept, how long ago was that now, six years or was it seven? It seemed like a lifetime. He bought a postcard of the Jardín Hidalgo, the pretty plaza in which he was sitting. The waiter had left a pen on the table and he picked it up. *Dear ma* he wrote. He stared at what he'd written, *ma*. He'd meant to write to Aurora. Only occasionally now did the memory of that evening creep out and startle him with its intensity, at other times it was almost as if he had dreamed it. He closed his eyes. The salt washed over them carrying an archipelago of freckles. He opened them. He picked up the pen, hovered. *I'm so sorry and I wish I could tell you that.* He looked at the card. Then he tore it up, and dropped it in the bin. He must be going crazy.

It was getting dark but he didn't want to leave this serene square for the bleak site. Perhaps he could find a girl. It felt like an age since he'd held someone in his arms, anyone he cared much about.

'Can we join you?'

Joey sighed, pulled out the seats next to him. How did they

know he was here? The others borrowed chairs from adjacent tables and ordered some drinks.

'This place is a bit smart. Have you got a secret stash of pesos you've not told us about?'

'Just fancied somewhere where you lot wouldn't go,' he joshed. 'I want to get used to it.'

As they were chatting, BuBu pointed his finger towards the street and nudged Joey, 'Look.'

Dimitri, his back to them, crossed the road, his hair tied back in a long braid. 'He's off again.' BuBu said.

'Where?'

'I don't know but he always comes back very late.'

'Yeah, he wakes me clattering over things and swearing,' Otavio said, slurping his coffee. 'My wife she says to me *Otty, he must have a woman in this town.* She's probably right but why does he come back drunk every night?'

'He can't be having a good time.' Joey said.

'Maybe he's found someone who isn't like tortilla dough, and it's breaking his heart,' ZuZu said.

'I heard he keeps his heart locked in a bank in Mexico City,' BuBu replied, to much laughter.

'As long as he's sober by show-time, that's what matters. We don't need any more *borrachos* in the circus.'

Joey looked away. He and Rodrigo had acquired a reputation for heavy drinking. He'd needed it once but not anymore.

'Now I have some news for you,' Otavio said turning to Joey. 'Robles told me he is coming to see your act, the one you've been working on.'

Joey gasped. 'Who told him? I mean, it's not ready yet.'

Otavio chuckled, and took a puff of his cigarette. 'I told him. And it is ready. He will watch it tomorrow.'

Joey stared around at the circle of grinning faces. 'You all knew?'

Otavio's boys clapped him on the shoulder. 'Yes, we did, some of us have been sneaking in to watch you so drink up you need an early night.'

Back in his lean-to, his head was spinning, running through the sequence of activities he had devised. He might get a spot in the show at last. He wriggled out so he could see the stars. His life really had moved on. Soon he'd be a proper performer in a Mexican circus with his own name on the posters, yet he still couldn't walk easily without the shoes. What would Doña Marta make of that?

His excitement was tempered by his anxiety about Sasha. He thought back to what Otavio had said and wandered if Sasha woke up too when his father fell in through the door, and did he lie in bed waiting for the sound of snoring before he could allow himself to breathe? Joey hoped that like him, Sasha had learned a way to disappear into another world. He decided to creep over to their trailer and check that he was safe. The light was on inside. He tapped on the door. There was no answer so he turned the handle and it opened.

'Sasha, Sasha. Are you in there?' He searched around but there was no sign of him. He went back outside. The night was thick with sound, the song of cicadas vying with the jabber of television sets and the plaintive songs from radios.

Joey began to search between the rows of trucks picturing all sorts of disasters and accidents. Images from Doña Rosa's newspapers flitted through his head. He hurried from the trailers to where the animals shuffled in their enclosures, their smell ripe and comforting.

'Sasha' he called quietly, then again a little louder. There was a high chattering reply from a recently acquired troupe of monkeys. He hushed them as he passed, slipping between bales of straw and a rigged-up corral for the horses. He found Sasha lying on a blanket in front of the lion's cage.

'Sasha, what are you doing here?'

He turned over, his eyes sleepy. 'I'm telling Don Carlos a story.'

Joey sat down next to him. 'What story are you telling him?'

The little boy leaned up on his elbow and rubbed his eyes. 'I'm telling him a story about the savannah. You know he comes from Africa but he's never been there, he doesn't know what it's like so I'm telling him.'

'Do you know what Africa is like?' Joey said pulling back the curls that almost covered his eyes.

'Aurora tells me. She has a big book with pictures.'

'Aurora?'

'The bird-lady who has been making the costumes; she is helping me to read.'

'Your papa doesn't hurt you does he?' Joey said quietly, 'when he comes home late, he doesn't hurt you?'

'Only if I'm bad. Mostly he talks to my mother and cries. I can't see her. I don't tell him that though.' He turned back to the lion's cage: 'Once upon a time there was a big lion that walked in Africa and he was very lonely and wanted some lion friends…'

In the cage the lion's big paws twitched. Joey put his arms around the boy and picked him up. 'I think he is dreaming about Africa and you need to go to bed and dream too.'

By the time they reached the trailer, the boy was already asleep. Joey laid him on his bed and tucked the blanket around him. His brow was a little furrowed, and his long lashes didn't quite seal his eyes. He appeared to lie in that fragile place between sleep and wakefulness. Joey left the trailer, quietly closing the door behind him.

26

Robles settled himself in his seat. Otavio checked the high-wire, and Joey mounted the ladder. Word had gone around that Limpy was having an audition so a few of the hands had gathered to watch. His head swum, his skin itched, his throat was dry, but his feet were calm and ready. He'd have to rely on them to carry him through.

He had chosen some traditional music to accompany his act, a slow ballad to begin with that built up into a fast rhythmic piece for his finale. His heart hammering, he placed one foot on the wire and closed his eyes. The music enveloped him. He placed the other and waited. Minute vibrations spread through his feet. His silver birdskin shoes felt like a mesh of tiny sensors. He walked to the centre of the wire and turned to face Robles.

He had perfected an unusual stunt rarely performed now. He slid down into the splits, balancing his body so that only his leg muscles and the arches of his feet held him in place. It was an audacious first move that he was sure Robles would not have expected. Keeping his balance he raised himself up, then jumped skywards, crossing his feet in the air like a dancer before landing back on his toes, with none of the teetering that irritated him in other performers. He didn't rock or sway even for effect, he felt utterly sure of himself.

On the tips of his toes he ran to the other end of the wire. 'Bravo,' someone shouted. He bowed then tried to screen them out, regain his concentration. He carried out some brilliantly executed acrobatic moves, and as he did so, glimpsed the familiar whisk of the hand in front of the mouth, the fear for the performer.

The music quickened. His finale was a series of two backward somersaults one after the other. This was a challenging trick even for a seasoned performer. Robles would be astonished that he had mastered it already. He crouched down on the wire, his head tucked into his chest. He felt the cable beneath his feet, pushed one foot in front of the other, rubbed his arch against it, breathed in. Then he rolled back, placed his feet, rolled back again, and the final move brought him to the platform at the other end, where he stood up and took a bow.

The audience stamped their feet and whistled. Nothing had gone wrong. He had excelled at all the moves. Everyone would say he was exceptional, but something was niggling at him. He'd not managed that extra thing he'd been grasping for. He hoped it would come to him but it hadn't. He was dogged and hard-working and tenacious like any other performer, and that had paid off. Perhaps he just didn't have that spark of genius. He was a Pachuca, not a Milagro. He climbed down the ladder and was surrounded by pats on the back, cheers and high fives.

'My man!' Rodrigo said thumping him hard on the back. Joey smiled, but couldn't shake off that internal disappointment.

Robles took his hand. 'Remarkable. You are a natural performer. When I have a slot, you will be on the billing. You may have to wait a few months. I will give you fifteen minutes but that is just the beginning.'

Joey's doubts disappeared and throwing his hands in the air, he cartwheeled across the ring.

That night Negrita and Blanca cooked *chiles en nogales*, green chilli peppers stuffed with minced pork in a cream sauce decorated with pomegranate seeds, a feast the colours of the Mexican flag. The tables were pushed together, covered with cloths and candles. He leaned back his belly full and his heart happy and gazed at his complicated family and knew he belonged.

One by one the women retired to their trailers, but the men were unable to finish their night and sat around nursing some cold beers. It was Rodrigo, of course, who recommended a cantina that served a strong *pulque* that they had to try. The young ones wanted something with dancing and DJs but Rodrigo, by sheer force of will, persuaded them otherwise.

It was the kind of place Rodrigo loved, cheap, dilapidated and probably full of *putas*. The others groaned when they saw it, but they burst through its doors around midnight ready for fun. Inside they found a small rundown bar with peeling plaster, a few tables and chairs and mirrors on the walls, etched with the names of famous tequilas. The air was thick with the acrid smoke from cheap cigarettes, and loud dolorous music poured out of the speakers behind the bar like the last cry from a broken heart. The place was half-full and the drinkers looked up as they stormed in.

There was a loud shout from Rodrigo. Dimitri was seated at a corner table staring at a glass of beer as if its honey-coloured depths would tell him something. He looked up, his eyes glazed. A smile appeared on his face then slipped off again. He dropped his gaze back to the table. Rodrigo pulled up a chair. Joey didn't want to join him but had no choice. This was not a good start to his teetotal regime.

Soon they'd taken over the table and when a nearby one was vacated they dragged that one over too. The *pulque* made from the Maguey cactus, was slimy, thick and very strong.

The evening to celebrate Joey's success soon degenerated. Women migrated to them, ready to help them spend their money. Rodrigo had two girls on his knees, one had her arm around Joey's neck, and even the boys with girls back at the site were enjoying their company. The only one on his own was Dimitri.

'Dimitri, you dumb Russian, no girls for you?'

Dimitri swore and spat on the floor. 'I want Elena,' he moaned.

Rodrigo, his eyes wide and glittering, banged his huge fist on the table. 'He wants Elena,' he roared. The others in the bar looked up and then turned away quickly. Rodrigo, drunk, was a terrifying sight.

He leaned in towards Dimitri and shook his arm. 'She's long gone *amigo*, you need to find another. Look at that piece of ass over there, she likes me, naturally, but hell, we can share her.'

Dimitri whose head was slumped on the table looked up, his hair straggling around his face, '*Yo quiero* Elena.'

Rodrigo and the others burst out laughing, and then Rodrigo made them stop, shushing them sloppily with his great hands, 'Hush now, shhh. Dimitri. Love is torture. It will only bring you misery.'

Dimitri shook his head from side to side slowly, repeatedly until the motion began to make Joey feel sick.

'He's got it bad,' Juan said.

'Juan, you are new, you don't understand. Dimitri here had a wife but she's gone,' Rodrigo said in a whisper.

'She had to go. She didn't want me anymore,' Dimitri said. The table fell silent. The men looked at each other uneasily.

'Hush *amigo*,' Rodrigo said, 'let's go somewhere else, this place is depressing me.' He signalled to the others, they began to stand up, but Dimitri wouldn't move.

'Elenaaaa, forgive meeee,' he bawled. Others in the bar stared in their direction and whispered to each other, mouths tilted in disapproval.

'Cut it out,' the barman called 'or I'll throw you in the gutter where you belong.' He dragged a cloth across the counter and muttered, '*cabrones, cirqueros.*'

Juan jumped up. 'What did you call us?'

An uncomfortable silence enveloped the bar. The music filled the emptiness with its booming rhythms but the atmosphere was tense. The barman stopped polishing his glass, opened his hands in a placatory gesture,

'I'm not looking for trouble here,' he vacillated, his eyes darting from side to side, ' but I have other customers, take your drunk friend out,' he nodded to Dimitri 'buy him some coffee.'

Juan, his fists balled, was breathing heavily.

'Let's go' Rodrigo said, 'We don't want to drink in this shit-hole anyway. The *pulque* tastes like piss.'

Rodrigo and Otavio's sons tried to pull Dimitri from his seat but Dimitri refused to be moved. 'I'll get up on my own,' he drawled

'Let's leave him,' Joey said. He could see the eyes of other men in the bar.

They staggered outside. The street was strangely quiet, and then they turned. Five men were heading for them, sticks in hand. Joey broke into a sweat and his stomach turned to liquid. Rodrigo whooped and shook his fists in the air. '¡*Bronca*! Fight!' he yelled.

The attackers, some of whom Joey recognised from the bar, looked nervously at each other as the shadow of Rodrigo's arms, enlarged by the streetlight behind him, slunk across the pavement and up the walls like two huge anacondas. Joey found himself grappling with a wiry boy, slippery as a greased watermelon and with nails that dug into his arm. He could hear the scuffles of others around him. He'd just landed his first punch when he heard the distant wail of a police siren. The boy backed off, his limp turning into a hobbled run. The other attackers scattered.

'Quick, we better move.' said Joey.

'Where is that Russian bastard?' Rodrigo said. Dimitri was lying in the gutter where he'd fallen or been thrown. They dragged him to an alley behind the bar, and then ran as fast as their injuries would allow, away from the sound of the approaching squad car.

'Do you think he'll be alright?' Joey said.

Rodrigo shrugged. 'He can take care of himself. Besides the barman won't want any fuss, he just wanted to scare us.'

They swaggered home along the highway oblivious to their bruises and cuts, high on adrenaline.

27

The next morning, Joey ached all over and his injuries, although superficial, were painful. A cigarette and a cup of coffee were required to restore some equilibrium. The first gulp made his intestines roll and he lifted his head to take a deep breath and there was Rodrigo heading towards him, his leg muscles bulging in his spandex leggings, a couple of hours of sweat soaking through his tee-shirt.

'Hey, what's happening?' Rodrigo said.

'How can you look so bright after what you drank last night?'

Rodrigo smiled, 'I have a liver like an ox, but I also drink a lot of water. I piss like an ox too!' He sat down and joined Joey and they discussed the night's events.

'So what happened to Dimitri?' Joey said.

'No-one has seen him since last night. He must be sleeping it off in his trailer.'

Joey walked over to the caravan. He knocked, and eventually Sasha's tangled head appeared.

'Where is your father?' Joey asked gently.

Sasha shrugged. 'I heard him come back very late, but he isn't here now. What's the matter?' He yawned, stretching his skinny body skywards.

'Nothing, you go back to bed sleepy head.'

Joey came back to Rodrigo deep in thought, 'Sasha heard him come back but now he's gone.'

'We need to find him. If he goes into town again he'll have us in deep trouble.'

'He's probably nursing his hangover somewhere, stupid bastard, he disgusts me.' Otavio said.

Joey was quiet. He had a bad feeling about it. 'Okay, let's go and have a look for the Russian. Perhaps he's fallen down a ravine, or is lying by the roadside.'

'Best place for him,' Otavio grumbled.

The three of them got up and separated, one to search the highway, the other to the Big Top, and Joey headed across the site. He looked between the trucks and the animal trailers, wandering past the horses to the edge of the site where the scrub was thick and thorny. There was no sign of him. Otavio was right: he was probably still lying in the alley where they'd left him. He turned back and stepping over the swags of cable he cut through the gap between the equipment trucks. Then he halted abruptly.

Don Carlos was sitting close to the bars of the cage gnawing at a piece of meat. A thick pool of blood, humming with flies, covered the cage floor and as Joey took in the horrific scene before him, he turned around and vomited. Dimitri in his dark-stained khaki jacket was lying on his side, his prostrate body blocking the unlocked cage. The back of his head had been clawed, the white bone visible through the matted hair and skin. The iron smell of the blood lingered in the air. A smashed bottle lay on the floor of the cage, the splintered glass catching the light. Don Carlos was chewing on his severed arm.

Joey ran back to the others. Rodrigo and Robles who'd been chatting together stopped and fell silent when they saw him.

'Christ, what's the matter with you?' Otavio said

'I've found him,' Joey said, 'I've found him.'

28

The area had been sealed off but the *cirqueros* all came to see the spot where Dimitri had been killed. The children clung to their mother's legs staring in fascination at the stains that were all that remained of Papa Afrika, and Don Carlos. It was Otavio who had shot the lion, at close quarters between the eyes, as soon as Joey had reported the news and before anyone else knew what had happened.

'What a way to die,' breathed Gustavo, shuddering.

'It is a good way,' said Juan, 'it is manly.'

'What kind of man was he?' Negrita sneered.

Josefina shook her head crossed herself, 'You must not speak ill of the dead. It is for God to judge him now.'

Negrita smiled wryly, 'I think God has done his judging don't you?'

'What will they tell the boy?' Blanca said.

Romulo shrugged. 'The truth I hope, that his father went into the lion's cage to feed him, and he was attacked and killed. We all know Don Carlos was mean.'

Joey looked around for Doña Rosa; she was not in the crowd. She would be disappointed that her investigations had led nowhere. He slipped away and found her in her trailer with wet eyes and shaking hands.

'You've heard then?'

She nodded. 'It's my fault he killed himself Joey. It's my fault. I should have kept my big mouth shut but I had to play the detective, tell him what I'd found out.'

She blew her nose noisily into a handkerchief and pushed a piece of paper towards him. The yellowed clipping from a Tijuana newspaper showed a picture of a young man,

'Dreyfus Mack, aka Sasha Mack, Dimitri Mackus, Dreyfus Chekhov, wanted in connection with a series of frauds, confidence tricks and sex with underage girls. A U.S. citizen, he was last seen in El Paso Texas. It's believed he may have crossed the border into Mexico.'

Despite the shorter, lighter hair and the less flamboyant clothes, the photo was almost certainly Dimitri. So nothing he'd told them had been true: the scientist father, escape from the Soviet Union, none of it.

'I didn't want him to commit suicide,' Doña Rosa snuffled, 'now the boy has no-one and it is my fault.'

Joey put his arm around her, 'Now the boy has everyone, Doña Rosa. Dimitri, Dreyfus, whatever, he made his own decision. Anyway it was an accident, nothing more. He was drunk.'

She patted his hand. 'If it had been an accident someone would have heard him scream. Still, I will to go to the church and say some prayers for his soul, he will need them.' Joey squeezed her arm and left her with her tissues and her evidence.

It was left to Señor Robles and his brother to deal with it all. There was no doubt in anyone's mind except Doña Rosa's that it was a nasty accident, but the police had to be involved. They looked uncomfortable on the site, as if they might be contaminated simply by proximity to the circus.

It was Joey who'd broken the news of Dimitri's death to Sasha. He took him to the far side of the site. One of the circus hands had cut an oil drum in half to make two seats and the sun had already begun to warm them. There were a few scrubby trees and two cacti dotted with red fruit bristled against the horizon.

Sasha listened, his eyes big and round his hands still for once on his skinny thighs. Joey waited for a response but none came. Joey put his arm around his shoulders. They were so thin. Where the collar came away from his nape, Joey could see dark marks on the skin.

'Will I have to leave the circus?'

'Of course not,' Joey said squeezing him gently. 'The circus is your home, you will stay with Robles and he will look after you, he said so.'

'Can I live with you?'

Joey looked down into the dirt. He had nothing to offer this little boy.

'I don't know, Sasha, perhaps you should live with Josefina and Gustavo, or Negrita and Blanca then you will grow up with some other children and a mama.'

'I don't want to be with them, I want to be with you.' Sasha's small chin was quivering and Joey could hardly bear to look.

'Sasha, it's not that I don't want you, it's just that I don't have a place to live myself,' Joey said.

'You can come and live in my trailer, we can share it. Then both of us will have a home.'

'We'll see,' Joey said. 'These are early days.'

Sasha stood up. His skinny legs stuck out of his threadbare shorts, bruised and dirty, but as he talked, his eyes filled with that familiar shine.

'You can learn how to train Don Carlos,' Sasha said. 'I will show you how to make him jump and roll over like a puppy. He is not like everyone says. He is friendly when you know how to handle him.'

Joey swallowed and he took Sasha's hands. The boy looked down at him, puzzled.

'What I have to tell you is difficult for me Sasha...Don Carlos is dead. We had to shoot him. Once a lion has tasted human blood, he becomes very dangerous.'

Sasha's face puckered up. He buried his face in Joey's jacket and howled. Joey wrapped his arms around him, feeling the desolation throb through his own body, the loss mirroring so many of his own. He swung him into his arms, and carried him back to the trailer, and handed him over to Josefina. He then took off into the surrounding hills and walked all day feeling his own emotions pouring through his feet making him run and jump and skitter as if trying to escape an invisible foe.

At the funeral for Dimitri, which was held in a local church, Joey and Sasha stood side by side, the child's face solemn and still. When Aurora had found out, she'd dropped everything and immediately driven up to the circus to be with them, but she refused to go to the funeral. At the cemetery, the tomb carried a small picture and the words:

Papa Afrika. A Great Performer died Oct 15th 1982, God rest his soul.

'A Great Performer', Joey liked the ambiguity of the inscription. Throughout the service Sasha said nothing. Only when the coffin was finally out of sight, he turned to Joey and whispered,

'Do you think he will be with my mother now?'

'But your mother isn't dead,' Joey said, holding his hands.

'I think she is. I saw her last night.'

Responses crowded Joey's head, that it was a dream, a shadow, the wind in the curtains but none of them crystallised into words.

'You can't hurt a ghost though, can you,' Sasha continued, 'so she can just slip away from him like this, pow!' And he squeezed his hand and opened it again, like a magic trick.

When they returned to the circus they were met by Rodrigo and Aurora. Seeing Sasha in his dark suit with his wild hair tamed, Rodrigo fell down on his knees and embraced him. Sasha comforted him, letting his small hands rest on Rodrigo's shaggy locks. Rodrigo leaned back on his haunches and rummaged in his bag.

'I have something for you,' he said. From his bag he pulled out

a long, thin
package. Sasha began to unwrap it. 'What is it?'

'It is Don Carlos's tail. I had it stuffed for you so you will always remember him.'

Sasha stroked it and smiled.

'And this is from me,' Aurora said, giving him the book on Africa. No-one had anything to offer in memory of his father.

After waking up several mornings in a row to find Sasha curled like a dog at his feet, it was finally agreed with Robles that Joey should move into the caravan with him. The three acrobats, busy as dragonflies, cleared away rubbish and bottles and old newspapers. Aurora and Negrita, with more sensitivity, came by afterwards to sort through some of Dimitri's personal possessions; photos and clothing and the bric-a-brac of the travelling life. Sasha and Joey came in as they were sorting through.

'Tell us what you would like to keep,' Aurora said 'then we'll throw away the rest.'

Joey watched the boy's eyes flicker over the piles of memorabilia and an assortment of whips and prods. He picked up a photo of his mother holding him in her arms, one of himself next to the lion, barely able to stand, and a flyer of his father as Papa Afrika with Don Carlos, his face surrounded by a flaming circle.

'Is that all?' Negrita said surprised. He nodded. She tucked the items into a cubby-hole behind his pillow, and dropped the rest into a rubbish sack. Aurora stopped her. She waited until the boy had left.

'Keep some of the photos. No-one should destroy all their past. Sometimes you need these things to know how far you've come.' She took the rest of the flyers and the best of the artefacts and wrapped them in a cloth.

'This looks like Sasha's birth certificate,' Negrita said. Aurora came over to look. '*Elena Luis Sandoval and...*' Negrita whistled, 'the father is down as *Ernesto Concha Morales (deceased).*'

Aurora looked over her shoulder, 'So he wasn't even Dimitri's son. Well there you go, and *she* called him Diego.'

She looked up at Joey, 'Are you okay?' Joey nodded. A thought had crossed his mind, but then he'd dismissed it.

'I'll keep this safe for when he is older and able to handle all of this history. Two deaths are enough. Let him have some peace.'

29

May 1983

'We will soon be the most famous circus in Mexico,' Robles said with a surfeit of braggadocio. He was sitting in his trailer on a pitch outside of Puebla, the home town of his brother-in-law.

It was eight months since Dimitri's death and the circus had continued on its southerly journey, stopping wherever Robles had managed to get a good deal or in this case, see a long-lost relative. Blanca and Negrita were chatting to Concepción, and her new boyfriend. It was late and the show had gone well.

'I better put you on the bill soon, Joey Pachuca, or I might lose you,' Robles laughed.

'Not yet,' Joey said, 'what you saw all those months ago was just the beginning. I have much more to offer.' He still hadn't got the chance he was waiting for to perform in his own right. He did acrobatics sometimes, and took part in the parade, but he had to bide his time. It was very frustrating. Still, when he finally got his chance they would never forget him.

Robles slapped him on the back, and plucked at the cuffs of his new shirt. 'I would like to introduce you all to Señora Forbes.'

Joey had noticed her, with her dark hair and tanned skin. She could have been a relative, or one of the many circus associates that Robles had but she didn't look the part. For starters, she was wearing hiking shorts and trainers. Most of the women Robles knew were squeezed into tight jeans and teetering heels. She smiled at the group, waved her hand around.

'Señora Forbes is a journalist, a Norte-Americana but we won't hold that against her.' Everyone laughed. 'She would like to write an article and take some pictures of us for the *National Geographic*.'

Joey's heart jumped at the familiar sound of those words, and he was there in his living room with his ma playing 'whereshallwego', leafing through the yellow- edged magazine full of its palaces and pagodas and pygmies and princes, his head bursting with wonder and longing. He rubbed his feet together.

'She is photographing Mexican circuses and has chosen ours.' Robles beamed. Excited gossip buzzed around the trailer.

Joey was exercising when Señora Forbes approached him.

'*Buenas tardes,*' she said, 'I join you?' Joey shrugged and indicated for her to sit down.

'*Yo soy* Janice Forbes.' She offered her hand, freckled and strong, with a gold wedding ring he noticed.

Joey shook it. 'Joey Pachuca'

'*Que raro*, un-usual,' she said. Joey tried not to smirk as she tried out English words with a Spanish accent. He'd heard rumours that the girls had made her repeat her mistakes over and over again for their amusement.

'I talk you your life in circus okay? How many years you have?' Her schoolgirl Spanish was charming and comical. She stumbled on through a few more questions and he chuckled.

'*Es mi Español. Oh que malo*! Usual I travel with friend. She talk Spanish good but she not able to arrive. I want to do this job very much.'

'Don't worry,' Joey said in English.

She looked up startled. 'You're American?'

Joey shook his head, 'Irish.'

She threw up her hands and cheered, 'Why didn't anyone tell me? You have saved my life.' She took out a tape machine. 'You mind if I use one of these, I never learned shorthand, too busy playing football with the boys, and running up mountains for all that girl stuff. Now I can't tell you how often I wished I'd taken a class.'

'You're married?' Joey said pointing to her ring.

She nodded and rummaged in her bag. She pulled out a wallet of photos.

'These are my kids, Kate, and Nick and Jessie, and that's my husband, A.O. He's a musician and a teacher.' Joey looked at them, their father's arms around their shoulders, their big white smiles. They looked lucky.

'They are beautiful,' he said giving her back the photo. 'Do you miss them?'

'Like crazy. I even miss the dog, but travelling is in my blood. So Joey, tell me about your role. You're a high-wire walker, I saw you practising yesterday. Incredible! You looked so completely in control. Aren't you afraid of falling?'

Joey smiled. 'I am not on the bill yet but I hope to be soon. I have excellent balance, sensitive feet.' Janice looked down at the feet in question, still in their birdskin shoes.

'What strange shoes. Are they specially designed for the high-wire?'

'They were made for me by a witch.' Joey laughed. He'd never told this to anyone at the circus, hadn't intended to tell anyone.

'A witch? If I buy you dinner will you tell me the story?'

There was freedom in revelation, he discovered, and he decided to unburden himself to this woman so far away from home. She would understand what it was to leave everything. She would understand about the geography of loneliness and loss, the topography of hope and disappointment. She would know what family meant. And she worked for the *National Geographic*.

They sat in a bar in downtown Puebla until the early hours, nursing their glasses, toying with the remains of a meal. They reminisced in English about first love and forgiveness, wanderlust and circuses, the smell of horses, the reek of poverty and despair, and the feeling of the ground moving beneath one's feet.

He told her of his father's violence and his fear that it lay in him too – that seed of destruction. Could he tell her the final element to his story? No, he couldn't. He remembered what had happened with Teresa, so when she asked about his mother, he simply said that he'd lost touch. She accepted that and for the moment it was the best he could do.

They got a cab back just as the sun was beginning to peer over the horizon, staining everything saffron, taking the chill off the air, and waking the birds. Joey walked as if he'd shed a life, left it with this journalist to turn into type and image, freed himself of its weight. How would Marta have described it? – freeing up his heart.

In the crisp light Janice took photos of him, arms outstretched, staring proudly into the camera, his feet barely touching the wire.

'Where will I send it? You'll be on the road again soon.'

'Poste Restante Mexico City. Aurora is our courier. She brings us the mail when she comes. I'll jot down the address.'

She took the piece of paper and folded it into her wallet.

'So,' she said the following day as she stood at her car door, 'what will be the end of your story?'

'Isn't it always *and they lived happily ever after*?' he joked, but inside a string of words was running through his head: forgiveness, absolution, resurrection, transformation, all those religious words that had meant so little to him before. He wanted free of those ropes that still anchored him to his past, dragging him down, making his feet heavy and awkward: the guilt, the self-pity, fear, rage, worthlessness. He wanted to rise above the earth and let the sun hit him full square. But they wouldn't just fall away, he had to release them, only then would he be ready to go where the air would take him. Maybe that's what Doña Marta had meant.

He looked at Janice, who was still waiting for a serious answer.

'Lightness,' he said.

She tipped her head, 'Of spirit, of heart, of body, of mind?'

'Yes, all of those please.'

She laughed. 'You don't want much then.'

It was his turn to smile, 'You know, it's not a wanting, it's a letting go.'

She leaned across and kissed him on the cheek, 'Good luck, Joey.'
'Let's not lose touch.'

Joey was truly sad to see her go. She had come from a place full of wild landscapes, of streams and horses. She was from the place of Joey's imagination, but she'd found him, given him respite from his dark places, and Joey felt grateful to her. He watched her drive away in the big hire car, the cream and beige of a palomino and wondered if their paths would cross again.

When the edition of the *National Geographic* arrived, they clustered around to look at the pictures. There was a beautiful one of the jugglers looking up into the sky together as the clubs spun in the air above them, and one of Concepción, practising the splits against the side of a truck, a book in her hand, 'Ay, I look so fat!' she said.

Then there was a double page of Joey. He was caught in the morning light, still and calm, and above him three of Aurora's birds fluttered, their wings a white blur.

'All that coverage and you're not even on the bill yet!' Concepción said enviously.

He grinned. 'It's my good looks, Concepción.'

He felt Sasha's hand in his. Joey, unable now to refer to him as Sasha, had taken to calling him Hijo, 'Son.' He loved the double meaning this had in English, my son, my sun. He'd tried to explain it to Aurora, and was grateful that she hadn't for once made fun of him. The rest of the circus soon picked up on it, and before long the name Sasha was almost forgotten.

Hijo pulled down the magazine and tried to peer into its pages. 'Is there one of me?' he said excitedly. They turned the page, a small picture showed him in a water fight with Dora, and a group of laughing children.

He frowned. 'There is nothing of me because I am not a performer. If Don Carlos was still alive they would have put a big picture of me in there with him. I'm just a nobody.' and he wrenched his hand free and ran off.

'Hey,' Joey called out, but Hijo didn't respond.

'Don't worry he'll get over it,' Blanca said squeezing his shoulder. 'He needs to find a new skill. Look, there is something about you in the article Joey!' Blanca began to read:

Joey Pachuca has a life from a fairy tale. He ran away as a youth from Ireland, stowed away on a ship, had a life of danger and struggle in Mexico City then finally found his true self in the ring of the Mexican circus. Although still a relative novice, he is gifted with extraordinarily sensitive feet, which make him a natural on the high-wire, or as shown here, practising more daring stunts on the low-wire.'

Blanca looked up at him, a puzzled smile on her lips. 'We know so little about you Joey!'

He reddened. 'She tells a good story, 'he said. 'She must be half-Irish.'

Throughout the summer of 1983 the circus wove its way through the states of Tlaxcala and Puebla where the snowy tops of Popocatépetl and Ixtaccihuatl dominated the horizon, with only the occasional thin plume of smoke to disturb the blue sky.

Robles decided in October to brave the more volatile regions of Mexico, drawn inexorably to the southern cities with their buzzing, tropical life. Joey was furious; they'd skimmed the edge of Mexico City and now instead of touring the city again, they were heading even further down country, but his fury soon turned to joy.

'We have had publicity,' Robles said, 'we must capitalise on it, a new venue and new audiences.' He was addressing them one morning as they sat drinking their coffee. 'I think we should go to Veracruz, somewhere with money and tourists. I will have posters made, like this,' he unfurled a mock-up, featuring some exciting new photos – *As featured in National Geographic* – was emblazoned across the centre.

'¡*Maravilloso Joey Pachuca!*' it read, finally his name and his face on a poster. He punched the air and whooped with joy. On the way back to the trailer he now shared with Hijo, he studied the copy that Robles had given him, unable to shift the smile from his face.

When Aurora arrived that weekend he showed her the poster and she hugged him, and swung him around overwhelmed with excitement.

'Oh, let me make you something special to wear,' she said, her eyes gleaming. Joey thought of her stitches next to his skin and he prickled with desire, but he shook his head.

'I promised myself I would wear the costume Lazaro gave me before he left. It is my homage to him but you will come, won't you, and bring your sister and your niece?'

She folded her arms and twisted her mouth into a pout. 'Well, I don't know. You reject my offer of a hand-made costume and so I'll have to think about it.' She pretended to turn on her heel and march away, but he pulled her towards him, and she didn't resist. He could feel the pulse racing in her wrist, as frantic as his own heartbeat. She looked up into his eyes and he leaned over her and kissed her very softly on the mouth. When he pulled away her eyes were still closed.

That afternoon, Joey unable to sit still, had jumped on a bus out to the edges of Puebla. He spotted, on a long wide street dotted with office blocks, a miraculous field of corn planted in an abandoned lot, and he jumped off the bus. He ran through the tall lush plants, dragging at the seed heads with his hands, gulping breath like free beer. Oh joy! Life jumping with sizzling fizz! Oh, the birds were crazy. And the insects were weird. What God had made those *and* love?

The ground beneath his feet was on the move. He took off his shoes and let his toes dig into the crumbly soil. There it was now, that sensation, waves and rumblings, rumours of something right there underneath the heel of his foot. He pushed in deeper, straining to understand it, like stretching to hear a conversation just out of earshot. But he didn't understand it. He just had to accept it, feel it, like this other thing. Like this Love.

And later in the night he thought of her again, that kiss still burning on his mouth, the feel of her body in his arms. Of all the girls he'd slept with, of all the things he'd done, nothing matched that thrilling brush of her lips. The bed was cool and then hot and he rolled over and she was there and he awoke, and she wasn't, she was just the sheet warmed up by his body heat.

He groaned, rolled onto his back, then got up and stood by the window. The moon over the Big Top was smeared by clouds, and at the edge of the encampment the horses stamped and shuffled and here in this trailer he thought of covering her naked body with his.

Even though he knew he shouldn't, with the boy sleeping quietly close by, he lay down on his sheet pushing and rising, thinking of her, slipping his tongue into the hollow of his fist – a poor replica for her mouth – and then, spent, he drifted into a fitful sleep, and woke early, wild and eager for the new day, with the knowledge deep in his bones that she loved him too.

30

His moment had come at last. He was edgy. Every nerve in his body seemed to be fluttering and hypersensitive. When one of the jugglers brushed past him on her way to the ring, he felt like he'd been stung. His audition had shown what he was capable of technically, but could he produce that extra something?

Aurora, here with her sister and niece, had agreed to meet up with him afterwards. He was relieved, afraid that if he saw her beforehand he would not be able to concentrate.

He had planned something impressive but also beautiful, full of difficult turns and dance steps. He stood in the wings, stepping from foot to foot, trying to keep his breathing steady. He was in the second half, a prestigious position for a new act. Blanca and Negrita stopped by and hugged him, still in their costumes after their performance. Señor Robles in his splendid ringmaster's jacket was performing a little magic and being a stooge for one of the clowns whilst the stage was cleared and the high-wire checked.

Joey closed his eyes, and felt his heart galloping. His feet were calm and still though, and soon his heart steadied too. She would be out there watching him and he would show her what he had become. He pulled the cloak she had made him after all around his shoulders, with its delicate embroidery invisible to anyone but him. He rubbed his cheek against it. Lazaro's silver costume hidden beneath gave him the courage he needed.

The clapping and laughter signified that the clown had left, taking Robles' giant underpants printed with the Mexican flag with him, a silly trick that the children loved. Joey took a deep breath, as Robles began his introductory patter. He rolled his shoulders, flexed his feet and at the mention of his name lifted his head, smiled broadly and ran into the ring.

The lights dazzled him and he spun on his heel and let the colours bounce off his cape. He unfastened it, handed it to Robles, bowed and ascended the ladder. At the top he stared down, looking for her face, and as if from the roof of the Big Top itself, a shaft of light picked out the side of her cheek as she leaned towards her sister.

Down below, the net shimmered, and he knew he would not need it. His feet, like greyhounds ready at the sound of the pistol, responded to his first step onto the cable. He danced down the wire, his feet barely touching it as he jumped and landed, twisting and leaping in time to the music. The splits followed by the triple backward somersault brought cheers and whistles from the crowd.

The fifteen minutes of his performance passed in a flash. It was almost instinctive and the sureness of his feet caused applause to erupt from the crowd. When he finally somersaulted off the net onto the ground and took a bow, the audience were on their feet, clapping along to the music. The sound of their cheering filled his body with energy and he wanted to run up the ladder and do it all again, convinced now he could produce something even more sensational. He took several bows before collecting his cape and slipping out into the wings to the pats on the back from the gathered performers. But away from the hectic crowd and despite an astonishing performance he knew that the extra thing had eluded him again.

Aurora, dazzling in a long green silk dress and coral-coloured beads, had come backstage to congratulate him. Her sister, older and thinner had shaken his hand shyly, and her niece Laura had clutched Aurora's hand, but stared at him constantly, barely uttering a word when he tried to speak to her.

Aurora had chucked her under the chin, and whispered 'Don't

be shy, *mi flora pequeña*. If he thinks you are lost for words he will get a very big head,' and the girl had giggled.

The celebration after the show was long and exhausting, and despite the handshakes and the luxury of genuine admiration, he was glad to get to bed. That night Joey thought about Aurora working in the city – in a bar, he'd discovered – earning extra money to support her sister and the niece whom she clearly adored. Her sister's husband had been killed in one of the frequent auto accidents in Mexico City when his daughter was just seven years old. Having someone else to care for had motivated Joey to work as hard as he could. Aurora, it appeared, was in the same boat but at least he was working at something he loved.

Earlier that evening, he'd sat on the edge of Hijo's bed, telling him half-remembered stories from his boyhood, Hans Anderson's tales, Aesop's fables, watching the story played out across his sleepy face and he was struck once again by his luck. This boy had chosen him to be his protector. The sheer improbability of it!

But along with the pleasure there was anxiety. Supposing he got it wrong? After all, his parents had. What had he ever done to warrant such trust? The responsibility frightened him. Sometimes if he thought about it when he was walking on the high-wire, he began to shake and lose balance. He didn't know anything about raising a child.

Then there was the fear in the night when some dream separated him from his boy and he'd wake up sweating with his pulse rattling away like an out of control express train. He'd have to get up and tip-toe across the trailer, pull back the curtain that shielded the boy's bed, and check. There he'd be, hand flung back, cheeks pink in the heat of sleep, mouth working at some invisible conversation and relief would wash over him.

Joey turned over but he couldn't sleep; the excitement of the evening had left him restless. The sight of Aurora still shimmered in his head. Quietly he got up, pulled on a sweatshirt and slipped out of the trailer. It was still, no-one was up. The traffic rumbled past in the distance and the night insects fluttered and buzzed around the lights. It was at times like this that he wished he hadn't given up smoking. He needed something to do with his hands, something to slow the night-train of his thoughts

He knew his performance had amazed the others but it hadn't been good enough for him. Tomorrow he would set to his new profession with increased determination. Now he no longer had to fulfil so many regular duties he could devote more time to his training.

Top of the bill were a trapeze act, from Guadalahara; the clowns were still a big attraction, and a knife-throwing act, Roberto and Juana, also pulled in the crowds. The *aerialistas* were due to leave in a month. Then perhaps, with some space freed up, he would move up the billing. He wriggled his toes in his birdskin shoes, grateful for the work they had done for him, calming the ferocity of this uneasy landscape. As he passed the animal enclosures, Dora poked out a hopeful trunk and he let her caress his face for a moment until, disappointed with the lack of food, she went back to hoovering the ground for some overlooked scrap. Negrita and Blanca's two horses stamped and steamed in the chill of the early hours.

Joey had steered clear of the horses; the smell of them reminded him of fields at home. Those days were like something viewed through smeared spectacles and before he'd met Marta he'd tried to keep it that way. But at that moment, he dropped his guard and Ireland was there with him; its dampness, its rich grass, a horse galloping towards him from the corner of a field for an apple and a good word.

He reached out his hand and made a clicking sound in his throat. Negrita's horse, Eng, lifted her head and stared at him. He called again, 'Come on girl, here now.' She turned, a rippling of muscle beneath the grey-white coat, and trotted towards him. Cheng, disturbed by the separation, tossed her head and followed behind. He felt the warm, pliant rubber of her mouth in his hands, the damp breath on his fingers. She tossed her head then pushed her nose against him. He took hold of her mane and rested his face against her cheek. The rich horse smell filled his nostrils, and he was there with the desert sky above him, the coyote wail of his mother a vivid memory. He felt his throat seize up. Eng shook her head from his grip, moved closer to him and stretched her head right over the fence to let her chin rest on his back.

Joey stood absolutely still, feeling the weight of her pressing on his spine. He gave into it, let her rest there. As he stood, the gentle snorts of Cheng in the background, he felt the weight of that memory lifting off his soul, and his feet resting a little more lightly on the ground.

31

Oaxaca, September 1983

The squeals and gasps of the audience and the explosion of applause turned Joey's blood to champagne. His pay packet was also increasing and he began to think about buying his own trailer, then he could move out of the one that Dimitri had owned, which echoed at night with the past. And something else had changed. Since his evening with the journalist, the sensations in his feet had altered somehow. He could still feel the earth writhing and stretching beneath him but it was as if the static had been turned down. Hope stretched before him like an open road, on which he might walk firmly and lightly into his future.

After months in the tropical villages and towns of Veracruz, Robles had decided to return to his beloved Oaxaca with its elegant squares and colonial buildings washed and faded by sunlight. He'd met his wife here, and tinged as it was with sadness, there was a melancholy pleasure to be had in a place that held so many memories for him. Whilst Joey was keen to visit the renowned city, he was becoming impatient. He viewed every new destination in terms of the ease with which Aurora might visit. It had been two months now since he'd seen her. Two months with only the memory of that one kiss. He'd thought about it so many times he feared he might wear it out. Was it possible to use up a memory, wear it paper-thin like a love letter until one day it disintegrated and disappeared into the ether?

All through his morning exercise routine with Hijo, he had been thinking about her, using the rhythm of her name to help him with the repetitions, when the boy had dropped the weights and whooped.

'Aurora!' he yelled out and ran towards her.

Joey looked up and there she was in a long dress, its sleeves gathered at the wrist, a scarf tied carelessly around her hair, walking towards them. Had he called her up like some ghost, forced her to come to him through the sheer force of his desire? She ducked her head to dodge a drying shirt and Joey caught a flash of her smile. Hijo bowled into her nearly knocking her to the ground.

'Hi there *niño*! I have missed you!'

'But I have been here all the time.'

She laughed and ruffled his hair. 'But unfortunately I have not.' She looked up as Joey approached wiping his hands on his towel. She waved her hand a little at him, and he smiled. His body ached at the sight of her.

'I hope he hasn't put his grubby hands all over your clothes,' he said, wagging his finger at Hijo. She looked down at her dress, which was smeared with black.

'No, don't worry, that's fabric paint.' Joey's eyes flitted over the marks, lingering too long on the curves that filled out her dress. They reached her face at last and met the amused look in her eyes. Caught out, his face burned.

'I hear you're the circus's great new hope. There was even a picture of you in the national press last week,' she said.

Joey bowed, clicked his heels. 'Thank you. I thought I'd never say this but I can't wait to get back to Mexico City.'

She laughed. 'I know – its pollution, its traffic, its dirt.'

'Its colour, its life, its music, its soul and…you,' Joey added.

She looked away. 'Well, I miss the circus too,' Aurora added, looking around her at the chaotic trailers, the washing and the piles of props. She sighed and played with Hijo's hair. 'He seems happy. I knew he would be in safe hands with you. And my sister and my niece needed me.'

'It's good to be needed, and it was great to meet them.' They were speaking like strangers. He felt like that idiot boy he was when they first met.

'I'm going to pick up some special fabrics in the next few days. Did you know that Robles has asked me to make you a new costume?'

Before Joey could reply, Hijo grabbed her hand. 'We are going to another circus tonight,' he blurted out. 'They have lions. Joey wants to see the high-wire lady. She is called…' his face clouded over, 'What's she called?'

Joey grinned, 'She's called the 'Unforgettable Ula'.' Aurora laughed and in that one burst of sound he felt the tension leave them both.

'Why don't you come?' 'We're leaving early and taking a couple of trucks, there will be plenty of room.'

She chewed her lip for a second as if deliberating and Joey's foot twitched a little. She grinned and whisked Hijo into the air, 'Well, how could I say no?'

'Let me take you to see my new friends.' Hijo said as she dropped him back on the ground. She looked up at Joey questioningly.

'He's found a family of iguanas over by that wall there. He's thinking of training them.'

She waved at Joey as the boy pulled her towards the edge of the site where the scrubland took over. Joey followed her until she disappeared from view. He checked his watch; how long did he have? He wanted to clean himself up, shave, put on a decent shirt. He hurried towards his trailer and then stopped in his tracks. Was this then the beginning of something at last?

In the dappled shadows of the Big Top, Hijo sat between them, his eyes glittering with the reflections of the lights around him. Just once Joey turned and glanced at Aurora. She was staring up at the aerial ballet, her mouth slightly open and her hands clenched in front of her.

He gazed around the ring. In the half-light, with the music rippling over them, the acrobatic dancer swirling and tipping on her red ribbons of silk, a strange sensation began to move through him. It trickled like a spring thaw; it made him draw a sudden breath. He hadn't even known he was frozen, now he wondered which parts of him were not locked up like dark green glaciers, and what might happen if this feeling continued, what might he be like under all this invisible ice, who might he be?

He turned to find Aurora staring at him, and pow!, another glassy piece of him disintegrated, floating away, filling his head with a gasp of oxygen, and he was up there with the acrobat un-rolling from the swags of red silk, hurtling to the floor, then stop-ping short, deliciously on the brink. He laughed and Aurora wrin-kled her nose and laughed back at him.

Oh, that was a night! He lay back on his bed, the light snores of Hijo his background music. Like a night of drinking it was blurred and shot through with sudden wild memories, his face reddening as he wondered what crazy things he'd said. He remembered dragging Aurora and Hijo in a mad run down a dark road lit by fireflies, as the others trailed along behind, her shriek of fear and Hijo's throaty chuckle. He remembered swinging Hijo between them, his stick legs pedalling in the air like a cartoon cat off the edge of a cliff. His feet had been full of sparks as he leapt and spun, dragging Aurora into his grasp, swapping her for Hijo until all three of them were bent over panting for breath, their ribs aching, laughter dropping out of them like quicksilver, enveloping everyone, until the whole party on that dusty back road was bewitched. It was an evening when the moon broke into his head and mixed it up spilling his dreams on the path in front of them where he was sure every person could see them and laugh at him.

And although she had said goodbye to him at her door he knew something had changed. When he woke up the following day, the circus was under a spell, sleepy and smiling, quiet and serene, performers stretching and exercising as if all their troubles had been eased. Josefina spent the entire day sitting on her stoop with a magazine. Concepción, her face a permanent smile, walked with her arms wrapped around Miguel, the boy she'd been desperately uninterested in for months. And just when it seemed the circus might collapse under the weight of its enchantment, fall asleep under its feathery lightness and never perform again, a bedraggled creature was spotted limping up the road.

32

It was Hijo who spotted it first – a dog, yellow and shaggy with huge paws and a tail that seemed to operate independently. 'Please let me keep her,' he pleaded with Joey. Joey tried not to look at the boy's eyes, so dark and deep they could swallow you up.

'We don't know where she has come from. Maybe she belongs to someone. Perhaps she is sick.'

Hijo stared at the yellow dog that had rolled onto its back and was shimmying endearingly in the dirt.

Joey could feel his resolve crumbling. 'She might not get on with the other dogs,' he said as Rodrigo's German Shepherd dog came bounding over and immediately wagged its tail. Hijo looked up and grinned.

'Rodrigo, help me here.'

'Don't ask me, I'm not going to be the big bad wolf.'

'Okay, we'll have the vet check her over and if she is healthy and if Señor Robles agrees, we can keep her.' Hijo threw his arms around Joey's waist and Negrita rolled her eyes.

The dog was returned to them, clean and clear of disease. 'The good news first, she's already been spayed, so no surprises on the way,' the vet had said. 'The bad news is she's going to be big, looks like a Golden Retriever /Great Dane cross. Not surprising she got dumped, she'll take some feeding.'

Joey opened his arms in resignation. 'We are used to feeding a strongman and an elephant – this will be nothing to us!'

'What are you going to call her?' Robles said

Hijo was gawping at the dog as it chased huge lumps of meat and biscuits around a bowl. Snuffling and grunting, she gulped back the chunks and swallowed them without even chewing.

'I'm going to call her 'El Lobo', because she eats like a wolf.'

Robles slapped him on the back and chuckled.

And that is how Hijo became 'Hijo del Lobo' – Son of the Wolf. The crowd loved the small boy, and the clumsy dog that got all the tricks wrong. She turned out to be a willing and enthusiastic animal with a gentle disposition. Joey stood by the curtain each night watching Hijo, the clattery soundtrack of Jungle Book throbbing around the tent. And when he bowed out to loud applause and cheering, Joey cleared the grit that had unaccountably got into his eye.

'My father used to do this trick with Don Carlos,' Hijo said one afternoon as he got the dog to roll over at the drop of a stick. It was the first time since his father's death that Hijo had mentioned him. Hijo watched as Lobo chewed on the stick. 'I think my father let Don Carlos kill him.'

Joey lifted the boy's chin, looked into his eyes. 'What? Why do you say that?'

'My papa knew lions and he knew Don Carlos.'

Joey sighed and pushed Hijo's hair back from his face. 'We will never know what happened to your father. He is gone but I will never leave you, do you understand me?'

33

The famed church of Oaxaca was the first one he'd been into in years. He'd only gone because Doña Rosa insisted. It was the mass for 'The Day of the Dead'. After much persuasion, Joey agreed to drive her there. He refused to go to any of the *ofrendas* and stare at the ghoulish collections of objects laid out on the decorated altars.

'I don't get it,' he said to her in the car. 'Why do the dead need bottles of tequila and cigars and special bread? If spirits of the dead exist then they don't have bodies do they, so what can they do with the food?'

Doña Rosa shrugged. 'It's tradition Joey, it's my tradition, and the spirits do exist, I've seen them.' Joey screwed up his face but said nothing.

Doña Rosa was a changed woman since Dimitri's death. She'd made a shrine in her trailer, offering prayers to the Virgin of Guadalupe and prayed each day for humility. Her remorse nagged at Joey. She hadn't really done anything, except present a man with the evidence of his crimes – surely that was a good thing? But Doña Rosa felt differently. She had done what she had no right to do, she had been his judge and perhaps he had turned into his own executioner.

'I have been a proud and vain woman, Joey and that is my sin.'

Not only did she pray but she also she tried to make reparations. She took up good works, organising performances in prisons and in places for the sick. He watched her counting the beads on her rosary and muttering to herself. He hoped she was saying one for him.

The church was overwhelming with its soaring ceilings and golden chapels, its statues robed in velvet and weeping blood. It turned his stomach. The smell of the incense made him dizzy and the lilting chant of prayers with the jarring amplification made him want to run. He made his excuses and slipped out into the sunlight.

Piles of flat *pan de muerte* – bread of the dead – were stacked at the back of the stalls. Comical and macabre skeleton figures jostled for space. At least they made sense. After all, saint or sinner, surgeon or high-wire walker, we were all a pile of bones in the end. He shivered. He didn't want to think about the end because he knew that for some it came brutally and with no warning.

The service over, Doña Rosa caught up with him. She was wreathed in smiles, her arm linked with that of a round and dapper man with a gleaming pate and a suspiciously black moustache. 'Go back on your own. I have met an old friend.' She patted his arm and smiled coquettishly.

Joey nodded. 'Can I borrow the key to your trailer and look through some of your books?'

Joey spent the afternoon trawling through her archives looking for inspiration but also for the answer to a more personal question. He must have looked at that photograph a hundred times of the travelling circus in Cork. He knew there must be more pictures here somewhere, the same circus in a different place perhaps, at a different time, maybe even a list of the performers. It was only a hunch, one he could barely give credence to, but still it nagged him. He approached it methodically working his way from left to right and from top to the bottom of each pile.

He'd spent hours doing this when he wasn't performing and practising, it helped to keep thoughts of Aurora from swamping him. She'd asked Robles if she could come back to the circus full-time after the Christmas season. She would do matinée and evening performances, and see her family when she wasn't required. Joey could hardly wait. The night they'd visited the circus was a template for happiness that had stamped itself on his heart. He was sure she had felt the same. Joey felt the ropes of the past giving way, freeing him a little more each day.

34

December 1983

The night of the 15th December she came to watch him again. He spotted her, in a white ruffled blouse sitting next to a laughing Otavio. Joey marvelled. She could even make that old misery smile!

Christmas was approaching and the circus bustled with holiday makers, chattering and laughing as the lights went down. He was wearing the cloak Robles had commissioned her to make for him. *'Maravilloso! Fantastico! Joey Pachuca!'* it exclaimed in red and blue on the shimmering fabric. He pulled it around his shoulders, felt the touch of her hand in it.

He steadied his breathing, and listened. He could hear the voice of Señor Robles winding the audience up, rolling his Rs out like red carpets to thrill them. He rubbed his eyes, feeling the silky dryness of the chalk dust against his lids and he imagined the scene beneath him, the gaping mouths of the children, half-chewed popcorn clogging their teeth, sticks of candy-floss tilting in their hands, their eyes fixed on the figure above them.

He shifted slightly, the platform juddered. He heard little gasps from the women as they bit their knuckles, and tried to look away. They'd all seen him climb up the swaying rope ladder, higher and higher, the spotlight following him with its gleaming finger, now he would give them something else, this time he would do it.

He stepped onto the wire, felt the music swirling inside him, closed his eyes and waited. His mind cleared, cold and still. The music hung in his head, suspended like mist and then his feet began to dance. His hands swirled around his body, his feet leaping, resting and pivoting beneath him. He imagined she was in his arms, her skin hot against his, dancing just for her. He forgot he was on a wire, forgot he was in a Big Top, in Oaxaca, Mexico. He could feel nothing but the music and his feet guiding him, controlling him.

The audience urged him on, but their sound became part of the music in his head, and as the rhythm slowed, his feet reacted to it gently, inching him forward on the wire. Delicately, he dropped to his knee and with his arms outstretched, he arched his back. The audience stilled.

Then it happened – up through his feet, a surge of energy like a beam of light, arcing through his body and into his neck. He felt it illuminate him, firing up each cell, every membrane and each capillary. It rushed through him like a flood over parched soil, percolating through fissures, drenching each particle, on and on, up into his skull until he opened his mouth and gasped.

He heard the sound mirrored in the crowd below, a huge indrawing of breath, but not fear, not anxiety, not even wonder; it was something else. Holding on to that moment he arched his back, stretching his neck and throwing his head back until it touched the wire behind him, and then the beam exploded.

It pulsed from his feet through his body into his head in a whirr of energy that made his flesh sing. He heard a stifled cry from below but he let it wash over him, he wanted to laugh, to spill notes from his mouth like a fountain, let them pour over those people below, soaking them in joy. And in all of this, through all of this, he saw her face smiling up at him. Aurora – her eyes shining, her skin emanating a radiance that mixed with his own.

As the music began to subside, he raised his head from the wire, felt the coursing light begin to fade like a firework in the night sky, and slowly he stood up, his arms extended outwards in an ecstatic embrace.

No-one moved or clapped. He heard sniffles in the audience. Joey stared into the crowd. Otavio was weeping, his grey jowls trembling with emotion. Aurora and Josefina were clutching each other, slack-jawed. The audience, all of them – children and couples and old people with sticks – sat absolutely still, their faces rapt, serene, exuding a strange lightness. He smiled. He'd found it, the moment of bliss, the glimpse of heaven.

Robles, his face pale and stiff, lifted himself out of his seat and began to clap. The others still appeared too stunned to move. Robles clapped louder, and the audience began to join in as if shaken from a trance. Still no-one uttered a word. Joey jumped into the net and back-flipped into the ring. The shock when he hit the floor was immense. His feet felt like they'd been pounded with rocks. It took huge concentration just to stand upright, when all he wanted was to sink to the floor. He was exhausted, but for a brief moment, he was Mozart.

35

When Aurora met him after the show, she was shy and awkward. He took her hand and walked with her silently around the outskirts of the site. The moon slipped out from behind a cloud, its face bleary with sleep. Joey felt calm and sure of himself. He stopped and he lifted her face to his own. She stared at him, her eyes full of wonder and perhaps a little fear.

'Don't be afraid of me.'

She shook her head and smiled. 'I don't know what happened there but...' her eyes began to fill.

'What did you see?'

'I saw you, your face as if you were right next to me. I even lifted my fingers to touch your cheek.'

Joey's smile broadened, 'And I felt your fingers wanting to touch me,' and he stroked her cheek with his hand as he'd dreamed so often he would and he kissed her very gently on the mouth.

At the first touch of his lips she shivered and breathed deeply, as if she was drawing him into her. Her eyes were shut, her lips slightly parted, he pulled her closer, felt her body against his chest, and he kissed her again, holding her fast against him, afraid she might slip away.

When they finally separated, she took him by the hand and led him to her trailer. He kissed the back of her neck as she opened the doors, and as soon as they were inside, he took her in his arms, but she pushed him away.

'Stop, Joey.' She groaned and sat down suddenly, her dress billowing around her like a burst balloon.

'What is it, what have I done?'

She looked up at him, her face pleading, 'You? Oh you've done nothing! It's me. There is something I need to tell you.' She pressed her face into her palms. 'I've been dreading this moment.' He saw the thin brown fingers massaging her forehead, as if trying to loosen the secret that was keeping them apart. She looked up at him through her splayed hands, her eyes troubled. 'No-one at the circus knows about it except Señor Robles and even he doesn't know the full story.'

'You're making me nervous.' He thought for a moment of the rumours of her burned and scarred skin, 'Nothing you can say will stop me wanting you,' he said laughing a little, hoping it was true.

She inclined her head as if she'd read his thoughts. She stood up decisively and rummaging under a pile of net skirts on the bed, produced a leather-covered book.

'Look at this while I pour us a drink. I need some courage.' He heard the bottle clink nervously against the glasses. The liquid glinted like amber in the string of orange lights draped along the inside wall of the trailer.

The book was an album full of photos. He turned the page, lifted the thin tissue that covered it. There was a small, smiling girl with two braids and a crisp white blouse. On the next page she stood awkwardly in a frilly dress, a flower in her hair, and then he came upon a more formal one, a family portrait. He held it up as she folded back the table, threw all the net skirts onto the floor, and piled a soft rug and some pillows on top of them.

'My family, twelve children.'

'Twelve!'

'Good Catholics from Ciudad Juarez, a border town. The USA was our back garden, we were their outhouse.' She laughed. 'We thought the USA was heaven, we all wanted to go there and hang out with Liz Taylor and go to Hollywood. Didn't think the closest we would ever get to Hollywood stardom was cleaning the pools of the rich and famous.' She patted the nest she had made. 'Come and lie here with me.'

He joined her and with his back against a big cushion and she resting against him, he turned the pages slowly. 'Did you ever go there?'

'No, not Hollywood, never made it more than one hundred kilometres over the border, but I lived in the US for three years until I had to run away.' He looked down at her hair, the glint of the brandy as she swilled it around in the glass.

'My family was very poor, as you can imagine with so many children. My father was a labourer. My mother spent all day working. It was a struggle. I went to school, we all did for a couple of years, but I managed a few more than the others. I could read and write, and I wanted to be a secretary in a clean office, with a pot plant and a shiny typewriter with its own cover.'

'Like the movies?' He tried to imagine her combing her wayward locks into a secretarial bun, walking in sensible shoes. It was impossible.

'Like the movies,' she said.

The smell of the brandy was intoxicating. He leaned over and took a mouthful, felt it slip down his throat, leaving its glowing trail. He loved the weight of her body resting against his, the warmth increasing his own but it wasn't enough.

'One Sunday, I met a man in church. He was much older than me, an *Americano*, from a small town across the border and he was down on business. He was a devout Catholic, unmarried. He had lived with his mother until she'd died earlier that year. He was not handsome, a little fat, a little pale, and he wore these thick glasses that made his eyes wobble, but he was American and he had a nice car, and for some reason he took a shine to me.

'I loved the flattery. All the girls in my neighbourhood were so jealous and I got carried away with the romance of it. My mother was keen – if he had money I could help support the family. He was so well-behaved too, did nothing but hold my hand and peck me on the cheek, of course my mother was always there keeping an eye on him. He sent me flowers and bought me little gifts, but he was very formal.' She pressed her palms together in mock piety and gazed up to heaven. 'I should have realised that wasn't normal! But I was barely sixteen and I thought he was being a gentleman.

'I was a bit of a romantic myself, the passionate and dreamy type. I longed to be swept away by a strong man with thick hair and cowboy boots, a *charro!* I used to practise kissing on my arm until I made myself come up in bruises.'

Joey laughed, felt the swell of her breast above his hand and longed to touch her. 'So you married him?'

'Yes I married him. My family was so proud and waved and cried as we drove away in his Buick to live in the US.

'Then I walked into his mother's house and I felt like I'd walked into a tomb. The furniture was dark and dreary and the place felt stiff and sad. I did the best I could. At first he didn't even want me to leave the house but I persuaded him to let me do my own shopping and I agreed to wear slacks when I went out so no-one would stare at my legs. At first I thought it was sweet. I thought his was a new lover's jealousy.' She shook her head. 'I was so naïve!'

'So what went wrong?' Joey turned the album and saw a woman in a short ballet dress, her arms and legs tattooed up to the wrists. '*La Princesa Pintada*'– 'The Painted Princess', was written beneath the photo in white ink. He looked more closely and his mouth fell open.

'Is this you?' he said holding up the photo. She looked up into his face searching his eyes for disapproval. 'The bits fit to be photographed,' she said.

She shifted around in his lap and took his hands in her own. 'I am worried you'll think less of me, if I tell you the whole story. Oh Joey, it has been so hard just to be friends.'

He leaned forward clutched her arms in his and kissed her so hard she could barely breathe. 'Aurora, whatever it is, I will still love you.'

He'd said those words. In his desire to have her, he'd said those words, and another rope broke free. He kissed her neck, skimmed her nipples with his thumb, felt them contract like something struck by fire. She jumped and he caught her lip with his tooth, tasted the iron sourness of blood and pulled away. She turned her back to him and he kissed the back of her neck sending a shudder the length of her body. She slowly pulled her blouse from the waistband of her skirt. He stopped breathing for a moment.

'What I did will sound crazy, but remember I was young, angry and foolish. I'd been brought up to believe marriage was for life, and divorce meant excommunication. I'd be dancing with the devil for all eternity if I asked for a divorce.'

Joey shrugged. 'Nothing sounds crazy to me anymore.' He nuzzled her ear, letting his hands stray up under her blouse, feeling the warmth of her skin. She lifted her body at his touch and her eyelids fluttered.

'Sometimes we do things and we don't know why,' he said, remembering Paco's uncle and the rustle of notes in his own pocket, then later the thrill of pointless violence. He suddenly had a yearning to unburden himself of his own past but he dismissed it.

'At first the marriage was bearable. It was a novelty to me. He was obviously a virgin too, but for me sex seemed perfectly natural, funny and embarrassing, but natural. After all when you come from a big family you live close, you kind of form a picture of what might be going on.' She rested her hand on Joey's thigh and when she lifted it to emphasise a point he was sure its imprint was still there. He thought he might burst with longing.

'He, on the other hand, couldn't cope with it at all. He could hardly keep his hands off me but afterwards he would turn his face to the wall and apologise for the sinner he was. I tried to be understanding but it made me so angry. But the more bitter and resentful I became the more he wanted me and then the worse he felt about it.'

Joey's hand touched her and she jerked away from him resting her head against the cool metal edge of the folded table.

'He began to go out a lot in the evenings. He said he had taken up cards as a way to ease his stress. He'd joined a local bridge club and it took place at different people's houses.

'He wasn't much of a liar, so curious, I followed him one night. He went into a house on the outskirts of town. At first I thought he had another woman, but when I peered in through a crack in the curtains I could hardly believe it. I saw a man beating himself with a little whip. Another was holding a Bible while a woman stuck pins into his skin. I was so shocked. I went back home and waited for him. When I confronted him, he quickly confessed. Turned out he'd joined an evangelical Catholic splinter group – The Church of the Three Nails – that's what they called themselves.

'It was a very small congregation but they were *muy extremo*. They met in each other's homes, because they knew the Catholic Church didn't approve of what they did.' She lifted her head, and took a swallow of brandy. He watched her throat rise and fall.

'As a result of this new craziness, things got harder for me. He began to blame me for his desires, said it was my fault, and that I must have a devil inside me. I suppose I should have just left then, but I didn't, I couldn't. I was brought up to believe that girls should do as they were told by their husbands and I thought it would change. Well, it did in a way I could not have imagined.

'He'd always worn these ugly glasses, he was very short-sighted but he started getting severe headaches. He went to see a specialist and was told he had a deteriorating eye condition. He would go blind and there was nothing they could do for him. He was horrified, understandably, but was convinced that this was God's punishment for looking at women with lust.'

'He sounds crazy. Where did he think babies came from?'

She shook her head, 'I don't know what he thought although I asked him often enough. He had psychological problems but I was utterly dependent on him and I hardly spoke any English. I was a healthy young girl and I wanted to be touched and held, not told I was the cause of his blindness.'

'So what did you do? Is that when you ran away?'

She shook her head and bit her lip. 'No, I did something completely reckless. Even now I don't know what got into me. It's funny. Your whole life can pivot on one decision made in an instant with barely a consideration.' With her back to him she lifted her hair. 'Undo the first four buttons of my shirt.'

His hands shaking a little, he did as she asked. He stared at the image that spread between her shoulder blades, tracing it with his finger, and sighed with relief. Was this old-fashioned tattoo, her terrible secret? He smiled to himself and pulled her towards him, until she nestled in his lap again, his arms wrapped around her waist.

'I was really bored one day, it was hot and the house was stifling. I'd cleaned everything until it shone. I'd listened to 'How to learn English' records and baked some cookies. So I took a bus to the next town. It was quite a long way. I wandered around its streets staring in at windows, looking at the couples walking along hand in hand and feeling sorry for myself, and then I strayed into a seedier district.

'The shops were tatty and shuttered, there were pawnbrokers and second-hand stores and then I saw this sign, 'Tattoo Parlour'. The window was full of elaborate drawings of hearts and flames and banners and birds, and there was one that caught my eye of Adam and Eve entwined, and they looked so beautiful, so free. Why not? I thought. I went in and I said:

I want a tattoo, that one in the window, like it was a dress or a coat, hah! I tell you he looked me up and down a bit suspicious, asked how much I had, and asked me if I was sure. I nodded. *Absolutely,* I said.

Where do you want it? That stopped me in my tracks. I thought for a while and then I said *My back, I want it on my back*. So that one you can see was the first one, it was four inches high and painful but I didn't care I was so excited.

'As he worked I gazed at the marvellous designs and photographs of men and women with their whole bodies tattooed. When I left my body was smarting, but the pain was a kind of release.'

'But what did your husband say?' Joey asked, fascinated

'I was very careful at first, but finally when he did notice, it was night time and he didn't wear his glasses in bed. So I told him it was a bruise I'd got from bumping into the sideboard. He accepted it. And when at night he would pull me to him, I would close my eyes and think of those lovers caressing on my back and imagine that he was a young strong man, with eyes that gazed at me with good clean desire, like Adam in the Garden of Eden.'

'Before the snake got in.'

'*Si, antes el serpiente*! And then the more his sight deteriorated the bolder I became. I would go as often as I could. In the beginning I chose romantic images, then I moved on to more graphic ones, innocent really but daring to a girl like me. After six months or so the tattoo man beckoned me to the back of the shop and showed me some special designs from Japan, based on paintings by a famous artist Hokusai, and I knew I had to have them.' She leaned forward, 'Undo the rest of my buttons.'

His blood thumping, he undid the last ten. 'Oh my God,' he breathed. Across her lower back, a naked Japanese courtesan, her kimono rumpled beneath her, writhed in the eight nimble arms of an octopus, one of whose tentacles was responsible for her ecstatic expression. Joey let out an incredulous laugh. 'Didn't you worry that the tattooist might tell people?'

'No, it was illegal for him to do them, especially on someone my age, so we were both sworn to secrecy. Each time my husband breathed on my neck, and then afterwards cursed me, I'd just think of those erotic images and disappear into my own world of pleasure, where I was not a devil. I saved all the money he gave me, and after a year or so I'd filled my back and started on my front.'

She turned towards him again, his mind was filled with the images that he hadn't yet seen and he held her hands, running his nail slowly across her palms, slipping his finger in and out of the gaps between hers.

'By this time, my husband was virtually blind. Now, I can feel sorry for him. What an unhappy man he must have been, so lost, so frightened but I was blind in my own way then and what I did was a kind of revenge – and I am ashamed of that. I tell you, Joey, anger can make you do some crazy things. Maybe I would have stopped anyway when my front and back were complete but something happened that changed everything.

'One night my husband came back from the Church of the Three Nails, and he had all his fellow worshippers in tow, all seven of them. They crowded into the garden shouting and crying and praising the Lord. I heard this commotion from the kitchen and I went to the door. There they were standing in my flower-beds, hands in the air. I was concerned the neighbours might call the police so I made them come in. And then I noticed it. He was walking without his white stick. He was staring at me without his glasses.

'Aurora', he said, 'I can see! God has forgiven me, I can see!'

Joey drew in his breath, 'Jesus!'

'Turned out that their little church had a healer who was the real thing. He'd laid hands on my husband's eyes, and a miracle had happened. I ran upstairs, my heart pounding. Whilst all the halleluiahs were going on in the front room I packed my bag as fast as I could, stole some money from his secret hiding place and snuck out the back door whilst they were all on their knees thanking the Lord. Luckily I didn't have too long before the bus came to take me to the border.'

She stopped, leaned back and searched his face for a reaction.

He burst out laughing with relief, and she did too. 'Oh, Aurora! That is quite a story, but you can't stop now. I want to hear the rest. How did you end up here?'

She stood up, and her hair sprang out in all directions. 'On the bus I suddenly panicked. I couldn't go home because my parents would send me back and I couldn't explain why I had left. At the border I took a bus to Chihuahua because it was the first one leaving.'

'To begin with I worked as a waitress but I was lonely and frightened, I made friends with the wrong people and I started taking drugs. I needed more pesos to keep myself high so I started to display myself for money in fairs, horrible places.'

The laughter that had shaken his body was gone. He didn't know what to say to this. It was hard to imagine Aurora, who'd seemed so aloof and even prudish, who'd kept him on tenterhooks for so long, stripping in front of customers. It excited him but there was something else, some feeling of disappointment, disgust even.

'After a friend died from an overdose I really thought that was the end of me. I just wanted to die too but somehow I picked myself up and I found a tattoo parlour. The feel of that needle on my skin, was the only thing that gave me respite from the grief, and from the need for drugs. As a contrast I suppose to the rest, I had my limbs tattooed with some of the great saints of Mexico.

'As you can imagine in the small towns of Central America I was a great attraction. People would queue to see me, and occasionally if I was very broke I would allow special customers to see the rest. It was the rumour that there might be more to see that encouraged them to come in the first place. I was twenty-one years old, an open book, with nothing, not even my dignity.

'It was Patricio, the man who died, who took me away and asked for nothing in return. He was a fire-eater in one of the shows I worked at. He was old, ready for retirement, and had some money put aside. He took me to live with him and he treated me like his own daughter. He was homosexual, although he never had a companion when I knew him. I think he understood what it was like to be an outsider. He was also the brother of Señor Robles' wife, which is why Robles allowed me to join this circus.

'I had been living with Patricio in Mexico City when he became ill and I nursed him until the end. When he could no longer speak,

I was his mouth and when he could no longer eat, I made him soups and fed him with a spoon and finally when he could no longer breathe, I closed his eyes and I wept for him.' She wiped the tears from her face. 'He was the last man to see my body, Joey.'

She stood up and slowly removed her blouse. Orchids trailed up from the image on her stomach and curved over her breasts. She loosened her skirt and let it fall to the ground and slipped off her underwear. There in front of him, patterned like some glorious Chinese ceramic, was *La Princesa Pintada*. The Virgin of Guadalupe adorned her right arm, El Niño de Atocha, the child saint, on her left. The gospel writers decorated her lower legs and Lucia and Teresa, Bernadette and Juana embellished her thighs.

His eyes moved from one astonishing tattoo to another, entranced as she slowly turned her body. He wrapped himself around her painted flesh. She wept as he kissed her stomach, licked the breasts of the dancer tattooed there, her geisha's face ecstatic as a samurai stroked the indigo jewel between her thighs.

Unable to wait any longer, he pulled Aurora down towards him. Shucking his shirt and jeans, adding them to the neon nets and petticoats, he kissed every one of her tattoos, following the lines with his tongue, her body opening up under his touch. He slipped into her and as she flinched and cried out beneath him, that same light, that energy he'd experienced on the wire, shot through them, their desire exploding with the brilliance of comets.

They lay beached in each other's arms, their damp bodies imprinted with sequins, feathers and the tangled streams of ribbon. Their breath had blocked the sky from view, and the trailer reeked of the brandy they had spilled in their haste to reach each other. Joey felt stunned, drugged almost, the room floated around him and the dust motes dancing in the orange light seemed like the stars in some vast galaxy.

'How could you have thought that would stop me wanting you?' Joey said his voice weak.

'You weren't horrified?'

'Absolutely! But now I'll never sleep with anyone but a tattooed lady,' Joey kissed her throat. 'I'm glad you stopped at your neck though. What about your family, all those brothers and sisters, do they know?'

'Only one of my sisters knows – the one you've met. The others only know I am with the circus. For some even that was too shocking and we don't speak. I have become used to covering myself. It is a kind of relief sometimes to hide after so many years of exposure.'

Joey closed his eyes. A thought flitted across his mind that for him it was the opposite, exposure would be almost a relief after so many years of concealment.

36

Joey had never known happiness like it. Each time he held Aurora and felt her body buck beneath him he wanted to say thank you to somebody. He now had everything he'd always wanted; a lover, a child, success and a home of sorts, even if it had wheels and was full of costumes.

The pages of the *National Geographic* plastering the walls of her van reminded him of who he'd become. He kept each poster that had been produced, circling his name and that of Hijo del Lobo. When he became an old man, fifty years from now, in his little stuccoed house, with geranium pots along the sills, he and Aurora would unroll these posters and laugh at their youthful photos, remembering the days when crowds had marvelled at their astonishing skills.

The circus travelled briefly, across the Isthmus of Tehuantepec, where the women, fat and jewelled, ruled the villages. The weeks passed in a dream, every cell thinking only of her, longing for her next visit. But now and then when the sky was full of hot rain and dish-cloth grey, he'd wake up in his bed his face clammy, the smell of blood in his nostrils, the red of her hair floating across the surface of his eye and his mother would come back to him, a phantom hovering over his happiness.

When it happened he'd roll over try to crush her out of his mind, hold onto images of Aurora's lithe and living body. It was the secret that still lay between them, the last rope that might just bring him down. But he couldn't tell her. The guilt hung around his neck until he thought he might die from the strain of holding it and this weight had increased with his joy. Was this the price he'd have to pay to keep her? Frustration made him want to punch the trailer's flimsy walls, its eggshell prison. He felt a headache coming on. He hadn't had one of these for months, this rolling thundercloud of pain, shutting down his brain, sending forks of lightning down behind his eyes. His happiness was a stolen gift, a prize won by cheating, and he didn't know what to do to deserve it. He began to understand what had driven Dimitri mad.

37

Exhausted by the tropical humidity, Robles finally capitulated and agreed to travel northwards again back to the centre of Mexico. Joey had wanted to celebrate his twenty-fifth birthday in Pachuca, which he'd discovered was a town in the state of Puebla, but Robles decided to take the Western route. August was spent in Cuernavaca, then Toluca and Morelia. The cities blurred into each other, losing their distinctive qualities, and Joey found it hard to remember their features.

December found them on the outskirts of San Miguel de Allende, a colonial town full of Americans. Hijo loved it because he could take part in the Christmas *posadas* – processions that walked from house to house reliving the search for a place at the inn. Joey loved it because Aurora was able to visit every weekend. Still it wasn't enough; without her his life seemed dull and grey. Hijo missed her too; she was the one who got him to stick to his schooling and learn about all the other things in the world that didn't involve animals.

By the time Lent came around with its feasting and fasting they were north of Mexico City in Querétaro. Robles called him in to his office. Joey knocked on the door and entered. Otavio was inside, and Francisco, whom Joey hadn't seen since their talk several years ago. Their faces were sombre.

'Sit down,' Robles said. Robles himself stood up and walked to the window.

'I have created this circus over many years, and I have watched performers come and go. Some I was glad to say goodbye to, others... well, others still have a place in my heart.' He turned and looked at Joey. 'When I first met you, nine years ago was it? Ten years?' He shook his head. 'Rodrigo brought you to me, a snivelling skinny pale thing like a feral dog. You asked me to give you a week, and you proved yourself to me in ways that are still secret between the two of us, Joey.

I do not want to see you go—'

Joey felt a huge weight pressing down on his shoulders, he leaned forward, rested his elbows on his knees steeling himself. He knew Robles had been visiting other circuses, he'd seen new Polish *trapecistas*, and The Unforgettable Ula was receiving rave reviews especially after her appearance in Las Vegas. He must be strong. He must be calm – no tears, no arguing, acceptance, graciousness, dignity.

'My wonderful *trapecistas* are leaving Joey, they have found a job in El Norte, they will be working with a circus *muy famoso* and I cannot stop them. I have talked at length with Otavio and Francisco and we have decided that you are more than ready to be top of the bill. You have a gift, Joey. I must not let you escape. That performance! Still when I think about it I cannot understand what happened, what I saw then, what I felt—' he shook his head.

A burst of choked laughter escaped from Joey. He beamed at Francisco. 'I thought you were going to ask me to leave.'

Robles threw his hands up, 'Leave, why would I do that, you silly boy!'

Joey looked around at their grinning faces, then jumped up and burst into a dance in the confines of the trailer.

'This is called a jig in Ireland. It's what you do when words aren't enough to say how happy you are.' Out of breath he stopped and shook hands with Otavio and Francisco, whilst Robles offered a toast.

'We'll be back in Mexico City in a couple of months, which gives you time to get a really special act together, and for me to get the publicity machine rolling. You are going to knock them out. They won't know what has hit them.'

'I wish you good luck, Joey,' Francisco said his eyes suddenly serious. 'I have never seen anyone take to the wire like you, it is like you are in tune with the universe. If you weren't so ugly I'd be jealous.'

Awash with bubbles of excitement, Joey jumped down the steps into the bright sunshine. He reached his own trailer in two back flips and three cartwheels, scaring a sleeping dog, and making a cluster of children laugh and try to copy him.

Aurora, who'd had been sworn to secrecy, joined him for the celebrations.

'I also have decided if it is okay with you, to stay at the circus, once you are back in the city, and to perform regularly again.'

Joey felt as if his heart would explode.

38

Mexico City, April 1985

Robles sent Joey ahead to some of the new sites in the south of the city to see what he could feel. Joey tried to explain the geology to Robles, that it was the soft clays of the old lake-bed that made the centre and north of the city more unstable, but Robles dismissed it.

'I trust your feet more than science. If you say we are safer in the south we'll tour here.'

That first night back in the city, Joey hoped Francisco, who'd told him about Angel Milagro, would come to watch him. When he heard his music begin, he skipped into the ring and searched the seats. The spotlights shifted and blurred, covering the crowd with pools of colour, and then he caught sight of him, sitting with Aurora amongst a group of prettily dressed girls.

Her niece had chosen to bring them here to celebrate her '*quinceaños*', her fifteenth birthday party. Aurora had spent weeks making her dress and planning with her sister the special day that would culminate with this show. He waved and Francisco waved back. Joey walked over to Robles and took the microphone.

'*Buenas noches,*' he said, 'I would like to dedicate my performance tonight to Franciso Sanchez Lopez, who is sitting here in the audience, and to the memory of Angel Milagro and also to a beautiful young woman, Laura, who is fifteen today.' He heard a bunch of squeals from the group. 'It is '*Semana Santa*', the time of deaths and new beginnings, and I hope my daring performance tonight will bring only new beginnings.' The audience clapped and stamped their feet.

He climbed the ladder as the drum rolled and stood on the platform. He performed his now famous dance steps to the vibrant rhythms of salsa, but then as the music slowed, he walked to the end of the wire. The music dropped to a low roll.

'Señorrrres and Señorrrras,' Señor Robles was bawling, 'this man, all the way from Ireland, but with the heart of a Mexican, is risking his life for your entertainment but also he will bring you something more. High-wire artiste extraordinaire, he will astound you by attempting an exceptionally dangerous move.'

The audience was absolutely silent as the *chamacos* came out and removed the safety net. He made them wait a little longer knowing their necks would be aching with the strain of waiting, their excitement turning to tension. Sometimes he was sure he could feel their eyes, little spots of heat like laser beams boring into him. Were they willing him alive or hoping for his death? Just a few seconds more. He was waiting for the signal, the sound of the second drum roll and then he'd perform a triple forward somersault, spinning high above the ground unable to see the wire the moment he left it, hoping his judgement was perfect and that his feet would find it as he landed. He went through it in his head, seeing the run up, the jump, the rolls, and then the final flourish to the mad exuberance of the mariachi music. The audience, released from their spell, would cheer and whistle and stamp their feet at his miraculous resurrection.

But the signal had not yet come and Joey, his head bent, closed his eyes. It was the smell that came first. The dark wet smell of the earth. Nowhere in Mexico had he found that exact smell, not even in the dank forests of the Isthmus where plants grew in the branches of giant trees. The smell was pure Ireland. He blinked and it was gone. He tested the wire, his feet sure and steady. The drums dropped to a soft rapid beat. Silence settled on the crowd.

He lifted his right foot, and then ran. A bend, a high jump, a tight tuck. For an instant he hovered above the wire between life and death, between earth and air, his thoughts somersaulting in his head, past and present, terror and utter serenity.

He was upright again, arms steady, perfect stillness, his toes listening to the steel rope vibrating beneath them, and at that moment hovering on the wire, the audience felt it again, that startling moment when the world seemed to stop, and the vacuum left by an absence of time was filled by the joys of the past, condensed into the essence of happiness that left them breathless.

Then it was gone. And amidst the wild clapping, the shrieking of the trombone and the din of Señor Robles roaring into the microphone, he thrust his hands up, unfurling his cape and as they whooped and whistled, Joey for a microsecond felt again that he *had* been reborn.

Robles was right. Joey's remarkable act was soon the hottest ticket in town. Celebrities came to his circus, and ticket sales soared. Joey had mixed feelings. It exhausted him to produce this effect to order. He wanted it to be something unexpected that came as a gift to the audience not something that they felt they had a right to experience. To his surprise Robles understood.

'Do only what you feel is right. Your kind of magic should not be wasted. It is for you to judge when to use it. I will not tell the audience what to expect.'

Joey was grateful for this. It meant that some audiences went away thrilled at the spectacle of his dangerous and skilled performance whilst others left with their souls transformed.

39

Monday 16th September 1985

The note arrived on the morning of Monday September 16th. The day had not been heralded by strange portents. The sky hadn't changed colour and no creatures fell from the clouds to warn him. It was an ordinary day, early breakfast, cold shower, exercises and rehearsals, swearing and bantering and hoisting Hijo out of bed and forcing him to have his weekly hair wash. His shoes lay in the drawer unworn.

Aurora had driven into the city to get some fabrics from her sister in the textile district. She had agreed to pick up the mail at the post office – mostly letters for the foreign performers. Hijo always begged for the stamps to stick in an album that she'd bought him for his birthday.

Joey received many letters these days, hand-written notes from star-struck children wanting to be like him. He had a couple in the drawer that he'd kept because he found them so touching. She arrived back, the bundle secured with elastic bands and she and Hijo had played postmen, delivering them to the various trailers, a job that he knew would take at least an hour as they caught up on gossip and discussed the costumes she was making.

Now they were back in Mexico City, she and Joey had become inseparable and her clothes had found their way into his trailer followed by her sewing machine and the endless bric-à-brac of her passion for stitch. He was forever stepping on pins and catching his feet on loops of thread and standing on chairs in feathered costumes as she altered a hem or fixed a tear.

They were planning to buy a new trailer they could share, with two proper bedrooms, and a kitchen. Now he was a star performer with a growing reputation, he could afford a proper place to house his family. They might even marry if she could trace her first husband and get a divorce. It would be good for Hijo and maybe he and Aurora would have children too. At thirty-one she had plenty of time and she yearned to be a mother.

It had a Mexican postmark, and the smudged stamp of The Hotel Regis but he hadn't opened the letter instantly. He rifled through the others: the laborious scrawl of young children, the typed officiousness of bills. Then he remembered the journalist from the *National Geographic* – she sometimes stayed at The Regis. He'd had a couple of notes from her since her article: a 'round robin' one Christmas with images of her family and a scribbled *thinking of you,* on the bottom, and a postcard of Utah National Park, which was pinned to the wall of the trailer. She preferred pictures to writing, it seemed. He picked the envelope up again.

Hijo burst into the trailer, clutching a kitten, chased by a screaming girl trying to get it back. Joey dropped the mail on the table, ushered them both out, and headed to the tent to practise, before the sun got too hot. But on the wire something wasn't right. More than once he thought he was going to fall and was glad for the safety net beneath him.

'That's enough for today,' he called down to Otavio, 'I'm tired, I'm going to have a rest. Have you seen Aurora?'

'Gone to the supermarket I think,' he yelled up. 'She had a long list from Josefina.'

Joey put on his wrap, slung his towel over his shoulder and headed back. Inside the trailer with the curtains drawn and the windows open, it was cool. He picked up the letter and he opened it, and then his whole world folded in on itself, collapsed like a dynamited building.

It was no more than a scrap of paper, a hurried message torn from a notebook:

Dear Joey,
I know about your mother. We need to talk. I'll be coming to the circus, around 18th September. J Forbes

He read it and re-read it, checked the envelope in case he'd missed something. The 18th – that was just two days away. After all these years, he'd been found out. He got up, pains stabbed at his feet. He put on his birdskin shoes and went out into the glare. He needed to walk and to think.

He headed for the main road. Huge trucks piled with goods roared past, stirring up grit, swirling rubbish in their wake. He walked along the hot verge, hoping the noise would still the chatter in his brain, help him in the midst of it all, to reach a quiet spot where he could find an answer, a way out.

His instinct was to run away but how could he? He walked for two hours, down small side streets and plazas, through public gardens and dark hectic markets. At last, hot and filthy he returned to the site, just as the light was beginning to fade.

The music had already begun to trickle out of the sound system, and the preparations for the night ahead had begun. Luckily he wasn't performing, he couldn't have done it, but he was leading the final parade. He went back to his trailer, washed himself down and lay on the bed.

There was a rapping at the trailer door. He thought about ignoring it but instead he called out '*Quién es?*'

A small head appeared. 'Papa, it's time to go.' Hijo climbed into the trailer and sat down at the table, playing with a pair of scissors and some cotton reels.

'I thought Roberto was gonna kill Juana today, man,' Hijo said shaking his head, and letting a long low whistle escape through his teeth. 'I wouldn't want anyone throwing knives at me if I'd just cursed their mother.'

He spun on the stool and made faces at himself in the mirror continuing all the while to fill Joey in with the backstage gossip. The whites of his eyes caught a glint of light through a crack in the curtain making them dance like little headlights in the gloom.

Joey massaged his temples, feeling a nagging ache beneath his skull. How could he explain the past to Hijo? He couldn't even think about it, let alone say it out loud.

'Oi!'

Joey turned. Hijo was looking at him crossly. 'You're not even listening to me. Have you heard even one word I've said?'

Joey shrugged then stretched out his arm and beckoned the boy. Hijo came over to the bed and lay down next to him. He could feel the small motor of Hijo's heart driving the skinny body and like an echo of love, his own slow gentle thud murmuring a response. The boy rested his hand on Joey's chest and the little fingers moved gingerly across his sternum.

'You okay, papa?'

'Yes, I'm fine, tired though and my bones ache.'

Hijo sat up, unable to be still for long. 'Lobo was really good today, that new trick I've been teaching her – I think she's finally getting it.'

'She'll be fine,' Joey said, 'If anyone can get her to jump through a hoop it's you.' His mouth uttered the words but they echoed in his ears as if spoken by some other version of himself, some version whose life was not about to fall apart.

'Yeah man! You wait, next time the hoop will be on fire,' said Hijo as he leapt up to demonstrate, his eyes shining. Joey watched him, wondering suddenly, if he would even be there to see Hijo's amazing new trick. The thought drained him and for a moment he felt dizzy and sick. There was another rap at the door, as someone called the five minute curtain up.

'Christ! It's like a bloody circus in this place,' Joey said and watched with a breaking heart as Hijo rolled his eyes and groaned at the corny old joke.

Hijo opened the door and bounded out. Joey sat down in front of the mirror and put on his make-up, his jaw clenching as he donned yet another persona. He tried not to think any more. He had to immerse himself in the routines, get on with the show. Maybe when he came back the letter would be gone and he'd discover the whole thing was a mistake, a misunderstanding.

With practised speed he put on his maharajah's robe and turban. He was leading Dora in tonight so Concepción could have an evening off. He had seen her climbing into Miguel's car, a new gold necklace shimmering at her throat. He envied the simplicity of her life.

The other performers were already gathered at the entrance to the ring. Through the striped awning he could see that the ticker tape had already begun to fall. It tumbled from nets in the roof, glittering in the lights like fragments of rainbows. The dazzled children squealed and cheered, filling their upturned hands with magic rain to throw at each other.

'Nearly over,' Florita yawned, gathering her hoops. Along with her sisters she'd already sold hot dogs in the interval and tickets before the show.

Normally when he saw their tired bodies and faces, pale and greasy beneath the paint, he was glad that he had his own trailer, with a mattress to rest on and curtains and quiet, where he could retreat undisturbed by the homesick sobs or night ramblings of another soul. Tonight though he would have welcomed the distraction, perhaps when the show was over, he'd get some tequila, kill the whole bottle and put an end to his thoughts.

A letter. Just those few words, like a bomb thrown in through his trailer window.

The mariachis were already circling, blasting out *Cielito Lindo* at double speed and the audience were stamping their feet. The four musicians had just enough time to set the mood before nipping out to change into their clown costumes and bring up the rear. By then the recorded music would be rattling out – assuming the generator was working. But for now, they were strolling casually, as if they were in the town square, trying to prise pesos from tourists, waving their huge red sombreros, trumpets squealing.

Dora had been led up to the tent flap and was already probing his chest with her trunk. He turned and patted her cheek, gazing for a moment into her dark, knowing eye. She would tell him what to do if only she could speak. At his signal, she wrapped him in her trunk and hoisted him onto her neck. He pressed his knees into the sides of her head and she hobbled forward, her trunk suddenly appearing through the curtains, responding with a blast to the whistles of the audience. He relaxed into Dora's rocking gait as he waved to the children, some of whom were standing now, their fathers' arms wrapped around them in a protective embrace.

The thunderclap of drums meant Lobo must have entered the ring. Joey turned and watched the huge dog pulling Hijo in a chariot. Hijo bowed extravagantly, calling Lobo until she barked. Children close to the front screamed and covered their ears. Hijo blew kisses and threw sweets to them from a leopard-spotted pouch that Aurora had made for him, turning the howls to laughter, as their hands moved quickly to scrabble for fallen candies. Joey waved back to the boy, his heart quickening at the sight of him.

I know about your mother.

The twins followed behind; Negrita in black satin on the white horse, Blanca in white feathers on the black horse, Roberto and Juana, bickering through their dazzling smiles, Aurora, then Victor and Valentino, princes of the trapeze, Evangelina (carried on Rodrigo's shoulders) and her performing dogs and finally, the clowns. One of them still sported his mariachi moustache, the fool. He would lose it if he rolled too sharply.

But even this noise and colour could not still the thoughts whirling in Joey's head. This was his family. He'd planned to retire here in Mexico spend his final years with Aurora. And there was

Hijo. He had a whole life ahead of him. The past would not come back and destroy it. He tried to whip-up this anger, let it build like a wave and ride it, but instead it dissipated into confusion and regret.

40

Tuesday 17th September 1985

'Come here and put this on.' Aurora held out a cape of reds and pinks. In the harsh light of the late afternoon it was brash, but under the spotlights of the Big Top he'd look like an emperor. Even the parade had exhausted him and his head still ached. He'd slept alone but it hadn't helped. He'd felt like cancelling this fitting and getting straight on with the clear-up but when he'd seen her waiting for him, her hands on her hips, her scissors dangling around her neck, he hadn't the heart. He shuddered.

'Did I catch you?' she mumbled her mouth full of pins as she tacked up the hem.

He shuffled. 'No, it's the ground, it's very jumpy today.'

She looked up at him. 'How jumpy?'

'More than usual but nothing serious I'm sure.' She dropped her head and went back to her work. He closed his eyes and concentrated on his feet. There were tiny sensations along his arches like little electric shocks. He could feel the ground moving under his toes, as if something was burrowing just under the surface.

They'd had a tremor back in May and Robles had become nervous all over again, insisting on weekly reports from Joey. Joey treated his concerns seriously but still, it was hard to be vigilant all the time. He'd wake up some nights convinced an earthquake was on its way, only to see, when he ran out into the night, the wobbling rump of a car transporter, juddering into the distance. On days like today he wondered if it was only his soul he could feel, its fears and anxieties travelling around his body in minute energy bursts gathering in a pulsating mass at his feet. Since he'd opened the letter, he'd had to wear his birdskin shoes all the time.

'There.' Aurora leaned back and took a look at her work. 'Turn, turn,' she said, slapping his arms. She re-pinned a fallen piece. 'OK, that'll do. So are you going to tell me?'

'Tell you what?' Joey said his heart beginning to race.

'Why you've been acting strange since yesterday.' She avoided looking at him. He could feel her breath against his foot as she snapped a thread with her teeth. A muscle twitched in his eye, sending motes racing across his iris.

'Who was the letter from?' she said removing the cloak from his shoulders.

'What letter?' He said stupidly. It was Aurora after all who had collected the mail from the post office.

'Joey. You're making me nervous. What's in it? Who was it from? Is there a problem?'

Joey stared out at the scrubby field, where litter and plastic bags bowled along in invisible breezes. He watched one caught in the branches of a thorn bush trying to fight its way out but snagging itself evermore resolutely on the deadly spines. Aurora put her hands around his waist. He could feel her temple pounding against his back.

'Aurora, I …I'll tell you later. I have some thinking to do and some clearing up.' Her arms dropped away from him and he walked out towards the Big Top without looking back, because he knew if he turned, her hands would be screwed up so tightly that her nails would leave red crescents in her smooth pale palms.

41

The animals had to be fed and watered, the Big Top had to be cleared and swept. He was amazed by how much rubbish the crowd left: jackets and hats, bags and groceries and once, the hand-written script of a novel which he'd given to Doña Rosa. It wasn't usually a job he enjoyed but today he was glad of the distraction it provided, glad of the excuse to avoid Aurora's hurt and anxious eyes.

The last of the audience were still dawdling out of the exit. Subdued and drained, mothers were scooping their drooping infants off the benches, and blinking in the darkness. It was still hot and now with the razzle-dazzle over, they were aware of it, as were their children who'd become fractious and whiney.

As Joey searched under the benches for forgotten belongings, a man stood around tapping his straw Stetson against his thigh whilst his infant took its last greedy suck. He stood up to stretch his back and caught the young man staring at him. He looked about eighteen, and behind him his wife, the baby now wrapped to her breast, was wrestling a crying toddler into a pushchair.

He knew that look. The boy was wondering what it was like to fling yourself through the sky for a living, to grab mid-flight the ankles of a beautiful woman or leap on a wire to tumultuous applause. That's how he'd been. Every image of another place or another life had him aching and twitching. But what was he really? A coward who'd killed his own mother and run away. He imagined what would have happened if he'd stayed and tried to explain it to the police. And his father – with his respectable face, swearing on the Bible that it was Joey who'd done it. Who would they believe?

The wife, upright now, was adjusting the sleeping infant and the young man turned away. What would they say and do when they got home, this couple? When he was out in the fields would she sew a few secret sequins onto her underwear, or when he stood alone in their shabby room, would he flex his muscles in a square of old mirror, dreaming he was Rodrigo El Fantastico? He felt like running after them shouting, *this is all illusion. You already have the secret of happiness*, but you couldn't tell a person something like that.

Whilst they were clearing up, Negrita and Blanca cooked food in the small outdoor kitchen, and laid it out on tables in front of the truck. This was normally his favourite time of the day, quiet, peaceful, reflective; the hum of the generator, the flickering strings of bulbs dancing with moths, the music drifting out from the radio, and Negrita and Blanca washing dishes, intent on the *telenovela* on their television.

There was no sign of Aurora. By the time Joey had finished bagging up the rubbish and sweeping the ring, Gustavo and Rodrigo had already pushed their plates aside and were smoking and playing cards. Roberto and Juana were arguing, threatening each other with loaded tortillas, and Doña Rosa was reading tarot cards for the Flores de Mexico – as the three young jugglers had named themselves.

'I see something bad in your future,' she was saying to Clarita. There was a squeak from the girl as her hand rushed to her mouth. 'Yes, your husband will be so well-endowed you will have to fight off all the other women.' Shrieks of appalled laughter ensued. Clarita, the shyest of the Flores, the shrinking violet, covered her face with her hands.

'You better give up juggling and learn to use a gun,' Rodrigo said between swallows of Corona.

'How about you, Joey? You in the mood for the cards tonight?'

Joey shook his head. 'Not tonight Rosa, I have a feeling the cards would bring only bad news.'

'You always say that,' she said shuffling expertly. 'What are you afraid of, Mr Pachuca?' Joey gave a short laugh, and pushed the salsa around on his plate.

Hijo, swigging from a bottle of cola, dropped into a seat opposite. 'Good crowd tonight.'

Joey gave him a napkin. 'Don't talk with your mouth open, Hijo. Have I taught you nothing?'

Hijo rolled his eyes, and then smiled, allowing the churned up food to show around his teeth, dodging Joey's open hand.

Maybe the journalist just wanted to help him? Fat chance. She was a mother herself wasn't she? He pushed away his plate, unable to eat. He felt nauseous.

'Go and sort out that dog,' he snapped at Hijo, 'I can hear her howling from here, and go sleep with Aurora tonight – I have a very bad headache.' The boy stopped mid-chew, his face dismayed.

Joey left the table, without looking back at him. He returned to the trailer and bolted the door behind him. It was full of shadows. Outside, the tinny wail of trumpet scales climbing into the night unsettled him and he knew if he looked out of his window, Tomás – one of the older members of the mariachi troupe – would be there in his singlet and mariachi pants, his big gut hanging over the waistband, shaking the saliva from the open valve onto the dirt floor.

He'd once been a big time jazz musician in Mexico City before he'd found religion, and had taken to the streets in honour of the Virgin. All these people, all these pasts – surely Aurora would understand.

It was gone ten but he could still hear raucous bursts of laughter outside. Perhaps it was the sight of his new costume hanging up behind him in the mirror or the smell of tuberoses that seemed to come out of nowhere to smother him but he got up and walked across to Aurora's van. The cicadas had taken over from the chatter of people, their manic buzzing, rising and falling in a frenzied chant. The heat clung to his shoulders, both suffocating and comforting.

A dim light glowed through the windows. He remembered the times they'd made love lying on piles of old costumes in need of repair and cleaning, the dust making them sneeze. They'd dressed as clowns and showgirls, decked in feather boas and masked like strange birds, the musky scent of her feeding his desire.

He stood at the door. Raised his hand to knock and then hesitated. He could hear her singing a sad old song, its high fluty sound like a thin dart piercing his heart. He closed his eyes and tried to imagine her face. He saw Teresa's face, that moment in Malinalco when she refused his love. His nerve left him. He turned around and headed back to his own trailer, sat at the table and picked up a pen.

Dearest Aurora and Hijo,

I have had to go to Mexico City to meet someone. I may not be back for a while. Please give the other letter to Robles and make my apologies. This is something I must do, and I'm sorry I can't explain it to you. Whatever happens remember that I love you both with all my heart,

Joey.

He stood in the dark. The gleam from the other trailers created patches of light on his floor and bed. He got up and turned on the low light over the mirror. He ran his thumb over a grinning gappy photo of Hijo that was tucked into its frame. He must have been six then, where had all the years gone? The letter was open on the dressing table. They'd be better off without him. He'd start somewhere else maybe, get a bus up north, change his name again.

He pulled a travel bag from under his bed and packed it quickly. He slipped off his silver shoes and added them to the top and zipped it up. He checked his wallet for cash. He picked up some flyers for their next show, a smiling picture of Hijo in the corner. He unzipped his bag and stuffed them in.

42

Wednesday 18th September, 3 a.m.

In the early hours of the morning when the audience were asleep in their homes, the children dreaming of spangles and terror, and the women with muscles like plaited loaves, Joey slipped out of his trailer closing the door quietly so as not to wake anybody.

Slipping between the shacks and trucks, every sound he made seemed magnified. The dogs lifted their heads as he passed and wagged their tails half-heartedly. Several times he stopped and ducked behind a car, or pressed himself against a truck, convinced he'd heard a cough or a footstep but it was just the snorting and stampings of the horses, the odd yowl from a cat, and the chatter of the television from Josefina's trailer. Still he felt observed, as if the inanimate objects watched his departure with invisible accusing eyes.

He'd longed to say goodbye to the sleeping boy, but he knew if he caught sight of him he'd change his plans. So he'd left, trying to forget the soft sounds of his breathing that settled in his head like fog, threatening to obscure the road that lay ahead of him. He walked across the site, past the van where Hijo dreamed and Aurora slept, angry and dismayed at his sudden coldness, and into the blue shadow of the Big Top, tethered to the ground by its net of guy ropes.

After he'd walked for some time out into the fields away from the circus, he'd finally allowed himself to look back. The dense angular shadows of the tents and vehicles formed an island in the dark landscape, an island where fire-eaters slept, and jugglers snored and an elephant, dreaming of *pan dulce* and fruit, trumpeted like the wayward horn in the school band.

He buttoned up his jacket and stared across a waste ground that bristled with towering cacti. Unseen creatures scuttled in front of him, alarmed by his unexpected presence. Ahead of him stretched the city, with its secrets and its tears.

Pains shot through his feet and into his ankles and he rested for a moment. In the chill of the night, he thought again of Hijo and Aurora. Gazing up at the last sharp stars, he imagined all the things he would have said if only he'd had the courage, but it was too late now. He knew he must cover as much distance as possible before the temperature rose and the women, skin-warmed like Monarch butterflies, began to flutter out of their front doors, with their cans of sprinkling water, ready to still the dust that swept in on the breeze and covered everything.

PART 4

1

Mexico City, Wednesday 18th Sept. 8 a.m.

He lay back on his hotel bed. Grey dawn light from an interior courtyard tried to make it through but failed. That was fine by him. There was something mocking in the eager Mexican light, something that made him feel exhausted.

He should have gone straight to the bus station and got a ticket out instead of wasting his money on a room. He rolled over and felt the blood pulse in his temple. He was twenty-five years old. He didn't want to run away again.

What if he told Aurora the truth – that it had been a terrible accident. But it wasn't as straightforward as that, was it? Of course he hadn't meant to kill his mother, but he had intended with every cell in him, to kill his father. Christ, what a mess! He saw the chain of events ahead of him; extradition, a trial, prison.

His feet ached. What had become of his father? The smell of those faded newspapers in Doña Rosa's trailer came back to him, the hours spent thumbing through looking for something, an excuse maybe. He closed his eyes and thought again of that long gone image of his parents dancing, his mother's radiance and his father's feet a dizzying blur. He tried to sleep but the room was hot and the air-conditioning clattered and hummed. He needed some coffee.

That journalist had given him this opportunity to make a run for it. Maybe he should be grateful for that. He went down to reception and left his key at the desk. Holding the wall to steady himself, he headed for the door. The pain in his feet was overwhelming. He spotted a chair in the foyer and dropped into it.

'*Està usted bien* Señor?' the desk clerk said.

Joey nodded, 'Altitude sickness.'

He peered through the etched glass of the window. People were striding confidently along the street and there was he, nerves frayed, waiting for his past to claim him. No wonder his feet were playing up.

If only the welfare authorities had sent him to a foster family or another home instead of that place. There had been a hearing, a court appearance, prolonged discussions, with his ma looking bewildered and his da grim and then it seemed he was there, in its echoing corridors full of other boys as bitter and angry as he was.

There were two ways to survive – to become tough or to become invisible. With his feet the way they were he took the second option and kept to himself as much as possible. His fights took place inside his head, endless rehearsals for the inevitable confrontation. She'd come to see him at the beginning but then her visits had tailed off. She wasn't well they told him and it was probably true. Then they sent him home, himself a live grenade and his father knowing exactly how to pull the pin. He sounded like one of those barstool failures, swirling their regrets around in their glass.

After a short walk, he hobbled in to the Casa de los Azulejos on Madero, a sumptuous colonial building that housed a department store and restaurant. He'd never had the nerve to go into it before, though he'd peered in to watch the waitresses in their starched headdresses and aprons, serving food on white platters. The outside walls were covered with blue and white tiles from Puebla that reminded him of the designs on Aurora's body.

He'd spent a long evening with that journalist in Puebla, spilling out his guts to her thinking he'd found a friend. She'd sensed that a piece of the puzzle was missing, poked her journalist's nose in and rooted around. He ordered a coffee and peered behind him. A large family were choosing a complicated array of dishes, arguing over the contents of the tostadas. He'd spotted the oldest one straight off with his extra nub of confidence and the angry one, with the longing in his eyes. Joey paid for his coffee and left.

Outside, the morning rush hour was in full swing. His headache was blinding and he thought he might throw up. He rummaged in his pockets for some pills, and his fingers closed on something hard and round. He pulled out a small red button decorated with a lion's face. Aurora had been so excited when she'd found these.

He closed his eyes and thought of the last time they'd slept together, the way her eyelids fluttered when he kissed her, the way her small brown feet tensed with desire. All the promises he'd made. The way he'd left her.

His own feet required him to walk slowly and to rest often. He'd never known the pain as bad as this. He'd thought at first it was just the emotional shock, but now he was certain it was much more serious. He caught sight of Popocatépetl, her thin plume, an admonition. He looked around at the scurrying traffic on Avenida Juárez, the bustling crowds, the solemn buildings jostling for space on the huge roads. He needed time alone to focus, to try and make sense of it. He felt a burst of pain run through the soles of his feet, he let out a cry and bent down to rub them.

'Are you all right?' a woman asked, her kind eyes crinkled in empathy.

Joey nodded and stumbled to a bench by the side of Parque Alameda. People hurried, children played, buses stopped and started. The mundanity was comforting. What nasty thing could happen on a day when children bought ice lollies and chased balloons? He opened his bag, took out his birdskin shoes and slipped them on. Immediately the pains dulled, but then he felt something that filled him with dread.

2

He hurried back to the hotel room as fast as his feet would allow him, and closed his door. Taking some deep breaths he tried to still himself and concentrate, but his blood was like a bass drum in his ears. Swamped with his other anxieties, he couldn't interpret the signals. He needed to be nearer the ground. Perhaps the building had a cellar. He went back outside, took the lift.

'In the event of hurricane, fire or earthquake, do not use the lift,' the sign in the lift stated.

Joey got out in the basement. It was warm and gloomy, just the low breathing of the boiler and the hum of a generator. He found a maintenance room and closed the door. Surrounded by mops and bottles of disinfectant he stood still and let his feet speak to him. When he closed his eyes, he was engulfed by a dense violet colour so intense it seemed about to absorb him. Cold crept over his skin and fear paralysed him. He was convinced that if he dared to open his eyes he would discover his feet in their silver shoes had fused with the ground. His head was pounding.

He forced his eyes open and took a deep breath. This was not like the tremors he'd occasionally had to warn Robles about, this was going to be big and it was coming soon. He looked up, thought of all the floors above him, all their concrete and tiles, the sinks and the wardrobes, the beds and their occupants, the crushing burden of marble and bone. He'd have to do something, tell someone.

He pulled open the door into the dusty corridor. A distant clank was the only sound of life. He leaned against the wall as his feet burst into spasms.

'When!' he shouted down to them. 'Where, in the *centro*, or somewhere else?'

He'd advised Robles to stay south of the city where the old basalt rocks were more stable. The circus should be safe, but it depended on the scale and origin of the quake. He'd go back to the circus. He would do the right thing for once, no more running. He'd tell Aurora everything, give himself up to the police and take the consequences.

Almost as soon as he'd decided on this course of action he felt a lightness permeate his body. The final rope released. But it was a tainted freedom, one that would take him from those that he loved, from the country that was in his blood and the circus he knew he was born to. He felt like falling on his knees and weeping at the irony.

He collected his things, checked out and walked into the street. People sidestepped him, bags of shopping in their arms. A party of school children, chattering and laughing, snaked past him along the pavement. He'd have to get moving.

He got a *colectivo* to Insurgentes then picked up a bus heading south. It was packed. He stared around him at all the faces, old and young, preoccupied and carefree. He needed to tell someone, but what could he say?

'Evacuate the city – my feet have told me the earth is about to break into a thousand pieces!' They'd lock him up.

3

He arrived back at the circus in the early evening, hot and dirty, to the sound of the final parade. He slipped into his trailer and collapsed on the bed. He yearned for sleep but his head was spinning. He rubbed his feet. What kind of blessing could this gift be if he couldn't really explain it to anyone? Through the window the crowd was thinning, laughing couples and tired children wending their way back to their homes and their normal lives and somewhere amongst them all were Hijo and Aurora. Hope began to trickle through him and encouraged, he went out to look for them.

It was Rodrigo who saw him first. Blanca and the others turned mid-conversation and fell silent. The look on Blanca's face was one of contempt. Joey could barely look at her.

'So you've come back to us then?' she said.

Joey dropped his head. 'Look, I'm not asking for forgiveness, but I need to tell you something important.' He glanced around at them, this family he was about to lose. 'There's going to be a big earthquake. I think we are on solid ground here but...' Blanca let out a cry and the other girls huddled together.

'We've not heard anything on the news about a quake,' Rodrigo said.

Joey threw his hands up. 'I can't explain all this, but trust me, my feet know. It's going to happen and soon that's all I can say. I've got to tell Robles and I need to find Aurora and Hijo.'

Blanca pulled away from Rodrigo, her face hard and angry.

'You are too late,' she said to him.

'Too late, what are you talking about?'

'You just disappeared and left that boy with no proper explanation. He thought he'd upset you, thought you'd left him for good.'

Joey felt the blood rush to his face and his stomach shrank into a tight ball. The others stood silent and accusing.

'He went into the city to look for you,' Negrita said

'And Aurora?'

'She went after him of course, with that journalist woman.'

Joey teetered and his legs gave way beneath him.

He stumbled through the night streets of Mexico City past busloads of workers and cars full of teenagers roaring by on their way to a celebration. But the sky knew something was up, the pollution formed a steel-coloured streak. He turned a corner and saw a fight had broken out in the street between the drivers of two collided trucks. One had shed its load. Crimson pomegranates, their skins split, covered the street winking and glittering in the flashing headlights. Joey shuddered and pushed on through the onlookers.

The Regis, the hotel on the journalist's note – that's where they'd be! Convinced he'd found them he followed Avenida Juárez to the corner with Balderas and hurried to the desk in the plush reception but the desk clerk shook her head.

He walked on blindly having no idea where in this huge metropolis he might find them. Panic made him irrational and after several hours he found himself back by the Parque Alameda. It was quieter now, the streets almost empty. He found a sheltered spot, opened a bottle, and drank until finally he fell asleep.

4

Thursday 19th September, 7.03 a.m.

It was the silence that woke him, that and the excruciating pains in his feet. The birds with their raucous chatter had vanished. Joey jumped up and immediately fell back to the ground as debilitating shocks ran along his arches, rendering him helpless. His head ached from the tequila, from the weight of sleep, but his feet knew what was coming. Earthquake. The word formed in his head, then exploded and the world collapsed around him.

Sweat had soaked through his shirt, and his throat stung. He groped around and felt above him the cold weight of stone and beneath his hands, dust and grit. The absolute darkness pressed down on him from all sides. If only his mother would come to him and take him down that tunnel to the light that people talked about.

Such a short life. But he'd had chances, more than many people and he'd wasted them. Anyway it was too late for regrets now, too late for confessions. He didn't believe in all that. There was no point being a hypocrite so near the end. Was she here watching over him? Could a spirit hear? 'Ma' he called out again.

A voice came back to him. An echo – the loneliest sound of all, he thought and began to weep. But it came again. He shouted out, a dry rasping growl. Somewhere under the rubble his feet prickled, making him wince and cry.

'I can hear you, are you hurt?' a voice called.

Joey gasped, 'I'm here! I'm okay!' Debris began to fall making him cough violently.

'Don't move. I will get you out. It's precarious out here but you'll be fine.'

'*Gracias a dios!*' Joey breathed as a small circle of light and a dark eye appeared from the gloom. He crossed himself, forgotten incantations pouring out of him. As wreckage was lifted in a flurry of dust, he began to shake uncontrollably then a hand grabbed his shoulder.

'Come, come, you must leave, it is very unstable. The building is in place but the roof has fallen in. I have removed the worst of the rubble from you. You should be able to get yourself out now.'

Joey looked at the man who was offering his hand, a metal crucifix and a black soutane, a man of God. Of course, he'd been in a church. It must have collapsed on top of him. Joey was about to take the hand and then sank back and shook his head.

'No. *Gracias*, I'm going to stay. I don't want to live anymore.'

The priest, groaning with effort, pulled him out with both hands, his eyes bright with impatience.

'Come with me, you idiot. You are alive and in one piece, apart from those cuts and I need help. There are people in the street who are trapped. Come with me.'

Joey heaved himself up and stumbled after him, through the grey light.

'What time is it, how long have I been there?' Joey said clutching his head and stepping over the fallen pews and scattered prayer books.

'It's after four, by the clock, but it's the end of time out there,' the priest said his head drooping a little.

Outside Joey stopped, stunned by what he saw. Just a few hours had passed but in that time, hundreds of lives had gone, crushed like insects inside the ruined buildings. He followed the priest along the edge of the buckled curb. Bodies littered the streets, water poured from hydrants and cars were on their backs like dogs, their engines smoking, oil leaking onto the road. In one an old woman dangled upside down, her head severed at the neck, blood congealing in her lilac flowered hat. In the back a child lay unconscious or dead. The priest pushed him towards the car.

'Get them out before the car explodes,' he said.

Joey spent the rest of the day and night working. He didn't rest, he didn't sleep, he dropped when he was too exhausted to move and lay where he dropped. His clothes caked with dirt, stank of blood and urine. Bodies lay under blankets, people pored over rubble listening for voices, dogs scrabbled and whined and children – their hands bleeding – hauled rocks as large as their heads. Under each block that he lifted Joey expected to see the face of Hijo, grey and still, or Aurora's corkscrew curls tangled and matted with blood.

Perhaps the three of them had escaped, found some bus or car heading out and were safely back at the circus listening anxiously for news of him, why hadn't he thought of that before?

'I need a phone, I need to call,' he shouted suddenly.

'You and ten million others.' Father Diego grunted, levering a piece of wood to remove a fallen beam. He rested for a minute and mopped his forehead. 'Most of the lines are down and the *Metro* system is out, we're trapped here for now. Your best bet is to leave a message with the radio station get someone to call you. Help me now with this, and I will take you there.'

The radio station was crowded, mothers wailing for lost children, husbands searching for their wives. After several hours Joey was finally able to leave his message and he silently promised a God he didn't even believe in, all the reckless things a man promises when he is desperate, things he can never hope to do.

Back outside in the gloom the ground shuddered and gasped beneath his feet. The job seemed impossible, the scale of the destruction apocalyptic; he wanted to throw himself to the ground and howl but Father Diego would have none of it. Tough and wiry, he shouted orders, lifted timbers and organised the stunned and grieving into parties to look after the sick, the old and the dead. He said prayers, he washed wounds, he rocked babies, and finally when Joey couldn't take it anymore he embraced him and let him sleep.

'You're not like any priest I ever met,' Joey said.

'I was a truck driver before I was a priest,' Father Diego replied, wiping some dust from his eyebrows. They were standing in line waiting for food. Women had come from their homes with pots of beans and tortillas: poor women with worn, lined faces, rich women in cashmere sweaters, their cheeks as soft as mink.

'And that is your church?'

The priest nodded. 'It *was*. I ran a project for street children there. They will probably cope better than anybody else. They already know how to live with devastation.'

Joey told him about his past, his life on the streets of Mexico City with Teresa, as they sat eating hot food, their faces lit by small fires. He told him about his childhood, about the holy family he'd destroyed, about his father and of finding a new family only to lose them because of his own cowardice, and finally he spoke of his mother. Father Diego listened, his sleeves rolled up his cassock tied into a knot in front of him.

'I absolve you', he said turning to Joey, '*In nomine patria e filio e spiritu sancto.*'

'No,' Joey shook his head, 'it can't be that easy.'

The priest laughed. 'Easy, you think that was easy? Look around you, look inside you, you have done your penance and you are doing it now. There is enough pain, let go of yours and move forward.' He sighed, rubbed his face with his hands.

'You know, Joey, I had a wife once and I killed her.'

Joey looked up, 'You killed her?'

'*Si*, I was a drunk as well as a truck driver, those two things don't really go together, not on big oil tankers. I killed her, in a truck I was driving. An accident? No, you can't call it that. I knew what I was doing. It was arrogance. And in my despair God found me and I found him, and we have been together ever since.'

'I wish I could find God, but I can't,' Joey said.

'Well, not everyone finds him in the same way, and some people never find him at all. I don't think it matters to God much. What does he have to gain? It only matters to us. Some people gain solace from God and some from God's creation.'

'But how can you look around at this and believe in anything but evil?'

'This isn't evil, Joey, this is nature. Men selling drugs to children – that is evil, buildings that collapse when they are supposed to be earthquake-proof – that is evil. You wait, we will find out a lot about people's capacity for evil and for good when the dust settles and the bodies are counted. Man can choose evil, but nature is nature.'

Joey looked around at the hunched figures, two sisters feeding from the same spoon, an old man wrapped in a blanket tended gently by a tattooed teenager with a ponytail.

'I'm going to carry on,' he said.

'Take care Joey, and I hope you find your loved ones.'

Joey never saw Father Diego again. He walked all night, discovering streets where the earthquake had barely dislodged a plant pot and then suddenly two blocks away, utter chaos. The electricity was out. The city, lit only by fires and dying car headlights, was strangely quiet. The smell of gas persisted and a trooper with a loudhailer warned against lighting cigarettes or matches. Like a huge rat, the earthquake had burrowed erratically under the ancient Aztec basin of Tenochtitlan, throwing off skyscrapers and schools like so many fleas from its back.

Exhausted, Joey found an improvised shelter set up by the Red Cross and spent the night there sleeping with hundreds of others who'd lost their homes and their families. He fell into a fitful sleep, disturbed by nightmares and the anguished cries of the grieving and the lost.

In the morning he heard external help was on its way. The Swiss were sending in crack rescue teams, the French were bringing sensing equipment. Radio Universidad transmitted messages from survivors informing friends and relatives of their whereabouts, pleading for others who were lost to get in touch. Joey returned to find a message from Señor Robles. Aurora and Hijo were not at the circus. They had not heard from them at all. Joey read the message – a flower that had bloomed inside him yesterday now withered to dust. He stared at the words as he was gently pushed away by the crowds of others eager for news. He was startled by a sudden piercing cry. He turned to see the old woman who'd been behind him in the queue sink to her knees. People moved aside giving her grief room. The guttural sound was unbearable, the sound of a soul dying within a living body. He shoved his own note into his pocket and elbowed his way through to the daylight. At least there was still a chance for him.

Men arrived at the shelters bringing van-loads of food to feed the rescue brigades and ordinary people had come in from all parts of the city to help.

'I have lost everyone,' a woman told him whose three children had been crushed in their beds, 'what can I do but be here, feeding you, talking to others, what else can I do with all this love I have inside me?'

Joey was astonished by what he saw. There was so much goodness amid the suffering. In all the months he'd lived in this city, he'd treated the ordinary people living around him as nothing more than a backdrop to his own dramas. His world had been the destitute living in the shack. He'd forgotten the existence of simple kindness and yet despite the circumstances, it surrounded him like air. People formed themselves into teams, working for twelve hours at a stretch to find bodies in the rubble and return them to relatives. They made holes in crushed buildings and disappeared into them like moles, risking their own lives for the sake of the dead.

And something odd was happening to him. Despite the turmoil, and his own anxiety and grief, his feet were calm. He put them on the ground, and found that he could walk more easily with only the occasional ache of regret and bitterness. He scrambled over the wreckage of hotels, clearing away rubbish with his bare hands using his agility to balance on beams and link ropes to girders so they could be hauled away.

It rained on the second day, which turned the dust into slurry and made the work slippery. Then an aftershock came as violent and destructive as the first. Buildings that had survived the first quake intact collapsed, killing thousands more, burying others, rendering still more homeless. The world had descended into chaos. After this second shock Joey wandered in a daze unable to concentrate his efforts. He'd start at one site and then imagining all the other places Hijo and Aurora might be, he downed tools and walked again. He couldn't rest. When he closed his eyes he imagined Hijo still alive in some small place gradually losing oxygen as he, Joey, slept.

5

In search of food, he found a street vendor, a pot of tamales steaming on some coals. All around him lay chunks of concrete and broken glass. Police vehicles sped past, and a jeep with armed troops rolled along towards the *centro*. A radio was churning out news. '*Centro Historico, Cuautéhemoc*'....the districts most affected were around the old Aztec heart of the city. The vendor nodded.

'It's the old lake,' he said making a bowl with his hands. 'The city is built on it, soft and yielding, that's where the damage will be. It started near Acapulco, but most of the damage is here.'

'What about the far south of the city?'

The man shrugged. 'I've heard nothing about that.'

Joey finished his food and went back to his search. The promised help came from abroad to supplement the efforts of the Mexican rescue workers and Joey was there when a child was pulled alive from the ruins of a school. Cheers went up among the volunteers and even the hardened workers wept. It gave him hope that maybe, at this very moment someone was pulling Hijo out of the wreckage.

Joey had attached himself to a brigade at the ruins of a huge residential block and was about to take a breather, when he saw a face he recognised. He left the digging for a moment and hurried over to the tall, slender woman, with her dark hair pulled back from her face. She was treating cuts and bruises on a whimpering toddler.

'Is it you, Doña Marta, the *bruja*?'

The woman turned and her eyes lit up in recognition. 'It's Joey, isn't it? Teresa's friend.' He nodded, beaming.

'How could I forget you?' she said. 'You were one of the most unusual people I ever treated. How are the shoes?'

'They have saved my life, I have them, look.' He delved into the pockets of the loose cargo pants he was wearing and pulled them out. She took the soft and battered shoes gently in her hands, and rubbed her fingers over them.

'I never thought I'd see these skins again,' she said quietly. She signalled to another worker and indicated that she was taking a break. She led Joey to a concrete slab, and sat down, her arm around his shoulders.

'And your feet?' Joey looked down at them and realised that in the novelty of their stillness, he'd almost forgotten what they were capable of.

'They are amazing,' he smiled. 'I'm almost able to manage without the shoes. I am a different person.'

She leaned back and gazed at him in admiration. 'That's marvellous. And what are you up to now?'

'I joined the circus. These shoes have made me a master of the high-wire.'

Doña Marta's mouth dropped open and she laughed and laughed. Joey joined in with her and for a moment, the injured, waiting for treatment, smiled too, relishing a sound that had become a distant memory. Then Joey asked the question that had been waiting impatiently in his throat.

'How's Teresa doing?' He loved Aurora, she was the woman he wanted to be with, but Teresa still lingered with him, and there were moments when her laugh with its clean, fresh sound, still came to him in his dreams. He hoped she was happy.

Doña Marta squeezed his hand and looked away for a moment. 'I'm afraid Teresa didn't make it, Joey. I'm so sorry.'

Joey opened his mouth and gulped in the air around him, as if his brain needed extra fuel to process what Doña Marta had just said. His eyes filled and his heart began to palpitate. He couldn't speak.

Doña Marta turned back to him. 'Oh, Joey. Oh, my poor boy!'

Unable to stop himself and oblivious to the crowd of people, bandaged and bloody, cradling their broken limbs, he sobbed. He tried to hide his face with his hands, but the tears flowed out between his fingers. Teresa, sweet Teresa. Despite all the horror he had seen, he had not shed a tear. He'd shouted and raged and looked away and cursed God but he hadn't cried. But this news had done for him. This one death had become the distillation of all the pointless loss and misery he had witnessed since the earthquake began.

The tears carried his grief in wet trails onto the ground beneath him, where they were swallowed up by the dust. Doña Marta let him be until his grief subsided.

'I should never have left her. I wanted her to come with me, but she said she wanted to stay with you. I was so angry with her.'

'Joey, she had her own problems. I think you know that her mother killed herself, and Teresa suffered the same depression. She took a lot of drugs to keep the demons from the door. I found her dead in my garden.'

Fresh tears welled up as he thought of Teresa's small body lying in the undergrowth.

'I tried to help her, but there are limits to my abilities. When someone has already made a pact with death, there is little I can do.'

He remembered then Teresa's mood swings, her fixation with that grinning skeleton which had disturbed him so much once but now signified nothing to him but another fiesta.

'She knew she was on the wrong road, that's why she wouldn't go with you Joey.'

'She told you that?'

Marta nodded. 'She thought that you would not be strong enough to save her and she would drag you down. She couldn't bear the idea of it because she loved you very much.'

Joey tried to keep his face from crumpling but he felt the edges of his mouth struggling to hold their shape. 'Her mother told her we had different roads and that my feet were the key to my future and my past,' Joey said, his voice cracking.

'Well, she was right. I don't know about the past but they seem to have given you a future.'

'Do you believe that her mother really spoke to her?'

'Yes, I do. I think some people do have contact with the dead, but it is not a good thing to have your ear tuned to the other world. It is a distraction. It makes it hard to live in this one. That's why we devote the 'Day of the Dead' to them, then the rest of the time we give ourselves to the living.'

Joey sighed. 'I hope if spirits do live on, that she is somewhere with roses. Where was she buried?'

'I had her body placed with her mother's in Catemaco. I thought that was the best thing.'

He nodded slowly then stood and stared up at the sky, his face tight with salt.

'Her death changed me,' Doña Marta said. 'I work with young-sters like Teresa now, but I can't always save them. I'm glad that she found happiness with you, even though it was for such a short time. She'd had so little joy in her life. And what about you, Joey, have you found love?'

Joey thought about Aurora and nodded. 'I was luckier than Teresa, Doña Marta. I have a wonderful girlfriend and a young child that I love but...,' he rubbed his hand through his hair and stared around at the devastation, '...but through my own stupid-ity I may have lost them. They are somewhere in all of this,' he said, spreading his arms to encompass the smashed buildings and the torn up roads. A sense of hopelessness tightened his chest. He breathed deeply trying to loosen its grasp.

'Have you tried Televisa Chapultepec? They have names of miss-ing and found people all over the walls. There are other places too throughout the city, and listen to the radio, they find new people every day. Look, I've got to go Joey,' she said pointing to the snaking queue, 'I have to return to my work. It's been wonderful to see you again, and I'm so sorry that I had to give you such bad news.'

They hugged goodbye and as he continued his search through the ravaged streets, he knew that he would never give up. He'd been spared. He'd been blessed with a cussedness that willed his body and his spirit to survive and he would use that same persistence to find them.

6

The night he left the circus, he'd grabbed a handful of flyers to take with him. Now he tore out the picture of Hijo's face and stuck it to each information board he saw, with a date and a time on it. But when he returned at the appointed hour, he found nothing.

Joey's feet were blistered from his explorations of the twisted piles of debris and ruins but still he hoped they might feel something. The army and the police were beginning to exert their authority, stopping the amateurs like him getting near the sites, waiting for the professionals to do it. Joey ignored their orders. He was determined to use his gift. It was like something out of the Bible, rolling back a stone and seeing a dusty hand clawing its way out into life. And all the time he walked and called out and prayed and pestered people about Hijo and Aurora.

At night around fires, while comforting each other, the recriminations began. Why had these buildings fallen and where were the government officials? Why weren't they getting their hands dirty breaking their nails?

'Placido Domingo has come to help,' an old lady told him, 'the world is watching and the world has good eyes.' She nodded her head wisely.

'This is a good sign,' an engineer said to him as Joey listened to some banker puffing out his chest and blustering on about corruption. 'When people have time to ask why, of man, rather than of God, things are looking up!'

Scenes haunted his nights: a young girl hugging her dead mother, and refusing to be dragged away; a bride still in her wedding dress, the flowers smashed and dirty, lying amid her train on a patch of glass-strewn ground; an old lady completely naked, too stunned to notice as she wept over the body of her husband.

Joey tried all the hospitals, those that had survived the destruction and the temporary ones set up by the relief organisations that had descended on the city. It was a bitter irony that the area with most hospitals had received the most damage. He wished he had Father Diego's faith and did not see this as the work of an indifferent God. He went to the morgues where the dead were laid out in rows and glanced at the swollen, ashy faces hardly daring to look. He hadn't found them alive, but so far he hadn't found them dead either.

Several days after the first quake, unable to sleep, he found himself by the remains of Hospital Juarez. It had been a focus of activity – the military and rescue organisations from around the world crawling over the rubble with specialised equipment, although after so many days the chance of finding survivors was almost non-existent.

'I was here when this bit opened in 1970,' a worker said, 'twelve storeys, and look at it now, all gone.' He shook his head at the destruction.

It wasn't just the place that had been devastated. Here more than anywhere else the people seemed devastated too, flattened by despair. Distraught mothers and fathers stood like wraiths unable to give up that last shred of hope that life would be pulled from the belly of death.

He'd heard many people thank the Lord that the earthquake had happened so early, before the schools were full of children. But here it was hard to be thankful. They'd already pulled out the body of a woman who'd given birth moments before the earthquake. The baby, still attached to her by its umbilical cord, had barely grabbed a breath before its life too was snuffed out. The nursery with all its delicate cargo had been destroyed. Piles of rubble seemed to mock the bodies, measured in pounds, that lay beneath. Sometimes, thin wails from the grieving burst through the blue sky, followed by murmurings of consolation.

It was too much to bear, and Joey decided to head off, find a place where he could be useful, where the weight of human misery was not so crushing. Then he felt something beneath his foot, something faint, a ripple of warmth. He stood absolutely still. A tiny vibration, different from those of the quake, tingled his instep. He walked gingerly over the lumps of concrete, carefully testing each one for stability, his blood pumping. There were more vibrations now, faint but definitely there. A mother stood, head bowed her tears flowing unhindered.

He whispered, almost to himself, 'I can feel them.' She turned sharply her eyes wide. He picked up a shovel and began to move the debris. Others, seeing this sudden movement, renewed their efforts too.

As the blocks lifted, a couple of dogs who'd been sniffing around searching for scraps began to bark. Suddenly there was pandemonium. Someone shouted for lifting equipment to secure the space. While they waited, onlookers and volunteers, invigorated by hope, began with infinite care to shift the rubble. Someone held up his hand. Everyone stopped. For a moment there was not a single sound, and then a tiny cry broke into the air.

A mother sank to her knees pulling at the broken cables and wrenching at masonry. Others helped her, scrabbling until an opening appeared. A retired miner, a wiry old man who'd come down from Zacatecas to offer his expertise, spoke up.

'We need to be careful here. Stand aside and give me some space.' He stretched his body out over the broken stone and shone a light down into the hole.

'I'm going in, when I kick, pull me out, but be careful – it might be unstable and we don't know what's down there.'

He wriggled in up to his chest until it looked as if the ground had swallowed him. The crowd moved back hands clutched, mouths muttering silent prayers. Joey joined the others eagerly waiting, as shards of light emerged on either side of the miner's shoulders. For a moment it seemed that no-one took a breath. Then the miner's foot kicked once, twice. Two men got down on their knees and pulled at his legs. Inch by inch he withdrew his shoulders, twisted his body around and slowly lifted his arms. In them he held a baby, its tiny fist uncurling in the daylight.

'She's alive and there are others!'

The miner sat on the debris holding the infant, his face suffused with wonder. It was as if the building itself had given birth, this wrinkled old man, the midwife of the moment. There was cheering and back-slapping, followed by sobs, and then quickly a line formed.

After some structural work to check that the space would not cave in, the babies were rescued, passed gently from one to another, each bundle with its fish mouth and struggling limbs a tiny miracle. Hysteria had broken out. He turned to the man next to him, and they both smiled and wiped their tears away with their filthy shirts.

'Pascale,'

'Joey,' Joey sniffed. He took the warm bundle that was offered to him and gazed at the perfect face with its delicate nose and black, living eyes. He passed it to the man next to him.

'You have a baby here?' Joey said.

'Me, no I just work in the city, but we must all do what we can. I can't believe what I am seeing here,' a tear dripped from his chin as the next baby took his finger. He eased it off and passed her to Joey. Her face puckered and he rocked her gently and passed her on.

'When I leave here,' Pascale said, 'I am going to paint, I've always wanted to and life is short.'

'If I ever leave here, I am going to make babies,' Joey said, 'for the same reasons.' There was loud laughter along the chain.

Joey walked through the broken city that night and thought about them, each tiny scrap of life hoping and hanging on, without water, without food, without human touch. If those little ones could survive then maybe the earthquake had spared his boy too.

He did his rounds again the following week, changing the dates on his posters looking for names, scanning the boards. The centre workers knew him by now, and tried to find ways to encourage him as his hopes faded; today, though, it was different. The young woman, her suit neat and tidy, her hair brushed smooth, grabbed his arm.

'I think I may have something for you.' Joey's breath caught in his throat. He grabbed her hands,

'Where, where? Show me.'

She pointed to a densely covered part of the wall. His eyes darted over it looking for news. Then he spotted it, a small drawing of a lion with a big grin and 'Nashonal Jographic' written above it.

'My boy, I've found him, I've found him!' He kissed her, and accepted the handshakes and hugs of the other searchers, their drawn faces renewed by his good fortune. He pointed to the address and she directed him; it was a temporary hospital three blocks away.

7

Aurora lay in bed, her tattooed arm with its drip startling on the white sheet. Her face was grey, her eyes dark windows shuttered against the outside world. When he took her hand, tears slid across her face but she didn't speak a word. He bent down and clutched her limp body to him. He held her close and felt the weight of her arms dropping by her sides. He looked up at the nurse.

'Catatonic shock. She has been like this since the death of her sister and her niece.'

Joey buried his face into her neck, whispering words of love and consolation into her ear. Her eyes moved towards his.

'Joey?' the word was more of a breath than a word, a husky sound escaping from her lips.

He lay next to her, stroking her face. 'Yes, it's me, I'm here, I've found you.'

'I lost them, Joey. I tried to get them out but I have nothing, not even their bodies,' and a wail broke out of her, like a lonely bird over an empty sea.

Her sister had been crushed along with six hundred other textile workers in the sweatshops around San Antonio Abad. Joey held her as she wept for the motherless children, for the poor workers whose bodies were left inside while the machines were rescued from the site. She cried for her sister and for Laura, who'd run after her mother to bring her lunch. She cried for the old people who wouldn't live to see their grandchildren grow and for herself when she thought she'd lost her love forever. And finally with Joey by her side she slept.

He slipped his hand from under her neck. He was desperate to see Hijo. The doctor had reassured him, as he'd tended to Aurora that yes, Hijo had been brought in with her, and that no, he was not injured and she'd sent one of the volunteers to find out where he was.

As Joey left Aurora to rest, the volunteer, a stocky young man with broken front tooth, grinned at him.

'He's busy,' he smiled, 'he's very busy but I'll take you to him.'

He led Joey through rows of people, the victims of a catastrophic war with no winners. He began to hear the sound of squealing laughter, the unmistakeable whoops of children without parents to interfere. At the end of another makeshift ward, Joey saw him, his nose reddened, his hair sticking out in all directions and huge trousers tied around his waist.

In a circle around him, children gasped with delight as he balanced a huge pile of toys in a teetering tower, tipping them backwards and forwards, heading for the nurses until they screamed and ducked, pretending to trip over invisible objects and generally playing the fool and when he'd finished and accepted the applause, Joey shouted, 'Bravo' and Hijo spun around, sending the pile of toys cascading to the floor.

The following day he met Janice Forbes. He discovered from Hijo that she had saved Aurora, had blown her own breath into Aurora's shocked lungs to keep her alive and he felt humbled and ashamed. What is more, with Hijo's help, she had put those notices everywhere in hopes of finding him.

He met her in the lobby of one of the least damaged hotels, and when he saw her, he struggled to say what he knew he must. She pushed a drink across to him,

'A coffee is okay I hope.' Joey nodded, took a gulp.

'And Aurora is recovering?' He nodded again.

'She was very sick, I thought we'd lost her, but she's in good hands,' she said. Joey coughed, felt his cheeks redden. 'I understand I have you to thank.'

She laughed. 'Hey, it was nothing. I've always had a lot of hot air to spare, ask my husband!'

Her smile faded and she toyed with her napkin. 'About your mother, Joey.'

Joey was about to speak but she hushed him up. 'Let me finish. You once told me that you and your mother read *National Geographic* together.'

Joey nodded, 'She called them the Geographicals,' he said. 'She'd get them from the church jumble sales, and we'd pretend to visit all the places in them.'

'Well, about six months ago, two years after the article about you appeared, I got a letter from someone claiming to be your mother.' She pushed a piece of paper across to him with an address and telephone number on it. Joey stared at the paper unable to pick it up, a clammy feeling creeping over his skin.

'What are you trying to do to me? My mother's dead. I know because...I, I killed her. You know this! You left me that note. I killed her with a knife that I grabbed from the tea table. My father was there, he told me she was dead and I ran.' Panic was rising inside him. Joey expected her to reel back in horror, but she carried on looking at him calmly and steadily. Was she playing some clever trick on him, some journalistic voodoo?

'I know something of what happened. I've spoken to your mother at some length. You see I needed evidence that she was who she claimed, after all you are now a celebrity. She sent me this to show you. It's a copy, she still has the original. She said this meant something to you, as it did to her.'

She handed him the photo, his mother's rapturous smile, and his father, with the dazzling feet – a man whom Joey now suspected he had never met. He leaned back in his seat, his thoughts as upturned as the city.

'I think I need a stronger drink,' he said, his hands shaking.

While Janice went to get him something, he looked at the address. Not the old house then, a flat by the look of it, in the city now, not away in the sticks. And a phone number. He could call her. A string of ordinary numbers, and he could speak to the dead.

8

Robles gave the entire proceeds of a day's performance to the fund for the *damnificados* – those made homeless by the earthquake. It was the biggest audience in the circus's history, and when Joey took to the wire that night, the light from his body made the Big Top glow like a planet.

Several of the performers lost family in the earthquake. Rodrigo's mother was killed in her home, and he wept openly for days. Like the country itself, a gloom descended over the Big Top, and black ribbons hung from all the trailers. But gradually life took hold and grief turned back on itself, becoming a private thing, tears in the dark, nights full of memories and regrets.

It was nearly the middle of October before Joey had the courage to telephone his mother and two weeks later, he was touching down in Cork, his hand clutching the photo, his stomach churning. Aurora had stayed behind. Her grief harnessed to a cause, she was busy with relief work, helping Doña Rosa organise shows to raise money and campaigning for the families of the textile workers.

He knew her at once, small, pale but with that mass of red hair. He held her close, alarmed at her fragility. Her hands were bird-like, the blue veins vivid under the surface, a miraculous network that had brought her back to life.

In the taxi they barely spoke. She clutched his hand in her lap, rubbing his fingers as he stared at the scenery, drab in the November rain, but laden with the smells of his childhood.

Her flat was small, on the ground floor of an old building with a well-tended garden. From the front door, he could see the docks where he'd stowed away all those years ago – a murderer he'd thought, with no soul worth saving but an instinct to survive. The air smelt salty and fresh and the seagulls surfed the air currents with a careless grace.

She poured him tea, and even the taste of that was a journey back through the frightening forests of his childhood.

'I've made scones, I'm sure you haven't tasted one in a while.'

He shook his head. He'd forgotten how young she was, forty-two, forty-three? She looked older though. The pictures of him from the *National Geographic* were framed and hanging on the wall. She saw him looking at them.

'What a day that was!' She pushed her hair back and leaned into the armchair. 'One of those miserable March days when you know you should have stayed in bed. I had an appointment with Mr Sharkey – do you remember him, he pulled out that loose tooth of yours – but when I saw the weather I thought about cancelling. The line was busy, though, so I got out the umbrella.

'There was just me and the receptionist – Veronica, he married her eventually you know – and that old drill whining in the background. It goes right through you that sound. I went to take a magazine to distract myself and spotted a copy of the *National Geographic*.

'I pulled it out and started flicking through it, and I was thinking about that game we used to play, do you remember? Then I turned a page and there was your face! I told myself it couldn't be you. This boy was on a tightrope in a foreign country – yet it was! I knew every inch of that face like it was my own. I jumped up shaking the magazine and pointing at the photo, shouting *'It's him, it's him!'* I could hardly breathe. I thought I was going to faint right there on the floor. Then I ran out of the office clutching the magazine, without a word of explanation. That poor wee girl must have thought I was crazy.

'Of course, when I calmed down enough to check the date the magazine was two years old, but I wrote anyway, and that journalist helped me find you. And then I heard the news of that terrible earthquake and I thought I might have lost you all over again.' She paused for a moment and looked up at him. 'It must have been a shock to hear about me,' she said.

'Shock! Ma, I thought I'd killed you, he told me I had.'

'Well, you nearly did. I lost a lot of blood, punctured a lung, but luckily you missed my heart. I spent some time in the hospital, and I still struggle with stairs but otherwise I'm fine.'

She picked up the teapot and poured more into his cup, stirring it slowly. The clink, clink of it was soothing, like the slow passing of time.

'And da, what happened to the bastard?'

His mother sighed, her mouth a twist of resignation. 'I thought of telling the police he'd done it but I didn't, I was too scared. He knew I'd done him a favour then and did the decent thing and left me. He had another woman anyway, up in Dublin I think, he'd gone on about her often enough.

'It was so strange to come into the empty house and hear my own footsteps, the sound of the door closing and know I didn't have to feel afraid anymore, that he had finally gone.' She sighed and plucked at the skin on her cheeks. 'You know, Joey, it takes so long to find out *who* you are and then you haven't enough time left to *be* who you are.'

'But you're still young ma, and look how far you've come, this place for starters.' He took in the clean willow-coloured walls, the spotless furniture, the painting of a calm ocean, none of it familiar, nothing with any resonance.

'The house was in my name so eventually I sold it, moved here for the sea, and went to college.' Joey's mouth tilted in surprise.

'Well, Joey, I was an ignoramus, as your nan would have said.

I wanted to do everything, make up for lost time, find out what makes us all tick but still I used to spend hours with my pen hovering over my essay looking out of the window imagining you sailing back to me. Daft, aren't I? Sure wherever you were you'd hardly come back on a sailboat now would you?' She sipped her tea.

'You know when he heard I'd sold up he wrote and asked for his share of the house so I sent him a piece of the gutter.' Joey slapped his thighs and the laughter burst out of him until his eyes watered. 'Oh ma, I've missed you!'

He rubbed his face letting his laughter subside slowly while he tried to compose himself for the question he needed to ask. His palms were sweating. He wiped them on his jeans.

'So tell me about my real da.' He felt the blood rushing up through his neck.

Like a reflection, patches of red spread up into her face, and she studied her hands for a moment before looking up. 'How long have you known? Was it the photo?' She rested her finger on it where it lay on the table, as if it still held the power to move her.

Joey shook his head. 'I'd always assumed that was you and da in the picture, I suppose I need to call him Brendan now. You looked so happy the pair of you. I blamed myself for being born and spoiling everything. But I didn't understand why he was angry with *you*. Then years after, a doubt began to creep in, and I knew there was something I'd missed. I also have a gift that's usually inherited, according to circus folklore, so I began to put the pieces together.'

'Are you ashamed of me?'

'Ashamed? No not at all! My God, I'd always feared that I was like him. He was like this voice inside me, telling me that was all I could be.' She nodded.

'So how did you meet my real father?' The words sounded strange in his mouth.

'It was 1960, I was seventeen. He was with a Spanish travelling circus that came here one Christmas and pitched on that big piece of ground that's a hypermarket now. His name was Luis. I walked into that fairground and saw him and that was it. He was an acrobat from Madrid, and a wonderful dancer. He spoke to the crowd in this halting, romantic English, and I was completely star-struck.

'I met him later at a dance in the town, and he picked me out. Of all the girls there, all the local beauties, it was me he chose. I was so naïve though, that when he told me he lived in a white castle in Spain and that when he returned he would bring me gloves made of peacock feathers, and silk stockings, sure I believed him. I fully expected that he'd come back and marry me and take me off in a silver boat with golden sails. God help us!

'Then my mother spotted the first missed month and she was onto me. All hell broke loose, my father wanted to send me away. Out of sight out of mind, come back from 'a trip to my cousins' nine months later and the baby in another country with a new name. Ma was having none of it. 'No-one will be fooled and that'll be our name talked into the dirt,' she said, so they hatched this plan with Brendan.

'He'd been interested in me, had taken me out a few times because he had his eye on the shop. He was in his late thirties then, more than twice my age. I shouted,

I threatened to run away – I was sure Luis would come back for me, you see. But in the end I had no choice. It was sorted in a month. When you were born they'd say you were premature. To the world, you would be Brendan's. He'd get the shop when your granddad retired and a monthly allowance for his trouble.'

Joey shook his head. 'That's just wicked, like the dark ages. How could they do that to you, marry you off, sell you almost, to a man you didn't love?'

'They were different times Joey, different rules applied. I'd sinned in the worst way possible. It's hard to imagine it now, when girls show off their bumps and no ring on their finger. The shame then was terrible. They probably thought they were doing me a favour.

'The day you were born was a strange one. Ma and da stood there pretending to be pleased yet even though I had so much to feel miserable about, I couldn't keep the smile off my face! I thought of all the things Luis had promised me and none of them were as wonderful as you. I still had the optimism of the young then. Of course things would soon start to sour but those first few years with you were—' her eyes filled.

'Oh ma.'

'I would read to you when Brendan was working, do you remember?'

Joey nodded. Snatches of those moments came back to him when he watched Aurora with Hijo. 'I remember Brendan singing to me too, ma, and I couldn't work out what had happened to change it all?'

'When my father, your granddad, died suddenly, God rest him, it turned out he'd left the shop to his brother. Do you remember when your granddad died? You must have been five. Brendan was kept on but there he was tied to me, a son that wasn't his, and as it turned out, unable to father his own child, though God knows he tried and not just with me. He was seething with the injustice of it all.'

'But that's what I don't get, ma, why didn't he just go, leave us alone and find someone else, why the beatings and the cruelty?'

Joey was up on his feet now, and as he paced around he saw that present from Tralee, that had sat on the table an innocent witness to his suffering. He wondered why she still had it after all these years.

'You know I've thought a lot about that. There were practical reasons – sure the monthly allowance was paid until you were sixteen, and he'd got used to the extra. As you know your fath… Brendan, liked the finer things in life but there was more to it than that. He knew he'd married me for the wrong reasons, and to broadcast it would shame him too. He needed someone to blame and we were the cause of all his problems. And that day when he saw you on the fence and realised what that might mean, what gossip might start—'

'So it was our fault? Ma, you're soft in the head. The man was a sadist.' Joey wanted to shake her as she sat looking into her lap, her shoulders bowed.

'I think he liked the power, Joey. Beating us made him feel more of a man.'

Joey thought back to those fights he'd had himself, swaggering around, his fists bloodied, and some poor dope lying in a heap, no match for his fury.

'And then you sent me away—'

'Being in that house without you nearly did for me. But I'd saved you, and that gave me a kind of strength.'

'But why did you stop visiting? That never made sense to me…' Joey couldn't finish, it was as if his throat had a hook in it.

'I wanted you to forget about me and I was a coward too, terrified of what he'd do if he found out I'd been to see you.'

'But couldn't you have told someone, got him arrested?' He wanted her to admit that she had failed to protect him, but it dawned on him as he said it, that she'd hardly been more than a child herself.

'I tried but they didn't believe me. He was charming and smart, and always had money in his pocket. He didn't look like a wife-beater. I felt if I could just keep you safe, it didn't matter about me. I'd brought it upon myself with my behaviour.'

She began to cry, and Joey stared down at the carpet.

'I wish I had killed him,' Joey said. 'I can't forgive him. I'll never be able to.'

His mother shook her head, 'I felt the same way for years but then I realised that he didn't care whether I forgave him or not. I've read a lot about it, Joey. If you give into hatred then they win. I've struggled with it though. I wish I was a better person. Yet here we are together. I can hardly believe it! Let's not talk about him.'

She straightened herself up, smoothed back her hair – a nervous gesture, Joey thought, as if the cradling of her own head made her feel safe – then she leaned across and took his hand. He squeezed it and let it go and walked to the window.

'Did he know about me?'

She shook her head. 'The fair was long gone by the time I found out about you.'

'Didn't you ever try to find him? Maybe we could do it together. I have contacts now, if you could give me some details, anything that you remember.'

She shook her head. 'He died in a car accident. I found out when they came back here again one winter, you were with me, do you remember? That was a bad moment for me, that last bit of hope gone.'

A wave of sadness coursed through him. But how could he feel grief for a person he'd never known, a person who'd never even known of his existence? Perhaps he was grieving for a dream lost, a hope drowned. He looked out at the tide. Already it had rolled back exposing a new vulnerable world. It had taken away the litter, the dried out remains, the messages scratched into the sand and had left it clean for others to leave their marks on its surface. Then the cycle would begin again and those marks would be obliterated by the next tide.

He watched the gulls circling, looking for scraps, feeding their young from the remains of less fortunate creatures. Life just went on, didn't it, endless cycles of death and renewal, only humans had the time to shed tears over it. He gathered himself and turned back to his mother.

'Looks like I've gained a mother but lost two fathers. Now that's what you call careless.'

She came and stood next to him at the window. He felt the tentative press of her hand on his arm.

'Come on now, let's go for a walk. Look. The sun is back.' She turned her face to him and patted his cheek. 'My son is back!'

A smile flickered on Joey's face, 'You know that's exactly what I always say about my boy.'

She turned from the door her eyes alight, 'You have a child! Oh my Lord and you didn't say!'

9

The fortnight he spent with his mother was both exhilarating and exhausting. During the day they walked arm-in-arm along wind-blown sands, the salt stinging their faces, and she told him what she knew about Luis: his mother was an acrobat, his father had been a trapeze artist and had died from a heart attack; he had a sweet tooth and cried at sad songs; he was a dreamer and full of stories. It was frustrating. The details were imprecise, worn into unreality by time. She remembered his feet though, the way he danced, the way they lifted him off the ground as if he were floating.

Each night they sat up into the small hours trying to squeeze a lifetime into fourteen days, but he was not prepared to open every door she knocked at. There was so much he couldn't tell her, about the humiliations of the homes she'd left him in, about the ordeals he'd endured. She wanted to know – he could see it in her eyes, those searching blue lights. Maybe she hoped that by sharing his suffering, she could be forgiven. He wasn't sure, but there were things he would never tell her because he knew that she would not be able to forgive herself. He knew all this because he felt the same.

The traumas she must have suffered haunted him. He saw it in the endless motion of her hands and the deep lines around her eyes, the medication she still had to take. It was not just altruism though. He didn't want the relationship to slip into an orgy of self-pity, culminating in accusations and blame.

He thought back to the days after the earthquake, when hearing a voice beneath the rock and rubble it was so easy to go crashing in like a superhero, ready to save a life only to destroy it with mis-directed zeal. Buried memories and buried bodies were much the same – they had to be uncovered with the greatest tenderness and skill.

It had been hard to leave her at the airport but at least they'd made plans. He finished his drink, and gave the glass to the air hostess. It was only his second time on a plane and he found the turbulence unsettling. He stood up and inched his way to the bath-room. The toilet cubicle was small and windowless. He liked the compactness of it, the way it muffled the engine's roar. It made him feel safe, like that wardrobe sanctuary of his childhood.

He washed his hands and looked into the mirror. There it was again, that momentary sense that he was looking at a stranger. Brendan was not his father. All his features now seemed subtly different in the light of that revelation. He blinked, recognised his mother's eyes and his old face came back into focus.

He sat down and opened his wallet and took out a photo, one of his mother and Luis, side by side. He'd looked at this new image a hundred times since she'd given it to him. His real father's face was strong, a generous mouth, the eyes pushed into creases by the smiling thrust of his cheeks. His hair had tumbled forward, and his left hand was caught in mid-air as if a gust of wind had played with that curl, thrown it across his eyes and he'd suddenly moved to push it back. Her right hand is resting on his chest. Her touch is teasing and there's joy in her tilted face.

When she'd confirmed that he wasn't Brendan's, that none of that man's blood flowed in his veins, it had been such a relief, he'd felt like singing. Once the initial euphoria had passed, however, he'd stood uncertainly before a blank page. Who was he now? All he knew of his real father could be found in this photo and his mother's memories, and they were just the gilded recollections of a love-struck girl. What had this stranger passed down to him? Sure his remarkable skills were a gift, but were there other darker elements that he hadn't yet discovered? He put the photo away. He was just being foolish, raw materials were part of it, but it was what you did with them that mattered.

There was an irritated rap on the door. Joey opened it up, apologising to the impatient woman in the rumpled sweatshirt who was shuffling from foot to foot as he pushed past her into the aisle.

Back in his seat he closed his eyes, and thought of Aurora. He had so much to tell her. He stretched his legs and his foot kicked against his bag. He smiled to himself. He had ten yards of the best silk in that bag, wrapped up in pale tissue and ribbon, a silk the colour of clouds, no, not clouds, creamier than that – the colour of milk. He imagined her face when she opened it, her hands running over the smooth surface, wrapping it around her body, exploring its possibilities. Her wedding dress, he hoped.

The first time he'd asked her she was still in the hospital, the bruises from the earthquake distorting the tattooed images of love. She'd looked away and said, '*There is no future.*'

The second time, when she was back on her feet and they'd lain in each other's arms in the trailer and made love like the last couple left alive, she'd said, '*Ask me again when I am back to my old self.*' Thinking of her, he drifted into a hopeful sleep, in which the fabric stretched out in front of him like the right road.

But when he arrived back at the circus, clutching his gifts and full of stories, he found her in bed, her hair matted and her face drawn. The indignation and fury that had kept her going in the first month after the earthquake had dissipated in his absence, turning instead into self-doubt and withdrawal.

In public she continued to campaign for justice alongside the relatives of each woman who'd died with her sister, but out of the public domain, she'd slipped into a deep melancholy. She refused to perform seeing nothing but mockery in the illusions of the circus. Joey did not know how to respond. He held her hand, he lay with her and spoke of the future they would have together, but her eyes were dull and lifeless. The future had become as alien to her as

Jupiter.

It was Hijo who coaxed her back from the edge. Joey watched as
he cajoled her out of her bed, forced her into her clothes, scolding
her gently and firmly just as she had done to him after the deaths
of his father and the beloved lion, Don Carlos.

He made her feed her birds and clean out their cages and he even
read to her from his book on Africa. Not wanting to hurt him, she
did what he asked. She sat for hours with her doves listening to
their susurrations, watching them strut and flirt, following their
instincts for nesting, hatching and then rearing their young.

Then at Christmas, Joey gave her the silk. And just as he had
hoped, her hands strayed across the yards of cream, and a look of
wonder flickered across her face. She picked up the fabric crumpling it in her arms, pressing it to her face and inhaling its smell.
Too afraid to mention why he'd bought it, he left it with her, hoping its beauty at least would bring her some kind of peace.

Through the months of convalescence, she spent hours embroi-
dering it. As the needle whipped in and out, her shoulders relaxed
and light returned to her face. She glanced up at him from the
ocean of fabric, her eyes engaged and alive. The simple action of
the embroiderer's needle had woken her up. Its single eye with its
narrow focus refused to encompass the harrowing memories that
hovered at the edges of her mind, threatening to dominate her waking hours as they did her dreams.

By March she was ready to perform again, and while there were
the occasional moments where sadness drifted across her face, she
had more or less returned to her old self – with one exception. She
no longer concealed her arms and legs, determined she said to be
truthful in the face of so much deception.

For the first week or so she could be found sitting on the stoop,
her legs stretched out in front of her while curious youngsters explored the faces of Mexico's most revered saints on her shins. He
listened, his throat tight, as she responded to their questions with
patience and enthusiasm. He recalled then his jocular vow as he'd

handled those miraculous babies during the earthquake. After all that had happened would she ever want to marry again, let alone bring children into the world?

On Easter Sunday of 1986, the day when according to the gospel writers, sun seeped into an empty tomb, and hope triumphed over despair, Joey asked Aurora for the third time if she would marry him, and this time, she said yes.

Epilogue

The 'wedding' of Aurora and Joey, was an extraordinary occasion. Performers from all over Mexico arrived to assist the celebrations, and photographers jostled for space at the entrance to the Big Top.

There was so much bunting that Aurora's doves refused to fly and pecked instead around the site, their throbbing throats inaudible in the din from the loudspeakers. The mariachis did their best to play the Irish music that his mother had brought with her, but then to everyone's relief returned to their own tunes with verve.

'Joey, Joey, hi!' He saw a figure running towards him, dodging the cameras, and the water pistols that Otavio's sons, in full clown regalia, were aiming at the press. It was Janice Forbes, and in tow were her husband and children, bemused by the scale of the event. Joey hugged her.

'I can't believe you made it! Does Aurora know you are here?'

'You know me and letters,' she said. 'I just thought I'd turn up, and if the weather stays like this, we'll be the guests that wouldn't leave. Where is Aurora anyway?' Joey shrugged and looked around him. He hadn't seen her since the morning.

'Well, I've got the camera, hope you don't mind if I just mooch round, and get some shots.'

Joey paced around the trailers and walked in and out of the Big Top, waiting for Aurora to arrive. He'd thought this day might never come after those dark grey months. But hope, Aurora discovered to her surprise, refused to die. She'd found it living inside her, indomitable and persistent. Maybe it was the simple triumph of life over death, that basic instinct to survive that Joey himself had felt on the boat from Ireland. Whatever the reason, he was thankful. He could so easily have lost her, he might lose her still. He looked around the Big Top, his nerves on edge.

A whoop of delight spread through the crowd, as Dora, her flanks painted with flowers, suddenly entered to a loud fanfare. Seated on her back was Aurora. The guests erupted, straining their heads to see this fabulous spectacle. As the elephant lowered her to the ground, Joey saw the dress, made from the cream silk and covered with dark blue embroidery. She turned proudly as the guests murmured their appreciation, holding out the skirt for them to admire. He marvelled at the complexity of the design, the way its patterns mimicked the skin beneath.

With no priest prepared to preside over such an event and no civil ceremony possible until her first husband was found, Robles appointed himself the master of ceremonies. He gave a speech of such poignancy, such yearning, that he was unable to complete it and Rodrigo finished the speech for him with tenderness and humour. Before the earthquake there would have been raised eyebrows and mutterings of disapproval by some at a union without the blessing of the Church or the State, but now after so much suffering, any joy, no matter how unorthodox, was a cause for happiness.

Nervously running through the vows he planned to make, Joey was only half concentrating. He looked down at Aurora's dress, the words of Robles floating around him. As he stared at it, the meandering lines began to reveal themselves. She had stitched the two of them love-struck on the back roads of Oaxaca, dancing like loons in the light of the moon. She'd stitched him on the wire, stars shooting out of his feet, his birdskin shoes glittering with silver threads, and she'd embroidered Hijo leaping around the Big Top with Lobo – and weaving in and out of the intricate scenes, decorated with the flora of Mexico; the nopal, the agave, the bougainvillea and the hibiscus – were defiant words in English and in Spanish:

'Cuando llegue la muerte, me enfrentaré a ella, pero mientras la vida me permita respirar, seguiré bailando.'

'When death comes I will fight her and while I have a breath of life I will dance.'

THE END

About the Author

Joan Taylor-Rowan is an award-winning short story writer. Her work has been broadcast on BBC Radio 4 and has been selected for numerous literary events. She has been shortlisted for The Asham Award, and has been a finalist in several international writing competitions. The first draft of **The Birdskin Shoes** was a finalist in the 'SpreadtheWord' novel pitch competition.

She has travelled widely including a year in Central America and Mexico and three months in the Amazon. She currently works in London as a teacher of Art and Textiles.

She has the Portsmouth Evening News to blame for her passion for writing. Growing up in Portsmouth, the local newspaper had a weekly children's page – 'The Chipper Club'. Joan discovered that a published letter doubled her pocket money and a star letter quadrupled it. A writer was born. This is her first novel.

Follow her blog for events and comments:
thebirdskinshoes.blogspot.com,
or email **joantaylorrowan@gmail.com**

Questions for Book Clubs

1. Did you enjoy the book – why, why not?

2. Did you feel that the book fulfilled your expectations? Were you disappointed?

3. What did you think the book was about?

4. Was the plot compelling – or did you feel you could see things coming?

5. Did you root for Joey and his situation or did he leave you cold?

6. Were you convinced by his actions?

7. Would you want to meet any of the characters? Did you like them? Did you know enough about them?

8. The novel has stories within stories – did these slow the plot for you or did you enjoy them?

9. The author is female but has a male protagonist – was he convincing?

10. Is this a "women's book" – or would its themes appeal to men too?

11. Do Mexico and the circus come to life?

12. Did you feel you were experiencing the time and place in which the book was set?

13. What are some of the book's themes? How important were they?

14. How are the book's images symbolically significant? Do the images help to develop the plot, or help to define characters?

15. Did the book end the way you expected?

16. Would you recommend this book to other readers? To your close friend?

(Based on questions by E. Lombardi in http://classiclit.about.com)

Made in the USA
Charleston, SC
29 July 2012